Also by Neal Shusterman

Everlost
Everwild
Unwind

EVERFOUND

NEAL SHUSTERMAN

SIMON AND SCHUSTER

SIMON AND SCHUSTER

First published in Great Britain in 2011 by Simon & Schuster UK Ltd,
1st Floor, 222 Gray's Inn Road, London WC1X 8HB
A CBS COMPANY

Originally published in the USA 2011 by Simon & Schuster Books
for Young Readers, an imprint of Simon & Schuster
Children's Publishing Division. 1230 Avenue of the Americas,
New York, New York 10020

www.simonandschuster.co.uk

A CIP catalogue record for this book is available
from the British Library.

ISBN 978-0-85707-182-8

1 3 5 7 9 10 8 6 4 2

Printed in the UK by CPI Cox & Wyman, Reading, Berkshire RG1 8EX

To my elementary school librarian,
who took me under her wing,
and turned me into a reader.
Thanks, Mrs. Shapiro,
wherever you are!

Acknowledgments

Everfound, and the entire Skinjacker Trilogy, has been a fantastic journey to write, and there were many people who made thate journey possible. First and foremost, I'd like to thank my editor, David Gale, as well as Justin Chanda, Navah Wolfe, Paul Crichton, and everyone at Simon & Schuster for believing in these books. Thanks to my parents for always being there for me, and to my children, Brendan, Jarrod, Erin—and especially Joelle, who read my early draft of *Everfound*, and gave me great editorial notes.

Thanks to Chris Goethals for being amazingly supportive, through *Everfound*'s birth pangs and a constant source of light. My deepest gratitude to my assistant, Wendy Doyle, who worked tirelessly doing everything from transcribing my incoherent ramblings to finding Russian and Swahili translations (even though I ended up never using the Swahili). And while I'm on the subject of translation, thanks to Gabriela Hebin, for correcting my questionable Spanish.

Thanks to Andrea Brown, Trevor Engelson, Nick Osborne, Shep Rosenman, Lee Rosenbaum, and Danny Greenberg, who keep my career from sinking to the center of the earth. Also a heartfelt thank you to Naketha Mattocks, Allison Thomas, Gary Ross, and Jeff Kirschenbaum for having the vision to see these books as films, and the passion to make it happen someday.

I'd like to thank Daniel J. Grossman for his airship website (airships.net), which has amazing information on the *Hindenburg*.

Thanks to Brody Kelley, Amber Loranger, Alex Easton, and all my other Facebook fans and Twitter followers for spreading the word about these books.

And thanks to that kid who asked, "What happens to a skinjacker who gets unwound?" That's the way to keep an author on his toes!

Prologue: Allie the Outcast's FAQs

If you've just woken up to find yourself in Everlost, you might be scared and confused. Don't worry, everything's going to be okay. Sort of. They call me Allie the Outcast, and I've put together a list of frequently asked questions for new arrivals. It's a pretty good idea to read them, even if you've been in Everlost for a while, because in Everlost it's so easy to forget. . . .

What is Everlost?

Everlost is a world in between life and death. If you're stuck here, then it means you didn't quite make it to the light. Of course, we can still see the living world, all around us, but we can't be a part of it.

Why can't I touch anything or talk to people? Why is the world around me so blurry and faded?

You're dead. Get over it. You're a spirit, or Afterlight. *We're called Afterlights because we give off a faint glow — which makes it easy to see things in the dark. We're like our own flashlights. We call newly awoken Afterlights "Greensouls."*

It was winter when I crossed into Everlost, but now it's fall. Why is that?

All Afterlights sleep for nine months when they cross over. That's how long it takes to be "born" into Everlost. We call spirits that haven't yet woken up Interlights.

Why do I sink into the ground if I stand still?

You're a spirit, and spirits can walk through walls—and the floor is basically just a wall beneath your feet. We sink faster through wood floors than through concrete, dirt, or stone. It's best to stay out of living-world buildings, or you might find yourself sinking to the center of the Earth.

If I'm a ghost, how come some places are solid for me?

Those are called "deadspots." Places that no longer exist, but were loved, or important in some fundamental way, cross over into Everlost. Spots where people died cross into Everlost as well, and so do beloved objects.

What's this weird coin in my pocket?

Don't lose your coin, and don't let anyone take it away from you! That coin will get you where you're going, when you're truly ready to go.

Uh . . . where was I going?

I wish I knew, but no one in Everlost can see into the light at the end of the tunnel, so no one knows what's there. Maybe it's whatever you believe is there . . . or maybe not.

How long will I be in Everlost?

That depends. If you're ready to go, and you still have your coin, it might not be long. But if you lose your coin, or you choose to stay, you could be here for quite a while.

This weird thing keeps happening. I keep getting stuck inside living people. I can hear their thoughts, and it's like I can take over their bodies. What's up with that?

If you can do those things, then you're a skinjacker. Congratulations! You have one of the most awesome powers in the world, because you can possess anyone you want. But be careful to use your power wisely. I'm a skinjacker, so I know how tempting it is to abuse that power. It's important to remember not to stay too long in any one body, or you can get stuck there!

Why can I skinjack?

Because you're not 100 percent dead. Your body is in a coma somewhere.

I can't skinjack, but I do find myself changing in weird ways. Why?

We are what we remember. If we remember we had big ears, our ears slowly get bigger. If we remember we have freckles, suddenly we're all freckles everywhere. I had a friend who died with a smudge of chocolate on his face. You don't want to know what happened to him. . . .

Why do I find myself doing the same things over and over again every day?

You know how ghost sightings always seem to have the ghosts doing the same things every day? Well, we're the ghosts now. Try to break the pattern if you can, otherwise you can find years have passed without you even noticing. It's easier to break the pattern if you're around skinjackers.

I can't remember my name, and it's freaking me out!

Unless you're a skinjacker, you'll tend to forget things. Maybe even everything about your life. That's why most Afterlights have nicknames—it's because they can't remember their real names. Skinjackers might take nicknames too, but for entirely different reasons.

I've been hearing a lot about Mary Hightower, and how she can help me. Should I look for her?

Absolutely not! No matter what anyone says, Mary Hightower is NOT your friend—and if you find one of her books, remember you can only believe half of what you read . . . the hard part is figuring out which half.

I just fell off a cliff, and I didn't even get hurt. How is that possible?

As far as I know, we can't feel physical pain in Everlost. Wounds heal instantly, broken bones unbreak—because they're not really bones at all, just the memory of bones.

I really hate this stupid shirt I'm wearing, but it won't come off. What's the deal?

Whatever you died in, you're stuck wearing it. It's a part of you now, just as permanent as your skin. You can cover it with something else, if you manage to find some clothes that have crossed, but you can't take off what you died in. Just be happy you didn't die wearing that tree costume from your third-grade play, or a Mexican wrestling mask.

Aren't there any adults in Everlost?

No. There are lots of theories as to why. Some people say that they cross with so much baggage, they all sink to the center of the earth, but I don't believe that. I think the older you get, the harder it is to break out of the tunnel. For grown-ups, that tunnel to the light is so thick, there's no way they're falling out of it. They get where they're going whether they want to or not.

Did I just see a giant silver blimp in the sky?

It wasn't a blimp, it was a zeppelin—a rigid airship. More specifically it was the Hindenburg, *which blew up in 1937. It's been here in Everlost ever since.*

What's a vapor?

It's what you call a group of Afterlights. You know; a pod of whales, a pride of lions, a vapor of Afterlights. Mary made that up. She makes up lots of things.

Actually, I'm pretty cool with all of this. In fact, I feel more content than I ever have before.

Then you're ready to move on. I wish you a safe journey into the light!

I have so many more questions, can't you tell me more?

I'm sorry, but there are some things you're going to have to learn for yourself. Good luck!

Allie the Outcast

PART ONE

Confernal Jamnation

CHAPTER 1

Jix

The boy jacked a jaguar, slipping into its sleek body and sending its simple feline mind to sleep. He owned the beast now. Its flesh was his. Muscular magic in a compact four-legged frame, perfectly designed for running, stalking, and killing.

He had taken on the name "Jix"—one of the many Mayan words for "jaguar"—due to his inclination toward great cats, and he furjacked one every chance he got. He preferred wild jaguars, living in the jungles of Mexico's Yucatan Peninsula—creatures that hadn't lost their will to hunt.

Reconnaissance was Jix's specialty: tracking and spying on Afterlights who His Excellency the King believed to be a threat. Afterlights such as the Eastern Witch—the one they called Mary Hightower.

His Excellency had created a barrier of wind upon the Mississippi River to keep her and other intruders out, but the Eastern Witch was shrewd and relentless. With the help of her own skinjackers, she had destroyed a living-world bridge, causing it to cross into Everlost. Then with a train full of followers and slaves, she rode a powerful locomotive across the river.

At least that was the story.

Others said that she never made the journey herself — that something strange and mysterious happened to her, but no one could agree as to what it was. She flew off into the sky. She melted. She turned to stone. She turned to flesh. Each rumor was more outlandish than the last, and no one knew for sure if any of them were true.

Jix was called in for closer surveillance. Discover their numbers, discover their intent, then report back to the king. If these trespassing Afterlights were truly a threat, they would be dealt with quickly, and would never see the light of day again. It all depended on Jix's report.

"You should skinjack the pilot of a flying machine," His Excellency had suggested to Jix, "for speed in this matter would greatly please us."

Jix, however, had resisted. "But sir, my skill to stalk comes from the jaguar gods. If I make my journey impure, they will be angered, and take the skill away."

His Excellency had then waved his hand dismissively. "Do as you will — as long as you bring us the results We require." The king always said "us" and "we," even when there was no one else but him in the room.

So, on a bright autumn day, Jix set out in the borrowed body of a jaguar, and within that speedy beast, he forged over mountains and rivers, resting when he had to, but never for long. When he came near human villages he heard many languages. Remnants of ancient tongues, Spanish, and finally English. Once he heard English, and saw signs written in that language, he knew he was getting close, yet never once was he spotted, for he had the best of both species now: the keen senses of the jaguar, and the full faculties of a human mind.

The ghost train had crossed the bridge in Memphis, so this was his destination. He was certain to pick up a scent of the supernatural there, and track them down. As he drew nearer, he could feel the thrill of the hunt filling him. The intruders wouldn't stand a chance.

CHAPTER 2
Figureheads

The one positive thing Allie Johnson could say about being tied to the front of a train was that the view was spectacular. The sunsets were particularly stunning. Even in Everlost, where the colors and textures of the living world appeared faded and muted, dramatic skies lost none of their majesty, and painted the turning November leaves of every tree, living and dead, into shades of fire, before the sunset dissolved into dusk. It made Allie wonder if the clouds, the stars, and the sun existed in both Everlost and the living world equally. Certainly the moon was the same to the living and the dead.

No, not dead, Allie had to remind herself. *Caught between life and death*... although Allie was closer to life than most others in Everlost. It made her valuable, it made her dangerous—and that was why she was tied to the front end of a ghost train.

Right now Allie didn't have much of a view. All she could see were the front doors of a white clapboard church. It would have been very picturesque if it wasn't a foot in front of her nose.

The train had been stopped at the church for hours, while Milos, Speedo, and a handful of Mary Hightower's best and brightest kids pondered what to do.

Mary herself was not available for comment.

Speedo, who was perpetually dripping wet in the ridiculous bathing suit he died in, always offered the most labor-intensive, solutions to obstacles in their path.

"We could backtrack again," Speedo suggested, "then find another dead track and take it," for a ghost train could travel only on rails that no longer existed in the living world.

Milos, their leader in Mary's "absence," shook his head. "It took very long to find a track that was not a dead end. What chance is there of finding another?" He spoke in slightly stilted English and a faint Russian accent that Allie had once found charming.

"Why don't you just give up," suggested Allie, who was in the perfect position to heckle them. "After all, Milos, you should be used to failure by now—and you're so good at it!"

He glared at her. "Maybe we should crash right through it," Milos suggested, "using your face as the battering ram."

Allie shrugged. "Fine with me," she said, knowing that it was impossible for her to be hurt in Everlost. "I just want to see the look on your face when the train derails and sinks to the center of the earth."

Milos just grunted, knowing she was right. One would think that ramming a wooden building would just shatter it, and the train would chug on through—but Everlost was not the living world. The church had crossed into Everlost, and things that cross into Everlost are permanent. They can't be broken, unless it was their purpose to break. They can't be destroyed unless destruction is what they were designed for. So crashing into the church was likely to derail the train, since the church's memory of staying put was probably more powerful than a speeding locomotive.

"How did it even get here?" Speedo asked, fuming. As the engineer, he had a singular mission: get the train moving. Anything other than forward momentum was his own failure as far as he was concerned. Typical for a thirteen-year-old. Milos, who had crossed into Everlost at sixteen, was a bit more calm about it. Still, Allie secretly relished the fact that every problem they came across made Milos look less competent in his role. Charisma went only so far.

"It got here," Milos calmly explained, "because it was built and torn down before the tracks were."

"So," said Speedo, impatient as ever, "why is it in our way?"

Milos sighed, and Allie chimed in her response. "Because, genius, if the living world tears two things down in the same place, and both cross into Everlost, we're stuck with both of them."

"We didn't ask you!" snapped Speedo.

"But she is right," Milos admitted. "Mary called it 'jamnation.'"

"Right. And then there's 'Marification,'" Allie added. "That's Mary Hightower making up words so she'll sound smarter than she really is."

Speedo glared up at her. "You shut up about Miss Mary, or your new place will be inside the boiler."

"Oh, dry up," she said, which irked Speedo even more, because, as everyone knew, he couldn't. Allie hated the fact

8

that Mary, the self-proclaimed savior of lost children, had been elevated into goddess status by her mere absence. As for jamnation, Allie had come across plenty of examples of it in her travels. The strangest had been a school from the 1950s built on the same spot where a Revolutionary War fort once stood. When the school burned down, and crossed into Everlost, the result was a bizarre juxtaposition of brick and stone, classrooms, and garrisons. In Everlost the two buildings both still existed in the same space, and were melded together in bizarre ways.

The evidence pointed to the same sort of thing here: that the foundation of the church and the train tracks had merged, leaving the train at a permanent dead end.

Allie, however, knew something Milos and Speedo didn't, and if she played it right, she could finally make a bargain for her freedom.

"I know a way past the church," Allie told them.

Speedo thought she was just taunting them again, but Milos knew her well enough to know she wouldn't say it unless she meant it. He climbed up on the cowcatcher, wedging himself between the train and the church so he could get close to Allie. Close enough to grab her—or slap her—but Allie knew he wouldn't. In spite of everything, Milos was a gentleman. Sort of.

"What are your thoughts?" he asked her.

"Why should I tell you?"

"Cooperation," Milos told her, "may help your situation."

It was exactly what Allie hoped he would say.

"She's just wasting our time," grumbled Speedo, but Milos ignored him, and leaned close to her so that Speedo couldn't hear. "I cannot offer you freedom," he whispered. "You are too much of a threat."

"But I don't need to be tied to the engine."

"It is for your own protection," Milos said, as he had told her before. "Mary's children need a scapegoat. They need to see you punished, and since we feel no pain in Everlost, strapping you to the front of the train looks far more punishing than it really is. In fact," Milos added, "I envy you. Your journey west is far more invigorating than mine."

"There are things worse than pain," Allie told him, thinking of the humiliation she had to endure by being a captive on display.

"How about this?" Milos said. "If what you have to say helps us, I will imprison you in a more comfortable manner."

"Untie me first," Allie said, "and then I'll tell you."

Milos smiled. "Not a chance."

Allie smiled right back. "Well, it was worth a try." She knew that Milos was vain and self-serving—and that his conscience only went as far as it met his needs—but he did have a moral code, if you could call it that. He was a man of his word. Odd that Allie felt she could trust him after all the terrible things she had seen him do.

"I see lots of things from the front of this train," Allie said. "Things that the rest of you don't see." She paused, stretching it out, making them wait for it. Then she said, "I saw something when the train entered this valley—about a mile back."

"What did you see?" asked Milos.

"If you're not going to untie me," Allie told him, "you're going to have to figure it out for yourself."

"Very well," said Milos. "We are in no hurry to leave anyway. We'll figure out our own way around it." Then he looked at the blank white face of the church before them. "In the meantime, enjoy the view."

Milos stormed away from Allie, refusing to be manipulated by her. She was the prisoner, not him—although more and more he felt like his own hands were tied. Around him dozens of Mary's children had already come out of the train. Some played hide-and-seek, or tag—always moving fast enough to keep from sinking into the living world. There were girls on the roofs of the train cars playing jump rope, and kids beneath the wheels, playing cards—as if they knew they would be stuck here for days, maybe even weeks. In fact, they had come to expect it.

Of course, they could always leave the train and continue on foot, but Milos decided long ago that it would not be wise. The train was a fortress for them. It could protect them against whatever they came across—and although they had not seen a single Afterlight since crossing the Mississippi, it didn't mean they weren't there.

In the weeks since commandeering the train, Mary's Afterlights had all settled into their own comfort zones, and the rail car population divided along predictable lines—or at least predictable by Everlost standards. There was an all-girls car, and an all-boys car, for those who bonded strictly along gender lines. There were a few "insomnoid" cars for souls who chose to give up sleep entirely, since slumber was optional for Afterlights. There was a car for sports-minded Afterlights who ran from the train each time it stopped, to play one ball game or another, and a car for those kids whose repetitive daily routines involved quiet, indoor activities — and of course the "sleeping" car, and the "prison" car — both of which served their own unique purposes.

To keep Mary's children happy and subdued, Milos made sure that the train would stop twice a day for several hours of playtime, and each day the games would eerily mimic the day before, down to the scores, the fights, and the things the kids shouted to one another. Each kid fell into his or her own personal pattern that was the same day after day — what Mary had called "perfectition": the perfect repetition of a child's perfect day. Milos figured the deeper the trenches of their personal ruts, the less Mary's children would bother him.

Then there were times like this, where the train came to one dead end or another, and was stuck for days until they figured out a proper course of action.

Milos looked back to the church, and wondered what Mary would do . . . but he wouldn't be getting advice from her anytime soon.

As he strode alongside the train, considering the situation, Jackin' Jill came up to him. As always, her blond hair was wild and full of nettles, as if she had been attacked by a tumbleweed. Was it Milos's imagination or were the nettles in her hair multiplying?

"If you've gotten us stuck again, then we should go skinjacking," she said. As a skinjacker, she, like Milos, was much closer to life, and did not settle as easily into daily routines. But Milos knew Jill didn't just want to go skinjacking. When she wanted to possess the living, she had a darker purpose in mind.

"Call it what it is," said Milos. "You don't want to go skinjacking. You want to go *reaping*, don't you?"

"My last orders from Mary were very clear," Jill said. "I won't put everything on hold just because you're a wimp."

Milos turned on her sharply. He would never strike a girl, but Jill often brought him to the very edge of his temper. "What I did for Mary proves I am anything but a coward."

"So why do you only let us reap once a week?"

"Because there needs to be limits!" Milos shouted.

"Mary's vision has no limits, does it?" The fact that Jill could stay calm made him even angrier, but he resolved to calm himself down. Losing his temper gave her control, and he was the one in charge here. He had to remember that.

"The difference between you and me," said Milos, "is that I reap because it is what Mary wants. But you do it because you enjoy it."

Jill did not deny it. "In a perfect world," she said, "shouldn't we all enjoy our jobs?"

Milos agreed to lead the skinjackers on a reaping excursion that night, but under the strictest of rules. "We will take no more than we can carry, and I will choose where and when."

"Whatever floats your boat," Jill said, caring only that she would get her chance to do her dirty work.

Moose and Squirrel were also part of the skinjacking team, bringing their number to four. Although Allie was also a skinjacker, Milos knew she would never come reaping, even if he did set her free from the train.

"Can I take two, Milosh?" Moose asked. "Pleashe?"

Moose was a linebacker who had made his unfortunate crossing into Everlost during a high school football game. As such, he was doomed to wear a blue and silver football uniform. That uniform included a helmet and an eternal mouth guard stuck between his teeth, so everything he said came out slurred.

"Yeah, yeah," said Squirrel, "Moose can carry mine back to the train."

"Thatsh not what I meant!" said Moose.

Squirrel was a twitchy rail of a kid. Milos never knew the manner in which Squirrel had crossed into Everlost, only that his exit from the world of the living had been supremely embarrassing, as evidenced by the way Squirrel's cheeks and ears would go red at the mention of it. Since Afterlights had no flesh or blood, one had to be severely embarrassed for the distant memory of blood to turn one's face red.

"As I said, we will take what we can carry," Milos told him. "Don't get greedy."

They set out from the train at dusk. Perhaps it was his imagination, or maybe just his misgivings, but Milos couldn't shake the uneasy feeling that they were being watched.

CHAPTER 3

Doomed Worthy

Jix, still in the body of the jaguar, had tracked the ghost train from Memphis to Oklahoma, following the faint scent of the supernatural. It wasn't a scent, really, but more of an absence of scent. It was that very specific feeling of fur standing on end for no apparent reason. No matter how keen the cat's senses, though, it could not see into Everlost. So when he knew he was close, he marched that jaguar into a public park in broad daylight, and allowed himself to be captured by animal control, before leaving the jaguar's body. He was himself again, and back in Everlost— but even as an Everlost spirit, he had absorbed enough from his feline hosts to be agile and stealth. He spent so much time furjacking cats that it had changed him. He had even begun to look like one. Although he still wore the tattered jeans he had worn on the night he crossed, he had crossed shirtless, and now his muscular chest had taken on a faint orange, velvety sheen—almost like fur. He had even begun to develop jaguar spots. His eyeteeth were slowly growing into fangs, and his ears had shifted higher on his head, becoming small and pointy. Jix was short for fifteen—at least by American standards—but he didn't seem young for his age, for his frame had filled out nicely, and his serious expression made it clear he was not to be trifled with.

Jix found the ghost train just south of Oklahoma City. It wasn't moving, because its path was blocked. Jix was not foolish enough to approach the train; there was some sort of demon attached to the front of it. Who knew what the demon was capable of? Jix kept his distance, watching and waiting.

Then at sunset, a team of skinjackers left the train. He knew they were skinjackers from the way they moved. Heavy on their feet, even though the earth threatened to pull them down. They walked with the brash arrogance of flesh, even though they had none of their own. It was the same way Jix walked—with the knowledge that living and breathing was only as far as the nearest heartbeat.

There were four of them. Their leader was a tall boy of fifteen or sixteen the others called Milos, there was a disagreeable girl with wild hair, there was a boy in a football uniform, and there was another scrawny boy who talked a lot but said nothing. Jix knew their language. He had become fluent in English, since much of his life had been spent selling trinkets to American tourists in Cancun. One's success depended on how much English one knew, and Jix had become exceptionally fluent. Even so, the small talk these four made didn't give him much useful information.

Were these the skinjackers who had destroyed the bridge? There was no way to be sure unless he followed them, but once they skinjacked, he wouldn't be able to keep up . . . unless he was in the body of a creature with keen senses.

When the skinjackers reached the highway, they leaped into four human bodies in a passing Cadillac that was headed toward Oklahoma City.

That's when Jix decided it was time to visit the zoo.

Finding a suitable cat was easier here than in the jungle. Here, all the perfect predators were assembled in a central location and locked in foul-smelling cages. Fortunately unlocking cages was not a problem for a skinjacker.

Since the Oklahoma City Zoo did not have a jaguar, and time was of the essence, Jix chose a panther, with charcoal-gray fur that looked blue in the moonlight. Good camouflage for a city night. Jix took over the body of a zookeeper just long enough to undo the locks on the habitat—but he left the gate closed. Then, once he had furjacked the panther, he pushed the gate open with his paws. There was something so satisfying in doing that part as a cat. It felt more like an honest and true escape.

The zoo was quiet now, and the night watchmen had no idea that one of their most dangerous predators was loose. They were more worried about kids with spray paint than they were about the animals. Watchmen were always easy to evade.

Out into the night, bounding through the shadows, he tracked his prey. Now he had a true scent to pursue— because the smell of a skinjacked human is strong, and as easy to follow as the blood trail of a wounded stag. A skinjacked human smelled of ozone and nervous sweat. It smelled like wet lightning.

He picked up hints of them on the air among the various scents of the city as he approached downtown. Keeping out of sight in such a densely populated area was a challenge, but challenge was something he lived for—and since city folk were not expecting to see a panther in the shadows, it was easier than one might have thought for him to go unnoticed.

The scent drew him toward a part of town still busy long after dark, a main avenue full of cafes and clubs. He quickly scanned the street for alleys and dimly lit crannies—places he could lurk without being seen—then padded off in the direction of the scent.

But then something happened. Something unexpected. Something terrible.

Jix felt the crash before he heard it—smelled it before he saw the flying shards of glass. The skinjackers' Cadillac had plowed into the front of a café.

Against all caution Jix loped forward to get a closer view.

The entire glass front of the café was gone, and the scene was full of panic. The scattering living, the groaning injured, and the silenced dead. Although Jix had no particular attachment to the living world, he could not help but ache with sorrow at the scene before him, and he knew instinctively that this was no accident—it was intentional! These eastern skinjackers were like angels of death, slipping in and out of flesh as the whim suited them, creating mayhem. His heart, which had pounded steady at the pace of his chase, now quickened, fed by both terror and fascination.

He leaped onto the hood of the Cadillac, and looked through the spider-webbed glass of the windshield into the car. Air bags and seat belts had saved the lives of the four passengers. They were as panicked and confused as everyone else—which meant that the skinjackers were gone. They had crashed the car, then had left their human hosts.

So where were they now?

Jix could no longer smell them, which meant they were no longer skinjacking. They were back in Everlost, and could be standing right in front of him, but as long as he was furjacking the panther, he couldn't see them.

"Oh my God! Is that some kind of tiger?" someone yelled, and Jix turned and growled menacingly, insulted for being mistaken for his brutish cousins. Then he peeled himself out of the panther, leaving the living world and transitioning back into Everlost.

There was a moment of disorientation as he left the world of flesh. The living world became blurry and unfocused around him. He was now back in Everlost, where the living world seemed a little less real, and the only things that were solid were things that no longer existed.

Immediately he saw the portals—four of them standing open before him. He knew exactly what they were, even though he had only seen a portal once—but the passageway to the afterlife is not something one easily forgets. It's the tunnel every soul sees at the moment they die. Most don't linger in Everlost—for the majority of people, Everlost is just a stepping stone—a springboard to launch oneself down the tunnel toward . . . well, toward wherever it is one happens to be going.

But every once in a while something goes wrong.

Standing at the mouth of the portals were the victims of the crash—high school age by the looks of them. They had been at the wrong place at the wrong time, and had been killed when the Cadillac crashed into the café. They stood in what should have been a brief moment of transition—and in spite of the shock of their sudden crossing, they seemed ready to move on, already reaching toward the light, which seemed both impossibly distant, yet close enough to touch. This moment was so personal, so private, that Jix felt ashamed to be watching it, yet he couldn't tear his eyes away.

That's when it happened. Four other figures came up behind the unfortunate souls. It was the skinjackers!

Each skinjacker grabbed on to a crossing soul, and held tight, digging in their heels, leaning away from the light with the full force of their wills, keeping the victims from going down the tunnel. It worked for three of them, but the scrawny one couldn't keep his grip and lost his victim into the light, cursing as he did.

In the end, the tunnels vanished, and, thanks to the skinjackers, three new spirits were committed to Everlost, collapsing into a deep sleep—the nine-month sleep all new arrivals had to endure before waking up as citizens of Everlost.

"You killed them!" Jix didn't even realize he said it out loud, until all the skinjackers turned to him.

"Who the hell are you?" asked the girl with wild hair. The one called Milos put up his hand to silence her.

"We freed them," Milos said. "We released them from a life of pain. We saved them from that world."

Jix hesitated. Until this moment, it had never occurred to him that people could be brought into Everlost on purpose—or that a forced crossing could be a desirable thing. He wanted to think about it, let his mind see it from every possible angle, but there was no time for thinking now.

"C'mon, c'mon, Milos. Let's get out of here," said the squirrelly one.

"No," Milos said, "I will not leave more of a mess than I have to." Then he turned back to Jix. "Are you alone? Are there others like you?"

But before he could answer, a scream rang out from the living world and a situation that was already bad, suddenly became a whole lot worse.

Jix had always been careful to leave the great cats he furjacked in places where they could do no harm, but in the heat of this extraordinary and terrifying moment, he had released his beast in the middle of a crowd. Confused and frightened, the animal did what frightened predators do. It attacked.

The cat turned on a girl who was no older than twelve. She wore a crimson dress. It was probably the blood color of the dress that got the cat's attention in the first place. Her life ended quickly with the panther's first pounce, then the cat bounded away, disappearing into the night. Jix wailed at the sight of his deadly mistake.

Now the girl's spirit stood in Everlost at the mouth of her own afterlife tunnel—and all because of him. Her eyes were fixed on the light, and she was already moving toward it.

"I got thish one," said the skinjacker in football gear, then he surged forward, and tackled the girl out of the tunnel like he was sacking a quarterback. She landed right at Jix's feet and her tunnel disappeared. Jix knelt down cradling her head in his hands.

"*Lo siento*," Jix said. "I'm sorry. . . ."

She looked up at him, her pupils wide and dilated, not yet understanding any of this. "I'm sleepy," she said. "Tell my parents I'm taking a nap. . . ." Then her eyes closed and her soul plunged into a nine-month slumber.

Milos knelt beside them. While the wild-haired girl seemed impatient, the squirrelly one just scared, and the football player proud of his accomplishment, Milos appeared to have genuine remorse. "What's done is done," Milos said. "At least she is at peace now. And when she wakes up, she will be young and beautiful forever, yes? Maybe someday she will thank you."

"Thank me? She'll never forgive me!" Jix shouted.

He held on to the sleeping girl, brushing her hair out of her face. She was Hispanic, with very strong Indian features, like himself. How could he have let this happen?

"I have a friend who is very wise," Milos told him. "Her name is Mary. She says that life in Everlost is a gift. She says we are all chosen to be here because we have been doomed worthy."

"*Deemed*," corrected the wild-haired girl. "*Deemed* worthy."

"Yes," said Milos. "Forgive my English. The point is, if she was chosen to be here, then there is no reason for you to feel guilt."

Jix turned to Milos, studying his face, and his eyes: bright blue with speckles of white, like a sky dotted with clouds. "What about you?" he asked Milos. "Do you not feel guilt for what you did?"

Milos took a moment before answering. "None," he said. "None whatsoever."

But they both knew he was lying.

Around them, in the living world, the chaos born from this awful evening was taking root. Crowds were gathering, loved ones were grieving, distant sirens drew closer. Jix was glad that the living world could be so easily tuned out by Afterlights. He did not want to witness further results of their actions.

"So what do we do with him?" asked the wild-haired girl.

"Push him down! Push him down!" said the squirrelly one.

"No," said Milos, "he is a skinjacker. He deserves better than that." Then he held out his hand to Jix. "Join us, and I promise you will be a part of something grand and glorious."

Still Jix made no move. Working under His Excellency, Jix had always dreamed he'd be part of something larger than himself. He even dreamed that he would be taken into the king's inner circle, for Jix was a well-respected scout. But scouting kept him at a distance, and when it came to the king, out of sight was truly out of mind. Whenever Jix returned with news, no matter how important, His Excellency would never even remember his name.

As Jix looked at these villainous, barbaric skinjackers, he found himself more and more curious about them, and oddly attracted to their way of life. Little was known about Mary the Eastern Witch—but here was an opportunity to learn more. What he ultimately did with that information would be entirely up to him.

He looked down at the sleeping girl in his arms, and made a decision. "I want to be there when she wakes up. I want to be the first thing she sees when she opens her eyes. Then I'll ask her for forgiveness."

The wild-haired girl rolled her eyes. "Whatever."

Jix gently lifted the spirit of the sleeping girl onto his shoulder. "Take me to the Eastern Witch."

The five of them made their way back to the train, everyone but Squirrel carrying a sleeping spirit.

"It's not my fault," complained Squirrel. "I couldn't hold on, my hands were greasy."

"Your hands are always greasy," Moose pointed out.

"Right—and it's not my fault!"

Jix spoke very little on the journey, but even so, he was still the center of attention. They all stared at him, some being more obvious about it than others. Jackin' Jill didn't even try to hide the fact that she was staring.

"I've seen a lot of freaky Afterlights, but I've never seen one like you," she finally said.

Jix was not bothered. He prided himself on his ongoing transformation. He hoped that in time his form would match that of his animal spirit. These eastern Afterlights knew nothing of animal spirits. They were like the living, disconnected from the universe, seeing themselves as solitary. So self-centered. Yet Milos had asked him if he wanted to be part of something larger than himself, which pointed to some higher purpose. These eastern Afterlights certainly warranted closer observation.

"There is art to what you have done to yourself," Milos said to Jix, and Jix nodded his acceptance of the compliment.

"So, are there any others in your litter?" said Jill. He didn't have to see her face to sense the sneer in her voice.

"Only me," Jix said, offering her as little as possible.

"You are the first Afterlight we have seen west of the Mississippi River," Milos told him.

"So, you're all on your own?" Jill pressed. "No leader? No friends?"

Jix considered how he'd answer the question before he spoke. "Cats are solitary animals."

They arrived at the train just after dawn, still carrying their sleeping souls. The kids who Jix had seen playing the day before were all in the train cars, but now that the sun was up, they would soon be out, and playing their games again. Jix had seen the train only at a distance, so as he drew closer with the skinjackers, he took note of everything.

First, and most obvious, was the little church, curiously blocking the train's progress. He had seen instances of jamnation before, although he had no such fancy word for it. This predicament made him smile. Such a little, unassuming building standing in the way of a mighty ghost train. It reminded him of a picture he had seen in a library book during his living days. A man standing in front of a giant tank in someplace Chinese. He suspected there was more to this church, however, than met the eye.

The demon was still tied to the front of the train, and now he could tell that it was a she-demon, perhaps *La Llorrona* — the crying woman — although she didn't appear to be crying. Not that Jix had actually ever met a she-demon, or knew for sure that such things existed, but he'd heard stories.

The next thing he noticed was a caboose at the other

end of the train, decorated with Christmas lights and shiny baubles that reflected the rising sun. He made a note to ask about it when he felt sure he'd get a truthful answer.

And then there was the fourth passenger car. All of the other passenger cars seemed crowded with children, but the fourth car was crowded in a very different way. In the windows, Jix saw faces pressed up against the glass. It was quite literally crammed with Afterlights—there had to be a thousand souls stuck in that cramped space. Jix recalled one time when His Excellency had commanded a group of Afterlights to squeeze themselves into a large ceramic vase that had crossed into Everlost. In the living world it had been big enough to hold no more than two or three—but Afterlights, who are pure spirit, and have no true physical substance, can fit just about anywhere. They kept climbing in, and his Excellency got bored when the count reached fifty. There was no telling how many souls were shoved into this train car.

"Wild, huh?" said Moose, looking at the crammed car. "Like clownsh in a car." The faces in the window didn't seem in distress, and Jix figured they had been in there quite a long time because they had gotten used to it. At most, it looked awkward and inconvenient, but they were still having conversations with one another as if this was just another normal day for them.

"Why are they in there?" Jix asked. "For someone's amusement?" That made Squirrel laugh, which was not a pleasant sound.

"They were an enemy army," Milos told him. "We defeated them a few months ago, and now we hold them in there for safekeeping."

"Yeah, yeah," said Squirrel. "Prisoners of war."

"Bet you've never sheen sho many Afterlightsh," said Moose.

For a moment Jix wanted to brag about the great City of Souls, but decided to keep that to himself.

The skinjackers brought their four slumbering spirits to an Afterlight who waited by a sleeping car.

"Leave them with me," the kid said, but Jix was reluctant.

"It is all right," said Milos. "Sandman will tag them, and mark them with the date they will awake."

Jix refused to give his sleeping girl to Sandman; instead he carried her into the sleeping car himself.

"Hey," said Sandman, "you can't go in there." Jix turned to him, bared his teeth and growled. Although his growl still sounded more like a boy than a wild cat, Sandman was intimidated enough to leave him alone.

The sleeping car was already crowded. Each upper and lower berth had two, sometimes three sleeping kids, their chests rising and falling with the memory of breathing, but none of them snored or made the slightest sound. Jix found a comfortable place and left his sleeping girl there, making sure she looked comfortable, then kissed her forehead, because he knew she no longer had parents to do so, and because he knew no one was watching. Then he left the sleeping car and went straight to Milos.

"I will meet Mary, the Eastern Witch, now."

"You will meet her," said Milos, "when she is ready to be met."

"And when will that be?"

Milos took a long look at him, perhaps trying to read something in his expression, but stealth also required a cool, unreadable face. Jix never gave anything away that he didn't intend to.

"Not today," was all Milos said.

"In the meantime," suggested Jackin' Jill, "why don't you go lick yourself clean like a good kitty?"

Jix suspected that he and Jill were never going to be friends.

CHAPTER 4

Green Goddess

Milos had not forgotten what Allie had told him, and although he hated the thought that she knew something he didn't, he had to find out what she had seen from her perch at the front of the train. *About a mile back*, she had said. *Figure it out for yourself.* Once the newly harvested souls were safely in the sleeping car, Milos decided to set off alone to do exactly that.

He left Jill in charge of Jix, which she resented. "I don't trust him," Jill said. "No normal person skinjacks animals."

"Would you rather Moose and Squirrel watch him?" suggested Milos. She just grunted in disgust. They both knew Moose and Squirrel had attention spans too short to effectively guard anyone. "Perhaps you could charm him into telling you more about where he comes from," Milos said, with a grin. "After all, you're a bit like a cat yourself."

She raised her hand like a claw. "In that case, why don't I just scratch that grin right off your face?" Still, Milos smiled. He had once been in love with Jill, as he had once been in love with Allie—but both times the love was bleached away by betrayal, leaving him with a wounded, if not broken, heart.

But then there was Mary.

All else in his life, and afterlife, had been mere preparation for her. She was his salvation—and in a very real way, he was hers as well.

Milos left the train in the afternoon, and followed the track, every couple of minutes looking around, trying to spot anything out of the ordinary, but nothing caught his eye. Looking back at the train proved to be a surreal sight: the locomotive, standing against the little white church right in the middle of its path. The way its steeple poked up at the sky made it appear as if the church was giving the train the middle finger.

Milos found nothing a mile back. Just a dead track, and the living world on either side of it. Whatever it was Allie saw, it was not revealing itself to Milos. He returned to the train, his afterglow faintly red with slow-boiling frustration.

When he arrived, all seemed the way it always did. Kids playing games, shuffling their feet to keep from sinking into the living world.

Speedo came running to him when he saw that Milos had returned. "What was there?" Speedo asked. "What did you see?"

"Nothing," Milos told him. "I saw nothing at all."

"So what do we do now?"

"I will figure something out!" Milos shouted at him. "Don't ask me again!" When he looked around, he saw that his outburst had gotten the attention of some of the kids playing around them. When Mary's kids saw him, they used to look away, too shy and respectful to make eye contact.

But now when they looked at him, they stared coolly, and their gazes were an accusation. *What are you doing for us?* those gazes said. *What good are you at all?* Now it was Milos who looked away when they stared.

He considered going up to the front car, and bargaining with Allie to tell him what she saw, or perhaps threatening her—but he would not give her the satisfaction of knowing she had the upper hand. Instead, he turned, and strode toward the caboose.

"Wait, where are you going?" whined Speedo.

And Milos said, "I need to talk to Mary."

When Mary's army had acquired the train from the Chocolate Ogre, it did not have a caboose. It had been a simple steam engine with nine passenger cars, each from a different time period. The caboose was added at Milos's insistence before they left Little Rock, Arkansas. He was adamant that they travel no further west until a final car—a *special* car—was found. No one argued. It was, in fact, the only order he gave that met with no resistance from anyone.

They finally found the caboose sitting on a slight stretch of dead track, hidden by a living-world apartment complex. Once found, attaching it to the train had been relatively easy. So was decorating it—because Christmas ornaments were both beloved and fragile, and so were naturally abundant in Everlost. The strings of brightly colored lights even stayed lit in Everlost without needing to be plugged in.

The caboose was decorated by Mary's loving children, and the entrance was locked to everyone but Milos, the only one who knew the lock's combination.

Now, as he spun the lock, and turned it to the combination, he took in a deep breath, for even though he no longer needed to breathe, the mere act of doing so helped him steel himself for the moment. Then, once he was sure he was ready, he stepped inside.

It was late afternoon now. Light poured into the windows of the caboose and onto an object that lay in the center. It was the only thing in the caboose.

The object was a coffin.

It wasn't made of wood as one might expect, or even of stone, as had been done in ancient days. This coffin was made entirely of glass—bits and pieces of it, meticulously glued together with bubble gum and anything else sticky enough to do the job. There were pieces of crystal taken from chandeliers that had crossed into Everlost. There were bottles, and window panes and sunglass lenses, artfully arranged, and little stained-glass window hangings that added color. The casket was strange and piecemeal, yet perfect in its own way.

Within the glass coffin lay a figure in a shimmering green satin gown, ever silent, ever still. A girl once lost to this world, but now ever found.

"Hello, Mary . . ."

Milos knelt beside the coffin, gently moving his hand across the rough edges of joined glass. Tears filled his eyes, but not tears of sorrow. Far from it. It was joy that filled him when he looked at her. This is where Mary belonged—in Everlost—a world she was determined to tame, and dominate. The Chocolate Ogre had found a way to make her live again, sending her back into the world of the living, turning

32

her spirit into flesh. Her untimely life was a shock to everyone, most of all to Milos—yet even in that dark time, Mary had orchestrated her own return to Everlost.

Bring me home, my love.

Those were the last words Mary said to him, before he took her life. She looked into his eyes, and steadied his hand as he thrust the blade through her heart. It was that singular act, as horrible as it was, that bound them together forever.

My love, she had called him—and in that moment Milos knew he had finally replaced Nick, that hideous chocolate-challenged spirit, in her heart.

In the living world Mary's heart had lain mortally wounded, leaking its last ounce of life in an alley—but as her body died, a portal opened before her spirit, and Milos was there to catch her. Just as he'd promised, he was there to grab her and hold her tight in his embrace, denying the gravity of the light and preventing her from being sucked down the tunnel to some mysterious afterlife.

Perhaps the light wanted her. Perhaps God had already set a table for her in eternity . . . but Milos wanted her more. With every ounce of his will, he held her back until the light retreated, the tunnel vanished, and Mary's spirit collapsed into his arms.

"I love you, Mary," he had said to her, but she didn't answer, and the moment after the light disappeared, her arms, which had held him so tightly, went limp and she fell into the deepest of sleeps, as they both knew she would. Nine months of dreamless slumber—for just as one is born to the world of the living, one must be born into Everlost. Not even the great Mary Hightower could escape that simple law of nature.

Even so, Mary had now accomplished something no one else ever had. . . . Never before had the same person lived and died twice. It changed everything.

Bring me home, my love.

And Milos did. On the day Mary re-died, he had carried her in his arms all the way back to the train. He walked with her through the crowd of Mary's children so that they could all see. She had left in mystery—for Milos had never told the others what had befallen her—and now she was back. Not just back, but transformed. They were all too awed to do anything but whisper and reach out to touch her, feeling the smooth fabric of her green satin gown. When she was forced back into the living world, her tight Victorian velvet dress had quickly been ruined by a mere week of living on the street. She had shed it, replacing it with this gown of emerald satin. Now she looked less like a governess, and more like a goddess—a fallen goddess, waiting for her moment to rise.

That moment would come, but Milos feared it wouldn't come soon enough.

Things had not gone well in the two months since he had brought Mary home. Just ten miles out of Little Rock, Arkansas, the ghost tracks had come to an end, and they had to backtrack, finding another set of rails that could carry them, and then another, then another—a constant series of false starts and dead ends. It was like navigating a maze, and finding alternate routes would take days. Even when they had forward momentum, they always moved at a snail's pace, for fear that the tracks would unexpectedly end.

And then the desertions began.

Those who were loyal to Mary were loyal to the end — but others who feared the prospect of a dying/rising goddess, or simply distrusted Milos, were quick to run off. At last count they were losing a half dozen kids a day. Mary's kids numbered close to a thousand when they started. He had no idea how many there were now. He was afraid to take a census.

"You'll be lucky if you have any left at all by the time Mary wakes up," Jill was quick to tell him. Milos did not want to face the prospect of explaining to Mary why he could not hold on to her children, and "protect them from themselves," as she would put it.

This is why Milos allowed the reaping expeditions. If there were a good number of sleeping souls, it might make up for all the ones they had lost. And sleeping souls can't run away.

"Everyone wants to know where we're going," Speedo had told him. "Did Mary tell you where she was leading us before you . . . uh . . . 'made her cross'?"

"Of course she told me!"

"Well, it might make us all feel a little bit better if you told us."

"That," said Milos, "is between Mary and me."

With all the starts and stops, backtracking and zigzagging, their journey was taking months. During that time, Mary's kids all fell into new routines . . . yet even in their routines there was a sense of impatience — as if they were all reluctantly passing the time until something happened — until Milos actually DID something that brought them closer to their unknown destination. More and more he felt like a leader in name only.

Now, as he knelt alone in the caboose, he looked through the glass to Mary's closed eyelids, trying to remember what her eyes looked like. Soft and inviting, while at the same time keen and calculating. It was an intoxicating combination.

"I have tried, Mary," he said, in barely more than a whisper. "I have tried to lead your children and to bring even more into Everlost, just as you had asked . . . but there is only so much that I can do." He found that he had forced his hands together, clasping his knuckles in something resembling prayer. "We face so many obstacles. And now this church . . ." He looked to the date she would awaken, written on the largest pane of glass. It was still more than six months away.

"I'm not sure I can do this without you, Mary," he pleaded. "Please, please wake up soon. . . ."

For an instant, he thought he saw a twitch of her cheek. But it was just a trick of the light sifting through the crystalline coffin.

Late that afternoon, Milos gathered all of Mary's children in a clearing just beside the train, then he climbed up on top of the caboose, and told them his plan. "We will build a bypass around the church," Milos told them. "But to do it, we'll need to find loose railroad tracks that have crossed into Everlost."

Speedo jumped at the opportunity to lead the expedition. "Leave it to me," he said. "I used to be a finder—I can find anything!" And since it was well known that he was, indeed, Mary's favorite finder, he was chosen to lead an expedition of twenty-five souls to scour the Oklahoma City trainyards.

The crowd seemed to approve of the idea, but then a

lone voice—it could have been anyone—called out from the crowd, "And then what? Where are we even going?"

The question brought absolute silence to the crowd. All eyes were on Milos, and Milos looked out at them, watching them watching him. They bobbed up and down in that odd way an Afterlight crowd did when trying to keep from sinking in living ground.

Milos cleared his throat, although there was nothing there to block his voice, and spoke as commandingly as he could.

"Mary wanted this to be a surprise, but maybe she won't mind if I tell you." Then he pointed off to the setting sun. "There is a deadspot in the West," Milos told them. "A deadspot larger than any you've ever seen. It is a beautiful place filled with everything you could ever want or need. A place where you can all be happy forever. This is where Mary wants us to go."

And the crowd applauded—some actually even cheered. There was one problem, though:

Milos was lying.

Mary's plan was to head west, and conquer . . . but "west" was a direction, not a destination, and while these children could blindly trust Mary to lead them, they weren't so blind when it came to Milos. He was afraid to consider what they might do to him if they knew Milos had no idea where they were going, or what to do when they got there.

CHAPTER 5

Allie in Distress

There were many things of which Allie was unaware. How could she know what went on behind her when her only view was the world in front of her?

She knew that Mary Hightower had been pushed out of Everlost, and into the living world, because Allie had been there, and had helped turn her back into flesh and blood. . . . Yet Allie did *not* know that Mary's second life was already over, and that she was just a few months away from awakening in Everlost again.

Allie knew that Nick, the "Chocolate Ogre," had finally been overcome by his chocolate cancer, and had dissolved into nothing—but she did not know that Mikey McGill, still deeply in love with her, had gathered the shapeless melted mass that had once been Nick, and had given him shape once more.

Allie had no way of knowing that Charlie and Johnnie-O—Nick's staunchest allies—were now hopelessly adrift in the *Hindenburg*, and that the massive airship was at the mercy of the Everlost sky.

And Allie didn't know about reaping.

She knew it was possible, but even if she had known what Mary's skinjackers were doing, what could she have done to stop them? To be imprisoned, unable to do anything was, for Allie, the worst punishment yet devised. She had been Allie the Outcast, an Afterlight to be reckoned with. Now she was a joke, and it burned her more than the heat of the earth's core ever could. She immediately flashed to that stupid old silent-movie image of the damsel in distress tied to the railroad tracks, helplessly wailing. If she ever got off this train, she vowed never to be so helpless again. She'd rather sink to the center of the earth than suffer the indignity of needing rescue.

There was a way out of this—there had to be. In theory, she could skinjack her way off the train by touching a living person passing by, slip into that person's body, and just walk away. However, the train never brought her in contact with the living. Even when they traveled through populated areas, the living never crossed directly into her path, and it wasn't like she could shout to them and call them over.

Still, she would find a way out of this, and once she escaped the train, she would leave Everlost. She would not go down the tunnel and into the light—that was for those who were truly dead. But skinjackers had other alternatives. . . .

She had learned the secret of skinjackers—the thing that no skinjacker ever spoke of, but every skinjacker eventually discovered. Skinjackers are not dead, but are in deep, deep comas . . . not quite dead, but not quite alive, either.

But if her body was still alive . . . maybe—just maybe—she could skinjack herself.

There was one problem, however. If she did it, it meant leaving Mikey behind. The thought of it challenged her resolve. Could she say good-bye to him, after the years they'd spent together? She loved him. It was not a simple love—it was as deeply complicated as true love should be, full of strength and vulnerability, joy and frustration. A powerful connection between them, more tangible than eternity. Could she sacrifice that for a chance at living? She wondered where Mikey was now, and what he would say. Would he talk her out of leaving, or encourage her to go? With Mikey there was no telling. He was a spirit who could be both selfish and gallant at the same time. It was part of what made her love him.

Of course none of her musings mattered as long as she was tied to the grille of a train.

On the day that Speedo left on his expedition to find railroad tracks, Milos and his skinjackers went off as well, for their own dark purposes. Allie assumed it was their usual "skinjacking for fun and profit."

Then, just a few minutes after they had gone, Allie was visited by the strangest spirit. A boy that seemed part cat. Clearly this was not one of Mary's children.

"I thought you were bound by a spell," he said as he approached, "but now I can see it's nothing but rope that has crossed into Everlost."

Allie had seen all sorts of body modifications in Everlost— some intentional, some not—but few were as exquisite as this boy's. "Who are you?" Allie asked. She waited for an answer, but he gave her none.

"They fear you," he said. "If they didn't, they wouldn't

treat you this way." She knew it was true, but it didn't change her sense of powerlessness.

"Are there many of you?" Allie asked. "Are you going to attack the train?" If there was a whole army of cat-kids, then this could be a good thing. If they saw Milos and the others as enemies, then they could see Allie as a friend, and might free her.

"I am here as a guest of the Eastern Witch," the cat-boy said, which, again, did not answer her question.

"There is no Eastern Witch," Allie told him, taking a little bit of pride in the fact. "She won't be back, no matter what her children think."

The cat-kid raised an eyebrow. "Then who is it who sleeps in the last car?"

At first she thought she had misheard him. Then she thought he was making some sort of joke. Then she realized he didn't have a sense of humor. He was dead serious. But if Mary was in the last car, she wasn't just sleeping, she was hibernating. She was in transition between life, and—

"No!" Allie didn't want to believe it. "No! Milos didn't! He couldn't have . . . he wouldn't *dare*!" But she knew he *would* dare. Milos was audacious to an extreme—he would have no compunction about killing Mary, then pulling her out of the tunnel. It explained so many things. It explained why they were still pushing westward, following Mary's directive, as if she'd be coming back.

Allie had thought that the one consolation of being on the front of a moving train was knowing that they were moving away from Mary. . . . Little had she known that Mary was with them all along.

This was the worst of all possible news—because Allie had seen into Mary's mind, and knew the monster she was. Allie knew what Mary planned to do.

"You have to help me," Allie said to the cat-kid. "Mary can never be allowed to wake up."

"And why is that?"

"Because she plans to end the living world. She means to kill everyone and everything."

CHAPTER 6

Cat on a Cold Tin Roof

Jix found Allie's accusation against Mary worthy of further investigation. He wasn't sure he believed that the Eastern Witch would dare to do such a thing as end the living world, or if she even could. Regardless, with so many months until Mary Hightower woke up, there were more immediate things to tend to.

Jix found that he had freedom to move through the train as long as Jill was with him. She was assigned to escort him wherever he went.

"I'm not an escort," Jill grumbled to Milos when he gave her the assignment. "I've got better things to do."

"I don't see you doing anything," Jix pointed out.

"Nobody asked you," Jill said in a threatening growl—a tone that suited her.

Milos had grinned. "I am beginning to like this guy." Which is exactly why Jix had said it.

Jix made note of everything. He learned how many kids were in the regular train cars—about fifty in each—which made it cramped but not unlivable.

More than once he witnessed kids deserting the train—usually in groups of four or five. Safety in numbers.

"Let them go," Jill had told him. "If we catch them now, they'll only run away tomorrow."

Once a day, Jix would go to the sleeping car, and visit the girl he had killed, making sure she was kept comfortable, and whispering his apology into her ear. In the living world, his younger sister would be much older than him now. He preferred to think of this girl as his sister, perpetually twelve, just as he was perpetually fifteen.

He would join in the various games the children played when the train stopped—everything from jump rope to hopscotch to tag. He got to know many of the kids, and although they were put off at first by his odd appearance, they always warmed to him.

Only the caboose was off-limits to Jix, which just piqued his desire to get in. He wanted to see the face of the sleeping witch. So great was her legend that gazing on her would be like gazing on the face of a queen. He couldn't help but feel a sense of awe each time he looked at the brightly decorated tomb—for a tomb is exactly what it was. In Everlost, however, a tomb was only a temporary thing.

After a few days, Jill seemed less and less attentive of Jix's comings and goings. On Thanksgiving night, the skinjackers went off to feast on turkey in the bodies of fleshies, and Mary's children, who had lost all track of living-world celebrations, settled into their evening routines. Jix decided this was the perfect moment to pay a visit to the Eastern Witch. He used his catlike stealth to climb up to the roof of the caboose, cold and rough beneath his bare feet. Then he pried open the small skylight, and quietly slipped inside.

The glass coffin in the center of the caboose was impressive, and the girl inside was at peace—as if she knew Everlost was still under her control even during her slumber. She was both unremarkable and extraordinary at the same time; an angelic face that could belong to any girl and yet also unforgettable. He knew that if Afterlights dreamed, Mary Hightower would be at the core of many of them . . . and perhaps at the core of many nightmares as well.

"Estos niños te veneran," he said, slipping into Spanish. "These children worship you—I'm not surprised you rest in such peace." He wondered which would be better: to be in the service of Mary Hightower, or to present her as a gift to His Excellency? Certainly Jix would be rewarded for it; in fact, the king might even remember his name.

"Take a picture. It'll last longer," Jill said.

Jix spun and growled, reflexively crouching to a pounce position.

Jill came out of the shadows—but how could she even *be* in shadow? Afterlights all have a glow about them—the dark provides no concealment. Even now Jill's glow filled the dim caboose as brightly as his own. How could he have missed seeing her?

"What are you doing here?" he growled, but it came out more like weak mewling.

"Waiting for you." She pointed up to the skylight. "I saw you climbing up to the roof." She produced the combination lock from her pocket. "Milos thinks he's the only one who knows the combination."

"So you were stalking me. . . ."

"Maybe you're just not as stealthy as you think."

Jix quickly composed himself. Jackin' Jill was shrewd and crafty. He already knew she was dangerous—he knew that on the night he met her reaping. The thought of how dangerous she must be made him feel the slightest bit electrified.

"You hid in the shadows. How did you do that?" he asked.

"I dimmed my afterglow."

"How?"

"You're in no position to ask questions," she told him. "I should go to Milos right now, and tell him I caught you breaking in on Mary."

"You're the one with the lock. I could tell him *I* caught *you*."

"Do you really think he'll believe that?"

"Yes," said Jix. "Because he trusts you even less than he trusts me."

The smug expression left her face, and she took an aggressive step closer. If she attacked him, it would be an interesting contest. Would she scratch or punch or slap? Or maybe she would move in closer than that, and wrestle him. Jix would often volunteer to fight for His Excellency's amusement, and he knew many impressive wrestling moves. Which moves could he use on Jill, he wondered? Would he choose to pin her, or throw her off? Again, the thought of it sent a wave of excitement running through him.

"Why did you come in here?" she asked.

"I was curious."

"Curiosity killed the cat," she quickly replied—exactly as he knew she would. It put him in control of the conversation without her even realizing it.

She glanced down to the coffin. "So now you've seen her. Is she everything you imagined she'd be?"

Jix shrugged. "She's just a girl who sleeps, *verdad*?"

"And yet she's more powerful asleep than most of us are awake." Jill looked him over, and he tightened his abs for the event. "I still haven't figured you out," she said. "Why are you even here on this train? It can't be because you want to be one of Mary's loyal servants. You're too much of a loner for that."

"Like you," Jix pointed out.

"I stay because I find it amusing. I like watching Milos spin his wheels and try to play 'daddy' to Mary's little snot-noses. But you don't have a reason to be here, and you never say anything about yourself. I find that highly suspect."

Jix smiled and gave her his best catlike stare. Jill was unfazed. What was it about her that intrigued him? She was not particularly attractive, and yet he enjoyed gazing at her. There was a certain . . . *rudeness* to her soul that Jix could not define. It was almost like a scent; sharp, but not entirely unpleasant. It made his nose twitch. When he had first met Jill, he had despised her . . . but there's a fine line between hate and certain other emotions.

"Are you going reaping tonight?" Jix asked.

"Mmmmmaybe," she said. It came out like a purr. "If Milos lets me."

How strange, thought Jix, *that she shows Milos such disrespect, yet knows which rules must be obeyed. So very feline.*

"You have an urge to hunt and to kill," Jix said. "As a human, that makes you a criminal. But as a cat, you'd merely be following an instinct."

She gave him an arrogant glare. "I don't furjack," she said. "If you ask me, I think it's sick."

"You say that only because you've never done it." He moved closer to her. "Don't you ever long to be something different? Something . . . *other*?" He reached out his forearm toward her. "Touch my arm."

"Why?"

"It's not just the color and the spots—it's beginning to feel like fur."

Cautiously, she reached out and brushed a finger across his velvet forearm the way one might touch a snake.

"It takes a very long time," he said, "but you can change yourself into what you choose to skinjack." Then he locked his gaze on hers. "There are no jaguars this far north, but there are mountain lions, I think. . . . If you became a lioness, I could be your male."

"Gross!" she said, but Jix just smiled.

"Your lips say 'no,' but your eyes tell a different story."

And at that, Jackin' Jill, who clearly never stepped back from anyone, took a major step backward.

"We're done here, Simba."

"For now," said Jix, the grin never leaving his face.

She turned and headed for the door, but didn't leave quite yet. "Think of something awful," she said, with her back to him.

"*¿Como?*" he asked. "What?"

"That's how you dowse your afterglow. Think of something awful, and your glow goes away, but just for a few seconds." And then she was gone, locking the door, and forcing him to leave the way he came in.

In her book *Tips for Taps*, Mary Hightower has this to say about human emotions:

"We in Everlost are bound by many of the same emotions that we had in life. Joy and despair, love and hate, fear and contentment. Only skinjackers, however, who still have access to flesh, are cursed with those unwholesome feelings brought on by biology, which includes all forms of burning desires. They should be pitied, because unlike the rest of us, they are closer to animals."

CHAPTER 7

What Allie Saw

After a week, Speedo's team of finders returned with a single railroad track.

"One down, about twenty more to go," Speedo said cheerfully, his oversized grin stretching quite literally from ear to ear.

While Milos was more than happy to stall as long as possible, Mary's hordes were getting restless, and nothing would quell the growing discontent but moving them closer to their imaginary destination.

Milos had no choice but to go back to Allie.

"Tell me what you saw," Milos said, "and I will set you free."

"Deal," Allie told him. And then she said, "This church isn't what it appears to be."

"If it's not a church, then what is it?"

"No—it's still a church but . . ." She sighed. "It would make much more sense if you saw it for yourself. Then you can honestly tell everyone *you* figured it out, and be the big hero."

"I went back along the tracks. I looked. I saw nothing."

"Did you go to the top of the hill?"

"That," said Milos, "is much more than a mile."

"My mistake," said Allie. "Hard to measure distance when you're tied to the front of a train."

Again, Milos backtracked alone, and when the tracks began to climb up the hill, he kept going all the way to the top, which afforded him a view of the train, and the terrain around it. There was a small living-world lake to the right of the train, and on the other side of the lake there was a deadspot, about the size of a house. Only a person with a wide view from the front of the train could have seen it as the train came down the hill. There was nothing on the deadspot—just a square made of stones, and a few stone steps that led nowhere. It was the foundation of a building.

It was not unusual for random bits and pieces of the living world to cross into Everlost, but there was something very wrong with this picture. Foundations did not cross into Everlost . . . entire buildings did.

Now he understood exactly what Allie had seen—and what it meant for all of them.

Milos raced back to the train, the memory of a heart beating in his chest, not out of exertion, but out of excitement and out of a fear he was not yet ready to admit. When he arrived back, the others knew right away that something was wrong. Perhaps it was in his eyes, or maybe his Afterlight glow had grown paler—maybe even a little sickly green.

Milos weaved through the groups of jump-roping, ball-playing, yo-yo–bouncing kids, and found Speedo preparing to go out on another rail-finding expedition.

"I will need fifty of our strongest Afterlights," Milos told him.

"What for?" asked Speedo.

Milos didn't bother answering him. "Gather them and have them meet me by the church."

Allie knew that Milos had figured it out, because he came to the front of the train with a huge group of Afterlights—too many for her to count.

"I told you you'd see it," Allie said, pretending not to be anxious. "All it took was a little perspective." Milos gave her a quick glance, but not a kind one.

"I don't understand," said Speedo. "Are all these Afterlights for my expedition?"

"There will not be another expedition," Milos told him. "Look under the church. Tell me what you see."

Speedo reluctantly knelt down, getting eye-level with the railroad ties. "I see the bottom of the church . . . and the tracks underneath it."

"Exactly," said Milos. "The church is sitting *on top* of the tracks."

"So what?" said Speedo. "It's still in our way."

Again, Milos glanced at Allie giving her a chilly look, then he returned all his attention to Speedo.

"Since when does a building cross into Everlost without a foundation?" asked Milos. Speedo could only stammer. "The answer is, it *doesn't*." Then he pointed across the lake. "The church's foundation is over there."

"So . . . if the church crossed over there . . . ," said Speedo, his voice shaking, ". . . how did it get onto our tracks?" But by the way he asked, it was clear Speedo didn't want to know the answer.

"Someone moved it here," Milos informed him. "Someone lifted it up, carried it all the way around the lake, and put it down right in our path."

"Milos gets a gold star!" said Allie.

Then Milos, always one to blame the messenger, turned on her in fury. "You keep your mouth shut or I will find some duct tape and tape it closed!"

To which Allie calmly responded, "Duct tape never crosses." Which was true. Things that cross into Everlost are usually loved, and nobody loves duct tape. Its use is, at best, an annoyance.

"If it moved once," Milos said, "it can move again."

"You . . . you want us to move it back?" asked Speedo.

Allie snickered, which only made Milos more irritated.

"We don't need to move it back, just off the tracks. Understand?"

"Oh," said Speedo as if it were a grand revelation. "I get it!"

Milos lined up the Afterlights on one side of the church. Then, on Milos's command, they began to lift and release, lift and release, over and over until the church began to rock back and forth. Even with fifty Afterlights, the church was so heavy, it took forever until they were able to build any sort of momentum.

Up above, the steeple wavered like a metronome, cutting a wider and wider arc across the sky. By now all the rest of Mary's children had come out to see what was going on. Moose and Squirrel watched like it was prime-time TV, Jill crossed her arms and feigned complete disinterest, and Jix observed stoically, without revealing how he felt about it either way.

The anticipation of all those assembled built as the church rocked on the tracks, until finally the building reached the edge of its balance, slid off the tracks, and tumbled over on its side, landing unbroken on the ground beside the train. Without a deadspot to rest on, the church began to slowly sink into the living world.

The Afterlights all cheered, giving Milos all the credit for clever thinking—although he knew it wasn't *his* cleverness that had solved their predicament. It was Allie's.

"Load up the train," Milos commanded. "And stoke the engine."

"What about me?" asked Allie. "Will you take me down from here now, like you promised?" Milos looked at her, thought for a moment, then said to Moose and Squirrel, "All right. Untie her from the train."

Allie relaxed, fully ready for freedom until Milos said, "Take her down, then tie her back to the train again. This time, upside down."

"What?"

Milos climbed up to her, getting right in her face. "All this time you knew, and you left us like sitting geese."

"Sitting ducks," Allie corrected, and then wished she hadn't.

"Did you think that whoever put the church here would attack the rest of us and set you free?"

Allie didn't answer him . . . because that's exactly what she thought.

"I am sorry," said Milos, "but you are far too useful as a

scarecrow for me to put you anywhere else." Then he turned to the others. "I want everyone who sees us coming to know that we are not to be trifled with. I want everyone seeing this train to fear it—to fear *us*. I want them terrified."

"Them?" asked Speedo. "Them, who?"

"It took fifty of us just to knock over that church," said Milos. "How many do you think it took to move it all the way around the lake?"

Speedo said nothing, clearly not wanting to consider the answer.

Allie struggled against Moose and Squirrel but it was no use. "Do you think that tying me up like that will scare them? Whoever they are, they're not scared of us, and they don't want us trespassing."

Milos responded by turning to the crowd and announcing in his loudest, most commanding voice: *"I hereby claim this territory in the name of Mary Hightower!"* and the crowd cheered even more loudly than before. "Now *they* are the ones trespassing," Milos told Allie. "Whoever they are."

With Allie tied back onto the grille upside down, the train continued forward . . . while beside it, the church lost its battle with gravity and, like a foundering ship, sank into the quicksand of the living world.

PART TWO

The Wraith and the Warriors

High Altitude Musical Interlude #1
with Johnnie and Charlie

There is no wind in Everlost. At least none that occurs naturally. No nor'easters heralding winter, no gentle summer zephyrs. Even Everlost trees that rustle in the wind are only going through the motions, moving with the memory of a breeze long gone.

That is not to say that Everlost has no atmosphere; it does. The air of Everlost is a direct result of the living, and is a blend of many things. The first breath of a baby and the last breath of a life well-lived. The charged air of anticipation that fills a stadium before the start of a game, and the electrified air of excitement when a band takes the concert stage—these all cross into Everlost. Every passage of gas that someone laughed at, every sigh offered up to a glorious sunset are here . . . but so are the screams of victims and the sobs of those who mourn.

Not every breath, but every breath taken and expelled with purpose, be it good or bad, are not forgotten by the universe. These things all blend and make up the air that Afterlights occasionally choose to breathe; air rich with emotions and with memories not entirely lost.

And since these moments are at peace with eternity,

they do not bluster and blow. One may ask, then, without a jet stream surging in the sky, how did the *Hindenburg*—the largest zeppelin ever built and burst by mankind—how did such a massive airship drift across the Atlantic Ocean? The answer is quite simple; one does not need a natural wind to be blown eastward, when there's an unnatural one.

"I've been working on the railroad, all the live-long day!"

On the day that Mary defeated Nick, and her army took over his train, Mary's former mode of transportation, the giant airship *Hindenburg*, was set adrift into the sky over Memphis. There were only two Afterlights aboard: the juvenile train conductor known as Choo-choo Charlie, and Johnnie-O; two kids loyal to Nick and caught in the wrong place at the wrong time.

"I've been working on the railroad, just to pass the time away!"

The control room of the airship was empty, sealed by a lock with no key—which meant there was no way to pilot the craft. Its engines were off, its rudder was stuck, and it would stay that way.

"Can't you hear the whistle blowing, rise up so early in the morn?"

That first day, they sat across from each other with a bucket of Everlost coins between them. Both Charlie and Johnnie-O knew what the coins were for. Holding a coin would pay the passage into the next world. The tunnel would open before them; they would remember who they were in life, and then they would be gone down the tunnel, and into the light. After all these years, they would get where they were going . . . if they held a coin.

"Can't ya hear the captain shouting, 'Dina blow your horn.'"

But neither of them had taken their coins. At the time, Charlie was just plain scared, and Johnnie-O knew he wasn't ready. Something deep inside Johnnie told him he had more to do in Everlost.

When their journey had first begun, the unnatural wind blowing them back from the Mississippi was powerful enough to give them an eastern momentum. The Everlost air offered them no friction, no resistance, nothing to stop their drift, and so a few days after leaving Memphis, they passed the eastern seaboard and were out over the Atlantic Ocean. That ocean seemed endless. Each day Johnnie would look out of the window to see yet more ocean around them, to every horizon.

That's when Charlie had begun to sing. At first he'd just hum to himself, then he'd mumble the words, and soon he'd become lost in the endless verses.

"Dinah won't you blow . . ."

For weeks Charlie had been singing the same song over and over again.

"Dinah won't you blow . . ."

He sang it twenty-four hours a day, with that same vacant, cheerful tone.

"Dinah won't you blow your hor-or-orn?"

He kept the beat with his head, endlessly banging it against the hallway bulkhead.

"Dinah won't you blow . . ."

Johnnie-O, who had very little patience to begin with, would have pulled out his hair, were it possible for an Afterlight's hair to come out.

"Dinah won't you blow . . ."

Johnnie squeezed his oversized hands into fists, wishing there was something he could bust, but having spent many years trying to break things, he knew more than anyone that Everlost stuff didn't break, unless breakage was its purpose.

"Dinah won't you blow your horn!"

"Dammit, will you shut your hole or I swear I'm gonna pound you into next Tuesday and then throw you out the stinkin' window where you and your song can drown and sink down to the center of the earth for all I care, so you better shut your hole right now!"

Charlie looked at him for a moment, eyes wide, considering it. Then he said: *"Someone's in the kitchen with Dinah!"*

Johnnie groaned.

"Someone's in the kitchen I know-oh-oh-oh!"

Unable to take it anymore, Johnnie grabbed Charlie and dragged him down to the starboard promenade, where the windows had a dramatic view of the clouds, and the shimmering Atlantic Ocean below.

"I'll do it!" Johnnie-O screamed, but Charlie just kept on singing. Maybe that's what Charlie wanted, or maybe he was just so far gone, he didn't even hear Johnnie anymore. Johnnie had seen spirits go like that. He had seen souls who were so ready to leave and complete their journey, that they had fallen into an endless loop, happy to pass the time, however long it took, until the tunnel opened before them. If that were the case, Charlie would be at home at the center of the earth, waiting for time to end.

But Johnnie-O, tough guy that he was, couldn't do that to him. He couldn't give Charlie a coin either. He knew he should, because Charlie was clearly no longer afraid . . . but then if he did, and Charlie went down the tunnel and into the light, Johnnie would truly be alone.

So he put Charlie down, and they sat in the lavishly decorated starboard promenade, and waited for happenstance to take them where it would.

Then, the day after he almost threw Charlie out of the window, Johnnie saw something in the distance that wasn't ocean. He shook Charlie in excitement.

"Look!" he said. "Look! It's China!"

Johnnie-O wasn't an expert in geography. He knew, however, that China was called "the Far East," and he assumed that their eastward journey would take them there. What he called China was actually the coast of Spain.

Once they reached the coastline, Johnnie contented himself with watching the view, listening to the faint sounds of the living below, and searching for deadspots on the ground. Then, the next day, to Johnnie's dismay, the sun rose to reveal that they were out over water once more.

"Oh, great," said Johnnie. "Where are we now?"

"Strummin' on the old banjo!" sang Charlie.

Johnnie-O suspected this was going to be a very long eternity.

CHAPTER 8
Half-lost

The old man was horrible to behold in both worlds. Half of his face had been ruined by fire. His left eye was dead and unseeing, and his left ear was deaf as a post. His left hand only had the memory of fingers, for it had fallen victim to the flames as well. Occasionally those nonexistent fingers itched. The doctors said it was a very common sensation for those who have lost a part of themselves.

He had long ago given up any attempts to disguise the scarring, or to hide it from the judgmental eyes of strangers—and everyone was a stranger now. Those who saw him always averted their eyes. Charitable people looked away in pity; others looked away in disgust—but in the end no one wanted to look upon him.

Who he had been in the first half of his life meant nothing anymore. The living world was unforgiving of old scars. Sure, there had been great sympathy at first, but sympathy has a short shelf life. The same people who once called him a hero now turned the other way when they saw him in the street—never knowing that this was the celebrated firefighter who had lost the left half of his life in a tenement inferno, while saving half a dozen people. All they saw was a ruined man in tattered rags, panhandling on highway exit ramps.

From the day his bandages came off, Clarence knew that something profound had happened to him—more profound, even, than the burns still raw on his face.

"I see things," Clarence would tell people. "I see impossible things with my dead eye."

If he had stayed quiet about the things he saw, he would have held on to his life, and adapted, as other burn victims do—but Clarence was not the kind of man who kept quiet.

"The things I see," he would tell anyone who would listen, "are terrible, but wonderful, too."

He would tell of the twin towers, still standing in New York, "touching the sky, just as sure as I'm standing here."

He would tell of the many ghosts he saw going about their business. "They're all children! They're dead and yet somehow they're not."

He would tell of the fears that kept him awake at night. "My dead ear can hear them sometimes—and some of them are up to no good. They'll kill you soon as look at you." And he talked about how his left eye could still see fingers on his left hand—and those fingers could actually touch all the things that no one else could see!

They gave him medication for a while, convincing Clarence that he was very, very sick—that his brain was damaged by the fire. The medication numbed his senses, and made it hard to get inside his own head—but none of that medicine made his visions go away. That's how he knew the problem was not him, it was the rest of the world.

"I see things, and I don't care if no one believes me!" he would yell in frustration. And, of course, no one did believe him. No one wanted to hear the ravings of a lunatic—much less the ravings of a burn-scarred lunatic. They just wanted him to go away. So the world forgot he was a hero, and instead labeled him a public nuisance.

For many years he wandered from city to city, state to state, looking for all the things he might see with his dead eye. He lived anywhere he didn't get thrown out of, which meant he never lived anywhere for long. Mostly he lived out in the open, everywhere from city streets, to country fields, trying to make sense of his visions—hoping that one day it would all fit together and he'd know why he was cursed with this gift of vision.

Clarence was in Memphis the day the Union Avenue Bridge came crashing down.

With his right, living eye, he saw the explosions, and the collapsing bridge . . . but with his left eye he saw the ghost bridge now standing in its place, and the spirit train that rode across it, heading west.

Indeed, things were brewing in the half-dead world, and the only way to find out how bad the brew had become was to capture a spirit or two. If he could do that, maybe he could prove they existed. Maybe a special camera could photograph them. Anything to prove to the world that he was sane and they were blind.

He took up residence in an abandoned farmhouse that looked one storm short of surrender, a few miles west of the

Mississippi. To Clarence's dead eye, however, that farmhouse looked as fresh and fine as the day it was built. There he came up with a plan.

He built himself a trap made of brass bed frames that no longer existed, from homes that were washed away in a flood. To anyone watching, he knew he must have looked mad—dragging invisible bed frames, with invisible fingers, but how he appeared to the world was of no consequence now.

Then, using that same dead hand, he hinged the bed frames with powerful springs, so when the trap was sprung it would snap closed, trapping the evil spirit inside.

For bait he used a glazed ham that would have been someone's Christmas dinner, had the delivery truck not hit a tree. The truck didn't cross into the ghost-place, but some of the meals it carried did.

For weeks he waited in the farmhouse, watching his trap out in the fallow field between the house and the highway. He knew something was coming before it even arrived, because he smelled it. It was not an aroma from the living world, because his sense of smell was lost in the fire. It came from the ghost-place, pungent and strong. Clarence had to smile. He had forgotten how much he liked the scent of chocolate.

CHAPTER 9

Assaulting Gravity

The earth is roughly eight thousand miles in diameter. Its center is four thousand miles down. While the living world is not solid enough to hold a stationary Afterlight on its surface, neither is it soft enough to make a downward journey quick. Still, sinking slowly, over a period of many, many years is no one's idea of fun.

Mikey McGill had been to the center of the earth, which, to an Afterlight, is no more hellish than waiting for one's father to come home for supper . . . if supper wasn't coming for a few billion years.

What had struck Mikey as the most annoying part of it was how everyone but he had developed a deep sense of contentment and peace. They had adapted to their situation, and had all come to love the waiting. Ask any soul who has sunk to the center, and they'll tell you that, at least for now, there is no place they'd rather be.

Mikey, however, never got with the program. He never felt "one with the earth." He never experienced the joy of Nirvana. The thought of patiently waiting until the end of time — or at least the end of the planet — was as unappealing to him as, oh, say, waiting for his father to come home for supper, which Mikey had actually found extremely hellish in life, because he never had any patience for anything.

There were those among the Centered Ones who believed that their very presence at the core is what allowed the planet to be a green, living thing, rather than just a rock hurtling through space—and that they were not lost to the living world, but a crucial part of the life cycle. Whether they were right or wrong didn't matter to Mikey. He just didn't want to be there. So he had decided to climb out.

Since strength in Everlost is determined by the power of one's will, and since Mikey McGill was the most willful spirit ever to sink to the center of the earth, he was able to climb back to the surface. He didn't just defy gravity, he assaulted it, and in so doing, became the only soul ever to return from the center. Of course when he emerged, he had transformed into the most heinous of monsters. He called himself the McGill, and struck fear into the hearts of Afterlights everywhere. Being the One True Monster of Everlost suited him for a while—but as much as his sister, Megan (better known as Mary Hightower), loved order and permanence, Mikey loved chaos and change. He couldn't stay the McGill forever—and although he now possessed the remarkable skill of tweaking himself into whatever form of monster he desired, he found, for the most part, he preferred the form he started with: a boy with slightly unruly auburn hair, who, according to Allie the Outcast, was somewhat decent-looking.

Just as his love for Allie had saved him, however, it now threatened to doom him . . . because in those days and weeks after the collapse of the Union Avenue Bridge, while Allie was taken hostage on a train headed west, Mikey was, once again, on his way to the center of the earth. This time, someone else was sinking with him; an Afterlight once known as Nick, but now more accurately called the Chocolate Ogre.

It had been a calculated risk on Mikey's part to try to travel beneath the Mississippi river, instead of facing the impassable wind—but he had to go after Allie. He had to rescue her, and this seemed the only way to do it.

The plan was to sink into the living world, move through the bedrock beneath the riverbed, then come up on the other side. He had managed something similar a few years back, diving into the earth on horseback, to rescue Allie from sinking.

This new challenge, however, had proven to be very different. Back when he saved Allie from the depths, he had more of the monster in him—a proud, arrogant fury that made it easier to assault gravity. But Mikey was not the monster he was. His time with Allie had left him far too human. Certainly he could tweak himself up a pair of spatula claws for hands, making it easier to move through the stone of the living world, but he had to face the fact that rising from the depths required more than that. It took willpower and a fury that raged hotter than the bowels of the earth. Mikey McGill certainly had willpower, but his love for Allie had taken the edge off of his fury.

And then there was the added burden of Nick. In the end Nick had become exactly what Mary said he would become. The small brown smudge on his mouth, left there from candy he was eating the moment he died, grew like a fungus until nothing was left of him but that chocolate.

He would have dissolved into nothing, had it not been for Mikey, whose skill at soul-tweaking extended beyond just the changing of his own form. Mikey took buckets of bittersweet spiritual fudge, and with more patience than he knew he had, Mikey had shaped it back into humanoid form.

But Nick was not the same.

He had only the faintest memory of who and what he was. He was like a small child, entirely dependent on Mikey, with no will of his own. He had truly become a Chocolate Ogre.

Still, knowing the risks, Mikey took them both down, letting them sink into the living world.

"I'm scared," the Ogre had said with a gurgling cocoa-rich voice.

Mikey had sworn to him that it would all be okay, and the Ogre had trusted him. It had taken only a few minutes in the ground, and away from daylight, for Mikey to realize that the task might be beyond him.

"Move your arms!" Mikey had commanded as they sank deeper and deeper. "Kick your legs like you're swimming."

"What's swimming?" the Ogre responded. The spirit that had once been Nick was now a dim-witted thing with no survival skills. And so they struggled, moving ever downward as Mikey tried in vain to move them up.

That's how it was for weeks. Mikey strained against gravity with the Chocolate Ogre clinging to him, a helpless weight around his neck. Mikey had no idea how deep they had gone, or even if they had moved far enough West to have passed under the Mississippi River, which now flowed somewhere far above them.

"It's dark!" the Ogre would say every once in a while, each time like it was the first time he had noticed it.

"Dark is good," Mikey would tell him. "If the rock around us starts to glow, and get molten, then we're *really* in trouble."

Molten magma would mean they were leaving the earth's crust, and entering the mantle. The heat wouldn't burn them, but they would sink faster, leaving them no hope of returning to the surface. They would sink until there was no direction but up, and they'd join all the others who were probably still singing *a trillion bottles of beer on the wall*, which Mikey had started when he was first down there, and calculated would go on for thirty-two thousand years.

But they weren't there yet.

As long as the stone of the living world around them was dark and relatively cool, they couldn't be more than a mile or two down, so there was still hope.

"Maybe we should just give up," the Ogre said to him in the midst of their endless struggle. "Maybe we should give up, and let what happens happen. Let the earth take us where it wants us to go. Is that a good idea?"

"No!" The suggestion infuriated Mikey. He wanted to tear the chocolate creature limb from limb for saying it—and he discovered that the anger gave him strength. Striking back at the Ogre would not help them—but taking that anger and channeling it into upward momentum—that would make a difference.

If Mikey let go of the Chocolate Ogre, he knew he could

save himself, but the days of the selfish, self-centered McGill were gone. He wouldn't do that to Nick. They would rise to the surface together, or not at all.

"This will not be our fate!" he screamed to the stone around him. Whether or not the earth was alive he did not know, but it seemed to have a will of its own. It wanted to draw them down into its womb, and hold them there until the world itself was no more. Perhaps that was acceptable, maybe even desirable for other souls, but not for him. He was not a Centered One. He was Mikey McGill, and he had things to do!

First of all, he had to save Allie! Without him, she would be a prisoner of Mary. Even worse, she would be at the mercy of that two-faced skinjacking slimeball Milos! Mikey could not bear to leave her in his clutches. The thought of it added to his fury, and his fury was transposed into muscle, moving them upward.

He renewed the struggle, and realized that arms and legs in this dense, gritty darkness were useless. He had the power to change, and realized there were forms more suitable for moving in dense, murky depths. He drew in his arms, and turned them into flippers. He fused his legs, and turned them into a fluke. He imagined himself a whale, but covered with sharp, toothlike ridges that could grip stone. Then he sprouted himself a dorsal fin.

"Hold on to that, and don't let go," he told the Chocolate Ogre, who, if nothing else, was very good at doing what he was told. Then Mikey began to force them upward through the stone of the living world, imagining all those things that made him furious—all those things that he knew he could change if he could only be back on the surface again.

He had no sense of direction now. But he knew they were moving upward because the earth around him and within him was getting colder and colder. Then after many days, he breached into the light of day, and the sun almost blinded him. It came so suddenly, he didn't know what to do next. He had almost forgotten what it was to be a spirit in Everlost. Before he could sink again, he found deep in his thoughts an image of who he was. Mikey McGill. Mary's brother. Allie's soulmate. Perhaps the one boy who could make a difference in the battle for souls in Everlost.

Before he knew it, his form transformed back into that of a human, and with what little strength he had left, he reached out and grabbed the hand of the Chocolate Ogre, who was already beginning to sink back into the earth.

"We've got to keep moving now," he reminded the Ogre. "If we don't, we'll sink again."

"It's bright here," the Ogre said. "Where are we? Where are we going?"

"We're going to rescue Allie," he told the Ogre. "I don't know where we are right now, but we'll figure it out soon enough."

Then a succulent aroma came to them, so pungent, it overcame the rich smell of chocolate.

"Do you smell that?" said the Ogre. "It smells good!"

Mikey was wary. He knew that in Everlost that which was pleasing to the senses was sometimes the tip of something much less pleasant. "Whatever it is, let's avoid it."

But like a dog fixed on a scent, the Ogre couldn't resist. He determined the direction of the smell, and took off after it.

"Nick, no!"

Mikey ran after him, trying to stop him—but found that his feet were still welded into a thorn-encrusted whale fluke. He fell flat on his face, and by the time he had transformed his fluke into two human legs, the Chocolate Ogre was bounding away.

There was a honey ham, glistening, as if it had come right off a holiday table, stuck into a post that had crossed into Everlost. Like all Everlost food, it was perfectly preserved and at the peak of flavor.

"Nick, don't touch it!"

But nothing could stop the Chocolate Ogre now.

Mikey caught up with him just as he grabbed the ham, and the instant he did, a trap sprang up around them both, locking into place. It was a cage! They were locked in a cage!

"Now look what you've done!" shouted Mikey, but the Ogre didn't seem to care. He just joyfully sunk his dark teeth into the ham, leaving behind a ring of chocolate with every bite he took.

There was a shout of glee, then strange maniacal laughter coming from a farmhouse that was slowly decaying itself into Everlost. A figure left the porch, approaching them. As the figure limped closer, Mikey could see that he was alive, but not entirely.

And for the first time in a very, very long time, Mikey McGill was truly afraid.

In her book *Everything You Wanted to Know About Everlost, but Were Ashamed to Ask*, Mary Hightower has this to say about scar wraiths:

"Scar wraiths do not exist, plain and simple. The very idea that someone could be part-way in and part-way out of Everlost is preposterous. Either you are blessed with admission into Everlost, or you are not. As for those awful legends about a scar wraith's ability to extinguish an Everlost soul and wipe it out of existence, those legends are entirely false. Nothing can hurt an Afterlight, much less kill one. Let me say this again, in case there is any doubt. Scar wraiths do not exist. However, if you see one, please report it to an authority."

CHAPTER 10
Wraith, Wraith, Go Away

Mikey screamed.

He had never screamed in all his years in Everlost, but this was something stranger and more horrible than anything he had ever seen: a man who existed part in and part out of Everlost. That steely gray eye, that cheek—and even one hand that almost seemed to hang in the air in front of the hazy blur of his living body— and where his Everflesh attached to his living flesh was an angry red line that sparked like a short circuit.

Mikey knew the scar wraith legend. It was second only to scary stories about himself when he was the McGill. According to the legend, just the brush of an arm, the grip of a shoulder, the caress of a cheek from a scar wraith's hand would "kill" an Afterlight. But worse than dying, the Afterlight would extinguish. No light. No tunnel. Nothing. The touch of a scar wraith meant absolute death.

"Well, well, well, what have we got here . . . ," the scar wraith said, his eagle eye zipping back and forth in its socket as he examined them. His voice was both rough and almost musical, too. There was a resonance to it, like there were two sets of vocal cords, one a little higher than the other; clashing dissonant tones like an air raid siren.

"Don't touch me!" Mikey screamed. "Nick, stay away from the bars! Don't let him touch you!"

The scar wraith circled the cage with a heavy chain that had crossed into Everlost, and locked it in place with a padlock.

Mikey tried everything to escape. He turned his hands into lobster claws, his fingers into tiny buzz saws, he filled his arms with muscles and tried to pry the bars apart, but he couldn't. He might have been able to push down the sides of the spring-loaded cage, but the chain and padlock now made that impossible. He thought of squeezing through the small chain-link holes of the bed frames, but he knew that wouldn't work either. Although Mikey could reform himself into all nature of monster, all his creations were big and bulky. He couldn't fashion himself into a creature slim enough to slither through the narrow bars and chain-link holes of a bed frame.

The scar wraith reached out his Everlost hand, dangling the key to the padlock, taunting him. Mikey jumped back, terrified that the wraith might touch him.

"No way out of there," the scar wraith said. "You're mine now, both of you. Whatever you are. You're stuck in there until I'm done with you . . . and then . . ." The scar wraith put the key in his pocket, then limped back to the dilapidated farmhouse. He dragged a wooden rocking chair from the porch, set it down in front of the cage, and was content to just sit there and stare at Mikey and Nick for hours. Mikey watched him, just as intently as the wraith watched them.

No one knew why a scar wraith's touch could extinguish, but Mikey had a theory. The living world had its natural laws, its life cycle, its science. Everlost also had natural rules. True, the rules of Everlost followed the beat of a rather syncopated drummer, but the natural laws of Everlost were sensible and consistent unto themselves. . . . But a scar wraith flew in the face of both realities. It was perhaps the only truly unnatural thing in the entire universe. Was it any wonder, then, that its touch could destroy?

"So, are you going to tell me what's going on?" the scar wraith finally asked, after much rocking.

"There's a lot going on," Mikey answered. "Be more specific."

"Fine," he snapped. "If you won't talk, then you can just . . . you can just . . ." Then he grunted, and stormed back to the farmhouse.

Once the scar wraith left, the Ogre, who had been content to gnaw on the chocolate-coated ham bone said, "Can we go now?"

"No, you moron!" shouted Mikey. "We're in a stupid cage!"

"Oh," said the Ogre pleasantly. "Never mind."

Mikey immediately felt bad for losing his temper, and for a moment he longed for the good ol' days when he could lose his temper as much as he wanted and not have to feel sorry, or apologize for anything.

"I didn't mean to call you a moron," said Mikey. "I'm sorry." But the Ogre didn't seem the least bit bothered, and that just made Mikey feel worse about it. "Just make sure you stay away from that . . . that *thing* that captured us. Trust me—you don't want to know what happens if he touches you."

Mikey shivered, which made his afterglow flicker like a failing lightbulb. To be extinguished. To not . . . *be* . . .

In life, people feared it. In Everlost, souls denied the possibility—but it was always in the back of Mikey's mind, lurking among thoughts of hell and the distant memory of pain. Mikey feared the light because he wasn't ready to be judged, if indeed he would be. However, *that* was a fear he knew he would overcome when he was ready. . . . But the fear of not existing at all? He doubted he'd ever get over that.

A few hours later, after it got dark, the scar wraith returned with a broken flashlight that cast its beam only in Everlost. He shined it in their eyes. "Third degree," he said. "Age-old technique of interrogation." Then he sat down in the chair with a bucket of chicken, and ate it in front of them. "Hungry are ya? It's like my grandma always used to say . . ." Then he went on eating without finishing the thought. The way he talked, one was never quite sure when he was done, because nothing he ever said was entirely complete. His words kind of trailed off, leaving a person waiting for more. It made Mikey just want to slap him—but he knew that slapping a scar wraith was not a good idea. He'd be extinguished in an instant.

Mikey was thankful that it was living-world chicken, because he couldn't smell it, and even if the wraith threw it to him, he wouldn't be able to eat it, or even catch it—it would pass right through him like everything else in the living world. Still, watching him eat it all right down to the bone was a little bit torturous. Third degree, indeed.

"Are you going to tell me what's going on?" the wraith said, his mouth full of food. "Because if you don't . . ."

Mikey wasn't sure if anything he could say would win their freedom, but staying silent on principle would definitely not help the situation. The wraith took another bite of chicken and washed it down with whiskey straight from the bottle. It made Mikey wonder if the man's liver had also crossed.

"There was a train," Mikey said.

The wraith leaned forward, the rocking chair reaching its limit. "Go on."

"It was heading west. We were chasing it."

"Why?"

"To rescue someone."

"Do you expect me to believe that?"

"Why would I lie?"

"Because it's what ghosts do," the wraith said. "Ghosts are the best liars. You have to be if you're gonna lie to death, and to yourself, making yourself think you're still alive." He pointed an accusing chicken bone at him. "But I know what you are. You're all demons, up to no good. And you know what they say about demons. . . ." But apparently he didn't know, because that's all he said.

"We can't be both demons and ghosts," Mikey pointed out. "We're either one or the other."

"You're whatever I say you are, so you can just shut up about it."

And then Mikey realized something. "You're not

convinced we're real, are you?" Mikey smiled in spite of himself. "They've been telling you that you're crazy, and you still wonder if maybe they're right!"

"Now you're making me angry," the wraith said. "And you know what I do to ghosts that make me angry!"

Mikey took a step away from the bars just in case, then said, "No, what do you do?"

The wraith stood, took a long swig from his bottle, and eyed Mikey in that sideways way with his Everlost eye. The moon came out from behind a cloud, and it made that crossed side of his face glow—almost like the glow of an Afterlight, but not quite. "You're a wise guy," he said. "I don't like wise guys."

"Mooooon!" said the Ogre. "Tranquility . . ." Then he pointed at the full moon. "Neil Armstrong walked in a Sea of Tranquility." Then he added, "It's made of cheese. But you have to take off the plastic before you put it on your burger."

Mikey sighed.

"What's his story?" the wraith asked.

"He's chocolate," Mikey said.

"I can see that," snapped the wraith. "Why is he chocolate?"

"Because it's all he can remember of himself." Mikey thought that the wraith would ask for more, but he seemed satisfied with the answer.

"You boys got names, or do you just . . . ?"

"I'm Mikey. This is Nick."

"Clarence," he said. "Can't say that I'm pleased to meet you."

"No," said Mikey. "The displeasure is mine."

That made Clarence laugh. He sat back down, drank

some, ate some, rocked some, and finally said: "If you're real—and I think you are—you're gonna tell me how to make other people see you."

"We can't do that," said Mikey.

Clarence didn't seem bothered. "Guess you'll stay in there forever, then. . . ."

Mikey rattled the cage in frustration. "We can't do everything!"

"But you can do *some* things. You can make yourself look like a monster. All those claws and bulging eyes, like you did when I first caught you." He leaned all the way back in the chair. "Do it again."

"No! I'm not a circus monkey."

"Well, seeing as you *are* in a cage," said Clarence, "maybe that's exactly what you are. . . ."

"I wanna see the monkey!" said the Ogre, thrilled at the prospect. "Mikey, be a monkey, aw, pleeeeze!"

Mikey ignored him. Not just because he didn't want to be a monkey, but also because he couldn't. Like a kid doodling in a notebook, Mikey was great at monsters, and twisted miscreations, but drawing up something real was beyond him. A monkey-faced lizard-thing was probably the best that he could do.

"Listen to me," said Mikey, trying his best to keep his temper under control. "The girl we're trying to rescue is a skinjacker. That means *she* can prove we're real. She can possess anyone, and that will make people believe you."

Clarence looked doubtful. "You're making a joke, aren't you? Having a laugh at my expense. You watch out, because . . . because . . ."

"Because what?"

Clarence stood up, hurling the bucket of chicken and his bottle far into the living world. *"Because I don't know what!"* Then he started pacing back and forth, almost tripping over his own half-dead foot as he did. "Now that I got you, I don't know what to do with you! All I know is that I can't let you go—not now and not ever." Then he looked off toward the moon, like it held some answer. "I can't go back to panhandling, and benches, and all those eyes that won't look at me. I can't go back to being what the living people see. You're my ticket . . . my ticket to . . . to . . ." Then Clarence collapsed back into the chair, buried his head in his hands, and began to sob. "I don't know where, I don't know . . . I don't . . ." He sobbed to himself for a while, like he forgot they were even there. Then the sobs faded into snores. The wraith was asleep.

"Can we go now?" the Ogre asked.

Mikey couldn't get mad at him anymore. "No, Nick," he said. "I'm sorry, but no." He gently patted his hand on Nick's soft shoulder. When he took his hand back, it was covered in a thin layer of chocolate

. . . soft shoulder . . .

The moment the truth dawned on Mikey, he realized what an idiot he had been—how narrow his own thinking was. If Allie were here, she would have thought of it right away. Even Nick would have figured it out if he were his old self.

"Yes!" said Mikey. "Yes, Nick, you *can* go. You can walk out of this cage right now!"

"Okay," said the Ogre. Then he stepped forward, then took another step, pushing himself up against the bed frames . . . then forced himself through, like fudge pushed through a screen. For a moment, he stood there halfway in, halfway out with the brass and steel of the cage right in the middle of him. "Feels funny," he said. Then he took one more step and he was outside the cage, leaving chocolate dripping from the frame.

"You did it!"

"Yes. Your turn now!"

But Mikey knew he couldn't squeeze through any more than he could become a circus monkey.

That's when Clarence woke up and panicked. He stood, the chair flying out from behind him and tumbling to the ground. "What? How did you? Don't you . . ."

Mikey leaned as close as he could to Nick and whispered, "Don't let him touch you."

But Clarence seemed more afraid of the Ogre touching *him*. "Stand back! Stand back or I swear I'll . . ." Then Clarence turned and ran back to the farmhouse.

"Go," said Mikey. "Go and find Allie. You can do it. I know you can. Just follow the tracks."

"Follow the tracks to Allie," repeated the Ogre.

"Think about her," Mikey told him. "Think about her as much as you can. It will help you to remember!"

"Allie," said the Ogre. "We met in the dead forest. Only it wasn't dead." For a moment, there was more shape in the Ogre's face, cheekbones and a firmer chin. A different shade of brown in his eyes. It lasted for only a moment, but then it was gone. "Find Allie," the Ogre repeated. "Follow the tracks."

The door of the farmhouse banged open again, and Clarence came out holding a sawed off shotgun — which was only sawed off in the living world. In Everlost the barrel was hard and solid and pointing right at the Ogre.

"Don't move . . . don't move or I'll . . . I'll . . ."

If the touch of a scar wraith could extinguish you, could the blast of the scar wraith's shotgun do the job too? Mikey didn't want to find out.

"Run, Nick!"

Nick did what he was told. He ran, and although Clarence aimed at him, he didn't fire. In a moment the Chocolate Ogre had disappeared into the night.

"Damn it all to purgatory!" shouted Clarence and aimed the shotgun at Mikey, who put his hands up.

"If you shoot me, you'll never know."

"Never know what?"

"Everything," Mikey said. "All the things you want to know."

Slowly Clarence lowered the weapon. "Tell me," he said. Then he went to get the toppled chair, set it upright and sat down again, laying the half-dead shotgun across his lap. "Tell me."

"Okay," said Mikey. "What do you want to know?"

"Everything, just like you said. Everything there is to know from the very beginning. And if I don't like what I hear, well, let's just say . . ." Then he stroked the shotgun like a favorite pet sitting in his lap.

Mikey sat down in the middle of the cage, took a moment to compose himself, and began.

"More than a hundred years ago, my sister and I were hit by a train as we were walking home from school. . . ."

CHAPTER 11

Chocolate Reign

Nick, Nick, Nick, Nick.

The Chocolate Ogre knew very few things for sure.

Allie, Allie, Allie, Allie.

So the things he did know, he held onto with a passion.

Mikey, Mikey, Mikey, Mikey.

He found that being a spirit of limited self-awareness, while frustrating, was also very liberating. He felt a freedom he suspected he had never felt in his previous life. He had few expectations, and fewer fears, and whenever he felt anxious it passed quickly like a summer storm cloud, too small to give rain.

All in all, it was good being the Chocolate Ogre, although he didn't feel much like an Ogre. Ogres have a bad temper, they ruin things, they chase people. Ogre was the wrong word. He felt more like a Chocolate Bunny. He told Mikey that, and Mikey instructed him never to say that again. "Bunnies are timid and fearful, and stupid," Mikey had said. "You're none of those things."

"Yes, I am," Nick had insisted. "I'm stupid!"

"No, you're not," Mikey had told him. "You're just not yourself. That doesn't make you stupid, it just makes you . . . muddled."

It only served to confuse him, because if he wasn't himself, then who was he?

Nick, Nick, Nick, Nick.

He ran from the cage and the farmhouse and the crazy scarred man, happily reciting the three things he knew that he knew. He kept to the train tracks as Mikey had said. They were easy to follow because the tracks had crossed into Everlost.

Allie, Allie, Allie, Allie.

He was content to live in the moment, but he sensed a certain sadness deep within himself. A longing for all the things he had once been, whatever those things were. He knew he had once been very clever. He had led hundreds of Afterlights, and, in fact the train he was following had once belonged to him. Mikey had said so.

Mikey, Mikey, Mikey, Mikey.

While he couldn't grasp the memory of these things, he knew that who he had once been, was not gone completely. The memories were still out there, divided among the people he knew and loved. Seeing Mikey had brought some of those memories back to him.

Allie, Allie, Allie, Allie.

And seeing Allie would bring back even more. Only in gathering those memories, could he gather back all the pieces of the boy called Nick.

Mary, Mary, Mary, Mary.

The name stopped him in mid-stride. It had come out of

nowhere—and he knew that nowhere often spat forth some very important things. A feeling came over him then, warm enough to melt him inside, but cold enough to harden him solid. It was joy poured hot into chilly foreboding. The feelings blended until he couldn't tell one from another—and when he looked at his hands, he could, for the first time, see something resembling fingernails.

Nick, Mary, Nick, Mary, Nick, Mary.

He felt a fluttering inside his chest that he mistook for an air pocket—probably left from when he pushed himself through the cage. He had no way of knowing that the fluttering was a single beat from the fleeting memory of a heart.

CHAPTER 12
Universal Justice

Mikey told Clarence everything he knew. The crossing of himself and Mary into Everlost, his many years at the center of the earth, and the many years it took to get out. He told Clarence of his time on the ghost ship, and how he was the McGill, the most feared monster of Everlost. Mikey told him about Allie, and although he tried to hide how deep his feelings for her were, Clarence saw right through it.

"'Love is the finest and foulest thing in the world. It will drive a man to greatness even while driving him into despair.'" Clarence proclaimed. "To quote the famous philosopher . . ."

"Which famous philosopher?" asked Mikey.

"If I knew, I would have told you."

Mikey knew both the fine and foul sides of love. It was his love of Allie that had lifted him up from darkness; letting him see a better way than the way of the monster. But once that love took hold, it also left a fear in him, which always lingered in the back of his mind, and made him intensely jealous. It was the fear of losing her.

"Love turns a heart to crystal," said Mikey. "Much more valuable, but much more fragile."

Clarence put down his bottle. "Who said that?"

"I did," said Mikey. "Just now."

Clarence raised his Everlost eyebrow. "You oughta be a poet."

Mikey was very pleased with himself. It had been a long time since anyone complimented him on anything he said or did.

"How's this?" Clarence said, and then he held up his Everlost hand, moving it before him as if the words were written in the air. "The face that launched a thousand ships . . . never heard of hurricane season."

Clarence laughed so hard it made Mikey laugh too. They were still laughing when the policemen came across the weedy field toward them—or more accurately toward Clarence, since they couldn't see Mikey, or the cage that held him.

"Looks like you're having quite a party," the bigger of the two men said. "Wish I could be in there with you." Then the two smirked to each other.

Mikey's first thought was that they had been skinjacked, until he realized that *in there with you* meant in Clarence's head. They took him for a lunatic talking to himself.

"I'm sorry but this here is private property," said the larger officer, clearly the leader of the two. "We're going to have to ask you to leave."

"You're renting!" shouted Mikey. "Tell them you're renting this place. They won't be able to kick you out until they check."

"You shut up!" shouted Clarence. "I don't need a freak like you telling me what to do!"

It was the wrong thing to say, because the officer thought that Clarence was talking to *him*. The man calmly reached his hand down to the hilt of his baton, and the other officer unsnapped the strap on his holster. "Now, none of us wants an incident," said the lead officer. "We could arrest you for trespassing, but it would be easier for everyone if you just moved on. You understand?"

"I'm renting," said Clarence. "Four hundred bucks a month. Check it out with my landlord if you don't believe me."

The officers looked to each other, then back at the dilapidated farmhouse, which, from their point of view probably wouldn't be worth four dollars a month, much less four hundred.

Clarence glanced at Mikey, more resentful than thankful, then took a couple of steps toward the officers, staggering as he went. Mikey figured Clarence was drunk most of the time Mikey had been in the cage—but he'd never seen Clarence *stumbling* drunk.

"Go on—get out of here, and maybe I'll pretend this harassment never happened."

"Tell you what," said the lead officer. "Come with us, we'll check out your story, and if it's true, we will bring you back here, no harm no foul."

"I got rights," Clarence said, "and I believe you are violating them right now."

"That's why you're coming with us voluntarily," said the second cop, speaking up for the first time.

The lead cop agreed. "Easier for everyone that way."

If Clarence was taken away, Mikey knew he would be stuck here. The thought of rotting in a cage until someone found him and freed him was more than he could bear.

"Throw me the key to the padlock!" said Mikey.

"No way I'm doing that!"

"Pardon me?" said the lead officer.

"Throw me the key!" said Mikey. "And I'll help you. I won't run away, I promise!"

"How do I know I can trust you?" said Clarence.

"Trust us?" said the second officer. "Since you are the one allegedly trespassing, I don't think you have much of a choice."

"Throw me the key!"

"I got this under control!" said Clarence. "Nobody's gonna—" Then Clarence stumbled once more, then fell to his knee—and to everyone's surprise he rose quickly and soberly, holding the shotgun, which had been lying forgotten in the tall grass.

"Clarence, no!" yelled Mikey.

Clarence swung it to the lead cop before he could pull out his weapon.

"Hands in the air!" Clarence ordered. The younger cop fumbled for his weapon. "Drop it or I'll shoot," Clarence said, very firmly.

The second cop quickly threw his weapon to the ground. "Okay, okay, okay—I dropped it, see? I dropped it!"

The lead cop never showed fear, though. "Sir. Put the weapon down. No one needs to get hurt."

"Oh! So now I'm 'sir'?" screeched Clarence, in that

two-toned siren voice of his. "I might only have one usable hand in this world but I can still pull a trigger!" With his finger on the trigger and the barrel of the shotgun resting across his ruined arm, he kept his aim straight at the lead cop's chest.

"All these years being chased from place to place, not able to be anywhere, not allowed to have a life. Well, from now on, I'm not going anywhere unless I want to! I'm done getting thrown around. I should . . . I should . . ."

"Clarence," begged Mikey, "you're making it worse. You're going get yourself killed. . . ."

"I don't care!" he screeched. "I don't care. Because if I do—"

Then in the blink of an eye, the lead officer pulled out his own weapon and fired.

The blast caught Clarence in the chest, his whole body twisted, and the shotgun flew like it had been launched skyward.

"NO!"

But the officers couldn't hear Mikey. Clarence wailed in pain, fell to the ground, and the officers were on him. Although the living world was a blur to Mikey, he could see that there was a lot of blood. Clarence writhed on the ground, while the second officer radioed in for an ambulance.

The first officer knelt down, trying his best to staunch the flow of blood. "Crazy old man, why did you have to go and do that?"

"M-m-monster in the cage," Clarence said. "Monster kid in the cage."

"Yeah, yeah," said the officer.

Mikey rattled the bars. "Clarence, the key!"

"Lousy kid," mumbled Clarence. "Don't think of no one but yourself." Then, with his ruined hand he reached into his pocket.

"Easy, old man!" said the officer. As far as the officer was concerned, the suspect had gone from dangerous lunatic to wounded victim, and he was doing his best as an officer of the law to comfort him. He saw the old man reach a ruined stub of a hand into a pocket but the hand came out empty. Still, he swung his arm, grimacing in pain, as if he was throwing something that the officer couldn't see.

"Stop moving," the officer told him. "An ambulance will be here soon."

"Go on," said Clarence. "Go back to hell or wherever it is you're from."

"Calm down. You're just making it worse," said the officer.

Meanwhile, in Everlost, Mikey watched the key fling from Clarence's hand, and spin end over end, making an arc in the air . . . but the throw was wild. Mikey reached through the cage as far as he could, but it was no use. The key landed on the ground more than ten yards away, and although Mikey grew a tentacle that stretched toward it, he wasn't fast enough. The key sank into the living world, beginning a long journey to the center of the earth.

The ambulance came and took Clarence away. He had fallen silent long before it arrived. Still, Mikey knew he wasn't dead—at least not yet. He knew, because Mikey would have seen his soul leave his body. Clarence, as frail as he looked, was a fighter, holding on to life, refusing to give up the ghost. It was a rare kind of strength, perhaps the same strength that left him a scar wraith to begin with. Mikey had to admire the kind of willpower that could defy mortality.

Once the ambulance and the police cars were gone, Mikey was alone, and knew he would be alone for a long time.

When he was a monster, he used to set out soul traps, not unlike this cage. He would snare unsuspecting Afterlights in his traps, and sometimes he would go a long time without checking if a trap had sprung. He hadn't cared if a soul was trapped there for weeks or months, and he showed neither mercy nor remorse when the souls were finally brought before him.

"Find out what they can do, and make them do it," he would tell Pinhead, his second in command. If a soul was useful, then he or she would become part of the McGill's crew. If the soul had no skills he needed, it would be strung up in the hold and stored like a side of beef. And now Mikey was caught in a trap himself, without even a prospect of a monster to come around to enslave him.

"Serves you right," Allie would have said, if she were here. She would call it "universal justice," or something annoying like that, and Mikey would grumble at her bitterly, but all the while he would know that she was right. You reap what you sow in Everlost just as in the living world, and Mikey McGill had sown some pretty nasty weeds.

Above him, storm clouds gathered in the living world, and it began to pour. Of course, Mikey didn't get wet. The living world rain passed through him, tickling his insides but nothing more. It was just another way for life to mock him.

Well, if Allie was right, and the universe was a place of justice, he understood why Clarence's key flew so far off course. It was because he had lied to Clarence. Mikey didn't have any intention of helping him. If he had been able to open the padlock, remove the chain, and pry the spring-loaded trap apart, Mikey would have bolted without looking back.

Mikey could accept that his actions could have an effect on the world, and on his own destiny—but could his *intentions* have an effect too? Could he be tried and convicted not because of the things he did, but because of the things he *planned* to do? They say that the road to hell is paved with good intentions, but bad intentions could certainly get one there faster, couldn't they?

He had no way of knowing if being trapped in this cage was merely bad luck, or some judgment from beyond . . . but either way, the result was the same: Mikey McGill was forced to think about who he was, what he had done, and who he might be, if he ever was freed from that cage. He knew he would never be entirely virtuous, but he also knew that there was enough virtue in him to make Allie love him. Perhaps his path back to her would have to be paved with good intentions . . . which meant not *all* good intentions paved a road to hell—so there was still some hope for Mikey, in this world, and maybe even the next.

It rained through the night and finally eased at sunrise, when the light of dawn broke through the clouds on the horizon. That's when Mikey shaped one of his hands into a claw, and his index finger into a sharp talon. He inserted the tip of that talon into the lock, and began moving it around.

Picking locks was not a skill he had ever cultivated, but he persisted day after day, turning the tip of his talon into different lock-picking shapes, and trying different ways of approaching the keyhole. He never tired, and he never gave up . . . because if there was any justice in the universe, he wouldn't be trapped there forever.

In her book *Caution: This Means You!*, Mary Hightower has this to say about gangs of wild Everlost children:

"It's true that Everlost has its share of feral children, often banding together in nasty little vapors. These bands of 'undocumented Afterlights' must be tamed with both force and love. We must put aside our disgust upon encountering them, and teach these savages all the things we know to be right. Unless of course there are too many of them. In that case, retreat might be a wiser course of action."

CHAPTER 13

End of the Line

The train tracks heading west were still alive.

That is to say, they were a part of the living world, and as such could not carry the ghost train anywhere but to the center of the earth. There was, however, a single track heading south, which wasn't ideal, but at least it was there. They took on a southerly heading, rolling at a cautious snail's pace into Texas, and through Dallas. No dead westbound tracks in Dallas, either.

"I'm sure we'll be able to pick up a western line once we hit Austin, or San Antonio," Speedo told Milos, with some confidence. "I think maybe I lived in Austin when I was alive. Or maybe Austin was my name, I can't really say for sure. I was in New Jersey when I died, though. At least I think I was. Do you think people from New Jersey would name a kid Austin?"

Speedo was always a blabbermouth when Milos came to visit him in the engine cab, since he was usually there alone with no one to talk to while the train was moving. The problem was, once Milos was in there with him, he couldn't leave and go back to the parlor car until the train stopped, so he was a captive audience, and Speedo knew it.

"If that church didn't fall off the tracks," said Speedo, "I would have been able to find enough tracks to build a bypass eventually—I'm the *best* finder—I used to find so much stuff—and then I'd trade up. I even traded up for the *Hindenburg*—that was mine, not Mary's—bet you didn't know that, did you? But I guess it's nobody's now, just floating out there with no one to pilot it. The best thing about a zeppelin is that it doesn't need tracks. If we coulda gotten it past that lousy wind, we would have been there months ago, wherever 'there' is."

Milos decided it was time to stop the train, give the kids a few hours of playtime, and himself a break from Speedo.

Whenever they stopped—which was still at least twice a day—Milos would wander among the kids as they played, doing his best to "play Mary." A comforting hand on a shoulder, and such. Usually though, the kids just flinched.

"This place that Mary wants us to go," they would always ask Milos. "Is it far?"

He tried to answer them the way that Mary might. "Distance and time mean nothing to us; we are Afterlights."

While this might have worked for Mary, they just stared at Milos like they were waiting for a punch line. It quickly became clear to him that whatever shining points he had earned the day they pushed over the church were losing their luster. Desertions started again—kids would even desert while the train was moving, like rats jumping from a sinking ship.

Each time they stopped for any length of time, Jill would insist they go out reaping. Sometimes Milos allowed it, sometimes he didn't, but when they went, it was always with strict orders to reap no more than one soul apiece.

"We should bring a few more Afterlightsh with ush," Moose suggested.

"Right, right," said Squirrel. "Once we make 'em dead, it doesn't take a skinjacker to knock 'em out of the tunnel. Anyone can do it."

"They're right," said Jill. "If we bring ten kids with us, they can carry ten more back!"

Milos didn't even dignify it with a response. As far as he was concerned he'd be happy if the three of them just left. He would be happy never to see Jill again—and as for Moose and Squirrel, well, their partnership had always been one of convenience—and Milos no longer found them very convenient.

Milos had come to realize how very much alone he was without Mary. The thought of having her back is what kept him going. All he had to do was hold things together until the day she opened her eyes.

There was still no sign of the mysterious western Afterlights who had put the church on the tracks. Perhaps the train had already passed through whatever territory they believed was theirs—or perhaps that church had been on the rails for a hundred years, and they were long gone— either into the light, or into the earth. There was no way to be sure. If Mary were here when they encountered "undocumented Afterlights," as she called them, she would probably talk them into joining her. Mary had a way of making everyone want to follow her—worship her, even. This was not one of Milos's skills.

* * *

Jix was also on edge now, because he knew things that Milos didn't. His Excellency had, many years ago, laid claim to all of the Americas west of the Mississippi. The king's forces had conquered many hordes of Afterlights, and had brought them all to the great City of Souls—first as prisoners, and then, when their memory of conquest had faded, as full-fledged citizens.

This was why there were so few Afterlights to be found— most of them had been relocated to the City of Souls, and occasional sweeps would catch the newcomers. There were only two reasons why there'd still be Afterlights in these parts. Either they had accidentally been overlooked . . . or they were too mean to mess with.

"Be on your guard," Jix had secretly told Allie, for he knew she was their best early-warning system. "Keep your eyes open always, and if you see something suspicious, call out to me. Wherever I am on the train, I will hear you."

"Tell you what," said Allie, "why don't we switch places, and you can be the one on upside-down lookout."

Jix did not take his discussions with Allie lightly. He appreciated the things she told him, because no one else was willing to talk about Mary, providing Jix with crucial information.

"Mary slithered her way into Chicago," Allie told him one night, while the other skinjackers were out reaping. "She charmed the leader there, then took over. That's what she does. I've never seen anyone so good at manipulating people."

Jix took note of everything Allie said, but he also knew that this was coming from a girl who despised Mary from the bottom of her soul. Jix could respect that, but he could also respect a spirit who could successfully manipulate thousands. For a moment he considered freeing Allie. No one would see him do it, for none of Mary's children ever came to the front of the train—they were all too afraid of Allie. No one would know it had been Jix that freed her, so what did he have to lose? Jix looked off to make sure the other skinjackers weren't coming back from reaping, then he leaned close to Allie.

"If you were freed," Jix asked her, "what would you do?"

Allie answered without hesitation. "I would stop Mary now, before she wakes up. I'd send her down into the earth, and that would be the end of her. Not even Mary can charm her way back to the surface." Then Allie got quiet, thinking for a long time before she spoke again. "Then, when I was sure that Mary was gone, I'd find Mikey—a friend of mine—and make him go into the light. He deserves to complete his journey. After that, I'd find my body, skinjack myself, and get back to my own life."

"Careful," said Jix. "Skinjacking your own body is not the same as skinjacking someone else's. Once you skinjack yourself, you're bound to your body. From the moment you jump inside, you can't leave it until the day you die."

"Why would I want to?"

Jix thought about the question. It brought back a memory that was painful to think about. "I had a friend who chose to skinjack himself. But his body had brain damage and a ruined leg. He couldn't speak, and he could barely walk, and he couldn't un-skinjack himself. He ended up begging on the streets of Cancun."

Allie squirmed in her bonds, and looked away. "Maybe it won't be that way for me . . . but unless you free me, I'll never have the chance to find out, will I?"

Jix picked up an Everlost stone from between the railroad ties, and tossed it into the living world. Allie had made her intentions very clear, but Jix was still neutral in this war, and his mission was to capture Mary, not to send her down. Perhaps Allie deserved to be freed, but freeing her would cause him nothing but trouble.

"If Mary succeeds," Jix asked, "and she ends the living world, what do you suppose will happen then?"

"Isn't the end of the world bad enough, without having to think about what happens afterward?"

So then he asked, "Is it so bad to end one world, when another world still remains?"

"Do you really believe that?"

"Maybe not," he told her. "Maybe I just wanted to see what you would say."

She struggled once more against her bonds, but they never got any looser. "So," she asked again, "are you going to let me go?"

"We'll talk again," Jix told her, as he always told her, and left.

Jix was not an insomnoid. He would choose to sleep when it suited him, and that night, he wanted to sleep, if only to keep his mind from pondering heavy things. Yet even though he tried, he could not settle his thoughts enough to sleep. Jix still told himself that he was traveling with the train just to gain information before returning to the City of Souls, and reporting what he had found to the king—but not even he was sure of his own motives anymore. At first he had told himself that he'd leave in Dallas, find a big cat somewhere, and furjack his way back home, but instead he stayed with the train. There was too much about this train of souls that intrigued him: the sleeping witch in the caboose, the train's destination—which the king himself would like to know about if, indeed, it was real . . . but most of all he stayed because of Jackin' Jill.

After their last encounter, Jill made a point of ignoring Jix, and yet he often caught her watching him out of the corner of her eye—but whenever he returned the gaze, she would get snappish and say, "What are you looking at?" It always made him smile.

As a skinjacker, he had the privilege of staying in the parlor car, so he and Jill were never too distant from each other, and when Jill got tired of pretending to ignore him, she would ask questions.

"How long have you been at this? Furjacking, I mean?"

But the real question was hidden beneath her words. She was more interested in knowing how much time he had left.

"The time will come that my slumbering body dies, and I can no longer furjack, just as that time will come for you."

"So you know about that. . . ."

Jix nodded. His Excellency had explained to him right away about how his body was in a coma—and how his gift of skinjacking was only a temporary one. "When I can no longer do it—when I become a normal Afterlight, I will find a coin, and pay my passage into the light."

"You mean you don't have your coin now?"

"No." The truth was, His Excellency had his own special use for Evercoins, but Jix wasn't about to tell Jill that. "Why is your hair like that?" he asked her.

"Tornado," she answered, and shook her nasty, nettled hair. "You hate my hair, don't you? Everyone hates it. I don't care."

"It's wild," he told her. "I like wild."

She squirmed at that. "How about you?" she asked. "How did you wind up in Everlost?"

"I was attacked in my sleep," he told her. What he didn't tell her was that he was attacked by a jaguar that had wandered into the village. He liked to think that maybe he had furjacked that same cat once or twice in his travels.

When the train reached Austin, Jill had asked Jix to join them when they went out reaping. "You can jack a circus tiger," she suggested, "and eat some really obnoxious kid in the crowd." Jix couldn't tell whether or not she was kidding, so he made up an answer that was equally unnerving.

"Humans don't taste good to a cat," he told her. "I only eat them when there's nothing better."

He did not join them, because he was not convinced the gods would approve of reaping. True, the Mayan gods were fairly bloodthirsty—particularly the jaguar gods—but there was a proper sense of nobility to those ancient stories of carnage. There was nothing noble about reaping.

When they reached Austin, there was finally a dead westbound track, heading toward San Antonio. Southwest, more accurately, but there was a very good chance that once they reached San Antonio, it would become a northwest track, heading toward the western states. Then, right around sunset the next day, as they neared San Antonio, the train came screeching to an abrupt halt.

All of Jix's senses peaked to high alert, and he instinctively knew there was going to be trouble.

Milos left the parlor car, furious at Speedo for bringing the train to such a jarring stop—but even before he reached the engine, he saw the reason.

"Problem!" shouted Allie from the front of the train. "We've got a problem here!"

"I can see that!" Milos shouted back.

Once again, there was a building on the tracks. Speedo had managed to stop the train about a quarter mile away from it this time—but seeing it from this distance was almost worse. It wasn't something so small and quaint as a clapboard church. You couldn't even call it a house. This thing was a mansion.

Speedo leaned out of the engine compartment, looking like he was dripping sweat instead of pool water. "H-H-How many Afterlights do you think it took to move *that* onto the tracks?" asked Speedo, nervously. Milos did not want to consider the answer.

"We'll send a team to investigate," Milos said.

The skinjackers now peered out of the parlor car at Milos for an explanation.

"What gives, what gives?" asked Squirrel. "Did you find out why we stopped so hard?"

Then Jix, leaning out of the entrance to the parlor car, pointed over Milos's shoulder, to the south. "There! Do you see that?"

Milos looked to where he was pointing. Night was falling quickly; the sky was already dark . . . and yet there was light coming from behind a nearby hill.

"Is that a city?" suggested Jill, probably hoping she could go reaping again.

"I don't think so," Milos said, his worry building. It looked like headlights in a haze, but the source of the light was still hidden by the hill. "It's getting brighter."

Jix released a growl that sounded much more like the real thing than any of his previous attempts. "We can't stop here!" he told them. "We have to leave. Now!"

"We can't leave!" Milos told him, pointing to the building in their path.

"Then go backward!" Jix shouted.

"Backwardsh?" said Moose. "Back to where?"

"Anywhere!"

Then there came a sound like the mechanical groaning of some infernal engine.

. . . *Grr-ah—Grr-ah—Grr-ah—Grr-cha! Grr-ah—Grr-ah— Grr-ah—Grr-cha* . . .

By now kids were looking out of the train windows, pointing at the light, murmuring to one another, while the sound coming over the hill got louder and more menacing by the second.

. . . *Grr-ah—Grr-ah—Grr-ah—Grr-cha! Grr-ah—Grr-ah— Grr-ah—Grr-cha* . . .

"What *is* that?" asked Jill. "Some kind of machine?"

"No," said Jix, just as the source of the light finally crested the hill. "It's a war cry."

Now it was clear what that light had been. It was the

combined glow of countless Afterlights coming over the hill toward the train. This was an invading force.

"*Bozhe moĭ!*" It didn't take a Russian translator to get the gist of what Milos had said.

As wave after wave of Afterlights came over the hill toward them, the awful sound resolved into the voices of a mob shouting their singular war cry:

. . . *Oogah—oogah—oogah-cha-ka! Oogah—oogah—oogah-cha-ka!*

Mary's kids were not prepared for this.

Months ago, when she had gathered her army of children, she had readied them for battle against the Chocolate Ogre—but back then, they knew exactly what they were up against, and had the advantage of being the attackers. This, however, was an ambush, and no one knew what to do, so everyone panicked.

Kids ran from the train, then ran back to the train, then ran out again. Kids screamed, they cried, and they fought with one another, as if that was somehow going to help.

"Stop it!" Milos demanded "Everyone stay calm!" But of course no one did.

. . . *Oogah—oogah—oogah-cha-ka! Oogah—oogah—oogah-cha-ka!*

The approaching marauders had faces painted with neon-bright war paint—green, yellow, and red—that glowed even more brightly than their bodies did, and many of them held what appeared to be weapons.

Milos ran up to the engine cab, where Speedo looked at him, wide-eyed and frozen like a rabbit before the radial. "What do we do?" warbled Speedo as Milos climbed in.

Milos looked toward the mansion, still a quarter mile ahead of them. "We ram it!" Milos said.

"Ram it? But . . ."

. . . *OOGAH—OOGAH—OOGAH-CHA-KA! OOGAH—OOGAH—OOGAH-CHA-KA!*

"I said RAM IT!"

Milos didn't wait for Speedo. He grabbed the control stick and pushed it all the way forward.

The couplers shuddered, the wheels moaned, and the train began to move, picking up speed, with the first of the invaders just fifty yards away.

"I don't like this!" Speedo complained, bracing himself against the bulkhead. "I don't like this at all!"

But Milos knew what he was doing. The mansion, just like the church, was resting on the tracks. The attackers had put it there—which meant that the train could knock it off of the tracks and barrel right on past, escaping the mob. All it took was enough momentum.

Jix, who still hung out of the door of the parlor car, was nearly thrown off by the sudden momentum, and Allie, who, as always, had the best view of the rapidly approaching mansion, screamed, calling Milos every foul name devised in the English language, but her voice was drowned out by the roar of the engine as they accelerated toward the mansion. She had no idea what would happen to her once she hit. The impact couldn't hurt or kill her, but what if the crash tore her soul to bits, and every bit, still alive and kicking, sunk down to the center of the earth? Whatever was coming, she knew it wouldn't be pleasant. She shut her eyes, and gritted her teeth as she, and the train, connected with the building at sixty miles per hour.

CHAPTER 14
The Neon Nightmares

In the early 1900s, a man who had made a fortune in oil decided to build a ranch in the middle of nowhere, complete with a thirty-room mansion: a showplace of a home fit for balls and galas and all those kinds of high society events that the rich attend. It was built on the right-of-way of an old rail line, but as that line no longer existed, no one thought it was much of a problem.

For a dozen years or so, the mansion was the talk of Texas; however, lightning strikes the rich and poor alike, and on one unfortunate night, a sizable lightning bolt set the place aflame. It burned to the ground in just a few hours. Now in the living world there's nothing but a hint of a clearing where the mansion once stood — but such a home, built with the blood, cash, and tears of a man who loved every inch of it, could not vanish from existence. The mansion crossed into Everlost in exactly the same spot where it was erected . . .

. . . which was right smack in the middle of the ghost train's path.

* * *

When the train struck the mansion, the building did not slide off the tracks, because, unlike the little church, it was exactly where it was supposed to be—and although the building was shaken down to its foundation by the locomotive strike, it did not yield. In the end, the mansion wanted to remain where it was more than the train wanted to barrel through—and so the train derailed.

The train cars uncoupled, folding together like an accordion, riding over one another, or just flying off the tracks like model trains running over a toy car—because every child with a train set eventually creates a massive derailing as part of the fun—and like toy trains, these train cars could not be damaged by the crash. They were simply thrown every which way.

Everyone experienced the crash differently.

Jix, who hadn't been able to decide whether to stay on the train or jump, had clung to the hand rail of the parlor car, and was sent flying by the impact. He could only hope he had enough cat in him to land on his feet.

Allie got the worst of it. She was shredded by the impact, but the shredding only lasted for an instant; then even before the engine stopped tumbling, her body was stitching itself back together. It felt like worms weaving through her insides. Meanwhile, the world spun as the engine tumbled before finally coming to rest. Allie thought the crash would loosen her bonds, but they didn't. She was still tied to the nose of the train. She was right side up now, which meant that the engine was upside down—but even though it had settled, it was still shifting, and she was tilting slowly backward. She quickly realized what was happening; the engine was sinking tail-first into the living world. In a minute—maybe less—it would sink all the way down and she would be submerged in the earth.

In the engine cab, Speedo was thrown against the control panel and dazed as the engine launched off the tracks, and when it finally stopped tumbling, Milos was no longer in the engine cab with him—he had been ejected out of the open door upon impact.

"Ooooh, this is bad," Speedo wailed. "It's worse than just bad, it's really *really* bad." The door of the engine cab was now almost entirely submerged in the earth as it sunk into the living world. With no time to lose, Speedo squeezed himself through the gap at the last possible moment. The fact that he was wet, for once, was helpful, because it made it easier to slip out. Then Speedo ran off into the night, and didn't look back.

Mary, as well as all the Interlights in the sleeping car, remained asleep through the whole thing, and the kids in the prison car had grown so uninterested in the outside world, they were barely aware of the crash. They felt the jolt as the prison car rode over the car in front of it and toppled to the side, but they had no idea what had caused it. "Earthquake?" one of the kids inside said, and since no one was quite sure, they just went on with their conversations.

Everywhere kids were scrambling to get out of the train cars before they sank. How successful they were depended on how their car had landed. There were only two cars that were not sinking—the parlor car, which had been launched clear over the engine, and had landed on the roof of the mansion, and the sleeping car, which had landed sideways across the tracks.

"What a mesh," said Moose as he climbed out of the parlor car and surveyed the situation below, happy that the parlor car was on the mansion roof, away from the worst of it.

"Nice one, Milos," said Jill, shouting down to wherever he might be. "Maybe next time you can just hurl us all into the Grand Canyon."

Milos heard her, but at the moment was too preoccupied to respond. He was now beneath the sleeping car, pinned to the rails, and struggle as he might, he could not free himself. What made it worse was that none of the kids running past him were willing to lift a finger for him.

"You!" he would command. "Come over here and help me!"

But they just glanced at him and hurried off without even answering.

Then, like thunder after the lightning strike, the invaders arrived—and they were so excited by this turn of events that their war cry degraded into random whoops and shouts of triumph. They had strange makeshift weapons. A skeletal umbrella at the end of a spear gun. A boomerang attached to long strips of flypaper—all items meant for snagging and catching Afterlights—and their bright war paint brought terror to all of Mary's kids.

"Get their coins!" one of them screamed. "Get their coins and send them downtown!" Little did they know that these Afterlights had already surrendered their coins to Mary. Not even the ones who slept had coins, because those never appeared until after one awoke in Everlost. If coins were what these invaders wanted, they would come up empty-handed, and be very, very angry about it.

Allie heard the battle, but couldn't see it. The engine had tilted straight up as the back end sank into the earth, so now her only view was of the stars and the moon.

"Someone out there had better untie me!" she yelled. She did not want to spend eternity like this. Going down to the center of the earth was bad enough. She would not go down tied to a stupid train!

Sure enough, someone climbed up to her—but it wasn't one of the invaders. It was Jix, his nose and fledgling whiskers twitching.

"So are you going to free me this time?" she asked. "Or are you just here to chat?"

He immediately began to pull at the bonds that held her there, but they were too tight to undo. He paused, but only for a moment. "You're a skinjacker," Jix said. "So skinjack. That's how you can get out of this."

"There aren't any living people here," Allie reminded him. "We're in the middle of nowhere."

"I don't mean people."

It took her a moment, but Allie finally got it. Still it made no difference. "Oh, so do you think a longhorn or an antelope will come bounding out of the bush on cue, and stand where I can skinjack it?"

"I see your point," said Jix, and then he leaped from the engine, leaving Allie to struggle with her bonds on her own. Around her the shouts of the invaders and the cries of Mary's kids filled the night. Allie could see them now when she turned her head. It was horrible. Kids wrapped in flypaper and dragged off by the marauders; kids tangled in nets sinking into the ground. And then she saw the caboose. It lay on its side, and around it a mob of Mary's kids struggled to keep it above ground, but their efforts were failing. If nothing else, Allie would have the satisfaction of knowing that Mary was going down too.

In a few moments Allie could see the dry brush around her, which meant that the train had sunk all the way down and was only a foot or so above the earth.

Just then, in the living world, something came bursting out of the chaparral. A coyote ran toward Allie and stopped only a few inches from her . . . as if on cue. Allie couldn't believe her luck, but it wasn't luck at all. Jix peeled out of the coyote. He had furjacked it and brought it right to her!

"Hurry! Before it runs away," Jix said. The coyote, perhaps confused at having been possessed by a human spirit, howled and took off—but Allie bent her hand up from her bonds, reaching toward it, and her fingertips touched the creature's leg as it passed.

There came a familiar rush and sudden dizziness. She felt the unmistakable heaviness of flesh, and—

—run run run, food food food, scratch scratch scratch—

Suddenly she was no longer tied to the train—she was no longer in Everlost at all! Her spirit had been drawn into the body of the coyote!

It felt—*run*—strange. Perhaps Jix enjoyed being in something nonhuman, but Allie knew she could never—*food food*—be a furjacker. The smells, the strange taste in her elongated mouth, and the feel of fleas on mangy fur—*scratch scratch*—were all just nasty—not to mention the maddening lack of opposable thumbs.

The living world around her was—*howl*—peaceful and

still. Only the simple sound of chirping crickets — *howl at the moon! Do it do it!* — filled the chilly night air. How strange — *sniff sniff* — that so much madness could be going on in this exact spot in Everlost, but to a living creature it was all invisible.

There was something — *run run* — very wrong, however. She could tell within an instant of furjacking the coyote. It wasn't just that she didn't like it — somehow her spirit was at odds with the animal. As if she were — *pant, pant* — somehow allergic. Could that be possible?

She wanted to — *run!* — stay, to make sure that Mary had sunk, but the coyote's instincts grated so coarsely against her own — *sniff-scratch-sniff* — she couldn't think clearly. The smells were so — *sniff sniff* — powerful it confused her thoughts. Why was she here? Who was she? She found herself darting back and forth, turning in circles, disgusted by her own dog breath. Her ability to — *run-howl-run* — think clearly had been — *food-food* — smashed by the scents and sounds assaulting the — *sniff-listen-sniff* — coyote's senses, then a rabbit — *chase!* — scurried through — *chase!* — the underbrush — *go!* — and she found herself — *food!* — racing after it — *catch!* — in pursuit — *chase!* — unable to control herself — *food!* — and she knew — *catch!* — that she — *food!* — was in serious — *eat!* — serious — *eat!* — trouble. . . .

Back in Everlost, the Neon Nightmares, as they called themselves, were beginning to realize that this train, which had seemed like such a ripe target, was not going to yield a single coin. Their last hope was the prison car. One of the invaders tugged open the door to find a bizarre twist of faces, legs, and arms all pushed together like sardines. The invader just stared, not sure what to do. "Give me your coins," he yelled.

"We don't got any," said one of the faces in the mass of packed kids. "Could you close the door, please?"

Now the invader was truly confused.

"But . . . but . . . you're sinking! Don't you want us to drag you out so you can beg for mercy?"

"Not really," said another face.

"We're quite comfortable, actually," said another. "Please close the door."

He had never seen Afterlights reach that state of perfect, imperturbable patience before. It annoyed him, so he did to them the only thing he could do to annoy them back. He refused to close the door.

Jix knew that what he did now was crucial; he needed to be quick and decisive. He could escape, and take news of all this to His Excellency, but that would be surrendering the prize. The Eastern Witch could not be allowed to sink to the center of the earth.

Most of the Neons were busy going after kids climbing out of train cars, and the ones that tried to go after Jix took one look at his strange coloring—even stranger than their bright war paint—and they backed off. He hurried toward the mansion, where the parlor car still sat on its roof, and called out to Jill.

"I need the combination!" he shouted.

Jill looked down at him, surprised, maybe even pleased to see him still aboveground. "Forget Mary!" she said. "She's done for—climb up here with us!"

"The combination!" he insisted. "Hurry."

Jill sighed. "Thirty-two—nineteen—twenty-eight—but you're wasting your time!"

He ran off toward the caboose, repeating the numbers in his head.

The caboose lay on its side, already halfway into the earth but the door at the very back of the caboose—the one with the combination lock—was still aboveground. The kids that had been trying to keep the caboose from sinking had either been pulled away by the Neons, or had scattered to save themselves. Using his own afterglow to light the numbers, he spun the lock left, then right, then left again. He tugged. Nothing happened. For a moment he thought that Jill had lied to him, but then on the second tug, the lock came loose. He pried open the sideways door and threw himself inside.

To his surprise, there were already Afterlights in there— about a half dozen of them. They must have climbed in through the skylight, but the skylight was now underground.

"Have you come to join us?" one of them asked.

Mary was still asleep in her unbroken glass coffin—she must have been tossed about by the crash, but these kids had put her back in, smoothing out her hair, keeping her the very image of peace.

"We don't have very long," Jix said. "We have to get her out."

But the kids didn't move. "Out?" one of them said. "But the maniacs will get her if we take her out."

"We're going down with her!" said another, gently rubbing a hand across the glass of the casket. "Then when she wakes up, she'll tell us what to do."

119

Jix roared with such frustration he surprised himself by the force of it. It got their attention. "Do you think she'll reward you for letting her sink? She'll hate you! She'll punish you! Better to be in the arms of the enemy than in the bowels of the earth! Now move!"

They didn't need a second invitation. They grabbed Mary's coffin, and, like pallbearers, moved her clumsily toward the door, which was quickly beginning to submerge.

Halfway out the door, the casket got stuck.

"Push!" said Jix, and, already up to his knees in the ground, he put all of his energy into pushing the coffin through, until finally it dislodged from the door and slid out into the night. Jix was right behind it, getting out at the last second.

Then, when he looked back, he saw there was still another boy in there. Jix locked eyes with him. The earth was up to his neck, and the doorway was now only a sliver above the ground. The boy was trapped. Still, Jix reached for him, and grabbed his hand, holding it tight, pulling—but someone wedged that deeply in the living world could not be pulled out, even by a strong Afterlight.

"Save her," the boy said, before his head sunk under. Even after the boy was completely underground, Jix held on to his hand. It was pulling Jix down too—he was in up to his elbow . . . but then the sinking boy squeezed Jix's hand to wish him a silent good-bye, and then let go. Jix pulled his hand out of the ground and when he looked up, the caboose was completely gone.

There were few things more humiliating to Milos than being pinned beneath a train car, and having no one—not even the ones he called his friends—willing to help him. He knew that they were out there; he had heard Jill call to him, as usual pointing out his shortcomings as a leader. Until this journey he had always considered himself quite a good leader. Why, then, was he such a failure here? He knew the answer. It was Mary. Even asleep, she was larger than life, dwarfing him, and as much as Milos loved her, he resented that he would never have the same commanding presence. Still he had to believe that there was something missing in her that only he could complete, and that together they would be greater than the sum of their parts. Now his greatest anguish was not knowing whether or not she had been saved from sinking.

He could see only the smallest glimpses of the battle, but he could hear everything. The shouts of the invaders were so confident, and the cries of Mary's children were so desperate, he knew they were losing. Then, when he heard Jill shout out the "secret" combination to the caboose, he was glad she actually knew it. He had no idea who was going after Mary, or if they would be able to get her out, but at least now he had hope.

Finally one of the invading Afterlights came up to him. Milos spat his best ecto-loogy at him, not caring what the kid would do in retaliation. The one good thing about being pinned between the train and the tracks was that they couldn't push him down into the living world while he was trapped there.

"Give me your coin or else!" said the kid.

"*Idi k chertu!*" Milos said. It gave Milos a little bit of satisfaction to be able to curse him out in a way he could not understand.

The kid kicked him in frustration. "How come you're all so useless!?" he yelled. "How come none of you got no coins? We gotta feed him coins or he won't tell us nothing — don't you get it?"

Milos looked at the face-painted boy like *he* was the one talking a foreign language. "Feed who?" Milos asked, but the kid just ran off to take his frustration out on someone who could fight back.

The sounds of battle diminished. All the other train cars had sunk. Then, with a dread that crushed him almost as fully as the train, he began to realize that if Mary had been pulled from the caboose in time and they managed to keep her above the surface, when she awoke she would never forgive him for this.

Moose, Squirrel, and Jill had the best view of the battle. The roof of the mansion was a fortress for them; they could look down from their shingled battlements and see exactly how bad the situation was. There seemed to be only about a hundred attackers, but they were so aggressive, and so well-organized, that Mary's kids didn't stand a chance. Some were captured, some never got out of their trains before they sank. But most of them simply scattered, running from the disaster as fast as their legs could carry them.

The Neons tried to get up to the mansion roof, but the doors and windows were all locked — and although one resourceful Neon managed to climb up the drainpipe, Moose hurled him right off and into the living world, where he sank as if hurled into pudding. After that, no one dared to climb to the top of the mansion again.

They watched as the Neons lay all the sleeping Interlights on the tracks to count them.

"Milosh is down there shomewhere," Moose told Jill. "I can't shee him, but I heard him."

Squirrel wrung his hands like an old woman. "What do we do? What do we do?"

"We save our own hides," Jill said. "That's what we do."

Unfortunately, Jill had trouble taking her own advice.

Jix found that his own exotic look had given him an advantage. Instead of being corralled with the other prisoners, he was brought directly to the Neon's leader. The kid was no older than fourteen, and beneath the streaks of war paint, he had bad skin with a whole host of whiteheads that yearned to pop, but never would. His greasy black hair looked like it had been cut by his mother, and his braces were caked with whatever he was eating when he died. Could be Oreos. All in all, he was definitely the kind of kid that got picked on while he was alive—but now, he got to be the bully.

Jix stood before him with beefy Neon guards holding him on either side, all of them shuffling their feet to keep from sinking into the living world.

"What are you?" Zit-kid asked.

"I am a son of the jaguar gods," Jix announced, trying to be intimidating. "And you have angered them."

Zit-kid was not concerned. He looked to the glass coffin that several of his Neon Nightmares now carried.

"Who's the girl in the glass box?" he demanded.

Jix considered how he might respond, and one of the

kids holding Jix smacked him. "Avalon asked you a question! Answer it!"

Jix growled, but held his temper. "She's the one with the answers," Jix told Avalon.

"What answers?"

"The answers to all of your questions. She is the all-knowing Eastern Witch."

Avalon, the zit-kid, was still unimpressed. "Never heard of her." He scratched his volcanic face, smudging some of his war paint. Jix noticed that his paint was slightly different. In addition to the bright streaks, he also had a silver W on his forehead.

"We already know all the answers," he said. "At least, we will when we have enough coins. You gotta coin?"

Jix shook his head.

"All right, then." Avalon motioned to his comrades. "Keep the girl in the box, and send the cat-kid downtown."

The two Neon guards began to push on Jix's shoulders, forcing him into the earth, making it very clear what they meant by 'downtown.'

"No!" someone shouted off to their right.

Jix turned to see Jill climbing down from the top of the mansion and she ran to them. One of the Neons tried to grab her, and she elbowed him in the nose, then made a beeline to Avalon.

"I've got a coin!"

"Don't!" yelled Jix. "They won't bargain—they'll just take it."

But she ignored him. "I'll trade you. My coin for his freedom."

"Search her," ordered Avalon, but she didn't give them a chance. She pulled the coin out of her pocket and held it up to Avalon. He looked at it with suspicion, then cautiously took it from her, holding it by the tips of his fingernails, then dropped it into the pocket of his T-shirt.

"All right, then," he said. "Send them both downtown." Then he turned and walked away.

"Push me down, and you'll never find the other coins!" Jill said. That caught his attention.

"You're lying."

"Oh, yeah? I can get you another coin right now."

He hesitated—and even Jix wondered if she were bluffing, but he decided not to interfere with Jill's scheme. He watched and waited to see how it would play out.

"Show me," said Avalon.

The guards plucked Jix, who was down to his knees, back to the surface, and Jill led them all toward the sleeping car, still lying sideways across the tracks.

"That car is empty," Avalon told her. "We already got all the sleepers out, and none of them will have a coin until they wake up anyway."

"Not in it," said Jill. "*Under* it."

They all went around to the other side of the car, to see Milos still helplessly pinned.

"Hello, Milos," said Jill, far too pleasantly to actually be pleasant.

"Switching sides, Jill?" he said. "I am not surprised."

"He's got a coin," Jill announced. Avalon looked at the train car, then at his mob.

"Check his pockets."

"You don't have to," Jill said. "It's not in a pocket. He keeps it wedged in the laces of one of his shoes."

Milos moaned, and Avalon pointed at Jix. "You. Go check." Jix knelt down and reached under the train for Milos's shoes. Milos kicked and struggled, but Jix was able to get a good hold on his shoes with his sharp nails. He checked the laces of both running shoes and found the coin wedged in the right laces, just as Jill had said. He pulled it out, spared a quick glance toward Jill and held it out to Avalon, holding it in his palm.

"Hey," said Avalon, "how come you can hold it and not get sucked into the light?"

"Because I'm a skinja—" But Jix stopped himself. Could it be that these Afterlights didn't know about skinjacking? If they didn't, he wasn't about to tell them. "I guess it's because I'm just not ready," Jix told them, then he gave it to Avalon, who carefully put it in his shirt pocket, holding it by his fingernails, just as he did the first one.

"All right, then," he said. "Where are the other coins?"

"Not here," Jill told him. "But there's a bucket that's so full of coins you can barely carry it."

Avalon glared at her, baring his Oreo-clogged dental work. "You think I'm an idiot? You're making that up."

"She's not," called one of the other kids that had been captured. "I saw it. The Chocolate Ogre's army had it when we fought them. But I don't know where it went."

"I do," said Jill, and she refused to say anything more.

Jix grinned like the Cheshire cat. Jill's ploy was cunning and clever. And to think she had done this for him!

"All right, then," said Avalon. "But you'll have to tell me

eventually." Then he ordered the Neons to send all the other prisoners downtown. "Two coins saves you and your cat," he told Jill. "I got no use for the others."

Jix tried to help them, but he was held back. In the end all he could do was watch as more than twenty kids were pushed into the earth. Then the Neons left, taking their two prisoners, all the Interlights, and Mary in her glass coffin, while behind them Milos spewed Russian curses at all of Everlost.

CHAPTER 15

Memory Makes the Man

Moose and Squirrel waited a good long time after the Neon Nightmares left before dredging up the nerve to come down from the mansion roof. Around them other kids were coming out of hiding as well—but just a handful.

"Where's Mary?" the refugees all asked. "She didn't go down, did she? Please don't say that she went down."

"They got her," Moose informed them. "The Neons got her and took her away, coffin and all." Which made the kids as miserable as if she had sunk.

Milos, however, was relieved—but it didn't temper his anger. "Are you two idiots going to help me or not?" Moose and Squirrel hurried to him, making all sorts of excuses, but Milos would have none of it. "You are both cowards! Now go get the kids that are left, and get this train off of me."

Moose and Squirrel went to gather the Afterlights who had hidden but had not run away. When Moose and Squirrel took a final head count, their number was forty-three.

"Forty-three?" wailed Milos from beneath the empty sleeping car. "How can there be only forty-three?"

"Most of 'em got scared off," said Squirrel.

"Fine. Get them to push this thing off of me."

But try as they might, forty-three Afterlights were not enough to leverage a train car off the tracks.

"That shucks," said Moose. "Sho what do we do now?"

As Milos struggled to find a solution to his dilemma, he began to smell something. It was faint at first, barely perceptible but growing. It was sweet, and reminded Milos of childhood; something pleasant in the midst of this most unpleasant circumstance. Then all at once he realized that this particular aroma was not a good thing at all.

"Do you schmell that?" said Moose.

"It's chocolate! It's chocolate," said Squirrel. "What do we do?"

By now other kids were scattering, terrified, knowing what that smell meant.

"No! No!" Milos shouted to them. "Stand your ground."

"Easy for you to say," shouted one of the escaping kids. "You can't move."

To their credit, Moose and Squirrel did not abandon Milos, although they probably both would have wet themselves, had they been alive.

The smell of chocolate quickly grew and became overpowering—intoxicating. Milos could not see anything from his angle, but Moose and Squirrel could, and what they saw made them quiver. The creature came lumbering down the tracks from the northeast, looking like some sort of swamp thing, but dripping chocolate instead of slime. Allie had told them that the Chocolate Ogre was just a boy—and that the monster legend was created by Mary to keep her children fearful, but this oozing spirit appeared every bit the monster that Mary had said it was.

The Chocolate Ogre strode forward at a steady pace along the track, the erie *ploosh, ploosh, ploosh* of his footsteps would have been comical if the sight of him wasn't so terrifying. He arrived at the breeched sleeping car, and looked at Moose, then at Squirrel, perhaps for an explanation.

"We didn't do it!" said Moose.

"Yeah, yeah," said Squirrel, "it was like this when we got here!"

The Ogre looked at Milos, then back to Moose and Squirrel. "I'm looking for Allie. Do you know her? Do you know where I could find her?" His voice, although slobbery and thick, was not exactly the voice of a monster.

"She's not here, she's not here," wailed Squirrel.

"Quiet!" yelled Milos. Even though he could barely move, he had a handle on the situation. The Ogre had never met them—he had no idea who they were! And so, Milos, using his friendliest voice, said, "We don't know anyone by that name, but maybe we could help you find her."

"Will you really help me?" asked the Ogre, overjoyed at the prospect.

To Milos he sounded like a very small child, innocent and trusting. This was not the way Allie had ever described Nick—but then, she hadn't described him as this freak of fudge either. Perhaps some of him was lost in transformation.

"Mikey said she'd be on a train," the Ogre said.

"Mikey?" said Moose.

"Do you know him?" asked the Ogre.

"Yeah, yeah," chimed in Squirrel. "He's . . . uh . . . uh . . . he's our best friend!"

"Really? He's mine too!" said the Ogre.

"And a friend of Mikey's is a friend of ours," said Milos. Then he added, "Of course, friends do not let other friends stay stuck beneath trains, do they?"

"No," said the Ogre. "I guess not."

"And I've heard that the Chocolate Ogre is as strong as a hundred Afterlights."

"You've heard that?" The Ogre was a bit confused.

"Of course!" said Milos. "Why, people have seen you lift entire buildings with your bare hands."

"Really?"

"Yes, really—so lifting a train should be easy for you."

Milos did not know all the physical laws of Everlost— but he knew that physical strength had nothing to do with muscles. Afterlights had no actual muscles, just the memory of them. In Everlost you are what you remember—and if memory makes the man, perhaps Milos could plant a false memory of superhuman strength within the Chocolate Ogre's mind. . . .

"I can pick up a train?" the Ogre asked.

"Sure you can! You could juggle train cars if you wanted to."

"Hmmm. I'd need three to do that."

Then the Chocolate Ogre knelt down, grunted like a weight lifter, and in one swift move, lifted the train car off of Milos, hoisting it high above his head.

"What should I do with it?" asked the Ogre.

"How far can you throw it?" asked Moose.

"A mile, I'll bet," said Squirrel.

The Ogre thought about it. "I don't think so, but maybe to those bushes over there." Then he let it go and sure enough, he threw it exactly as far as he believed he could. It landed in a copse of living-world tumbleweeds, scattering the Afterlights who were hiding behind it, then the sleeping car slowly began to sink into the ground.

Now that Milos was free, he took a moment to study the Ogre, looking into those murky eyes sunken into that mess of a face. This once-human creature seemed lost in a fundamental way. *Well*, thought Milos, *finders keepers!* Milos reached his arm out and shook the Ogre's hand heartily. His whole hand was enveloped in chocolate. "My name is Milos. This is Moose and Squirrel. You are one of us now."

"I'm . . . I'm . . ." The Ogre searched his thoughts and finally said, "I'm Nick."

When Milos pulled back his hand, it was covered in chocolate. In a world where food was rarely seen, the sight of chocolate was tempting. He didn't *need* to eat—no one in Everlost needed to eat, but that didn't stop the craving for food—especially something as uniquely satisfying as a taste of chocolate. Milos couldn't help himself. He licked the chocolate from his hand, and it was absolutely delicious! No wonder the Ogre was able to gather followers. He may not have had Mary's beauty or vision, but he was a virtual fountain of the thing kids most wanted!

Milos turned and called out to the brush around him. "Come out, all of you!" he said. "The Chocolate Ogre is on our side now. He's going to help us."

Bit by bit, the frightened Afterlights cautiously came out of hiding.

"Come see what he has for you," Milos said. "It is a peace offering and he gives it freely!"

They came forward, and dozens upon dozens of hands reached toward the Ogre, touching his shoulder, his arm, and even his face, taking little bits of him away. One taste of the chocolate was enough to win most of them over.

"But, but . . . Mary told us he was a monster," said one of the reluctant ones.

"He was," said Milos being careful to choose his words just right. "But it was Mary's dream to rehabilitate him, and to make him see her way. Now her dream has come true."

"Mary . . . ," said the Chocolate Ogre. He looked off, searching his sopping sweet memory of a mind. "I loved Mary," he said. This next part came out as a question. "And . . . Mary loved . . . me?"

Milos stood with his mouth open. Moose and Squirrel were wise enough to stay quiet and waited to see how Milos would handle it.

"Yes," Milos finally said. "Yes. Mary loves all of us, and we all love her."

The Chocolate Ogre shook his head "No, this was different. . . ." And as Milos watched, it seemed that his features began to look clearer and more defined, less like a thing, and more like a person. Even his voice sounded less slippery. "Yes, we were in love."

Then Milos let out a calculated laugh and Moose and Squirrel took the cue to laugh as well, until Milos put up his hand to silence them, and became very, very serious.

"Loss of memory is not a thing to laugh at," Milos said. "All Afterlights must face it. I am truly sorry, and I hope you will forgive me. But you see, Mary has only one love—one soulmate in Everlost . . . and that would be me."

The Ogre said nothing at first, and Milos didn't give him any time to think it through. "In all the stories I have heard about the Chocolate Ogre, no one ever mentions Mary—but there *is* a girl to whom the Ogre is devoted. Let's see, what was her name again?" Milos pretended to think for a moment, then snapped his fingers. "Jill! That's it—her name is Jackin' Jill."

"Jill?" The Ogre took in the lie, and his face began to lose some of its form again, his identity moving away from the boy once known as Nick.

"Yes, you love Jill," Milos insisted, "and you long to wrap your arms around her, and smother her in chocolate, and sink with her down to the center of the earth."

"And . . . and this Jill . . . she loves me?"

"More than anything," said Moose.

Squirrel snickered. "Yeah, yeah, a match made in heaven."

The Chocolate Ogre's muddy eyes now darted back and forth between the three of them in confusion.

"Do whatever I tell you," said Milos, "and we will make sure you find Jackin' Jill, the girl you love."

The Chocolate Ogre sighed, resigned, and Milos turned to the gathered kids, who still reveled in the tiny taste of chocolate they all just had. "We will track down our attackers and bring Mary back," Milos told them. "I promise you this."

"But there are so many of them," said one fearful Afterlight. "And they have weapons."

Milos waved the worry away. "Who needs weapons when we have the Chocolate Ogre on our side?"

"Wait," said the Ogre, trying to remember something. "What about . . . uh . . . what about . . . Allie?"

To which Milos replied, "Allie who?"

The Chocolate Ogre opened his mouth as if to say something—as if there was something he was supposed to remember—someone he was supposed to find. But whatever memory he was trying to save, it sank into the mire of his mind just as the sleeping car sank into the earth.

In her book *My Struggle: The Quest for a Perfect World*, Mary Hightower expresses her feelings on "lost souls."

"I believe every wayward Afterlight can be rehabilitated. It begins with the purging of living memory, and ends with the joyous discovery of one's perfect day, to be relived forevermore. On occasion we can find powers we never knew we had—all the more reason to leave behind as many memories as we can!"

CHAPTER 16
Wurlitzer

There is a vortex in south Texas.

A place that exists both in the living world and in Everlost that is rife with unpredictable supernatural properties. It is much like the Intolerable Nexus of Extremes in Memphis—also known as Graceland—the vortex which accelerated the transmutation of Nick into chocolate. It is similar to the Orlando Frost Vortex, a curious spot that exists underneath a huge faux castle and will cryogenically freeze any Afterlight that stands there.

But to say any one vortex is like another is misleading. All vortices are unique in their effects—and the Vortex of the Aggravated Martyr—also known as the Alamo—had the power to give any army garrisoned there courage. A ridiculous amount of courage. The Neon Nightmares were not much of a fighting force until they chose to live at the Alamo—and although they numbered only a hundred and ten, their courage gave them a boldness that made them seem like twice as many. It was the type of courage that in the living world would get counties, TV shows, and knives named after you, particularly when that courage got you killed.

Due to the fact that the Alamo was a living-world tourist attraction, the place was often very crowded—especially during the day. Such a place is maddening for Afterlights—mobs of flesh-filled bodies walking through you was irritating enough in a normal spot of Everlost—but in a vortex where the two worlds kissed each other, an Afterlight can actually feel the passage of a fleshie, and fleshies can hear, feel, and sometimes even see Afterlights within a vortex—which accounts for various ghost sightings around the living world.

And so, the Neon Nightmares decided it was best if they bunked in the secret part of the Alamo where no one ever went.

The basement.

In the living world, tour guides will tell you that it doesn't exist. Indeed, Texans may mock you at the mere suggestion. But the truth is, there is a series of tunnels beneath the Alamo connecting chambers and storerooms in a secret cellar that has crossed into Everlost. It was here, beneath the vortex, that the Neon Nightmares called home.

Avalon led their captives to the secret passage behind the paperweight shelves in the gift shop, then down narrow stone stairs. The stairs gave way to a low tunnel that finally opened up into a large, dim chamber filled with bedrolls; a common room where most activities took place. The sleeping Interlights were carried off down a winding corridor to be stored elsewhere until they woke up, but Avalon had the bearers of the glass coffin lay it before him, so he could have a good long look at the girl inside.

"What's her name?" he asked Jix, and shouted, *"Answer*

me!" before Jix could open his mouth, so that anything Jix said would sound as if he were responding to Avalon's demand, rather than his question.

"Mary Hightower, the Eastern Witch," Jix said, and the Neons all murmured to themselves, already building Mary's powerful mystique in their minds.

Seeing the Neons' reaction, Avalon said, "She belongs to me now. When she awakes she will be my personal servant," although Jix suspected it would be the other way around. Avalon told the pallbearers to take her away with the other sleeping Interlights, dismissing her as if she were completely unimportant—but clearly she was already sparking the imagination of the Neons, whose eyes followed the coffin until it was down the hallway and out of sight.

The Neons had far less respect for Jix and Jill, who had their hands tied behind their backs, and were repeatedly taunted and prodded.

"Funny war paint you got," they said to Jix.

"It's not paint," he proudly told them. "I am a son of the jaguar gods."

"Stop that," Jill whispered to him. "The 'jaguar god' stuff is getting old."

Jix whispered back, "If only one in five believe me, that's more than twenty who'll be afraid to fight me when we try to escape."

Jix looked around to see if there might be an escape route. There were several other doorways, leading to other rooms, or tunnels. Until he knew where they led, there was no sense trying to run. At the far end of the room, Jix noticed a large object covered by a flowery quilt. It was about four feet high with a rounded top. He couldn't imagine what it might be.

"We have two coins!" Avalon announced to his warriors, tapping his shirt pocket to make sure they were still there. The Neons cheered. Then Avalon gave Jix and Jill an unpleasant Oreo smile. "If it was up to me, I'd lock you both in the old storeroom and forget about you for a year or two—but it ain't my decision to make."

"I thought you were the leader," Jix said.

Avalon shook his head. "No, I'm the high priest."

Jill gave him her best diminishing look. "You don't look like much of a priest."

Avalon made a sudden move as if to slap her with the back of his hand, but he didn't do it. He was only trying to make her flinch. Jill, however, never flinched at anything.

Then Jix locked eyes with him and said very calmly, "If you hit her, I will open my mouth wide enough to swallow you whole, force you through my bowels, then out my other end."

Avalon scowled at him. "You can't do that."

"Try me," Jix said. Avalon backed off, then angrily stormed away, and Jix winked at Jill. "One in five."

They watched as the rest of the Neons stood at attention and Avalon went toward the blanket-covered object in the front of the room.

"What is it?" Jill whispered.

"An altar, I think," said Jix. Then Avalon got down on his knees, and the minute he did all the others knelt as well.

"On your knees!" ordered one of the guards, forcing Jix and Jill down.

Then Avalon removed the blanket.

There were many unusual objects in Everlost, with unusual properties. While there were things that had crossed that had made Jix raise an eyebrow, there was nothing as strange as the object beneath the blanket. He wasn't surprised that it had crossed—what was bizarre was how it was being used.

The object was an old-fashioned jukebox. Jix had seen them before in the restaurants and bars that tourists visited. The old ones used small vinyl records to play music; the new ones had CDs or digital files, but still were made to look old. This was the real thing: a classic round-topped machine built in the 1950s with lots of chrome and neon—red, yellow, and green—the same colors as their war paint.

"Now I've seen everything," said Jill, and one of the guards shook her. "No talking once Wurlitzer is revealed!"

The device, which did bear the company name "Wurlitzer" sat patiently waiting for someone to select a song. But of course, the songs were not free.

"Mighty Wurlitzer, we beseech thee," chanted Avalon. "Answer us what we ask."

"Oh, brother," mumbled Jill, and was shaken again.

Avalon deposited an Everlost coin into the slot. It rattled down into the machine's mechanism and jangled as it dropped into the coin box. Then he asked his question. "What shall we do with these two prisoners?" Then he pressed a selection button.

Wurlitzer whirred and spun through a number of records.

"How fair is it," Jix said to his guard, "if he gets to choose the song?"

"Don't matter what he chooses. Wurlitzer's got a mind of its own."

The jukebox finally settled on a song, and through its little window, Jix could see a 45 vinyl record lifted up and dropped on the turntable. The needle moved toward it, the record popped and clicked, and an old crooner's voice began to sing:

"Please release me, let me go . . ."

The crowd breathed a singular moan and Avalon turned to them. "Silence!" he shouted, as pompously as he could. "Wurlitzer has spoken."

The guards immediately removed Jix's and Jill's bonds.

"I'm glad Wurlitzer didn't play 'Fly Me to the Moon,'" said Jill.

As the song continued, Avalon came up to both of them. "I suppose Wurlitzer doesn't care about keeping you until we get your stupid bucket of coins," he said. "You're not important enough to him."

"How do you know it's a 'he'?" Jill asked snidely.

"Shows how little you know," Avalon said. "For your information Wurlitzer can be a boy or a girl. It all depends on who's singing."

When the song ended, Avalon covered the jukebox and the warriors went about their normal business of entertaining themselves much the way Mary's children had—but the Neons' games and conversations were wilder and ruder.

Avalon, resigned to Wurlitzer's decree, said, "All right then, you're free to go."

And to Jill's absolute horror Jix said, "I prefer to stay."

"What?!"

"You go if you want," Jix told her. "I want to learn the way of Wurlitzer."

"Tell me you're joking."

"I don't joke like that."

Avalon smiled broadly, exposing what looked like railroad tracks in mud. "You want to be one of us?"

Jix didn't answer, but Avalon took his silence as acceptance. "All right, then! You won't regret it." He looked back at the blanket-covered jukebox. "See? There was a reason why Wurlitzer chose to let you go. It was because he knew you would stay." He looked at Jill, in mild disgust, then pointed to one of the guards. "You—take her upstairs and throw her out."

"No!" said Jill, clearly furious at Jix. "I guess I can stay for a while. I mean, it's not like I've got anywhere better to go, right?"

"All right then," said Avalon. "But you don't get war paint until you prove yourself worthy."

Jackin' Jill was not a good girl. She was not a nice girl. In life she had been a constant source of trouble to her family, and was even more trouble as a skinjacker. She always thought her parents would see her coma as a blessing to them, and wondered why they hadn't just pulled the plug years ago.

Whether or not her sociopathic streak was hardwired or was a reaction to the harsh realities around her, she didn't know and didn't care. She liked doing bad stuff. She was bad. That's what she was always told, and so she had embraced it.

Reaping souls from the living had begun as a way of maintaining status in the inner circle. First in Pugsy Capone's Chicago, and then for Mary—dear, sweet, goody-two-shoes Mary Hightower, who loved all children, and wanted to protect her widdle babies from the big bad world, by having Jill reap them into Everlost.

Jill didn't know why she enjoyed reaping. All she knew was that there was an exhilaration in doing something so horribly wrong, and yet being rewarded for it. She would never admit that she had mixed feelings about it. She was good at it, and when her conscience tried to rear its ugly head, she would smack it back down, reminding herself that her only worth was in what she could do.

And then along came this feline freak, who cut through all of it every time he opened his lousy mouth, and made her see herself in a new light. Jix called her a huntress—and said that there was nothing wrong with it, nothing evil. All she had to do was leave the path she was on, and find a better, nobler path for her tendencies. No one had ever suggested that there could be anything remotely redeeming about her. Did he really believe it?

Jill cornered Jix in a saddle room where half the saddles were crumbling to dust and the other half had crossed into Everlost. It was just one of many hidden chambers in the old Alamo tunnels.

"What were you thinking?" she demanded, pushing him against the wall. "You want to stay here with these nut jobs?"

Although Jill thought she caught him by surprise, Jix

had actually seen her coming. He could have dodged her, but he let her rough him up. She needed to get it out of her system, and besides it was the first physical contact they'd had.

"If we left, they would have Mary," he told her.

"Why do you care about Mary?"

Jix pulled away from her, spun her around, and put her in a firm, yet tender headlock. "There are things you don't know about me," he told her.

Jill struggled, but he knew it was only for show. She could have gotten out of his grip if she had wanted to.

"What? That you're on a mission from the jaguar gods?"

"Close," said Jix, "because His Excellency does think of himself as a god."

"His Excellency? I thought you were alone."

"I never actually said that. You just assumed." Now the struggle was for real and so he let her go.

"I gave up my coin to save you! You owe me the truth."

"Very well," Jix said. "But not now. There are too many others who can hear us." And sure enough, a few Neons passed by the saddle room, taking note of them.

Jill nodded her reluctant acceptance. "I really hate you, you know that?" Then she stormed away.

In truth there were several reasons for Jix to stay. Bringing Mary to the king was just one of them. But there was also something about this jukebox which caught in his mind. Only a fool would worship a ridiculous machine—and while the Neons weren't the smartest, they had been able to avoid detection and resist being conquered by His Excellency. Did the jukebox have something to do with that? Was their devotion to this machine based on something real?

Jix knew there were signs in Everlost. Signs that truly pointed to something beyond all of this. The most obvious ones were the coins: objects which were from neither the living world nor from Everlost, and had the ability to transport a soul to the next world, whatever that might be.

And then there were the fortune cookies—which they knew about even on the Yucatan peninsula, although they were harder to come across there. Everyone knew how in Everlost, all fortunes were true. Each one provided actual guidance, speaking to every Afterlight individually.

There was one time Jix had been sent to scout out a band of Afterlights that had been gathering newcomers in Mexico City with hopes of raising an Everlost Aztec Empire at Tenochtitlan. Thanks to Jix's help, His Excellency conquered them. Jix was rewarded with one of the king's own personal fortune cookies. Not just an ordinary one, but one coated in white chocolate—and those were supposed to contain the most powerful fortunes in all of Everlost.

Jix's fortune had read, *"You will free them."*

When His Excellency had asked what it said, Jix told him *"The jaguar gods smile on you."* It was the only time Jix had ever lied to the king. That fortune was always at the back of Jix's mind and he often wondered who it was he was meant to free.

When it came to the jukebox, it also said exactly what needed to be said—so in that sense, it was not all that different from the fortune cookies.

CHAPTER 17

And Then Along Came Mary . . .

A few days later, Mary's coffin mysteriously disappeared from the root cellar, where all the other Interlights were being kept, and appeared in the middle of the common room. No one knew who had carried it there. Avalon, too proud to admit things were going on behind behind his back, made it seem as if he meant for it to happen.

"You may look at my property," he told everyone, "but you may not touch it."

There was a small African-American boy who walked around with a big ceramic piggy bank as if it was his only friend in the world. Everyone called him Little Richard. One day Jix caught him staring at Mary, as if she might open her eyes. Impossible, of course, considering she still had several more months of hibernation before her.

"Wurlitzer meant for her to come here," said Little Richard. "It's like that 'Let It Be' song. You know, 'In times of trouble, and all that.'"

"Did Wurlitzer ever play that?" Jix asked him.

"No," said Little Richard. Then he said with absolute

confidence, "But he will when she wakes up." Clearly he was part of whatever conspiracy had moved her here.

The Neons, fancying themselves a military unit in everything they did, set up a twenty-four-hour watch over Mary's coffin, in case someone moved her again, or as some Neons secretly believed, she teleported herself to a different location.

By now, both Jix and Jill had come to understand the nature of the Neons' constant battle-readiness, and why everyone there was macho to the extreme—even the girls.

"This place oughta be called the Abyss of Abysmal Aggression," Jill told Jix, after getting into an all-out brawl with another girl.

It was Jix who figured it out. "The vortex above us is filled with the *adrenalina* of all the men who died here, I think. Down here, we still feel its effects. It can turn anyone into a warrior."

"So how come it doesn't affect *you*?" Jill asked.

Jix smiled and puffed out his bare chest. "It doesn't get more macho than this."

Jill scowled at him. "You're an idiot."

In truth, Jix did feel the effect of the vortex. There was a powerful urge to fight, and to challenge Avalon. But he was also disciplined and knew how to control those impulses. He had to have that much discipline to control the impulses of the cats he furjacked.

By now both Jix and Jill had come to see that the Neons' various activities were, like so many Afterlights, repetitive day after day until they had become like rituals. The group of kids who played poker, then fought; the girl who read the same book cover-to-cover every day, then fought; the gym-rats who bench-pressed a barbell that would be far too heavy for them to lift in the living world, then fought. Only scouts and lookouts left the cramped labyrinth to search the city for Afterlights with coins, and to protect their hideout from nonexistent attackers. The Neons lived their deaths as if they were an army under siege.

While Jill wanted nothing to do with the Neons, Jix smoothly inserted himself into their routines, just as he had done on the train, making sure that each Neon knew him, and was comfortable with him. Comfortable enough to answer innocent questions that they wouldn't even remember he had asked.

"How long has Avalon been high priest?"

"Since Wurlitzer played 'See You Later, Alligator' to the last one."

"How did Wurlitzer even get down here?"

"Probably the Crocket Street tunnel—it leads to the old Grenet house."

"Has it ever played on its own, without someone asking a question?"

"No—why would it?"

There was one girl rumored to have been here so long, she had no memory of being anywhere else. Her name was Dionne, and she spent much of her time polishing a Bowie knife—perhaps the original one. He saved the more important questions for her.

"How many songs does Wurlitzer play?" Jix asked. "Thirty? Forty?"

Dionne shook her head. "There are more songs in there

than you can imagine," she told him. "And sometimes it'll play songs some of us have never heard before."

Her answer confirmed what Jix had suspected; that this machine was not a simple mechanical device. It was something much, much more. Wurlitzer held the memory of every song that anyone has ever loved.

Then he asked the big question: "Has Wurlitzer ever been wrong?"

Dionne paused her knife-polishing and took a moment before answering.

"Once," she said. "But if you ask me, it was Avalon's mistake, not Wurlitzer's." Then Dionne leaned closer and whispered, "A few years ago, Avalon asked Wurlitzer for a mission, and Wurlitzer played two songs in a row when only one coin had been dropped in. The first song was 'The Chapel of Love' and the second was 'Chattanooga Choo Choo.' Avalon's usually pretty good at figuring out what it all means, and he seemed pretty sure about this one too. He made us trek all the way out to this little town called Love, Oklahoma, looking for a chapel that had crossed over—and sure enough, we found one. Then he said we had to lift it up, and move it over to some railroad tracks that had also crossed over. We went home, and nothing ever came of it. Crazy, right?"

"*Sì*," Jix agreed, "*loco*." But Jix knew it wasn't *loco* at all. The only reason Milos rammed the train into the mansion was because of that church. If that church hadn't been on the tracks, Milos would never have been led to think the mansion could be knocked off the tracks, too. If it hadn't been for the church, they would simply have sealed up the train when they saw the Neons coming, like a turtle pulling into its shell—which means Jill and Jix and Mary would not have been here now . . .

. . . which meant they were here because of Wurlitzer.

Jix felt a phantom shiver run through his entire spirit. Wurlitzer didn't just advise the Neons on matters of the present; it also anticipated the future—which meant it was truly a force to be reckoned with. Was it friend or foe? Jix wondered. Or was it fickle and unpredictable in its intentions?

When Jix crossed into Everlost, he had taken on the beliefs of his Mayan ancestors—for in this mystical world, a rich tapestry of magical beings suddenly seemed to make sense to him. Mayan gods were often mischievous, reveling in human folly, and there were dozens of them. It would have been less complicated if it came down to Wurlitzer being either the voice of God or the devil—but for Jix, there could be many other alternatives.

Or maybe it was just a talisman, a powerful luck-object. If it were like the coins and the cookies, then it was a messenger of comfort—a lifeline, thrown out to those caught in this middle realm. He wanted to believe that, but the only way to know for sure would be to ask it a question. The machine, however, was always guarded. And besides, Jix had no coin.

Jix discovered that, while Wurlitzer was fed every coin the Neons stole, there was one "emergency coin" inside Little Richard's piggy bank. One problem, however: The piggy bank was the old-fashioned kind—it didn't have a rubber plug on the bottom, it was solid all the way around. The only way to get the coin out was to smash the bank . . .

but in Everlost, things didn't break unless it was the object's purpose to break. One might argue that a piggy bank's purpose was to eventually be shattered, but the universe would argue back that such a thing could not happen until the bank was full. In such arguments the universe always won. Thus, the piggy bank was about as secure as Fort Knox.

Little Richard spent much of his days holding the piggy bank upside down and shaking it to make the coin come out of the tiny slot. He had been at it for several years.

"It will come out when it wants to," Jix told him. But that didn't stop him from shaking the bank.

Jill, who was listening, looked at Jix doubtfully. "You talk like the coin has a mind of its own."

"Not a mind," Jix said. "But a purpose. Nothing exists without a purpose."

Jill smirked. "Did the jaguar gods tell you that?"

Jix knew it was meant as an insult, but he chose not to take it as one. "No," he answered. "My mother did."

Jill was not impressed. In fact, she was never impressed by anything. Ever. This fact impressed Jix a great deal. At least once a day, Jill would get in Jix's face, insisting that they leave. "We're skinjackers, we need to skinjack," Jill said to him one day. "Even if you don't, I do!"

They had been there about a week, by Jix's reckoning, although the days did blend together—especially when they couldn't see daylight.

"You would leave Mary?" he asked Jill.

Jill looked over to the glass coffin. It sat like a center-piece in the common room, like a diamond in the middle of its setting. While Wurlitzer was covered with a quilt, Mary's glory remained unhidden. More and more Neons had begun to revere the beautiful girl in the green satin gown. They knew nothing of her, had read none of her writings on the nature of Everlost. She arrived here without the thunderstorm of legend that usually preceded her arrival. Yet still, these Afterlights were drawn to her.

Jill considered Mary for a moment more, then said, "I don't owe her anything, and right now she's useless to me."

Jix smiled. "Self-interest suits you, *verdad*? But sometimes a predator needs to look further than the eyes can see."

"What are you blathering about? More of that jaguar-god nonsense?"

"No. I'm talking about successful stalking." He looked around, and saw that the poker kids were beginning to get louder, preparing for their daily fistfight—which included a crowd of others cheering them on. Jix took Jill to the corner farthest away, so they could not be heard. "Cats stalk with their instincts—but you and me—we stalk with our minds. The way I stalked all of you on the train."

Jill gave him a twisted grin. "You didn't stalk anyone—we let you stay."

"Why?" asked Jix. Jill had no answer for him. "I'll tell you why. Because you never saw me as a threat. And yet I was. I knew you all so well—and had earned the respect of so many of Mary's children, I could have easily taken over the train if I wanted to."

Jill looked a little shaken. "Was that your plan? To take over?"

"No," he told her, then leaned in closer. "But it is now."

* * *

The following day, one of the lookouts—a skinny kid they called Domino—came down from up above, announcing that he had been seen by a group of refugees from the train crash. Avalon was not pleased. "I should push you down myself!" Avalon yelled at him. Then he ordered the Neons to prepare for battle. "We beat them once," he said, "and we'll do it again. And this time, we'll send every last one of them downtown!"

"But they've got a monster now," said Domino.

"What do you mean, monster?"

"I don't know what else to call it. I've never seen anything that strong. And here's the weird part," he said, looking around, almost afraid to say it, as if they wouldn't believe him, "It's made . . . of chocolate."

Jill gasped, then pretended she hadn't.

"It's true!" said the lookout, and showed them the brown stains on his clothes where it had grabbed him.

"And you led it right here, didn't you?" said Avalon in disgust.

The lookout began to stammer. "I . . . I . . . I didn't know what else to do."

"Imbecile!"

Up above them, in the Alamo complex, a woman screamed and an alarm began to blare. Even though living-world business meant nothing to them, today it added to the tension. The Neons were all looking to Avalon for direction, so he pulled out the one remaining coin from his pocket. "We'll ask Wurlitzer what to do." Everyone agreed. He strode toward the machine, tugged off the blanket, and all the Neons fell to their knees. Even Jix did, for fear of angering it, whatever it was. Jill had to be forced to her knees.

Wurlitzer's light cast a multicolored glow around the common room, caught and refracted by the many bits of glass that made up Mary's coffin, which sat just a few yards in front of the jukebox. It almost seemed as if her coffin was a part of Wurlitzer now: an altar before the figure of a god. Jix couldn't help but wonder if Wurlitzer wanted it this way—that even the attention given to Mary somehow reflected back on the mystical machine.

Avalon dropped the coin in and waited for it to clink its way down to the coin box and then he asked his question. "Mighty Wurlitzer, what do we do about this chocolate monster?" He pressed a random button on the machine's console, and Wurlitzer came to life. It pulled a record from its apparently infinite spinning rack, dropped it on the turntable, and with clicks and pops the song began to play.

"Oh, don't it hurt, deeeeep inside . . ." sang a man in falsetto.

"I don't know this one," said Avalon.

"What does it mean?" someone asked.

"Shh! Let me listen." Avalon put his ear to the glass as if that might help his hearing, then he squinted through the next few lines as if squinting might make him smarter. "This is a difficult one."

But then Jill said, "Wait for the chorus. . . ." because she did know this song. In fact, it had been one of her grandfather's favorites.

The music built to the chorus, and Frankie Valli sang, *"Silence is golden . . ."* and there was a collective gasp from the room.

"Wurlitzer has spoken," Jill muttered, clearly a little freaked by it.

"Quiet!" yelled Avalon, then realized his error, and whispered, "Quiet . . ." Avalon went to the back of the machine and turned the volume down as low as it would go. In a couple of minutes, the song ended and when it was done, silence fell and it remained. No one spoke, no one moved. From the Alamo gift shop above them, they heard a voice.

"I know you are here somewhere!" someone yelled. Someone with a Russian accent. "And I won't rest until I find you!"

Jill stood up.

"No!" whispered Jix.

"I'm done with this place," said Jill. "I want out. Even Milos and his morons are better than this." The others threw angry gazes at her, and Dionne brandished her knife—but silence was not golden for Jill—not when her fate was being decided by a glorified music box.

Jix grabbed her, getting face to face. Then looking into her eyes, he said, "It's time for you to choose, then. Choose that life . . . or choose me."

Jill looked at him with bitter fury.

"You must make your decision now," he demanded.

She glared at him a moment more, then she pulled him close, kissed him hard, then slapped him even harder.

"I really, *really* don't like you," she said.

"Will you be quiet!" snapped Avalon. Jill sat back down in silence, not sure whether this was victory or defeat . . . while up above, things began to break.

CHAPTER 18
You Put Your Whole Self In . . .

Milos's team of refugees had been scouring San Antonio for days, but it was a big city. There was no telling where the Neons were holing up. Wherever they had gone, they were well-concealed.

"Maybe they're not here," Moose suggested. "Maybe they went shumwhere elsh." But Milos was not ready to give up. There were still too many places to look.

Shortly before Wurlitzer played its song about silence, Milos and his crew finally caught sight of a single Neon watching them, trying to appear like a Christmas elf in a department store's holiday display. The kid ran when he was spotted, but Moose caught him and brought him to Milos.

"I will make a deal with you," Milos told him. "Tell us where you are hiding and return Mary to us, and we won't send you to the center of the earth."

The kid laughed in his face. "I won't tell you a thing." Clearly, he meant it. He would rather sink than give away the location of the Neons.

"Very well," said Milos and he called for the Chocolate Ogre, who came lumbering forward. "Say hello to my little fiend," said Milos.

"I think you mean 'friend,'" Squirrel corrected.

As soon as the Neon saw the Ogre, his face filled with terror. "What is that thing?"

Milos ignored the question. "Now I'm giving you one last chance. Tell us where you are holding Mary."

"And Jill!" added the Ogre.

The kid still shook his head, but all the while stared at the Ogre. He seemed almost ready to break. Milos turned toward the Ogre. "Show this miserable Afterlight what we do to those who don't cooperate with us."

"Okay!" Then the Ogre thought for a moment. "What do we do?"

Milos sighed. "We show our strength in a way that they will never forget."

"That makes sense," said the Ogre cheerfully. Then he grabbed the Neon, lifted him off the ground, and threw him all the way over the building in front of them.

Milos stood there, stunned. "Why did you do that?"

"Because I didn't think he'd ever forget it," said the Ogre.

The whole mob of Afterlights ran to find him, but he wasn't on the next street, or the next, or the next. Milos had begun to think that maybe he had landed hard enough to sink — but then they finally saw him in the distance, turning a corner. Once they reached the corner he was long gone — but then one of the other Afterlights noticed something. "Hey, what's that?"

They went down a narrow alley that opened up to a street with stone-paved sidewalks and crowds of living people. On one side of the street were older, living-world buildings, but their facades were insulted by garish, blinking signs advertising everything from a wax museum to a mirror maze, and across a large plaza was an old stone mission.

"I think itsh the Alamo," said Moose. "But I thought it would be bigger."

"Look at it, look at it!" said Squirrel, pointing at the familiar face of the structure.

The entire building, and the stone walls that surrounded the complex almost seemed to be squirming; randomly shifting in and out of focus. The stone itself appeared to swirl in and out of phase, as if it couldn't decide whether it was in Everlost or in the living world.

"It's a vortex," Milos said. Milos didn't even try to hide his disgust.

"You don't think they're in there, do you?" asked Moose.

"You can't make me go into a vortex!" said the complaining Afterlight—the one who always doubted Milos. "You never know what a vortex will do to you!"

"If you don't go, what *I* do to you will be much worse," said Milos. No one else gave him an argument.

They crossed the plaza, then stepped into the main building, a stone church full of arches and iron chandeliers called "the Shrine." The ground felt strange beneath their feet; one moment soft, the next moment solid.

"We shouldn't be here. . . . ," complained the complainer.

It was midday, and there were way too many tourists for Milos's taste. He had been denying himself his skinjacking

159

pleasures, putting the search for Mary ahead of his own desires, but having so many living, breathing bodies around him was insanely tempting. "We need to clear this place out," Milos told Moose. "Go skinjack someone and pull a fire alarm."

Then a living woman, blueberry-plump in a cranberry pants suit, looked at Milos. Not *through* him as if he wasn't there, but *at* him — and she screamed. The vortex had made at least a part of his face visible for an instant. It was a complication he did not need.

The alarm began to blare before she stopped screaming, and guards ushered the living out. Milos was startled by the woman, but he could not be deterred from his mission. Vortex or not, he was finding the Neons.

After the living left, it was easier for Milos to move through the Alamo grounds and look for signs of Afterlight activity. Unfortunately, the alarm masked any sounds that hiding Afterlights might have made. He sent teams into every building, and through each courtyard and garden of the compound — and while voices in the Long Barracks were promising, they turned out to be the trapped words of soldiers, spoken more than a hundred and fifty years ago. A vortex could be annoying that way.

When the fire threat was determined to be false, the alarm was reset, and the living were allowed back into the building — including the cranberry woman who was as loud as she was large, and demanded that security be on the lookout for ghosts. She insisted that a ghost had probably pulled the alarm. Security, however, had already nabbed her nephew as a suspect, an obnoxious boy with a history of lies and mischief. The woman insisted that Ralphy had been possessed.

Milos could not stand listening to her endless nattering. "Will you go skinjack her," Milos told Moose, "and make her shut up?"

"Do I have to? She's really not my type."

"Just do it!"

Reluctantly, Moose jumped into the woman, and she immediately stopped talking. Then, commandeering her body, Moose took her out into the middle of the courtyard and started her doing the Hokey Pokey. By the time she was putting her left arm in, other tourists had begun to join in the spontaneous fun, until about a dozen Alamo visitors were doing the Hokey Pokey in the courtyard. Not to be outdone, Squirrel skinjacked an elderly gentleman in the Arbor Garden, and started doing the Chicken Dance, but nobody joined him.

Milos went back into the Shrine, and saw the Chocolate Ogre standing beneath a stone arch, looking at a series of historic Texas flags. He seemed thoughtful—which worried Milos. He did not want the Ogre thinking too much.

"People died here," the Ogre said. "A hundred and fifty of 'em." And he pointed to a full-fledged deadspot in a small grotto that didn't shift in and out of phase like the rest of the building. "Jim Bowie, Davey Crockett, William Travis . . . I did a report on the Alamo once. . . ." And as he remembered, his shapeless face started to change. "I wonder if I could find the spot where Bowie died. . . ." The memory was strong enough to bring form back to his face. Cheekbones and a jawline.

"But what about Jill?" Milos said quickly. "Remember. That's why you're here; to find Jill."

"Right," said the Ogre, losing his focus. He looked around as if coming out of a trance—never realizing that *this* was the trance. "Well, she's not here," the Ogre said, then strode out to search another building.

Milos walked the grounds' inner perimeter, getting increasingly frustrated—and then he heard something. Music—and it didn't have the hollow timbre that living-world music had to Everlost ears. It was coming from the gift shop!

By the time Milos had gotten to the gift shop building, the music had stopped. Now the only sounds were the inane conversations of the living.

Milos stood in the middle of the gift shop and called out, "I know you are here somewhere, and I won't rest until I find you!" Then he wandered the room, listening for something, *anything*. Finally he heard whispering. Yes, he was sure of it! It was coming from behind the southern wall. Then he heard the distinctive sound of a slap.

He leaped at the wall.

The first time, he bounced off of it, so he waited until the wall shifted out of phase with Everlost, and he leaped at it again, this time going right through it and out into the courtyard where Moose was still leading tourists in the Hokey Pokey. Milos jumped back through the wall again and again but found nothing—no secret passageway, no concealed Neons, just stone, several feet thick. He tried to leap through in another spot, and just as he passed through the wall, it began to shift into phase again. He felt it solidifying around him—but he was out of the wall an instant before it became solid. He didn't want to think what would happen to him if he was caught within the wall the moment it solidified.

Would he become a permanent part of the wall? He didn't want to find out, and he knew he couldn't risk it again.

A sudden fury filled Milos like a rush of adrenaline, spiking his anger. He wanted to battle, he wanted to defeat the Neons and he wanted to do it *now*. He knew the sudden surge must have been an effect of the vortex—but it was serving him, and as long as it served him, he had no need to fear or fight it.

He knew what he had to do.

While Moose, still as Madame Cranberry, put his whole self in, Milos decided to do the same. He went to the gift shop entrance and skinjacked the guard who stood there. A sudden rush—the beat of a heart, the taste of a mint, and—

—*uniform's tight / gotta lose weight / gotta work out / when's lunch?*—

Milos felt a moment of vertigo as he took hold of the man's body, and the thrill of skinjacking once more. He listened to the man's thoughts for a moment, then he sent the man to sleep.

Milos, now wearing the body of the security guard, looked around him. To the living, nothing appeared unusual about the Alamo. The living felt a sense of history, and a sense of power to the place, but they did not see it shifting in and out the way Afterlights did. If there was a secret passage within the walls, a living body was the only way to find it. A living body, and brute strength.

"Something wrong, Wayne?" the girl behind the counter asked him.

"Yes," Milos said. "But it will all be fine soon."

Then he went over to a display of Alamo chess sets

against the wall and began to knock them to the floor, ripping out the whole shelving unit. People gasped and the cashier called for other guards, but Milos didn't stop. Shelf after shelf—mugs, T-shirts, pewter figurines. Tourists raced out in a panic, then another guard came in.

"Wayne, what the heck—" He tried to grab Milos, but Milos shoved him into a glass display case, shattering it. Milos destroyed everything against the western wall, ripping out bookshelves, looking for the telltale signs of a passageway hidden behind them, but there was nothing but the same coarse stone walls.

He began to doubt himself. Maybe the voices had come from the living after all. Maybe the Neons were elsewhere—the mirror maze or the wax museum. Or maybe that escaping Neon ran to a different part of the city entirely.

Just as he was about to rip down a shelving unit full of paperweights, three more guards came in, grabbed him, and pinned him to the ground. Milos peeled out of Wayne the wayward rent-a-cop, leaving the man to deal with the aftermath of Milos's rampage.

Filled with furious, yet exhilarating, determination, Milos gathered all the Afterlights in the Shrine where the effect of the vortex was its greatest—knowing he could use the vortex's power to help rally them.

"The Neons are not here," he announced. "But we will find them, and when we do, we will show no mercy because they showed no mercy to us!"

And they all cheered, the battle fury of the vortex filling them. "Remember the Alamo!" Squirrel shouted, and Moose smacked him.

"So what do we do until we find them?" someone asked.

And all at once Milos realized what they needed to do. All this time Milos had resisted, but now he was ready to accept his mission—his purpose. He had lost nearly a thousand of Mary's children. Well, by the time Mary woke up, he would make absolutely sure that there were at least twice that many; maybe three times; maybe ten. It could be done, if they all worked hard enough.

"Mary made it very clear what she wanted us to do," Milos said.

"Go west?" someone shouted.

"No," said Milos. "We stay here. We stay here until we find her. And in the meantime we increase our numbers . . . by reaping."

Milos never enjoyed reaping, but maybe that was because Jill had done it in such a cheap, sleazy manner. But with nearly fifty Afterlights waiting in Everlost to catch crossing souls, Milos's reaping extravaganzas would not be sleazy at all. In fact, they would be nothing short of epic.

PART THREE

The Gates of Grief

High Altitude Musical Interlude #2
with Johnnie and Charlie

*S*he'll be comin' round the mountain when she comes
. . ."

Johnnie was more than ready to hurl himself out
of the *Hindenburg* window.

"She'll be comin' round the mountain when she comes . . ."

More than once, he thought they were actually beginning
to settle back to earth, and he got his hopes up . . . but it
wasn't them coming closer to the ground, it was a living-world
mountain rising to meet them.

*"She'll be comin' round the mountain, she'll be comin'
round the mountain . . ."*

The problem was, in spite of Charlie's inane singing, they
weren't comin' round the mountains at all: they were going
directly *through* the mountains. Over and over they were forced
to suffer an unpleasant violation of granite and limestone as
they traveled sideways through living-world mountains—which
wasn't all that different from sinking into the earth except that
you came out on the other side.

"She'll be comin' round the mountain when she comes!"

And beyond the mountains and the plains there was always

another vast expanse of sea. Johnnie had no idea there were so many oceans, so many seas. Then, when they finally hit land again, he realized that there was something a little bit too familiar about the coastline.

Finally he spotted a landmark in the foothills. A sign on a mountainside said HOLLYWOODLAND, although the LAND part was clearly in Everlost.

"No!" wailed Johnnie-O. "Are you telling me we've gone all the way around the world?"

To which Charlie responded, *"She'll be ridin' six white horses when she comes . . ."*

It was enough to make Johnnie-O cry. He knew the world was round, but in his mind it sort of went on forever before coming back around on itself again. There was no telling how many times they had circled the globe and no way to know if it would ever stop.

"We deserve better than this," he told Charlie, who just smiled and continued to sing his song.

It was late the next day that Johnnie saw something out of the ordinary from the window. They had been traveling mostly over desert, and were still over the western United States. Johnnie-O had seen many odd living-world things from the *Hindenburg* windows—a road whose random twists and turns spelled out the word "haha"; a fighter jet parked for no apparent reason in a suburban backyard, giant crop portraits made by living people with way too much time on their hands. But nothing was as strange as this—and it wasn't in the living world—it was in Everlost!

"Is that a deadspot?" asked Johnnie, mainly to himself, because he knew Charlie wouldn't answer. "Yeah! Yeah, I think it is!" But this was more than just a deadspot—it was a massive patch of earth, dull gray in color, miles across, and perfectly round.

"Charlie, you gotta see this!" But right now Charlie, was all about killin' the old red rooster when she comes.

Johnnie peered out at the deadspot as they approached. What first looked like a flat gray disk wasn't flat at all; it was covered with tons of stuff! Johnnie couldn't tell what kind of stuff it was, just that it was stuff.

And that's when Johnnie had the big idea!

The *Hindenburg* had passed many deadspots; buildings that had crossed over, intersections where accidents had occurred. None of them, however, were big enough to land a bull's-eye from the *Hindenburg*. This deadspot, however, was so big, you couldn't help but land a bull's-eye!

The idea of jumping thousands of feet from an airship was not exactly Johnnie's idea of fun, but it was better than the alternative. And besides, they were Afterlights. Sure, they would hit the ground hard, but they would be no worse for it, and they would be off the infernal airship for good!

"Get up, Charlie, we're going!" But when he turned to look for Charlie, he was gone. "Charlie?" He could still hear Charlie's singing, but it wasn't coming from the starboard promenade anymore. He was somewhere else in the ship.

"Charlie, get back here!"

The airship crossed into the airspace over the strange deadspot, and Johnnie could feel a sudden difference in the air around him. An unexpected density—if Everlost air could even have density. Static began to spark in the walls around him, and the airship began to turn as if being acted on by a new force. "Jeez, what is this place?"

With the sudden spinning motion of the airship, it was hard for Johnnie to walk without stumbling into walls, making it harder to search for Charlie. Still, Johnnie bumped his way to the port promenade, the galley, and all the staterooms. Charlie's song was coming through the vents, but it seemed to be coming from everywhere and nowhere. Meanwhile, below, they had already sailed halfway across the deadspot.

Finally Johnnie climbed up through a ceiling hatch, from the passenger compartment, and into the airship's massive aluminum structure. There, on a narrow catwalk sat Charlie. He wasn't singing anymore. And he was holding the bucket of coins, as if protecting it.

"What the heck are you doing here?"

Then Charlie pointed up. Johnnie looked to see the airship's massive hydrogen bladders, like giant internal balloons all around them. Static electricity sparked through the entire space, coursing over the bloated bags of hydrogen . . . and wasn't it static that brought down the *Hindenburg* to begin with?

"It can't blow up again, right?" said Johnnie. "This is Everlost." But there was something about this deadspot that made anything seem possible. He grabbed Charlie's hand. "C'mon, we're getting out of here!"

He practically dragged Charlie down from the infrastructure and back to the starboard promenade, opening a window. "I know it's scary," Johnnie said. "But we have to jump. We'll probably just bounce anyway."

But suddenly the air changed again, and the static sparks stopped, and when Johnnie looked down, he saw the border between the deadspot and the desert moving away from them.

They had missed their chance. They were out over the living-world desert again.

"Noooooooooo!"

The airship stopped spinning, and went back to its normal drift—although the interference from the deadspot had shifted its direction by a few degrees to the south—but otherwise, their predicament was exactly the same as before.

Johnnie-O curled his big fingers into oversize fists. "Why couldn't you have stayed put! We could be out of here!"

But Charlie just smiled and sang, *"Camptown ladies sing this song; Doo-dah! Doo-dah!"*

Johnnie-O peered sadly, longingly, out of the window at the huge, perfectly round, gray deadspot as it receded on the horizon.

Funny, but from this angle, he couldn't help but notice how it resembled a giant Everlost coin.

CHAPTER 19
Roadkill

Three weeks.

Allie lived the sordid life of a coyote for three weeks—although to her, the time was immeasurable. All she knew was that the days were many. Each moment was a nightmare for her because she never forgot who she was, or what she needed to do—but the senses and biological demands of the animal's body held her in an iron grip.

Allie had never suffered from an addiction. Yet as she suffered through this, she'd come to know what it must be like; how a person could be unable to resist, knowing full well the depth of the consequences, yet still traveling that path to one's own doom.

She had always been a willful person, but resisting this was like trying to stand firm against a tsunami. Humbling couldn't begin to describe it. She didn't think Jix intended this when he gave over the coyote for her to skinjack. How could he have known that the animal's base instincts were stronger than her will to resist them?

As the first few hours passed on that first day, she knew that she would be permanently stuck inside the coyote if she stayed much longer—for no skinjacker can separate themselves from their host if they stay there too long—and yet the desire to hunt, to eat, to howl at the moon, made everything else feel trivial. Soon it was too late. After the first day in the animal, she knew she was bound to that mangy, flea-ridden body for the rest of its life. Perhaps someone else— someone with a canine kind of soul—would have enjoyed this, but that wasn't Allie.

The feral spirit of the coyote would occasionally surface in her mind. It had grown used to its new reality, but Allie knew she never would, and when she gathered with other coyotes, they all bared their teeth and kept their distance, knowing she was not one of them.

Day after day, she suffered the living hell of this existence, until late one night she chased a rabbit across the highway, and was hit by a truck.

The coyote was killed, and Allie was painfully ejected from its body. The animal's faint spirit leaped into its own particular light, presumably going off to dog heaven, or wherever it is that roadkill coyotes go, and Allie was back in Everlost, sinking butt-first into the living world.

She pulled herself out of the ground, but it wasn't so easy to pull herself together. Now that she was herself once more, she was wracked with sobs, and she couldn't stem the tide. She was not a girl given to tears, but this had been too much even for her. Life inside the coyote had been by far the worst experience of her life and afterlife, and such an experience deserved to be exorcised by a violent wave of emotion washing it from her soul.

She let her tears flow until the storm within her calmed.

Then, when she was done, she got her bearings and made her way back to the train—or at least where the train had been. She found the spot as dawn began to light the eastern sky. The only sign that anything had happened there was the strange sight of the parlor car on top of the mansion.

She was free now. She could go back to Memphis and find herself, skinjack her own comatose body, returning to her life and putting all of this behind her. . . . But how could she do that now? She had no idea if Mary was still a danger to the living world.

Feeling more alone than she ever had, Allie sat down on one of the rails, trying to decide what to do. For a moment she thought she smelled chocolate, and it reminded her of Nick.

Poor, poor Nick. He had lost his battle with the chocolate that plagued him. In the end it had completely consumed him, and he dissolved, leaving nothing but a bubbling brown puddle at Graceland. Allie knew it was Mary's doing. She had lured him to the Graceland vortex, knowing it would accelerate Nick's strange condition. Even if Allie had been able to escape from Milos, there was nothing she could have done for Nick. In the end, he was just one more of Mary's casualties . . . and if Mary had her way, there would be many, many more. Mary would bring indescribable grief to the living world—and for what? So that Mary could reign over more and more children, becoming queen over this lonely, bittersweet world between life and death.

. . . *Bittersweet* . . .

Again, that scent of chocolate came to Allie, and although she was sure it was just her imagination, she looked around her in the growing light of dawn, trying to find its source. There, on a railroad tie was a brown footprint—then another, and another! She knew there had to be some logical explanation for this. She refused to allow herself to hope that maybe, just maybe . . .

She reached down and touched one of the prints, and brought the tip of her finger to her mouth. It *was* chocolate!

Could it be?

Was it possible?

Could Nick somehow have risen from that molten miasma he had become? Yes! There was only one Nick; only one "Chocolate Ogre." These prints could be made by no one else!

Allie followed the footprints to where the chocolate pooled thicker. He had stopped here for a few moments. There were others who had stepped in it as well, leaving tread marks of different textures and sizes on the railroad ties. Was he attacked here? Were the other tracks from friends or foes? Perhaps he had been captured by the invading Afterlights—she had no way of knowing.

She found his last footprint on the iron of a railroad track and then nothing. He had stepped off the tracks and onto living ground, which left no footprints behind, so there was no way to track him. All she had was the direction of his final step: south, toward a city in the distance. San Antonio. Allie set off toward the city with renewed passion, and a strong sense of hope.

CHAPTER 20
Home Body

Allie did a systematic search of the city, traveling between locations by skinjacking, then peeling back into Everlost to look for signs of Nick. As much as she despised Milos, she had to admit he had taught her well. Her skinjacking skills were cutting-edge, better even than his own. She could surf her way through a crowd, relaying body to body like an electric charge. On a busy day downtown she raced a speeding car and estimated she could travel at close to sixty miles per hour if there were enough fleshies in the street to conduct her spirit.

She found Nick's telltale chocolate footprints in the Alamo, and was thrilled at first, until she realized it was a vortex, and feared it might have dissolved him again. Then she saw a trail of his prints leaving. She was relieved, and although she couldn't track him from there, she knew he couldn't be too far away. It appeared that he wasn't a captive—and there were plenty of others who tracked his chocolate around the old mission. Who was he traveling with? Had he found himself more followers? Was he still trying to bring Mary down? Did he even know that Mary was in hibernation and would stay that way for months?

Allie knew the Neons had to be around somewhere too. She didn't fear being captured by them. Now that she was in a bustling city, no gang of Afterlights could capture her. If they tried, all she had to do was step into a fleshie and she'd be a whole world away. . . . Unless, of course, the Neons had skinjackers of their own, and she doubted that. Still, just to be safe, when she skinjacked, she always made sure that her subjects were in good physical condition in case she had to run.

She had chosen a girl in the living world to be her home base. Or "home-bod," as Allie came to think of it. She was about fifteen, and reminded Allie of herself in some ways, and in some ways not. Her name was Miranda Womack, and she lived downtown with her family in a historic brick home on a street lined with massive old magnolia trees. Allie had found her sleeping over her homework at a nearby Starbucks, and was quick to discover that Miranda was somewhat narcoleptic—that is to say, she fell asleep at the most inopportune times, probably because she stayed up all hours of the night, much like Allie used to. Allie realized that her own body had caught up on all that lost sleep as it lay in a coma somewhere for the last four years.

Four years! It suddenly occurred to Allie that her sleeping body would be eighteen years old. She would not even recognize herself, if and when she finally chose to go back.

Well, at least when she skinjacked, she could be the age she felt.

Whenever Allie skinjacked Miranda, the girl never knew that Allie was there, because Allie was such a masterful skinjacker. She only jacked when Miranda was drowsy, putting her instantly to sleep. She always freed Miranda in the same place she started, and never spent more than half an hour within the girl's body at any given time. After each skinjacking, Miranda simply assumed she had nodded off again.

"Honey, you really need to get more sleep," her mother would say, and Miranda would always protest, saying things like "I'll sleep when I'm dead" and such. The irony was that most of the dead—at least those in Everlost—rarely slept at all.

Allie used Miranda to take care of living-world business, such as creating a map of all the Everlost deadspots she found, and all the places she had explored in her search for Nick. She couldn't create such a map in Everlost, since on the rare occasions that she found paper and pen, she would always use them for something much more important: refuting the things that Mary had written in her self-serving and deceptive books. Allie had no idea if anyone read the "books" she herself wrote, but all the same, she always left them in highly visible deadspots for anyone who might find them.

Each day Allie searched Everlost for clues of the whereabouts of Nick, Mary, and even Milos and his cohorts—for if the Neons hadn't pushed them down, they could still spell trouble in any number of ways. Yet each day, Allie spent less and less time in that search. The more she skinjacked, the more compelling the living world became and the less important Everlost seemed to be.

Even observing the daily activities of Miranda Womack

become obsessive. The girl's life was so full of ridiculous drama, it was like watching a soap opera; fairly inane, but totally mesmerizing. Like the time her boyfriend, a somewhat sincere but woefully hormonal boy, confessed to kissing one of her friends at a party and tearfully asked Miranda for forgiveness. Apparently this was not the first time it had happened. Well, Miranda might have been forgiving of a multiple offender, but Allie was not—and saving Miranda from herself was the least Allie could do in payment for the use of her body. Allie skinjacked Miranda just long enough to tell him to go grow a spine, and she broke up with him. Then Allie skinjacked Miranda in school, and flirted a bit with a boy who Allie had already scoped out and knew was much more worthy. He asked Miranda out, they became the perfect couple, and that was that. In this way Allie had cast herself as the girl's fairy godsister.

After all Allie had been through, delving into the ordinary was like submersing herself in a warm bath. It was comforting, and it made her want to put aside the heavy responsibility that came with being a skinjacker, and knowing the things she knew. Milos had tempted her with the craving every skinjacker had to skinjack. He spoke of the joy of it and she could not deny how wonderful it was, how *powerful* she felt—not just to be whoever she wanted to be, but to be able to change the course of people's destinies by taking over just the right person at just the right time. She began to wonder if perhaps this was the true purpose of skinjacking. Maybe the world was full of such spirits, tweaking the living like spiritual mechanics, getting into the works of their lives and fixing whatever was broken.

. . . And these days, there was so much that was broken. One needed only to look at the news to see it. San Antonio alone had enough heartache. The twenty-car pileup on the interstate, the horrible high school fire, and half a dozen other disastrous events. Allie could not prevent the disasters, but as a skinjacker, she had the power to ease the pain of a troubled world.

For instance, the day after the deadly fire at Benson High School, she had gone into the homes and into the minds of grieving parents. She didn't put them to sleep, however. Instead, she spoke to them loudly and clearly within their minds in the guise of an angel, telling them that their son or daughter had gone into a bright and welcoming light. These people heard her voice and were powerfully comforted.

When Milos had showed her this trick, he had called it *terminizing*—because he had gone into terminally ill patients, to ease their minds. He did it just to show off—she doubted he used the skill much. He also taught her *justicing*, which was much more aggressive and even more intrusive. It involved going into the mind of alleged criminals to find out if they were guilty or innocent. Allie had no real desire to go justicing; it was far too much of a violaton. And yet, there was one situation that she couldn't get out of her mind no matter how much she tried: the case of the boy accused of starting the school fire.

His name was Seth Fellon—a very unfortunate name under the circumstances. Seth was a sixteen-year-old high school dropout who worked at a gas station near Benson High. His mug shot showed a pierced eyebrow, nose, and lip. There were also violent tattoos up and down his arms.

Allie knew this because he was all over the news. They were calling him "the Benson Burner," and although he insisted he was innocent, the evidence was incriminating. Word was that he would be tried as an adult.

If there was one thing that Allie had, it was insight into the soul, having seen through the eyes of so many people — and every time they showed Seth Fellon on the news, there was something about him — something about the whole situation — that didn't sit right with her. She couldn't say why.

"They ought to give him the death penalty," Miranda's father said while watching the news one night. "Lower the age for capital punishment, and be done with him."

It was Miranda herself who gave Allie a crucial bit of insight. Allie was there in the room, observing but not skinjacking at that particular moment, so the thought was Miranda's all on her own.

"I think he's innocent," Miranda said.

"That's only because you think he's cute," her brother teased.

Miranda smacked him, then she said, "His tattoos have skulls and roses but no fire. If he's a pyro, his body art would have fire in it, don't you think?"

Allie couldn't help but be a little bit proud of Miranda; she was absolutely right!

In her book *Caution: This Means You!*, Mary Hightower says this about the hazards of entering living-world buildings.

"Don't. Plain and simple. Don't enter a living-world building unless you have no other choice. Living-world floors are deceptively thin. Stand on a wood floor, and you may just find yourself sinking through to the basement too quickly to escape the relentless pull of gravity. Step into a living-world elevator, and you may just find it rising to higher floors, leaving you behind to plunge down the shaft.

Do not be tempted by curiosity, and do not accept a dare. Limit yourself to buildings that have crossed into Everlost. They are the only buildings worthy of our attention anyway.

CHAPTER 21
The Benson Burner

I t was a simple matter for Allie to get into a high security detention center, walking right through every
security door as an Afterlight. Unlike most Afterlights,
she didn't have to worry about sinking through living-world
floors, because she simply jumped inside of living hosts,
piggybacking rides inside of them, hiding behind their con-
sciousnesses, rather than taking them over completely. Such
"half-jacking" made it easy for her to get around without
being noticed. First she half-jacked a correctional officer on
his way to the main cell block, hanging on to the edge of his
thoughts as he went about his business. Then she jumped
to another, and another and another, until she had a good
sense of the detention center's layout, and had gotten some
inside info about the Benson Burner, who was the subject of
quite a few conversations.

Apparently the public defender's office had assigned
Seth Fellon a lawyer who came to see him daily, because his
family had disowned him.

Allie lingered until the lawyer showed up; a very efficient-
looking woman in neutral beige, and wearing an air of confidence.

Allie piggybacked inside her mind, studying her. Allie had no intention of probing her thoughts, but being that close to someone's mind revealed many things. The woman believed the boy was guilty, but she was also dedicated to her profession and would do everything within her power to give him the best possible defense. Well, now that Allie was here, he'd be getting something better than that. He'd be getting exactly what he deserved, one way or another.

Two guards brought Seth Fellon to the room where his lawyer was waiting to see him. The guards sat him down, and then left, closing the door. It was called client-attorney privilege. Although the guards waited outside the door, they couldn't listen in. In that room Seth and his lawyer had absolute privacy. It was exactly what Allie needed.

Seth Fellon looked the part. He was a punk with scraggly hair, a stony gaze, and an orange prison jumpsuit that seemed like something he was born for. He had no facial rings now; they had been removed when he arrived. His jumpsuit had short sleeves, and Allie could see the tattoos up close. Not a single hint of fire.

Before the lawyer could speak, Allie made her move, pushing her own consciousness forward and tweaking the sleep reflex deep within the woman's limbic system. The woman instantaneously went to sleep, and Allie took full control of her body, rolling her neck to get a kink out of it.

"Hi, Ms. Gutierrez," Seth said. "Any luck changing the trial date?"

Allie had no idea. With the woman's mind asleep, there was no way to look for the information. Seth took her hesitation as a "no."

"Didn't think so," he said. "I don't suppose you would have a cigarette, would you?"

Although Seth's eyes were anything but friendly, Allie forced herself to look deeply into them.

"I want you to think about the fire," Allie said, getting right down to business. "Everything that happened before, during, and right after."

"What's the point?"

Then Allie asked the big question. "Are you guilty, Seth?"

He looked away uncomfortably. "You said you wouldn't ask that."

"I'm asking."

Now Seth looked scared. "They found my fingerprints on the gasoline can," he said. "Why does it matter what I tell you? They've all made up their minds anyway."

"You work in a gas station. That's why your hands smelled like gasoline, and that's why your prints were on the gas can—you probably filled it for someone."

"Yeah," he said. "But nobody believes that's true. Not even you."

"If it's true," Allie said, "I'll believe it. Now close your eyes and think about the fire."

"No," he said. "I don't want to think about it. All I ever do is think about it!"

Allie held eye contact. His gaze was still cold, still mistrustful, and now that she was here with him, she couldn't tell anymore. What she thought was innocence might have just been shell shock from having been caught.

"Don't move," Allie said. Then, making sure the lawyer stayed asleep, she leaped out of her body across the table and right into the mind of the prisoner.

—*Cold in here / cigarette / this is useless / I need a cigarette*—

She probed his thoughts, poured through his memories like she was rifling through a filing cabinet.

—*Hey what the / how the / who the?*—

She didn't try to hide herself, because that didn't matter. In fact, it was better if he knew exactly what was happening. Finally, she found it. Or rather, she *didn't* find it. There was no memory of starting that fire! He had a lot of other crazy stuff going on in that head of his, but none of it had anything to do with arson. He was at the gas station cash register a block away, and once the fire had started, he had actually gone into the building to try to help people. He didn't start the fire—he was trying to be a hero!

Now that Allie was convinced of his innocence, she left him, leaping back into the lawyer. But something had gone wrong. Her face was down on the table.

Suddenly the guard—who must have glanced through the small glass window in the door—burst into the room, ripping Seth from the chair and throwing him back against the wall.

It was Allie's mistake, and a stupid one, at that. When she had leaped from the woman's body, she hadn't stabilized her in any way. The woman, still asleep, had fallen forward. Now that Allie was back inside of her, she raised her head off the table, but the guard was already restraining Seth.

"What did he do?" the guard asked, then yelled at Seth, *"WHAT DID YOU DO?"*

"He didn't do anything," Allie shouted, and, thinking quickly, she added, "I had a dizzy spell. I put my head down.

Are you going to beat my client because his lawyer got dizzy? I'm sure the media would love to hear about that."

The guard backed off instantly at the mention of media.

"Now please, leave me to consult with my client."

The guard reluctantly backed off and left, but not before throwing a suspicious glare at Seth.

Once the door was closed, Allie took a deep breath to get her thoughts settled, and to make sure she was still in complete control of her body. When she looked at Seth he was staring straight at her, still backed against the wall.

"Muh . . . Muh . . . Ms. Gutierrez," he said. "Something just happened. Not the guard, something else."

Allie took a deep breath. "Just sit down."

"But Ms. Gutierrez—"

"I'm not Ms. Gutierrez."

He stared at her with the same lost expression Allie had seen on TV. He came forward and lowered himself into his chair, never taking his eyes off of her.

"Listen to me very carefully," Allie said, "and don't do anything that might make the guard come in again, okay?"

Seth nodded, clearly frightened beyond words.

"I saw into your mind. I know you're innocent . . . and I'm going to get you out of here."

"But . . . but my fingerprints," Seth said, "and all that evidence they planted . . ."

"It doesn't matter, because you're never going to go to trial. I'm getting you out . . . do you understand?"

When he realized what she was saying, he nodded and bit his lip nervously. "How?"

Allie tried to explain it to him as best she could. "I can

be whoever I want to be. I jump into people and I take them over. And no, you're not crazy, this is really happening."

"You . . . can read my mind from over there?"

"No, I just guessed what you were thinking."

"Good guess."

Allie leaned closer to him. "If this is going to work, you're going to have to trust me, and do exactly what I say."

"Oh, yeah. Sure. Why not?" Clearly he still wasn't convinced that this was real, and that was a problem, because if he doubted her for an instant it would all fall apart.

"Listen to me," Allie said as sternly as she could. "If you don't do what I say, you are going to be tried as an adult— and you won't last very long in a real prison."

That made him squirm. "Okay," he said. "What do you want me to do?"

"Tonight," Allie told him, "you're going to hurt yourself. Not enough to cause any real damage, but enough so that they have to take you to the infirmary."

"There's security at the infirmary, too," Seth said.

"That doesn't matter," Allie told him. "It's not the guards I'm worried about, they're predictable. But if the other prisoners figure out that something's fishy, there's no telling what will happen."

"Okay," said Seth. "Okay. So . . . how will I know you? I mean, if you can be anyone, how will I know who you'll be?" It was a good question.

"Code word!" Allie said. "I'll say a code word, so you'll know."

"Great. What is it?"

Allie thought for a moment. It had to be something no one would accidentally say.

"*Hightower*," Allie told him, and shivered at the name spoken aloud in the living world.

"High tower," said Seth. "Got it."

"Now, I'm going to wake up your lawyer and leave. But you've got to act like nothing happened; as if she just walked into the room, sat down, and you've been waiting for her to say something. Can you do that?"

"Hey, I'm not an idiot," said Seth. "I even had an acting class before I quit school."

"Right," said Allie. "Okay, then I'll see you tonight." Allie prepared to wake up the woman but just before she did, Seth said, "So, who are you?"

Allie was about to say that it didn't matter, but you know what? It did matter, *she* mattered. She didn't need the world to know that she was doing this good deed, but if he knew, that would be enough. "My name is Alexandra Johnson." Then she added, "I'm not from around here."

Allie had no idea why this was so important to her. Perhaps it had to do with that sense of helplessness she felt when she was tied to the front of the train. Wrongful imprisonment struck a very deep chord in her, especially when she knew she could do something about it. Somehow this punk represented every one of Mary's kids—every kid denied the right to move on. Allie knew it was crazy, but freeing him would be satisfying in a way that she could not explain.

Deep down, she knew there was more to it—something tickling the back of her mind that she couldn't get at. Right now she didn't really want to try. It was time to act, not to think.

Now she was glad that she had been humbled by the coyote, learning that she was not all-powerful, that she could not do everything. Because this skill was enough to make anyone arrogant beyond belief. To know the truth of every situation, in anyone's mind, to be able to dispense justice without any oversight. To be judge and jury and know absolutely that your assessment is correct. No human being had the right to have such power, and yet every skinjacker did. She had to hold on to some of that humility she experienced so that she would use this power wisely.

Allie didn't leave the detention center that day. She waited on a deadspot, and there were no shortage of them in such a place. She watched the movement of the guards. She piggybacked on several of them just to learn the procedures of opening and closing security gates and doors.

Seth was in solitary confinement; all high-profile prisoners were. But the only way out was through the main cell block. Moving a prisoner anywhere in the detention center always required two guards. Allie could skinjack one guard, put him to sleep, then leap to the other guard and run with Seth—but that wouldn't go over well in the middle of a crowded cell block—especially one where the inmates wanted to see the Benson Burner lynched just as badly as the public. Allie knew the only way to get Seth out was to get him out of the cell block first in some legitimate way. . . .

* * *

That night Seth Fellon broke his nose. His wails echoed in the halls of solitary. "I deed a doctor!" he yelled. "My doze! I deed a doctor!"

One of the guards on duty reluctantly came to check it out, peering through the little window into the small concrete cell. He cursed about the bloody mess that was all over the room, then went to get a second guard so they could escort him to the infirmary.

"You think you've got it all figured out, don't you?" one of the guards said, as they pulled him out of his cell. "Mess yourself up, then claim that *we* did it to you." Then he pointed to the corner of the hallway. "See that? That's a security camera, moron. It'll prove you did it all on your lonesome."

Once they arrived at the infirmary, the doctor on call took his time in getting there. Both guards remained while the nurse took care of him, doing her best to stop the bleeding and disinfecting the gash across the bridge of his nose.

"How did you do this?" she asked.

"Fell and hit my face on the toilet."

"Ouch," said the one of the guards, then laughed, so that no one could accuse him of being sympathetic to an arsonist.

Then, when the doctor finally arrived, the nurse turned to him and said, "It's about time you came down off your *high tower*."

"Don't start," said the doctor as if it were a perfectly natural thing to say.

Seth met the nurse's gaze, recognizing something in her eyes.

* * *

As far as Allie was concerned, this was all about timing. She knew there were five security doors between them and the main entrance. She knew where she needed a magnetic swipe, where she needed a code, and where she'd have to be buzzed in by a guard. She was only a single skinjacker, but if she had her timing down, she could do this.

"We'll take X-rays in the morning," the doctor said, after he had sewn up the gash, "once the swelling goes down a bit." Then he pulled off his surgical gloves, tossed them in the trash, and was gone.

"All right," said one of guards. "Back to your cell."

But Allie handed him a clipboard. "Not until you fill out the accident report." Then she excused herself to the restroom where she promptly left the nurse's body asleep in a stall.

In the examining room, Seth watched as the guard filled out the report. "See," the guard said. "Doing that to yourself was a waste of time."

"And," added the other guard, "it'll hurt even worse in the morning."

Seth kept waiting for Allie to return, but she didn't. Then as the two guards led him out of the infirmary, the one on his left said, "You'd better not try anything funny; this place goes into computer lockdown the second you try to escape. With technology like that, who needs snipers in *high towers*?" Then he said, "Come on. The warden is waiting."

The other guard looked at him strangely. "We're taking him to the warden?"

"You know our orders. If anything unusual happens to

the Benson Burner, we're supposed to take him straight to the warden."

The other guard wasn't convinced. "That's not protocol." He pulled out his walkie-talkie. "Let me call it in."

Allie leaped out of the left-hand guard, through Seth, and into the right-hand guard just before he pressed the button to talk—but she had leaped so suddenly that the first guard—who she had put to sleep while skinjacking him— was jarred awake. He didn't even stumble.

"Hey," he said reaching for his weapon, knowing something strange had happened. "How'd we get in the hallway? What's going on?"

Damn! Allie leaped back again into the left guard—she never even had the chance to put the right guard to sleep, and he knew something had been possessing his body.

"Something's wrong here!" he said.

There was no time to think now, so Allie tried something she had never done before; she leaped from one guard to the other and back again, over and over, back and forth, staying just long enough to keep them from doing anything she didn't want them to. Faster and faster she bounced, until she was seeing double—two separate images from two pairs of eyes. She kept increasing the speed of her jumps, images flickering like a projector getting up to speed, until she couldn't tell whose body she was in anymore. Then she realized that she was skinjacking them both at once! Allie settled into the rhythm of this alternating current. It was exhausting, but she had no choice.

"What's going on?" Seth asked.

"Move it," she said and found that the words came out

of both men's mouths simultaneously. Striding in unison, they came to the first set of security doors, and punched in the code, bringing them one step closer to escape.

They needed to be buzzed through the next door, and the guard on duty asked,

"Where are you taking this prisoner?"

Both guards said in unison, "Prisoner transfer."

The guard on duty chuckled at the apparent coincidence, and buzzed them through. Allie realized that both men were sweating profusely, but she couldn't do anything about that. They were also fully awake, and knew everything that was happening to them—and although they struggled to get control of their own bodies, they had no experience with such a thing. As long as she kept hammering them down, she would stay in control.

They made it through one more door without incident. Ahead was one more guarded door, then they'd be in the prisoner admissions area—kind of like a criminal's lobby. After that they would be home free.

But before they got through that last security door, from an adjacent corridor came a small, bald man with an unforgiving face.

"What are you doing? Why isn't this prisoner in his cell?"

Allie's hearts sank. This was the warden. She couldn't bluff her way past him, because any transfer would have already gone through his office, and he would know about it. And so she did the only thing she could. She began leaping into him as well, turning her two-step dance into a waltz.

One-two-three, one-two-three, one-two-three . . .

The warden tried to speak, but it came out as a stutter. "Uh . . . Uh . . . Uh . . ."

Left-right-forward, left-right-forward . . .

And in a moment, Allie was seeing through three sets of eyes instead of just two. It was the hardest thing she had ever done. It was like juggling, *body-juggling*, and if she bobbled any of them, it was all over. But perhaps it was worth the risk, because the guard at the admissions door wasn't going to question the warden.

"Good evening, sir," said the guard as they approached the door.

All three skinjacked men nodded, and the guard buzzed them out to the deserted admissions area, watching with only mild interest as they strode out the front door into the chilly night.

"I'm gonna get shot now! I know it!" Seth said in a panic.

Allie had all but forgotten Seth, the single member of the foursome she wasn't skinjacking. "Quiet!" she said in a three-voice chorus. It took even more energy to speak with three sets of vocal chords under her command, so conversations had to be kept to a minimum. She reached into her pocket, all three men mimicking the same exact motion. While the guards came up empty-handed, the warden had his car keys in his hand. He hit a button and the Lexus in the warden's parking space unlocked.

Seth, who took the passenger seat, mumbled to himself all the things that could go wrong as they drove out into the city, and Allie simply could not deal with the distraction. "Stop! Talking!" her three voices told him.

She hadn't lived long enough to get her license, and on top of it, it was near impossible to drive when she had three points of view, but with the aid of the warden's muscle memory she managed to keep the Lexus on the road, and mostly in her own lane. Soon she was able to narrow her focus, and make the warden's eyes her primary ones, although the two guards in the backseat perfectly copied the motions of the warden's hands on the wheel.

She drove down a frontage road, afraid to get onto the freeway. Then, when they were about ten miles out of the city, she turned onto a residential street, dead quiet at this time of night. She pulled over to the curb, turned to Seth, and struggled to say, "Get! Out! Good! Luck!"

Seth hesitated for a moment. "Right here? But—"

"Go!"

He didn't need another invitation. "Well . . . Thanks. I mean . . ." And since there was nothing he could say that would be adequate, he gave her a genuine smile, then opened the door and ran, disappearing into the dark neighborhood.

Once he was gone, Allie turned off the headlights, turned off the engine, and continued to jump. Guard to guard to warden; guard to guard to warden.

There would be a manhunt. Seth would be hunted down like an animal—and with those bandages on his face he'd be easy to spot . . . but Allie suspected he was streetwise, and much smarter than people gave him credit for. With any luck, they'd never catch him. And if they did, she could free him again.

Why did I do this?

Why do I care?

She knew the question was important, and her answer crucial—but she couldn't think about that right now.

One-two-three, one-two-three, guard-guard-warden. The three men were drenched in sweat but she kept them under her firm control for almost an hour, making sure she gave Seth a substantial lead. Then, when she could juggle no more, she let all three men go.

One guard began to scream, the other began to pray, and the warden pounded the steering wheel in frustration. Allie knew these three men would face the full wrath of the judicial system, and their claim of being spiritually possessed would be laughed at. *Perhaps*, Allie thought, *I could skinjack the judge at their trials, and get them off.* And it occurred to her that every event changed in the living world through skinjacking required even more skinjacking to offset the consequences.

Allie didn't linger to watch what the men made of their experience. Now that she was back in Everlost, she felt as if her soul had been shredded. She was so weak, she could barely lift her feet and found that she was beginning to sink deeper and deeper into the living world because she couldn't move fast enough to keep it from taking her down. She knew she would sink over her head if she didn't do something soon, so she made her way to the nearest home, practically crawling, and skinjacked the first person she came across, just to escape from sinking. A woman, home alone, watching the home shopping network. Once Allie was inside, and had taken control, she instantly knew that the woman was drunk. Very drunk.

Between the fleshie's blood alcohol level, and all the

turmoil in her own soul, it was more than Allie could stand. She stumbled into the bathroom and retched into the toilet. She could have found a neighbor to skinjack, but she didn't. She stayed there retching until there was nothing left to purge. . . .

. . . Because now that it was over, now that she had done the deed, she knew why she had to free Seth.

Seth had no memory of the fire—but it was more than that. He also had no memory of leaving the gas station and going into the school. Somehow all the evidence pointed to him, and there were witnesses who swore they saw him start the blaze.

How was that possible?

How could a person have no memory of something their own body did?

The answer had been in front of Allie all along, but she had refused to see it until now.

Seth Fellon had been skinjacked.

There could be no denying it. So Allie heaved over the porcelain bowl, hoping she could flush away the truth.

CHAPTER 22

A Balance of Power

I t had taken two weeks of endless tweaking and tinkering until Mikey McGill finally picked the lock on the cage he was trapped in. Then, once he was free, he immediately set off on the railroad tracks, following Nick's prints. If nothing else, Nick was single-minded; each footprint was spaced exactly the same distance apart. Nick had marched like a machine, slow and steady, but he had a two-week lead on Mikey now.

When Mikey reached Little Rock, he ventured into the city, hoping to find Afterlights he could convince to join him. His ability to become a monster was impressive enough to get their attention, and if he played it right, they would respect him instead of fear him. Fear was easy, but it had gotten tiresome. He would much rather have Afterlights who joined him because they wanted to, not just because they were afraid not to.

Mikey found no Afterlights in Little Rock, or anywhere else west of the Mississippi, for that matter. He pondered this as he rested on a sizable deadspot in a hotel lobby. He didn't even want to guess how the deadspot had gotten there. In the living world, a TV played a twenty-four-hour news network. Someone was being interviewed about a car wreck. Mikey didn't pay much attention until he heard—

"It's bad, it's bad. I'd never seen so many cars piled up!"

Mikey's eyes snapped to the TV. There was something familiar about that voice. The focus was blurry, like everything else in the living world, but he could make out two middle-aged men being interviewed.

The second man said, "Yeah, I never shaw shush a bad crash."

Mikey stood and stared at the TV, trying to tell himself he hadn't heard it, that it was a trick of his own twisted mind. He had heard enough of the report to know that this had happened in San Antonio, Texas. The driver of an eighteen-wheeler claimed to have fallen asleep at the wheel. A witness in one of the cars, however, claimed that she saw the driver jackknife the truck on purpose.

Mikey tried to dismiss it. The two voices couldn't belong to Moose and Squirrel. These were deeper, older . . . but Mikey had heard their skinjacking voices before. The vocal chords change with each fleshie, but the way a person speaks does not.

. . . And the driver turned the wheel intentionally.

Mikey knew that Moose and Squirrel had been on the ghost train. Could they be causing greater and greater mischief for their own amusement? Was Allie still captive on that train?

If Moose and Squirrel were creating disasters, Mikey figured there would be other occurrences, other awful events that seemed random, but were not. The problem was, Mikey couldn't access the information. He couldn't turn the page of a living world newspaper, or read the blur beneath the headline.

What Mikey needed was someone who could be in both Everlost and the living world at the same time. What he needed was a scar wraith.

Clarence did not die when he was shot that day at the crumbling farmhouse. Had the bullet pierced his heart, or even nicked an artery, his story would have ended. He would have faced the tunnel and the light—and in that light, maybe he would have found some of the answers as to why his life had been so unfair.

But the officer who shot him hadn't been aiming for the heart. He had aimed merely to disarm him. The bullet had imbedded itself in Clarence's shoulder, fracturing his collarbone, leaving Clarence with a whole host of internal issues—but none of them life-threatening.

And while it was true that the living world had mostly forgotten his heroism, good deeds have a nasty habit of coming back when one least expects them to.

When it came to light that this crazy old man was once a firefighter who saved many lives, the officer who fired the bullet felt a bit of responsibility. It was nothing quite so fervent as guilt—after all, he had fired in self-defense—but the man felt enough responsibility, and had enough compassion, to downplay the shotgun attack, bringing the charges down to trespassing and resisting arrest.

He was sentenced to six months in prison, but his sentence would be thrown out if Clarence agreed to commit himself to a hospital . . . the kind of hospital where they put people who talk to dead kids and see things that no longer exist.

So Clarence agreed. On that day he gave up his quest to show the world what he knew about Everlost . . . and that was the day that Clarence began down that long, slow road, toward his death—and a sorry death it would be, meaningless and hopeless, a funeral attended by no one except for those who were required to fill out paperwork.

Clarence knew that would be his fate, but what did he care? He had failed, and he had to accept that. He had captured two evil spirits, he had plied them for information, and even with all of that, it had brought him no closer to proving to the world the things he knew.

Well, it didn't matter! Why should he care about the world anyway? There, at Hollow Oak Hospital, his own personal world was safe and sterile. His pillows were fluffed regularly, he had a somewhat warm bed. The best part of it was that there were no ghost children.

At least not until the day one paid him a visit.

Clarence yelled out loud when he saw Mikey standing in his bedroom. Fortunately, random shouts were more the norm than the exception here, so no one thought much of it.

"Why are you back?" Clarence asked. "Haven't you done enough damage?"

"We need to talk," Mikey said, "but I can't stay here, this floor is too thin."

Clarence could see Mikey struggling to keep from sinking through it. It made Clarence laugh, but Mikey ignored him.

"Meet me on solid ground," Mikey said. "Out in the garden." And then he walked through a wall and was gone. Clarence had half a mind to make him wait an hour or two, but he was too curious about what this troublesome spirit had to say.

Tracking down Clarence in the living world had not been easy for Mikey. He had gotten so accustomed to traveling with Allie, he had forgotten how disconnected Everlost was from that world. Without her, the living world, as close as it was, was a universe away. Mikey could turn himself into any monster he could imagine, but he couldn't change the path of a single speck of drifting dust in the living world. He could walk through walls, but he couldn't lean on one. He could raise his Everlost voice, sounding like the voice of God or the devil, but couldn't ask a single question to the living. He felt powerless, and it was a feeling he despised.

In all his years in Everlost, his inability to interact with the living world hadn't mattered. Although both worlds coexisted, it was easy for him to ignore that other place, and tune it out the way the living tuned out the tick of a clock, or the flicker of a lightbulb. To Mikey the living world had been little more than an annoyance.

But things were changing.

For as long as anyone could remember the two worlds had coexisted, and aside from the occasional haunting, or random skinjacking, the living were not troubled by the world they could not see.

Mary had changed that, however. She used skinjackers to blow up a bridge, and that bold act set in motion a clockwork too intricate for anyone to see. Anyone, that is, but Clarence, who could see both worlds at once. It was that connection to the living world that Mikey needed . . . but Mikey had other things in mind for Clarence as well.

"I need your help."

"Oh, really?" said Clarence. "And why should I help you?"

They were out in the garden now, a spot that even in December was frequented by patients. The staff had hung some ornaments from the bare-limbed cherry trees, but all it did was draw attention to how bare the branches were. There was an attendant on duty in the garden to make sure that none of the patients did anything problematic. Apparently talking to oneself did not count as a problem.

"You should help me, because I can prove to people that you're not crazy," Mikey said. "I can't prove it to everyone. But maybe to a few people. The people who really matter to you."

"Nobody matters to me anymore." But Clarence was not convincing. So Mikey waited until Clarence said, "My son, maybe. But he doesn't even know I'm alive, so maybe it's better if—"

"I know someone who can make your son believe from the inside out—but I need your help to find her."

"In case you haven't noticed, I'm in a 'psychiatric facility.' I might be here voluntarily, but if I leave, those charges they dropped will come right back."

To which Mikey said, "Only if they find you."

Clarence thought about it. "You know, I'm beginning to

like you. And that scares me." A breeze blew in the living world, knocking loose one of the sparsely spaced ornaments. It fell to the ground and shattered with a dainty tinkle. The attendant went to clean it up.

"So this friend of yours—is she an incubus, or a succubus, or a poltergeist, or a ghoul?"

"None of those things. She's just a girl."

"And you're in love with her."

That caught Mikey by surprise. "How did you know that?"

"We talked about it, remember? And besides, that glow you've got—when you talk about her, it turns a little bit purple."

"Right. So the first thing I need you to do is read me some newspapers. Living-world things are too blurry to read in Everlost."

"What are we supposed to be looking for?"

"Accidents," Mikey said. "Accidents in Texas."

Clarence took a long time to consider it, scratching his beard stubble. Then he held out his Everlost hand to Mikey. "It's a deal. Let's shake on it."

Mikey instantly backed away. This was a scar wraith. He had to remember that. If the legend was true, he could be extinguished by a single touch.

Clarence still held out his hand, waiting. "A gentleman's agreement requires a handshake. Didn't your mother teach you manners?"

Mikey considered telling him the truth, but instead he said, "I'm unclean! Yeah—I'm an unclean spirit. And out of respect for you, I shouldn't touch you."

Clarence looked at him, but didn't drop his arm just yet. "How does a spirit become 'unclean'?"

Once the lie had been launched, Mikey found it hard to change its trajectory. "It's not my fault—I had a curse put on me by . . . uh . . . by a graveyard ghoul. That's why I walk the earth."

"Graveyard ghoul, huh?" Finally Clarence put his hand down. "In that case, we'll skip the handshake. Because, you know what they say . . ."

"Yeah," said Mikey. "Yes, I know what they say. Boy, do I know what they say!"

As it turned out, they didn't need newspapers. Over the next few days Clarence scoured the Internet from the computer in Hollow Oaks's recreation room. What Clarence found confirmed Mikey's suspicions. San Antonio, Texas, had become a center of bad luck. Not just the car pileup, but a school fire and a bleacher collapse, and a freak electrocution. Although Moose and Squirrel never appeared again in any of the news clips, the circumstances were all similar. There was always a suspect or two, who had been seen by reliable witnesses—once even caught on surveillance video—and yet each suspect claimed to have no memory of what happened.

There was no question in Mikey's mind that this was where the ghost train went—which meant Allie was there too. More than anything, Mikey wanted to find Allie, but he also knew he had to stop these random crimes against the living.

Mikey had no particular love of the living world, but

he did not despise it the way his sister did. He tried to tell himself that Mary wasn't the one behind all these terrible things—but he had to accept the truth: Milos, Moose, and Squirrel were now working for her. Alone, they had been just a nuisance, but in the hands of someone like his sister—someone with vision—they were incredibly dangerous, and could manipulate the living world in ways too frightening to imagine. Yes, they were Mary's weapons, whether she was standing there with them or not.

So how does one fight against weapons that powerful? By having one's weapon: a weapon could wipe out the very existence of Mary's skinjackers. Clarence would be Mikey's weapon—his "balance of power."

Of course Mikey couldn't tell Clarence that. If he knew, he'd be gone in a heartbeat. That's why Mikey had to lie about why they couldn't shake hands. It wasn't the worst of lies, Mikey figured. In fact it was bound to help everyone. And besides, Mikey had turned over so many new leaves, the ground before him was practically carpeted green. He could afford to turn one back. He could afford one simple white lie.

Only much later would he realize that he was very wrong. Not only couldn't he afford it, but there weren't enough coins in all of Everlost to pay the cost.

CHAPTER 23

Uptown Boy

While Allie was freeing the innocent, and Mikey was preparing his ultimate weapon, the Neon Nightmares were hunkering down in their lair, lying low.

With the threat of the Chocolate Ogre somewhere in the city above, the Neons had set their security alert on red. All lookouts were given orders to sink themselves if spotted, rather than lead the monster back to the Alamo again. They had been lucky the first time, but would not escape detection a second time.

After the first few days in lockdown, Jill went through a sort of skinjacking withdrawal, aggravated by the adrenaline rush infused into them all by the vortex above. It was like being wired on caffeine twenty-four hours a day, and since sleeplessness was the normal state of Afterlights, it only made things worse. In the Alamo basement, everyone was an insomnoid.

Knowing how hard it was on Jill, Jix decided to give her a gift.

The Crockett Street tunnel was guarded by two Neons

whose routine involved endless knock-knock jokes. Unfortunately they only knew about twenty, and so they just kept repeating the same ones over and over.

"I'll tell you a new knock-knock joke," Jix told them, "if you let Jill out the back entrance, and let her return without telling Avalon."

The two Neons agreed that it would all depend on the joke . . . and so Jix introduced them to the Interrupting Cow, which is perhaps the only knock-knock joke in existence that is actually funny.

The joke sent the guards into a giggling fit that lasted the better part of an hour, and it bought Jill the right to come and go as she pleased. When Jix told Jill, she was thrilled by the possibility of escaping the dungeon, if only for a while.

"Why don't you come with me?" Jill asked, but Jix had inserted himself into so many of the Neons' routines, he knew his absence would be noticed.

"Go skinjack," he told her, "but I see no need for you to reap."

"I'll do what I want," she answered.

Jill left first thing the next morning for her day on the town, and once she was gone, Jix went about his own day; the same games, the repeated conversations. In this way he maintained a foothold in the routines of as many Neons as he could—because by becoming a cog in the routine, it gave him the power to bring the gearwork to a grinding halt if he wanted to.

After he made his obligatory rounds, he took some

time to visit the root cellar, which was the farthest, darkest room in the maze of the Alamo underground. Few places were actually dark down there, because there were so many Afterlights that their glow illuminated most spaces—but this room was where they put all the Interlights captured from the train—those sleeping souls waiting to be born into Everlost. The Interlights gave the Neons the creeps because they didn't glow, so Jix could go there and not be bothered.

He found the girl he had inadvertently killed, and sat beside her. He had no idea what her real name was, so he called her Inez. Inez was his sister's name, and it comforted him to think of this girl in that way. As he sat there, he thought about Jill. It intrigued him that she felt no remorse for the souls she had intentionally brought into Everlost, but also troubled him. It troubled him enough to find his own Afterlight dousing the room into darkness, just as Jill said a truly bad feeling would. He practiced it, strobing his light on and off. He couldn't say he enjoyed it, but as stealth was an important part of being a scout, the ability to feel miserable, and douse his afterglow, was a skill worth knowing.

Then, at a point when his light was fully doused, he realized there was still a glow in the room. He looked up to see Jill standing there at the entrance to the chamber.

"I thought I might find you here," Jill said. She wove through the sleeping Interlights, and noticed which one Jix sat closest to. "What is it with you and that girl?"

"I stole her life. The least I can do is look after her."

Jill crossed her arms and shook her head. "I still don't get you," she said, which was fine. Jix still wasn't sure he wanted to be "gotten." Then Jill sat down beside him. "You promised you would tell me about yourself. So far you haven't told me a thing."

Jix *had* promised her that, but he also hoped the opportunity would never present itself. His specialties were reconnaissance, stalking, and observing. Putting himself out in the open and making himself vulnerable was something he just didn't do.

"Don't you dare make me say 'please,'" Jill said. "I don't do the *P* word."

"Tell me about your day skinjacking."

"Don't change the subject."

"Did you reap?"

"I said don't change the subject."

"You didn't come to the chamber to find me," Jix said. "You came to bring a new Interlight, didn't you? Where did you leave it, in the passageway so that I wouldn't see?"

Jill looked at him coldly. "I do other things than just reap," she said. "How do you know I didn't go to a ball game or eat a lobster dinner?"

"Did you?"

"No," Jill admitted. "But I didn't reap, either." Then she paused and looked away from him. "Maybe it's like you said; I have better things to do with my 'hunting instincts.'" She reached out and touched Inez's hair. It gave off a dark, smooth sheen, reflecting their afterglows. "She has nice hair," Jill said. "Not all of us are lucky enough to die with nice hair."

"Now who's changing the subject?"

She gave him an irritated sigh. "If you must know, I skinjacked a girl in her twenties, which is how old I would be if I wasn't here. I chose her because she was pregnant, and I wanted to see what it was like to feel a baby kick."

Jix never dreamed that Jill would have such a thing in mind when she went skinjacking, but he didn't show her any sign of his surprise.

"I took a long bath," Jill continued, ". . . and then I brushed her hair."

Jix reached out to touch Jill's hand, but she pulled it away before he could. "Your turn," she said. "Tell me all the things about yourself that you don't want me to know."

Since she didn't back off, Jix had to keep his word. He wouldn't lie to her, or tell her half-truths. She would probably know if he did. He told her the truth as clearly and as simply as he could.

"I am the long-distance scout for His Excellency, Yax K'uk Mo', the Supreme King of the Middle Realm. My mission is to find out if Mary Hightower poses a threat to him, and capture her if I can."

If Jill was shocked, she didn't show it. In this way, she was a lot like him. "The Middle Realm?" she asked.

"What you call Everlost."

"So . . . there are more like you?"

"There are many Afterlights in the City of Souls . . . but only one like me."

Jill smiled. "Good," she said, then she got up to leave. "As far as secrets go, I'd give that a six out of ten." Then she added, "I thought you were going to tell me you were an alien."

The next day, one of the Neons' lookouts found a stray Afterlight.

It wasn't one of the train refugees; it was a *Greensoul*,

a new spirit, freshly woken from some accidental crossing nine months before.

"He was just wandering around, calling for his mama," the lookout told everyone. The Neons all laughed at the poor kid, and his lip quivered. He couldn't have been any older than six. He had a runny nose, which would now continue to run for as long as he stayed in Everlost.

Avalon stomped up to him. "Give me your coin!"

"I don't got money," the boy said.

Avalon turned to the Bopper—one of the more intimidating Neons. "Take it from him!" But Jix firmly grabbed the Bopper's shoulder.

"I'll do it." Jix said, and since Jix had become a regular in the Bopper's daily poker game, he politely said, "Oh, sure, Jix."

"I didn't ask you!" Avalon snapped.

"But I can grab the coin without going into the light," Jix reminded him.

Avalon never changed his unpleasant expression. "All right, then."

Jix knelt down to the boy. "Do I scare you?" Jix asked.

The boy shook his head, then nodded. "Only a little," the boy said.

"I won't hurt you," Jix told him gently, "but *they* might, if they don't get what they want."

"Yeah, but I don't got money, just some tissues in my pocket," the boy whispered.

"You wanna see a magic trick?" Jix asked. The boy's answer was a wet sniff. Jix then told him to take out his tissues.

"Now," Jix said, "unfold them."

The boy did, and as the tissues spread apart, a coin dropped right into Jix's open hand. The boy gasped. "Where did that come from?"

"Magic," Jix said, because indeed it was.

The boy grinned, and wiped his nose.

Avalon had no patience for this, or anything else for that matter. "Put it in my shirt pocket," he ordered Jix. Jix went over to Avalon and gave him a wide smile.

"Here you go . . ."

Then he grabbed Avalon's hand and slapped the coin right into the center of his palm, forcing Avalon's fingers closed over it.

"*What?* No!"

Avalon struggled, but Jix held Avalon's fist closed. Everyone was so shocked, no one knew what to do.

"No! No!" Avalon shouted. "I'm not ready! I'm not ready!" But apparently he was, because he looked off toward something that no one else could see. No one, that is, but Jix and Jill, for only skinjackers can see someone else's tunnel. A look of resignation came over Avalon, and he heaved a heavy sigh. "All right, then . . ." And before everyone's eyes, he lurched forward, and vanished in a rainbow twinkling of light.

There was absolute silence. No one spoke until a kid called Foul-Mouth Fabian declared something holy that wasn't holy at all.

"He sent Avalon *uptown*!" someone said. "What do we do? What do we do?" But without a leader, no one could agree.

"Send Jix down!"

"Throw Jix out!"

Jill looked at Jix incredulously. "You're crazy," she said. "You've lost your mind!"

But Jix just winked at her, and said loudly enough for everyone to hear, "Ask Wurlitzer!"

Everyone fell silent again.

"We can't ask Wurlitzer," the Bopper finally said. "You gave Avalon the only coin!"

"There's one more," Jix reminded him, then he looked to Little Richard. Everyone's eyes turned to the kid, and he backed away.

"Not my problem," Little Richard said. But it was. The Bopper pointed to the bank, and Little Richard went to pick it up. Turning the bank upside down, he shook it. The coin just rattled around inside, as it always did. "See?" Little Richard said. "It's not going to—" And then the coin fell out of the tiny hole and onto the dusty ground.

"No way!" said Foul-Mouth Fabian, although he did squeeze in a third word in the middle.

"Wow . . . ," said Jill.

"Just like my mother said," Jix told her. *"Todo tiene su propósito.* Everything has its purpose." It had been a wild gamble, but he had a feeling that the coin was waiting for him. It frightened him that he had been right, almost as much as it would have frightened him if he had been wrong.

The Bopper, now taking the role of High Priest, carefully lifted the coin up in his fingertips and went over to Wurlitzer. Then, with his free hand, he pulled off the quilt. Wurlitzer's neon glow lit the room in shades of yellow, green, and red. The moment the jukebox was revealed, the Neons fell to their knees, including the little Greensoul boy, savvy enough to get with the program.

The Bopper dropped the coin into the machine, and it rolled around, then dropped into the coin box with a *clink*. Then he said, "Oh, mighty Wurlitzer, what should we do with Jix and Jill?"

"Avalon already asked that," Jix reminded him. "It said to let us go."

"That was then," said the Bopper. "But things change."

Then he pushed a button, and Wurlitzer came to life, its record bank spinning like a wheel of fortune. Everyone waited in anticipation, and Jix grinned, wondering what song it would choose.

In her book *Caution: This Means You!*, Mary Hightower has this to say about Objects of Power, or O.O.P.s:

"One may, on occasion, come across Objects of Power. These are, like many things in Everlost, best left alone. They usually come in the form of a machine that has crossed over — often due to sunspot activity — never because someone loves it. Nobody loves an Object of Power. Thus, love is exactly what it craves. It will, however, settle for subservience. There are those who feel that these objects are possessed by some unknowable spirit, but I say they are merely filled with some faint leftover consciousness of creation, like the irritating static spark when you grasp a door handle on an exceptionally dry day.

Foolish Afterlights will argue until the end of time whether such objects are forces of good or evil — but I know the answer. They are neither. These so-called Objects of Power serve no one but themselves. Therefore if an entity or object:

A) takes something of value from you,

B) claims to know things it can't possibly know, and

C) draws followers like rotting meat in the living world draws flies;

then lift your slowly sinking feet out of the earth, and run as fast, and as far, as you can, for the thing in question will never do you any good."[1]

---

1 In her book, *Mary, Mary: Trite, Contrary*, Allie the Outcast points out that A, B, and C paint an accurate description of Miss Hightower herself.

CHAPTER 24

Face the Music

The smile lingered on Jix's face, his mouth refusing to accept what his ears were telling him. *When you're alone, and life is making you lonely, You can always go . . . Downtown!*

The Neons all looked to one another—this was one song it didn't take a high priest to interpret. They all listened to a mockingly upbeat woman repeat the word "Downtown" in almost every line as she sang about the city's energy and itsneon signs.

"It said Neons!" Someone shouted! "The song knows our name!" and they turned to Jix and Jill with sudden singular purpose, becoming a raging mob.

The friendships that Jix had formed, the way he had delicately woven himself into the Neons' social structure—none of that mattered now . . . because Wurlitzer had spoken.

"Downtown!" shouted the Neons. "They're going Downtown!"

And all at once Jix realized his folly. It was the coins! They should have been a tip-off. Anything truly helpful—anything truly *good*—would never demand an Afterlight's coin. Such theft was reserved for monsters and dictators, and, yes even "His Excellency," who, when it came down to it, was not excellent at all, only power hungry.

As the song reached its chorus, both he and Jill were grabbed by dozens of maniacal hands that practically tore them apart as they lifted them off the ground. *Downtown!* The song sang, *Everything's waiting for you . . .*

And as Jix looked one last time at that shining, faceless jukebox, he couldn't help but feel that it was laughing at him.

The Neons had to take Jix and Jill up before they could push them down. For the first time since the attack on the train, all the Neons climbed the stone steps and walked out through the gift shop wall into the Vortex of the Aggravated Warrior. It was daytime, and although the Alamo was open, it was a slow day. Only a few tourists milled about the grounds in the living world—and none of them within reach of either Jix or Jill. There were so many hands holding them, they could barely move, much less reach out toward a fleshie and skinjack their way to freedom.

"Take them out the front gate," the Bopper ordered, then he turned to Jix, offering a moment of sympathy. "Sorry," he said, "but Wurlitzer knows best." Jill spat at him, which did not help the situation. He scowled at her then turned to the Neons and said, "We'll throw them into the river. That way, they'll be sure to sink fast."

Then, as they were carried out through the Alamo's main gate, Jix saw a glorious sight.

Boy scouts!

At least twenty of them, milling around just outside the main entrance. Never had Jix been so pleased to see living, breathing human beings.

"Do you see that?" he called to Jill.

"I'm way ahead of you!" she answered.

The Neons, who never paid much attention to the living, just walked right through the mob of scouts, and the moment they did, Jix pushed himself into the first fleshie he came in contact with and—

—*candy / candy toys candy / gift shop / twenty bucks / how many toys / how much candy / and a keychain with my name too*—

He quickly put the scout to sleep, took full control of his body, then looked around to orient himself. It never ceased to amaze him how the same spot could be so full of turmoil in Everlost, and yet be so calm in the living world. No sign of the Neons anywhere around them. He could just walk away from here, and never have to face any of this again if he wanted to. Jix looked around and caught sight of another scout looking just as disoriented. "Jill?"

The other kid nodded. "In the flesh."

A few other kids in troop thirteen looked at them funny. Jix motioned for Jill to step away with him, for a moment of privacy.

"Hey," said one of the other kids. "Scoutmaster Garber wants us to wait here!" But fortunately the scoutmaster was at the ticket booth, too busy to notice.

Once they were far enough away for no one to hear them, Jill said, "The boy scout look suits you. Now let's get outta here."

And although he knew it wasn't what she wanted to hear, Jix said, "I'm going back."

"What?" She stared at him, shaking her head. "No! No way! Not this time. If you go back, you go alone."

"Don't you see—*the Neons don't know about skinjackers!*"

"Yeah," said Jill. "Lucky for us."

"More lucky than you think!" Then without any further explanation, Jix peeled out of the scout and returned to Everlost, leaving both the scout and Jill completely bewildered.

In Everlost, the Neons were at a total loss. As far as they were concerned, the two prisoners simply vanished into thin air. It was at least ten seconds until someone asked the obvious question: "Uh . . . where'd they go?"

"I don't know," said the Bopper, "but I don't like it."

Then, just as quickly as he'd vanished, Jix appeared, standing ten yards away.

"Grab him!" yelled the Bopper, but when they tried, he vanished once more into a flurry of live people, only to appear somewhere else a few moments later.

Now the Neons were scared—which is exactly what Jix was counting on. Then an exceptionally annoyed Jill appeared beside him. Jix was counting on that, too.

"Wh . . . what are you?" someone dared to ask.

It was Jill who answered. "He is the son of the jaguar gods," she said in a commanding voice, "and the jaguar gods are very . . . *very* . . . *angry!*"

Eyes widened, jaws dropped, and some of the smaller kids ran back into the Alamo to hide, but the rest were too shocked to move at all. In fact they were so frozen in place, they were sinking in up to their ankles.

"You mean there really are jaguar gods?" said Little Richard, timidly. "And they're mad at *us*?"

"Furious!" Jill said. "But they can be calmed, if you do exactly as Jix says."

Even though Jix never told her of his plan, she instinctively said all the right things. They were working as a team now! Jix puffed out his chest and matched her commanding tone. "You no longer serve the music machine," he told them. "You will feed it no more coins, and its name will never be spoken again."

The Neons all looked to one another. "But . . . But . . ."

"Do as he says, or you will face the wrath of the jaguar gods!" Jill threatened.

Jix wanted to grin at how well their ploy was working, but he kept his face dark and menacing, staring down as many Neons as he could. "You are all now subjects of His Excellency, the Supreme King of the Middle Realm."

"The who of what?" someone called out.

"Silence!" shouted Jill, clearly relishing every moment of this.

"So . . . there are jaguar gods, *and* a king?" asked Little Richard.

"Yes," Jix told them. "But mercy will be shown to those who are obedient . . . and come with gifts."

"Whaddya mean, 'gifts'?" the Bopper asked.

"The girl in the glass coffin," Jix told him. "She will be your gift to the king." Then he stood there waiting to see what they would do.

The Neons had a very difficult decision to make. For as long as they could remember they had done Wurlitzer's bidding. Their entire purpose had been to steal coins from stray Afterlights, just so they could hear Wurlitzer "speak." But Wurlitzer did not move, or disappear, or threaten as this son of the jaguar gods did. In fact, Wurlitzer didn't do anything without a coin. This gave Jix an advantage—and although Afterlights by their very nature resisted change, they could also adapt when they had to.

The Bopper looked around, gauging the Neons' reaction to the ultimatum. No one rose in defense of Wurlitzer. The Bopper, who now spoke for all of them, turned to Jix and Jill and made his decision. "What do you want us to do?"

Once Jix made his plans known, the Neons were quick to carry out his orders. They were, after all, an army that was used to doing what they were told—and Jill was more than happy to be their taskmaster.

The first order of business was to move Wurlitzer out of the common room. Jix had them move it into the small room full of old saddles. The Bopper, a bit repentant for how he had treated Jix, led the moving team, and in just a few minutes, this device that everyone had worshiped was now nothing but a relic.

"You know, in all this time, that machine never played a song I liked," the Bopper said, after setting Wurlitzer in its new resting place. "It's good that you sent Avalon uptown."

With Wurlitzer out of sight, Jix hoped it would quickly be out of mind, and when the Neons all began to take off their bright war paint, he knew the machine had truly been defeated.

"We're leaving here," Jix told them. "There are boats in Corpus Christi that have crossed into Everlost—enough to carry all of us, and all the sleeping Interlights, south to the Great City of Souls."

"So . . . ," said Little Richard, who now followed Jix around. "There're jaguar gods, a king, *and* a city of souls?"

"Yes," Jix told him.

"In Mexico?"

"The living call it Mexico," Jix said, "but the City of Souls existed before there were nations."

It was on the evening before their departure that Jix dared to go into the saddle room to face Wurlitzer one last time. He did it because, deep down, he still feared it. Jix knew the jukebox would give him nightmares if Afterlights were able to dream. He didn't know why—it had neither arms to grab him, nor legs to kick him, and it had no voice but the one the Neons allowed it to have. Perhaps *that's* what he feared—how much power a thing could have when it was given permission to have it.

"You are nothing now," Jix told it. Wurlitzer said nothing. "Your own greed has left you with no one to worship you." Still, the machine said nothing. "And now you will stay here undiscovered until the end of time."

And then a voice behind him said, "Wurlitzer made all this happen." Jix turned to see Little Richard standing there with his empty piggy bank. "He played that 'Downtown' song because he knew we would take you outside and you would show us your powers." Then with enough arrogance

225

to make his point, but not enough to incur the wrath of the jaguar gods, Little Richard said, "Wurlitzer did this for you. You should thank him."

Then the boy left, and Jix covered the machine, so that its light couldn't attract anyone else to the room. There were no more coins, and no one to give the machine a voice . . . but Wurlitzer was destined to play one last song before falling silent forever.

CHAPTER 25
The Souler Eclipse

Allie had no choice but to introduce herself to her "home body," Miranda. She needed an ally in the living world—not just a body she could borrow, but someone who could work on her own, and help track down the skinjackers responsible for these crimes against the living. Allie was quick to figure out that the Benson High fire was not an isolated incident. Whoever these psycho-jackers were—and Allie suspected there were more than one of them—they had to be stopped. She had her suspicions as to who they might be, but she wasn't ready to pass judgment quite yet. She had always believed a person was innocent until proven guilty, and suspicion was not enough to convict Milos and his cast of idiots.

Allie introduced herself to Miranda slowly, carefully. She hid behind Miranda's consciousness, and gave her a single stray thought one evening before Miranda went to bed. *"I'm a friend and I am in here with you."* And then again, just as the girl woke up in the morning. *"My name is Allie. Don't be afraid."* Both times, Miranda thought it was just part of a dream, but she was wakeful enough to remember . . . so when Allie spoke to her deep within her mind in the school cafeteria that day, it didn't come completely out of nowhere.

"I've been with you for a while," Allie said in her mind. Miranda nearly choked on her chili, excused herself from her friends, and hurried to the bathroom.

"You're not real," Miranda said aloud. "You're just in my head. It's because my mom's right, and I don't get enough sleep."

"I am in your head," Allie told her. *"But I'm also real. We'll talk again later."* Then Allie pulled out, giving Miranda time to process this new wrinkle in her life.

That evening, as Miranda did her homework, Allie moved inside her again. She didn't take over Miranda's body, just met with her mind.

"Please," said Allie. *"I need your help. And if you help me, I'll tell you things—amazing things that no one in the living world knows, as long as you promise to keep it a secret."*

But Miranda just put her hands over her ears as if she could shut out Allie's voice. "No! No! I'm not listening! Go away! Go away!"

"Why don't you and I go for a walk?" Allie told her.

"I don't want to go for a walk. I'll exorcise you." Then she rummaged through her jewelry drawer and came up with a little gold cross which she held out to herself in the mirror. When that didn't work, she ran into the kitchen thinking, *"I'll get garlic and eat an entire bulb of it. Garlic scares away demons!"*

"No," Allie said calmly. *"That's vampires. And besides, you're allergic to garlic."*

Miranda stopped short. "How do you know that?"

"Let's just say we're much closer friends than you think." Then Allie sensed Miranda dredging up thoughts of silver bullets and stakes through the heart. Allie did her best to control her temper and remind herself that she was the one trespassing in this girl's very personal space.

"Listen," Allie told her. *"We can do this the easy way, or we can do this the hard way."*

"What's the hard way?" Miranda asked.

"This way." And as smoothly as slipping into a bathrobe, Allie pushed herself forward and skinjacked Miranda, taking control of every muscle of her body—but didn't put her to sleep. Miranda was awake, but now just a passenger in a body that Allie controlled.

"Now," Allie told her out loud, "we are going out for a walk, and I promise you, I'll tell you everything."

They walked until after dark, but Allie was able to give Miranda control of her body after the first ten minutes. Miranda was a sensible girl. Once she realized that Allie meant her no harm and that having her own personal ghost was a really cool thing, Miranda agreed to their partnership.

Allie told her everything, just as she had promised: how a car crash had landed her and Nick in Everlost. How they found Mary and her "children" in the eternal towers. Allie told her about the awful monster called the McGill and the wonderful boy named Mikey who remained once the monster was gone. Then she told Miranda the dark secret behind the Benson High fire.

"I knew it," Miranda said. "I knew that Fellon kid was innocent. I'm glad he escaped." And then she gasped. While

Allie was pretty good at keeping her mind separate from the people she skinjacked, she had let her guard down and Miranda caught a brief glimpse into Allie's thoughts. She knew Allie had been the one who helped Seth Fellon escape, and it impressed her almost as much as it scared her. "You're like a superhero," Miranda said. "The Souler Eclipse."

"Let's not go there," Allie said, because losing one's humility was a dangerous thing for a skinjacker . . . although she had to admit she liked the name.

The next day, Miranda took the money she was saving for a new phone and bought a police scanner, which she listened to in all her free time, while Allie wandered the streets night and day looking for signs of Afterlights. Now every single police action, every single accident, every siren blare got their attention. There was no telling where the psychojackers would strike next or what nature of terror they would bring upon the living world. Then one night, the police scanner pulled in emergency chatter on more than a dozen different frequencies, calling all cars to the Regency Theater.

The police scanner had been a good idea, but it could only tell of things that had already happened, not what was about to happen. Allie and Miranda arrived at the scene an hour too late; the street outside the Regency theater was already blocked by police tape. Allie had never seen so many squad cars in one place. Or ambulances.

The theater's marquis advertised a much-anticipated concert by teen singing sensation Rhoda Dakota . . . But Rhoda wasn't singing anymore. In fact, she'd never sing in the living world again . . . but that wasn't the half of it.

Apparently there had been a combination of deadly "coincidences." The fire sprinklers came on for no reason, hitting a damaged electrical line at the front of the stage. The short circuit should have tripped the circuit breakers, but somehow it didn't, and the result was disastrous. The panicking crowd had raced out of the theater, but Rhoda and more than thirty fans never had a chance. News crews were already on the scene, and even the most jaded of reporters were fighting back tears.

"Go home," Allie told Miranda. *"There's nothing you can do here."*

"What about you?" Miranda asked.

"I've got work to do." And with that, she peeled out of Miranda.

In Everlost the chasing squad car lights were muted, and the voices of emergency workers faint. Allie raced into the theater, but there was no sign of the culprits. They were long gone, leaving only carnage and deadspots—so many deadspots—and each one marked the place where someone's life had ended.

"Who would do this?" Allie said furiously, knowing that no one was there to answer her. But someone did.

"Us," said the voice of a young girl. *"We* would do it."

Allie turned to see a single Afterlight there, standing all alone in the center aisle. She couldn't have been any older than seven or eight when she crossed.

"He said Mary wanted us to, but I don't believe it. Ever since Mary found me in the playground, and took me up in her silver balloon, she's been nice to me. She would never do such a horrible thing."

Well, obviously this girl hadn't been watching when Mary had her skinjackers blow up the bridge—but this wasn't the time to argue.

"I know you're Allie the Outcast, but I don't care. If you do something terrible to me, maybe I deserve it anyway."

But Allie just took the girl into her arms and held her. Allie never considered herself the motherly type, but this girl needed someone to comfort her from the things she had seen, and maybe the things she had done.

"What's your name?" Allie asked.

"They call me Lacey."

Allie could see why. Her shoelaces were untied and must have been that way since arriving in Everlost.

"What happened here, Lacey?"

Lacey closed her eyes. "He told us to do it."

Although Allie already knew the answer, she had to ask, "Who told you?"

"Milos," she said. Now it was Allie's turn to close her eyes and swallow the news. To think that once, she had trusted him. To think that once, she had even been attracted to him. But how could she know way back then, that this type of darkness was lurking inside his heart? How could she know he could become a . . . She couldn't even say the word. So, holding on to Lacey almost as desperately as Lacey held on to her, Allie asked, "Why?"

"Because we need more," Lacey said. "More and more and more. That's what he says."

"More what?"

And for the first time, Lacey looked her right in the eyes, as if trying to read something there. "More of *us*," she said.

"More Afterlights. They don't glow like Afterlights—not yet anyway—but they will once they wake up."

When the truth hit Allie, it hit with force enough to pound her halfway to the center of the earth, and it might have too, if she wasn't standing on a deadspot.

More Afterlights . . .

Now it all made sense in a horrible, twisted way.

"Milos and Moose and Squirrel make them cross, then we're supposed to grab them before they disappear," Lacey told Allie. "We grab them, and hold them, and then they fall asleep—but I don't think it's right."

Allie knew on some level this had to be Mary's idea, but she couldn't tell Lacey that. Allie had seen into Mary's mind. She had seen that this was only a fraction of what Mary truly wished to unleash upon the living world. Had Milos seen her mind too? Was he now some sort of dark apostle?

"How many?" Allie asked Lacey. "How many kids have you . . . have you . . . taken?"

"We've reaped almost two hundred, but there's gonna be more," Lacey said. "A lot more." Allie shivered. It was almost as if she had flesh herself.

"I'm going to hell!" Lacey cried.

"No," Allie said. "It's not your fault. And besides, you're never going to do it again, are you?"

Lacey looked up to her with wet eyes and shook her head.

"Well," said Allie, "the decision to stop has got to count for something, right?"

Lacey didn't seem convinced, but nodded anyway.

Allie told Lacey she had to go back to Milos. She didn't

want to send her back, but she knew that if Lacey was missed, it could make Milos suspicious. "You'll be a spy," Allie told her. "A double agent. Just don't tell anyone, and you'll be fine." And then Allie asked the million-dollar question. "Do you know where they're going to strike next?"

"Yes," Lacey said, then looked sadly down at her own dangling laces. "It's happening next Friday," she told Allie. "In a playground."

CHAPTER 26
The Angels of Life

The Chocolate Ogre was confused.

It would have been fine if he hadn't known the depth of his confusion, but he was fully aware of how confused he was. He knew, for instance, that he was being used by Milos, and yet, Milos was so very kind to him. According to Milos, he and the Ogre were best friends now. He seemed so sincere, it was easy for the Ogre to believe it. Sometimes.

Then there was the Ogre's alleged devotion to this girl named Jill. He had no memory whatsoever of her, and yet Milos, Moose, and Squirrel all insisted that he and Jill were in love and that if Jill ever showed up he should sink with her to the center of the earth, so they could be together until the end of the world. It all sounded very romantic. And yet, not.

In his mind, the Ogre had a memory of two girls. One all dressed in green whom he loved, and another who he believed may have crossed with him into Everlost. Milos just laughed when the Ogre suggested that.

"You did not cross into Everlost," Milos told him. "You

are the Chocolate Ogre; you have always been here." There was a distinct possibility that it was true, but the Ogre only believed it once in a while.

Milos was certainly clever—there was no doubting that. He was very good at planning exciting excursions for the Afterlights in his care. "Angels of Life," he called them. Their excursions made special places—and people, too—cross into Everlost.

This did not sit well with the Ogre. There was a powerful sense in him that these excursions were wrong.

One day as they sat in the crossed bank building that they called home, the Ogre brought his concerns to Milos. "You're killing people," the Ogre pointed out. "Even if it's for their own good, I don't think you should be doing it."

Milos dismissed his concerns as if he were a small child. "Words like 'killing' and 'dying' are living-world lies. The living fear crossing because they do not know we are waiting here for them, to save them from the light." Milos looked out over his Afterlights. "Do you think any of them are sorry to be here? And when the souls we have reaped awake, do you think they will despair, and despise us for having cared enough to bring them into Everlost? No!"

Well, that remained to be seen. There would be no way to gauge their gratitude until they awoke. So far the souls they had reaped were sleeping out their hibernations in the bank vault. According to Milos, they belonged in a vault, because they were treasures. Gifts for Mary, if and when they found her.

The thought of Mary made the Ogre flutter a bit inside, as it always did—but now he knew the feeling was just the devotion all good and true Afterlights had for the girl sent to Everlost to care for them. At least he thought that was it. He wasn't really certain about anything except the knowledge that he was uncertain.

As for Mary, they were no closer to finding her. There had been no further sign of the Neons and every time it was mentioned, it was a reminder to everyone of how badly Milos had screwed up.

"My mistakes only make me stronger," Milos said whenever it came up. "Stronger and more determined to make a better world for Mary when she awakes. It is like they say, 'We burn from our mistakes,' and now I burn with more determination than before."

Once in a while Milos would send Moose and Squirrel out alone for smaller missions—the ones that didn't involve people, just real estate. So far Moose and Squirrel had caused a coffee shop, a bowling alley, and a post office to cross. The post office had been an accident. Now, however, they received a daily supply of dead letters to read, and some were highly entertaining.

Things took a definite turn for the worse when Milos announced his plans for the concert. Certainly the so-called "Angels of Life" wanted Rhoda Dakota among them—who wouldn't? But they weren't convinced that reaping fans at a concert was a good thing.

"Of course it is a good thing," Milos told them. "It is what Mary wants, and when she returns I will make sure she knows who did their job and who did not." That seemed to convince some, but not all of them . . . and so Milos offered them something else. "For all of you who do your duty, you will get as much chocolate as you want."

This was news to the Ogre.

"Uh, I don't know if that's a good idea," the Ogre whispered to Milos.

"Nothing to worry about," Milos told him. "You have more than enough to spare, yes?" And so, in this way, Milos convinced all forty-three Afterlights to go to the concert. The Ogre didn't go. He never went because his hands were too slippery to prevent crossing Afterlights from getting where they were going. The Ogre was glad he couldn't reap, because he didn't know whether he had the heart to do it.

When they all came back from their mission at the concert, the Ogre saw that it must have been successful, because Moose came into the bank holding Rhoda Dakota herself, asleep in his arms, followed by every other Afterlight, each carrying a sleeping Interlight.

The Ogre did not expect what happened next.

After depositing an Interlight in the bank vault, one of the Angels of Life went straight for the Ogre, and thrust his hand into the Ogre's side. It didn't hurt, but it didn't feel all that good, either.

"Milos said we could have some," the kid said, "and after what I had to do today, I deserve a whole handful. No, I deserve *two* handfuls!" Then he thrust his other hand into Nick as well and went off with two fistfuls of fudge.

Until now the kids would only dare to touch a finger to him once in a while, to get a taste of chocolate. That had been fine with the Ogre—after all, he oozed the stuff like thick, dark perspiration. He did have, as Milos said, plenty to spare . . . but every resource has its limits.

After the first Afterlight exacted his pound of fudge, a second Afterlight came, then another and another. One grabbed his shoulder, another stripped chocolate off his leg. Before he knew it, the returning Angels of Life were mobbing him, and taking pieces of him away. He screamed, but they ignored him. He fell to the ground, and tried to crawl. But mob mentality had taken over, and there were too many of them to fight off.

Finally Moose pushed his way in and yelled, "Shtop!", pulling the Afterlights off of him. The Ogre tried to rise off the floor, but he couldn't. Then he looked at himself, and was terrified by what he saw. There was barely anything left of him. He was like something you might find on Halloween, a chocolate skeleton. Finally Milos arrived, shooing everyone away and helped the Ogre into a chair where he just shook, barely able to hold himself in a sitting position.

Milos didn't apologize, he only said, "Perhaps this was not the best idea."

"Maybe," the Ogre said to him, "you'll burn from this mistake too."

The weakened Ogre was left in the care of a girl with wide eyes and untied laces. She was one of the few who didn't partake of the feeding frenzy.

"I'm sorry about what they did to you," she said to the Ogre. "But at least you're getting better." And indeed he was. Slowly chocolate began to grow on him again, oozing out from that sweet spot in his soul. He had, however, lost most of his ogreishness. He was now just a slender chocolate boy, much less intimidating than he had been before — but also more human. He liked that. Even though his face only had the barest hint of a form, at least now he could think of himself as something other than an Ogre.

Seeing himself as a boy made him remember a few more things. He was now certain that he had crossed over from the living world, and had not been here forever. He knew he once had a name, although he could not recall what it was. He was fairly certain, though, that it had begun with an *N*.

Knowing that much about himself made him bolder, not so easily manipulated. Milos, he finally concluded, was not his friend—and Milos probably knew a lot more about the Ogre than he was admitting . . . so the Ogre gave him a simple, but firm, ultimatum.

"Tell me my name, or I'll breathe chocolate so deep into your soul that it will make you too heavy to skinjack. So deep that your Afterglow will turn brown."

Milos looked at him with fear, and something far from friendship, and said, "Your name is Nick."

"Nick . . ." He nodded. "Thank you." Nick reached up and brushed his fingers through his hair. It was the first time he realized that he even had hair. "I've decided that I'm going on the next mission with you. I'm going to watch what happens, and if I don't like what I see, I'm leaving."

Milos looked guarded. "That is, of course, your choice. But remember, if you leave you will never find Jill."

"I don't know anyone named Jill," said Nick, realizing that it was true, and for the first time realizing that everything Milos had told him from the moment they had met, had been a lie.

CHAPTER 27

Last National Life

It would soon be one of the tallest buildings in San Antonio. It was still months from completion, but one could already see how impressive it would be. Just the kind of high-profile office building Last National Life Insurance Company needed.

. . . And across from the construction site sat Blue Harvest Academy, a very private, very expensive school, preparing the next generation for whatever future their parents left them. Blue Harvest boasted the best teachers, the best computers, and an awesome jungle gym. The one-of-a-kind play apparatus was a blue and gray starship made of the newest polymer plastic, guaranteed not to fade in the sun or crack under the abuse of countless children. Filled with slides, tubes, and climbing bars, as well as a "landing gear" swing set, it was easily the coolest playground in San Antonio — maybe the coolest one anywhere.

Since no nearby play-places had crossed into Everlost, Milos had decided one was needed for the Afterlights in his care — and this was the one he chose. Since playgrounds were much loved, causing it to cross would be a simple matter; the trick was bringing a fresh harvest of souls along with it. But Milos had that covered too.

Thanks to Lacey's tip, Allie arrived long before the so-called "Angels of Life." In fact, she had been waiting for them since dawn, hiding within walls of nearby buildings, and slipping in and out of people to keep herself concealed from Everlost eyes. She had spent much of her time since the concert disaster going into the minds of grieving families to comfort them. She knew it had to be done, yet she couldn't help but feel that cleaning up the emotional mess Milos had left behind somehow made her an accomplice.

Miranda wanted to help, but Allie worried that it might put her in danger. She didn't want her to become an "accident" victim as well. Allie came to Miranda one last time, visiting her in a dream to tell her good-bye. Allie could no longer justify using her, even if Miranda was willing. It made Allie feel dirty. It made her feel like Milos.

Now, on Friday morning, Allie scoped out the spot where Lacey had said the next reaping would happen. Finally, halfway through the morning, while a group of schoolchildren were out in the playground for recess, Allie saw Afterlights approaching—but it wasn't what she *saw* that stopped her cold, it was what she *smelled*.

The unmistakable aroma of chocolate.

She saw Nick almost immediately, walking side by side with Milos, Moose, and Squirrel. The last time she had seen Nick he was a bubbling mess of molten chocolate, without form whatsoever. Now he looked unusually thin, but at least he had something resembling human form. She wanted to leap out and call to him, but she fought the urge. First things first. She didn't even know why Nick was with Milos. Certainly not as a coconspirator. No matter how much Nick had changed, he couldn't have changed *that* much. Even when he had served Mary, Nick had known enough to quickly switch sides—even if he *was* in love with her.

Allie lingered, peeking out from behind trees in a street-corner Christmas tree lot. She watched as Milos directed dozens of Afterlights to position themselves all around the school playground. The living moved through them, never knowing that almost fifty invisible spirits were there, waiting. Lacey was among them and she looked around conspicuously, obviously waiting for Allie to show up and stop them—but Allie couldn't reveal herself—not even to Lacey. Allie also noticed that Nick did not join them; he waited across the street.

"It's time," Milos said. Moose rolled his shoulders and stretched as if he were a linebacker coming off the bench for a big game. Squirrel rubbed his hands together, which was a nervous gesture, but in a way was also threatening, like a burglar getting ready to pick a lock. Then the three skinjackers vanished into pedestrians, taking over three living bodies.

Allie quickly made her move, knowing she could lose them if she didn't quickly skinjack. She leaped into a woman who was picking out a Christmas tree and—

—Too small / too tall / too dry / too expensive
the fake trees are looking better and better—

Allie quickly put her to sleep and hurried off the lot. She

looked at the street in front of the school, searching for anyone who seemed to have a moment of sudden disorientation. Three people were standing still among the other moving pedestrians: a mailman, a well-dressed woman, and a jogger in shorts that were too bright for his pasty legs. They nodded to one another, then split up: The mailman and the woman went into the school, while the jogger trotted across the street toward a busy construction site.

Allie had no idea who was who, or which of them it would be best to follow. She chose to go into the school. If need be, she could pretend to be a parent picking up a child.

Once inside, the mailman turned right and went into the main office, but the woman continued on. Again, Allie had to decide who to follow—but even before she could make a decision, the well-dressed woman was stopped by a portly teacher with a gray goatee.

"Excuse me," he told the woman, "but you'll have to check in at the office first."

"Right, right," said the woman—but then both the woman and the teacher seemed to change. The woman reached out to the wall for balance and looked around, disoriented, while the teacher suddenly looked . . . well . . . squirrelly. Then he turned and hurried off down the hallway.

Allie leaped from the tree-lot woman, and skinjacked a passing school janitor. She quickly gathered her senses, and continued down the hall, keeping a distance behind the bearded teacher. The teacher turned a corner, but when Allie caught up with him, the man was just standing there bewildered.

"Strange," he said. "Very strange . . ."

Clearly Squirrel was gone, but there was no one else in the hallway he could have jumped into.

"Damn it!" said Allie, and the teacher, forgetting his confusion, looked to her, appalled.

"Watch your language, Mr. Webber," the teacher told the janitor. "After all, this is a school."

Meanwhile, through the wall, and in a classroom that opened to a different hallway, a somewhat squirrelly student excused himself to go to the bathroom . . . but his real destination was the bicycle racks.

The fourth graders were let out into the playground for recess, then, just a few minutes later, the fifth graders came racing out of the school as well, immediately commandeering the plastic starship. Mixing grades in the playground was not the usual routine, and when the principal stepped out behind the flood of fifth graders, one of the teachers on duty was quick to ask what was going on.

"I thought they could use a little bit of extra playtime," said the principal.

This was odd, because the principal of Blue Harvest never came to the playground unless he was showing it off to prospective families, and never suggested more playtime for anybody.

The teacher looked toward the space-age climbing apparatus, which now held an overabundance of Starfleet personnel. "Do you really think this is a good idea?" she asked. "It's so crowded—someone's bound to get hurt with all those bodies."

"Well," said the principal, "it is like they say, 'The morgue, the merrier.'"

Allie had no idea where Squirrel had gone, and so she decided to go out into the danger zone itself. Still in the body of the janitor, Allie found her way out to the playground where kids were fighting over the elaborate equipment. To her right, a teacher was having a heated discussion with a man in a suit who must have been the principal.

"Yes, you did," said the teacher. "You said the fifth graders needed extra playtime, so you brought them out here."

"I most certainly did not!" the principal insisted. "What would ever possess me to say such a thing? I don't even remember coming out here."

Then Allie noticed a boy in the middle of the playground who was not playing with the others. He was looking up. She followed his gaze to the skeletal skyscraper across the street. The construction site was filled with activity, with workers welding and hammering on almost every floor.

Allie looked down at her janitorial uniform, to remind herself who she was, then knelt down to the boy.

"What is it?" she said, in a gruff male voice. "What do you see?"

The boy never looked at her. "Nothing," he said. "Just the building." And then he added, "It is big, yes?"

Allie recoiled. This was Milos! He must have skinjacked the principal, and was now skinjacking this boy—but he was too absorbed in his mission to notice that the janitor had been skinjacked too. Milos then ran off into the starship, disappearing into the many tunnels . . . and the moment he did, a shadow crossed over the playground.

Allie looked up to see a load of steel beams being raised by a huge sky crane high above the construction site. Allie realized with a sinking feeling that the crane had an arc wide enough to swing out over the playground, if that's what the crane operator—or the person *controlling* the crane operator—wanted to do.

"We have to get out!" said Allie. "Everyone! We have to get out of here now!"

But nobody listened. After all, the janitor had little authority over children in a school. Allie quickly leaped out of the janitor and into the teacher closest to the door, and tried to open it. The door wouldn't budge. Then when she turned toward the side gate, which was the only other way out of the playground, she saw a kid securing it with a bicycle lock, so that no one could get out. This time something about the way he moved allowed her to see right through his disguise.

"Squirrel!" she yelled.

He looked up at her and ran. She knew she had given herself away, but that didn't matter now. All that mattered was getting those kids out of there. Moose must have already been in the sky crane, because as the massive load of girders rose higher and higher, the crane began a long, slow arc toward the school.

The principal called to the students, not yet realizing what was going on. "Enough playtime," he told them. "Everyone line up by your teachers." The kids all grumbled but immediately abandoned the starship until Milos, skinjacking a scrawny blond boy, poked his head out from one of the tunnels.

"Look, everyone! There is money in here." Then he held out a few dollar bills. "This is why they sent us out here, to find Christmas money!" Suddenly the kids ran happily back to the starship against their principal's orders.

"I found a dollar!" said one.

"I found five!" said another.

It was an easy trick to pull off. Allie wondered how many kids Milos had skinjacked just long enough to empty their pockets into the tunnels. They were all finding their own lunch money. Allie peeled out of the teacher and took over a girl climbing through the starship. She found Milos, and pushed him against the curved tunnel wall with a thud.

"You're not going to get away with this," she said.

Milos recognized her right away, and smiled. "Allie!" he said in that little-boy voice. "I thought you had sunk. So good to see you."

She pushed him against the tunnel wall again. "This isn't going to happen," Allie told him. "I won't let it."

But Milos lost none of his composure. "You cannot stop it now. Why don't you sit back and enjoy it. It will be quite a spectacle."

She would have pounded him through the wall if it wouldn't hurt that poor boy he had skinjacked.

Meanwhile the adults in the playground were beginning to realize that the sky crane across the street was being very careless with its load. "If it doesn't change its trajectory," said the principal, "that load of girders will be right above us. What is the crane operator thinking?"

Allie knew there was no time to lose. She leaped out of the fifth-grade girl and began the most important relay race of her life. She hurled herself to another child, then to a pedestrian on the other side of the fence. She body-surfed her way from fleshie to fleshie, until she was in the construction site, then she paused just long enough to get her bearings. She was a construction worker, and the workers around her were already looking up, wondering why the I-beam load had swung so wide.

Allie turned to leap again, determined to make it up into the crane rising above the tower's highest floors, but she came face-to-face with Milos in the body of one of the other workers.

"Don't forget I am better at this than you," he said, and he grabbed her. "I taught you everything you know!"

Instantly Allie leaped into the worker behind Milos, then to his right, then to his left and back again, creating a pattern of four—moving faster and faster until she was skinjacking all four men. Then she swung at him: identical punches from four different directions, powerful enough to bring Milos to his knees.

"Not everything!" she said in four voices. Then she pulled herself together, and leaped away, leaving Milos reeling from the blows.

Allie launched into a construction worker on the second floor, then to one on the fourth, the seventh, the tenth, up and up, relaying it in leaps and bounds as if the building was a skinjacker jungle gym. It was just as she had done at the Grand Ol' Opry so many months ago when Milos taught her to body-surf this way, swinging from fleshie to fleshie as quick as lightning. They had tied that first race, but this time Allie had to win.

Twentieth floor, twenty-third, twenty-sixth. It was hard finding construction workers now to leap to and the most she could leap through was three floors at a time in the living world. Finally she found herself in the body of a welder on the top floor. Up here, the building was nothing more than a steel frame. It was windy and treacherous . . . and hanging in space before her, almost parallel with her line of vision, was the load of girders nearly in position above the playground. Far below, kids were desperately trying to climb the playground fence to escape. Had it been a chain-link fence, they might have done it, but it was wrought iron—vertical bars with spiked tips—and the kids couldn't get a foothold. No one was getting out.

Allie looked up to where the spine and horizontal boom of the crane met. That's where the control cab was, still far above her. There was no way to leap that far. She would have to climb the ladder in the body of the welder—but just then she felt a hand on her shoulder.

It was Milos. He was in a lean and sinewy worker. He looked like a man whose body knew how to fight. "I'm sorry, Allie, but I can't let you ruin this. . . ." And he elbowed Allie in the jaw. She felt excruciating pain as the welder's jaw shattered, and she fell to the naked beam, which was barely a foot wide. She tried to scramble away, but the pain from the broken jaw made her weak and unable to focus. Fortunately they were both tethered to a safety cable . . . but unfortunately Milos unhooked their safety wires.

"More interesting this way, yes?"

As he moved in for the fight, Allie thrust her legs out, kicking Milos, and knocking his feet out from under him. He landed on top of her, pinning her to the beam. His face was just inches away from hers. She could smell the remains of a rancid cigar on his fleshie's breath.

"If you were in a different body," Milos said, "I might kiss you again. But then, no. Mary is a much better kisser."

And then Milos did the unthinkable.

Holding on to Allie, he rolled off the girder, taking Allie with him, and they began a thirty-story plunge.

"No!" Allie felt that horrible falling sensation, a roller coaster without a track. The whole world spun around them. In just a few seconds, their fleshies would be dead and their own spirits would be injected deep into the earth by their momentum. But when Allie met eyes with Milos as they fell, all she saw were the eyes of a horrified construction worker. Milos was gone . . . and right beside them a construction elevator carried Milos, in a freshly-skinjacked worker to the top floor.

Now in the last few moments of the plunge, Allie did the only thing she could do. "I'm sorry," she said to the two doomed men. "I hope you get where you're going." Then, just before impact, Allie peeled out and leaped up and away like a pole-vaulter, putting all the force of her will behind the leap. She shot through the Everlost void searching for flesh, *anyone's* flesh, to give her safe harbor, and—

—don't sweat don't sweat / and stick to more buzzwords
upward trend / target demographics
and if you get lost point to the graph—

Allie forced full control over whoever's body she was in,

and found herself staring at a dozen dark-suited people in a conference room, pointing to a graph. It was such a total disconnect from the moment before, she thought she must have actually died, or at the very least lost her mind. It took her a moment to realize that she had leaped so powerfully, she had landed a block away, in an entirely different office building.

"Go on," said the man at the far end of the table, obviously the boss. "What was that about our target demographics?"

Then, one of the executives at the table stood and looked out of the window. "Hey, did you see that? I think two people just fell from the Last National Life building!"

Everyone got up to look, but only Allie noticed the load of girders still hanging thirty stories above the playground. She was relieved the load hadn't been released yet, but had to wonder why.

At that same moment, Moose sat in the control cab of the sky crane in full control of his fleshie, staring at the release button. He had been staring at it for at least a minute now. The load of girders was positioned exactly where it was supposed to be, but he couldn't hit the button. He thought back to the part he played in the concert disaster. It had been hard to make himself set off the sprinklers at the Rhoda Dakota concert.

"She is for you," Milos had told him. "When she wakes up, she will be yours."

Although Moose was thrilled at the idea of just meeting Rhoda Dakota, much less a date-after-death with her, knowing he was responsible for ending her life made it all seem a little bit dishonest, didn't it?

And now this.

In all the other disasters, his acts were just a small part of a larger whole . . . but this time, it was all him. He would be releasing the load of deadly beams. Not Squirrel, not Milos—him.

And so he stared at the button.

The girders were still dangling from the end of the cable when Allie body-surfed her way out of the nearby office building, and down the street toward the playground once more, but since her eyes were on the load of girders, she wasn't watching the fleshies she surfed. She miscalculated, overshot the fleshie she was aiming for, and stumbled to the ground.

She was back in Everlost again, still down the street from the school. But something had changed. To Allie's surprise, there were Afterlights running all around her— Milos's Afterlights—and they were running *away* from the playground. Allie saw Lacey and caught her. "What is it? What's happened?"

"It's horrible!" Lacey said. "You have to run before it eats you!" And she raced off with the others.

Then Allie saw it. It was perhaps the most horrific thing she had ever seen: a puke-green creature covered with scales as sharp as razors. Its head was a giant bloodshot eyeball sprouting tentacles instead of eyelashes, and at the end of each tentacle was a hungry tooth-filled mouth.

. . . And at the sight of the horrible beast, Allie's afterglow flushed purple with a deep and powerful love.

* * *

The journey of Mikey and Clarence to San Antonio was not an easy one. Suffice it to say that it involved many unorthodox methods of travel in two different worlds.

It was Nick's sweet aroma that had led Mikey and Clarence to the playground. Without it, they would have wandered the streets of San Antonio as Allie had, no closer to solving the mystery of the psycho-jackers than she had been all these weeks. But once Nick came out into the open, without even knowing it he became a beacon for anyone trying to find him.

They found Nick right about the time Allie and Milos battled on the thirtieth floor. When they saw Nick, and the many Afterlights waiting in the playground, Clarence was hesitant. He had never seen so many "ghosties," in one place. Mikey, however, went straight to Nick, who looked at him, bewildered.

"Mikey?" The change in Nick's face was almost immediate. The unnatural roundness of his head took on a more defined shape.

"Have you found Allie?" Mikey asked, never realizing that her spirit had just shot past them, and into the office building a block away.

"Allie!" Nick said with intense joy. "That's her name." Now eyebrows formed, and lids that blinked over brown eyes.

"Of course that's her name. Have you seen her?"

Nick shook his head. "No. But I remember her now. We crossed together, didn't we? In a forest." And when he smiled, there were now teeth where just a hollow hole had been.

"Something's wrong," said Clarence, who pointed with

his Everlost hand to the playground. "These children are trapped." At first Mikey assumed their screams were the sounds of play, but they were screams of terror. Kids futilely tried to squeeze through the bars and climb over the spikes of the wrought-iron fence, while all around them the Afterlights just stood there, as if waiting for something to happen.

"Nick, what's going on?" Mikey asked.

Nick pointed up, and for the first time, they saw the load of I-beams hanging directly over the playground. "They're reaping souls," Nick told them. "But I don't think it's right. Do you?"

Mikey didn't need to answer him. The answer was right on his face.

Clarence, still a rescue worker at heart, sprung into action first. "I'll help the living, you go do something about those freaking ghosties." Then Clarence smashed the driver's window of the nearest parked car, popped the trunk, and grabbed a crowbar in his living hand. In an instant he was racing toward the playground gate, where he pounded the bicycle lock with the crowbar over and over.

Mikey knew he had no power to help the living, and the only weapon he had against the Afterlights was fear. So digging deep into the darkest pit of his imagination he drew forth the most frightening miscreation he could dredge up and transformed himself into a foul-looking, fouler-smelling tentacled thing, the likes of which had never been seen in this or any other world. Then he threw himself into the playground roaring, turning the tips of his tentacles into tooth-filled mouths, each of which roared in a different dissonant pitch.

One look, and all the Afterlights scattered in terror, abandoning their mission, but that didn't do a thing for the living children still trapped in the playground—and no matter how hard Clarence hit that lock, it wouldn't break. So instead he used the crowbar to pry the gate from its hinges. . . .

"What's wrong with you?"

The sky-crane control booth had flown open and Moose was faced with a furious construction foreman.

"I . . . I . . ."

"Why haven't you dropped them?"

Moose quickly realized that it was Milos, but he was no more relieved. "Maybe we shouldn't do it, Milosh. I mean, itch jusht a bunsh of little kidsh."

"We need all ages, you idiot! Mary would expect no less." And when Moose made no move toward the control panel, Milos said, "Either you do it, or I will."

"Okay," said Moose. "Then you do it."

Milos glared at him. Then, without the slightest hesitation, he reached out, pushed the button, and released the entire load.

Mikey, still in beastly form, frightened the last of the Afterlights away, then turned to see Clarence pry the gate off its hinges, just as the girders above them began a thirty-story drop. A flood of living children escaped from the playground as the girders fell, and just then Mikey heard a voice behind him.

"Mikey, is that you?"

It was Allie! The sound of her voice chased the beast back to the depths of Mikey's mind in an instant and he became himself once more. She ran toward him, but before they could embrace, a crash exploded in the living world violent enough to feel in Everlost.

No matter how strong the climbing starship was, it could not hold off a crushing onslaught of tempered steel. The load of falling girders didn't just destroy the jungle gym, it shattered it. Fragments of plastic exploded in all directions, and even the ground beneath it fractured from the weight. The principal and teachers, who were the last out of the gate, were hit by plastic and asphalt shrapnel, and although those wounds were painful, they were not deadly—and their larger bodies shielded the escaping children.

The playground was destroyed but the children were saved.

Then as Allie and Mikey looked to the spot where the climbing starship had been, they saw something amazing. The space-age jungle gym was gone from the living world, but in Everlost a strange swirl of ectoplasmic smoke, almost alive with purpose and design, began to condense and change color resolving from green to shades of blue and gray. It took shape as if the cosmos itself had breathed into a huge invisible mold the exact size and shape as the jungle gym. For a moment it shimmered like a mirage, and then became solid. The entire playground, lost to the living world, was now a part of Everlost.

"Wow" was all that Mikey could say. In all his years in Everlost he had seen many things but had never witnessed a place cross into Everlost. Finally he turned to Allie, ready for that long-overdue reunion, but Allie's eyes were still locked on the jungle gym, because she saw something he had not yet seen. Not all the children were saved . . . because crawling out of the newly crossed jungle gym was a little boy who Allie recognized. It was the blond boy Milos had skinjacked. Milos must have put him to sleep so soundly that when Milos left his body, the boy remained unconscious within the starship tunnels and was still there when the steel came crashing down.

"There's always one," said a man's voice Allie didn't recognize. "No matter how many you save, there's always one." There, standing just a few yards away from Mikey, Allie saw a man who seemed half in Everlost and half out—but before she could process what she saw, something else stole her attention. A brand-new tunnel now opened before the boy, much different from the climbing tunnels he had just crawled out of . . . and the light at the end of this tunnel was blinding.

That's when Milos barged furiously past her. "I will not leave this place empty-handed!" He ran, determined to tackle the boy out of the tunnel, and trap him in Everlost—but out of nowhere a brown blur launched itself at Milos, knocking him to the ground before he could get to the boy.

"This ends here," said Nick with such fury that his chocolate ran as dark as tar. "Let the boy go!" Even as he said it, the blond boy's eyes lit up and a smile filled his face. He reached a hand toward the tunnel, it drew him in, and the tunnel vanished. Whatever his destination, he got there without any further interference.

Everyone was speechless. The only sounds now were

from the living world; the creak of settling steel, the cries of all the kids who survived, the soothing voices of adults trying to comfort them, and the distant sound of approaching sirens.

Milos, now smeared with tar-dark chocolate, pulled himself away from Nick and looked hatefully at everyone around him. In his mind he was the only one wronged here. He was the only victim. Even Moose had betrayed him, and was still up in the sky crane bawling his eyes out like a baby, just because Milos dropped the load of steel. Well, at least he still had Squirrel, who now came up beside him. Then he saw Clarence, and froze.

"Oh my God, oh my God!" said Squirrel with a terrified warble in his voice. "Do you know what that is?"

"I know." Milos had heard the scar wraith legend, but he had never believed it was real. He figured it was the Everlost version of a fairy tale, a story meant to frighten little children into obedience. Yet here before them was the real thing. Then he realized who had brought it. He turned to Mikey with the kind of disgust usually reserved for the times he was a monster.

"You brought a scar wraith?"

"A what?" said the wraith. "What did you just call me?"

Mikey kept his eyes on Milos and smiled. "The killings stop now," Mikey told him, crossing his arms. "Surrender, or be extinguished."

"Run, run!" said Squirrel. "We gotta skinjack and run!"

But Milos stood his ground. He thought about Mary, and how she could stand in the face of anything, how she would never retreat. If he were ever to be an equal in her eyes, he would have to learn that kind of courage, that kind of commitment. Maybe then, he would earn the kind of respect she commanded. Maybe then, he would feel worthy of her. "We will leave here, and you won't stop us," Milos said, forcing himself to look fearlessly into the scar wraith's Everlost eye. "I don't care what evil you threaten us with!"

"Evil?" said the wraith. "What do you mean 'evil'? I just saved all those children!"

"You condemned them!" Milos screamed. "Condemned them to live! I offered them salvation. *I* am the one Mary chose to see her vision through. *Me*. And I will not let any of you stop that vision."

"What is wrong with you?" the scar wraith snapped. "Are you the one who caused all this?" Then he advanced on Milos.

"Clarence, wait!" said Mikey, but Clarence was too worked up to listen.

It would be easy to say that what Milos did next was out of selfishness and cowardice—but at the moment, he wasn't thinking of himself. Instead, he was thinking about Mary and her children. If he were touched by the scar wraith and extinguished, who would lead them? Moose and Squirrel? They couldn't lead themselves out of an open grave. Without Milos, it would be over. Mary's dream would die and when she awoke she would be alone, with nothing. He couldn't allow that to happen.

And so when the scar wraith approached him, he took a diagonal step backward putting himself behind Squirrel like a king retreating behind a pawn.

"Don't you hide from me!" said the scar wraith. "Face me like a man, if that's what you are!" Then he reached out to push Squirrel out of the way.

"Clarence, no!" screamed Mikey, but it was too late. Clarence grasped firmly on to Squirrel's shoulder to push him aside.

Squirrel was not the finest spirit around, but consoled himself with knowing he wasn't the worst one either. His existence had always been one of ignoble embarrassment. He had crossed into Everlost when he had fallen from a tree while trying to peek inside the window of a girl who would have nothing to do with him. As a skinjacker, his simple pleasures were not all that different, peering into people's lives for his own amusement. He was not an enlightened spirit and was less concerned with good and bad, right and wrong, than he was concerned with just making it through the day in one piece. That, and having a good laugh. Lately, however, there wasn't much laughter and he had been trying to convince Moose it was time for both of them to bail. After today, they might have done it too.

But today, Squirrel was touched by a scar wraith.

The power of belief is a very real thing in Everlost. The way one looks, physical strength, is all determined by what an Afterlight believes—and no one can truly control what they believe. We can lie to ourselves, saying we believe one thing, and sometimes we convince others it's true, with the hope that by convincing others, we can convince ourselves. Wars are often waged not because of what we believe, but because of the things we want others to believe.

Squirrel was not sure of any of his beliefs. He was not so deep that he pondered such things. But when Clarence reached for him with a hand that was clearly a part of Everlost, attached to a body that clearly was not, Squirrel, in the furthest recesses of his soul, believed that the touch of a scar wraith would extinguish him forever and ever.

So that's exactly what it did.

To those watching, it was undramatic and instantaneous. Clarence grasped on to Squirrel's shoulder, Squirrel uttered the tiniest little squeal . . . and then he was gone.

No tunnel.

No shimmer of rainbow light.

One moment he was there, and the next he wasn't. He simply dissolved into nothingness. Extinguished.

Clarence was thrown off balance by Squirrel's unexpected vanishing act, and Milos, forgetting his resolve to stand against the scar wraith, turned and ran in terror, skin-jacking the first fleshie to cross his path.

Clarence didn't bother with Milos. He was more concerned with the spirit who had disappeared at his touch.

"Where'd he go?" Clarence asked. "Is this another ghostie trick?"

Mikey shook his head, not wanting to believe it. There was a stirring in his soul now, building toward pain—the kind of pain the living felt. "No trick, Clarence."

"So, where did he go?"

"Nowhere," Mikey sadly told him. "He went nowhere."

CHAPTER 28
The Tears of Eternity

The very fabric of the universe mourns the extinguishing of a soul—both in Everlost and the living world. If Squirrel had still been there to see it, he would have been proud, maybe even a bit embarrassed, to see the tribute paid to his memory by all of creation.

In Nevada, an unprecedented thunderstorm formed where none should have been, pouring forth a deluge of water, salty as tears, on the parched earth below.

In Africa, a seven-point-five earthquake rumbled like a heaving sob through the vast Serengeti, a place where no fault line existed before.

In Brazil, a furious tornado cut a path from one edge of the nation to the other, with not a single storm cloud anywhere in the sky.

And ninety-three million miles away, the sun itself fell into sorrow, inexplicably dimming by one hundredth of one percent, henceforth and forever.

Of course such events have never been seen by human

eyes, because a true extinguishing has never happened in the history of human life on earth.

Until now.

In the living world, these impossible events would be seen as signs—although no one would agree as to what they were signs of. Global warming? The Second Coming? Solar collapse? Armageddon? The living would come up with endless theories to argue, because the living were exceptionally good at arguing, especially when no one knew the answer.

In Everlost, however, the effect of a mourning universe was very simple and very clear. It was a silent wail that echoed through every soul, culminating in a powerful twinge of pain—yes, pain—deep in every Afterlight's gut. And with that pain came a sudden awareness that something undoable, something irreparable had occurred.

Awareness.

Few things are more powerful than awareness, and it resonated within the sleeping, dreamless souls of all spirits in transition between the living world and Everlost. The sudden spark touched every Interlight regardless of how long they had slept, and jarred them all back to premature consciousness. It was a Great Awakening borne from one of the most profound pangs of mourning ever to be felt by the universe.

The Interlights in Milos's bank vault all sat up, wondering where they were, and how they got there.

The Interlights in the arms of the Neon Warriors, who had left the Alamo that very morning, were suddenly walking on their own two feet, and asking lots of questions.

And in a glass coffin, a girl dressed in glorious green opened her eyes and smiled.

"Well, now," she said to herself. "Let's see what I've missed and what still needs to be done."

... While in a lonely chamber deep beneath the Alamo, a Wurlitzer jukebox, without coin or question, began to play 'Eve of Destruction.'"

PART FOUR

Mary Rising

High Altitude Musical Interlude #3
with Johnnie and Charlie

*L*ondon Bridge is falling down, falling down, falling
down . . ."

Sing-alongs, Johnnie-O had decided, were
invented by the darkest forces of evil as hell's ultimate horror.

"London Bridge is falling down . . ."

Johnnie was convinced that whatever memory of a brain
he had, had been eaten by big fat everworms, and all that
remained were the ghosts of swiss cheese holes.

". . . my fair lady!"

And maybe cobwebs.

There was no telling how many journeys they had made
around the world. Now, thanks to the gravitational tweak the
giant deadspot had given them, each revolution left them a few
hundred miles farther south. They were spiraling toward the
equator. Eventually they would pass it, and wind up spinning
in circles at the south pole.

"Take the keys and lock her up, lock her up, lock her up . . ."

With no contact from any of their friends on the
ground since that fateful day Mary attacked the train, they
had no way of knowing who had won that battle. They

could only hope that their sacrifice was not for naught.

"Take the keys and lock her up . . ."

For many weeks now, looking out of the windows had provided no solace. Deadspots were few and far between, and the sight of them was nothing more than a cruel tease from a cold world.

". . . my fair lady!"

Yet even with his Swiss-cheese, cobwebbed, empty head, Johnnie-O still didn't reach the same absolute mindless, happy, sing-along stupor that Charlie had found.

"It's gotta mean something, don't it, Charlie? The fact that I'm not a complete blithering idiot like you?"

Charlie's answer was just a vacant smile, and another verse.

. . . But halfway through that verse, a shadow swept across the bulkhead.

"Wait! Did you see that?"

Charlie must have, because he actually stopped singing. At first Johnnie thought that it might be a living-world airplane cutting through their airspace, but as he rose to look out of the window, he saw something flash by. A colorful flash of feathers, and a powerful beat of wings—and then another, and another.

"I think they're angels, Charlie! The angels came to save us!"

In a moment, he could hear what could only be dainty angel feet setting down on the silver surface of the airship above them.

For the first time in a very long time, Charlie made eye contact with Johnnie-O, and together they sang, *"Off we go . . . into the wild blue yonder . . ."*

CHAPTER 29

The Great Awakening

Mary could see faces looking down on her, although it was all quite distorted due to the bottles, eyeglass lenses, and random glass objects that made up this strange box she found herself in. Her pallbearers had placed her on the ground and now just stared at her. Mary pushed on the lid, but it wouldn't give, so she turned to the pallbearer with the sweetest face.

"Excuse me," she said, "but would you be so kind as to undo the latch?"

"Yes, ma'am." He knelt down, fumbled nervously with the latch, then pulled open the lid.

As soon as Mary stood up, about half the Afterlights knelt before her respectfully, as if they had been in the habit of doing so. The other half just stood about, looking lost, confused, and startled by living-world traffic that barreled past them.

At first she assumed the kneeling Afterlights were the children she had gathered, but none of their faces were familiar, and there were only about a hundred. When she had been so rudely dragged back to the living world and summarily killed by Milos, there had been close to a thousand.

Mary quickly surmised that the confused ones were all Greensouls — new arrivals to Everlost who had all just woken up from hibernation. But why had they all woken up at once? Clearly something out of the ordinary had occurred here.

"Thank you for the warm reception," she said. "But there's no need to kneel." The kneeling Afterlights reluctantly rose to their feet. "Where is everyone else?" she asked. "Where's the train?" But no one would field the question.

"Yeah . . . about the train . . ."

Mary turned to see a familiar face at last. "Jill!"

"Hi, Mary," Jill said. "Uh . . . long time no see?"

Mary stepped out of the coffin and went to her, grasping her hand. Jill, she knew, was not an affectionate girl, but Mary believed everyone could benefit from a warm greeting. "It's good to see you," Mary said. "I have so many questions."

"Yeah, me too!" shouted one of the newly awoken Greensouls. He was rapped in the arm by one of the more respectful Afterlights.

"Quiet! Show respect before the Eastern Witch."

The Eastern Witch, thought Mary. Not a title she cared for, but for the time being it would do, if it brought her this level of respect.

Another Afterlight came up beside Jill — a strange one. He wore no shirt and his oddly colored muscular body bore spots and a velvety sheen. His eyes were vaguely nonhuman and where other boys his age might be sprouting facial hair, he was sprouting whiskers. Mary would have laughed, but he seemed way too serious for laughter.

"Jill, please introduce me to your friend."

Jill opened her mouth to speak, but the spotted boy spoke first.

"My name is Jix," he said. "And you should not be awake."

"Well," said Mary as politely as she could under the circumstances. "It appears that I am, doesn't it."

"It was not meant as an accusation, just a fact," Jix said. "Things will change now. The three of us should talk."

Mary studied Jix closely. "Are you the leader here," she asked, "or some sort of mascot?" The question was meant not so much to belittle him, but to gauge his confidence. If he bristled, he was weak and easily manipulated. But if he let the insult roll off his back, then Mary would have to carefully finesse this relationship.

Not only didn't Jix let the insult bother him, he chose to answer the question in a way that gave no answer at all, which meant that, in his own subtle way, he was a force to be reckoned with.

"They fear me because they know what I can do," Jix said.

"And what can you do?"

"Skinjack."

"Is that all?"

He offered her a very cool, catlike smile. "What greater power is there?"

"Hey! What about us?" chimed in the same loudmouth Greensoul from before. "Is anyone gonna tell us what's going on?"

The other Afterlight hit him again, harder this time.

"All questions will be answered," Mary announced. "Just as soon as mine are."

Mary looked around to take in her surroundings. They were standing in the middle of a street on the outskirts of a city. By the look of it, they had been marching away from the city. Living-world traffic would occasionally barrel right through them, causing great distress to the Greensouls, who were yet to understand any of this. She turned to address all the Afterlights.

"Thank you all for taking care of me in this difficult time," she told them. "Now I think it's best if we all go to a deadspot to sort everything out, for I can see so many of you struggling to keep yourselves from sinking into the living world."

"Back to the Alamo basement?" suggested someone. Well, at least now Mary knew what city they were in.

"No," said a girl toward the back of the crowd. "There's a closer place. I was one of Avalon's scouts. I know all the deadspots in this city. There's one just south of here."

"Wonderful!" said Mary. "Lead the way!" The girl, thrilled to suddenly be important, marched off and everyone followed.

Mary walked with Jix and Jill on either side of her. "Now," she said to them, "why don't you tell me what happened while I slept. Start from the beginning and don't leave anything out."

"All right," said Jill. "But you're not going to like it. . . ."

The deadspot was a miniature golf course that had been bulldozed by the living world, thus crossing it into Everlost.

As it came with a fully stocked ball shack, the Neons, who had been sequestered in the Alamo for so long, were more than happy to entertain themselves playing a few rounds of miniature golf. The Bopper made all the Greensouls act as caddies, as if this were some fraternity initiation.

Jix and Jill sat in the shadow of the pint-sized windmill as Mary processed everything they told her. She began to make some decisions, although she didn't share all of them. Not yet, anyway. The hardest thing to swallow was the news about the train, and how so many of her children were lost.

"Only some of them were pushed down," Jill told her. "A lot of them just scattered."

"Well," said Mary. "We'll just have to gather them back, won't we?"

Although Jix did not respond, Mary could tell that he was not pleased by the suggestion.

Milos was apparently still in San Antonio looking for her. She was pleased by this, if only because she might have a chance to reprimand him for the horrible job he had done . . . but then, perhaps she should be more gracious and charitable to him. After all, Milos had courage and loyalty enough to bring her back to Everlost by his own hand. She could still remember the intense pain of his cold steel blade in her chest—indeed there was a tear in her dress in that exact spot over her heart—and she remembered the conflicted look in his eyes when she died. She also remembered the joy in his eyes when he tackled her from the tunnel. He was clearly in love with her, although her own feelings toward him were still not entirely defined. She did love being loved, though. As for whether she could forgive him for losing so many of her children . . . well, she supposed she wouldn't know the depth of her forgiveness until she looked into his eyes again.

"We think Milos is with the Chocolate Ogre now," Jill told her, which was, of course, impossible. Mary had seen Nick dissolve into a pool of dark liquid. He was gone. And yet, the very idea that he might have come back from that horrible end sent the memory of her heart fluttering with the faintest of fear. Not fear of Nick, but fear of the love she once had for him. Mary told herself she felt no such love for the boy anymore. And if she told herself enough, perhaps she might believe it.

"If Milos is here with some refugees from the train," Mary said, "we will seek him out and bring those Afterlights back into the fold." Again, Jix stared at her, not giving a hint of a reaction, and so she said, "I trust I'll have your full cooperation."

Jix didn't answer her right away. He thought about it, then he said, "I think instead you should come with me to the City of Souls."

"I have no intention of voyaging to some distant land," said Mary, "when I have so much to accomplish in this one."

Jix nodded. "How might I convince you?"

In spite of her desire to just dismiss the idea, Mary gave the question serious thought. In Chicago, she had come to a dictator, only to be thrown into shackles and humiliated. Of course, Mary eventually rose above all that, and took over his petty dictatorship. But this Mayan King sounded a much more formidable foe than Pugsy Capone.

"I think you should go to the City of Souls," said Jill — which surprised Mary. Jill never had an opinion unless there was something in it for her. Then Mary realized there was: Jix. Jill was in love with him. Mary smiled at her realization and patted Jill's hand ever so condescendingly.

"You two go. I'm sure you can skinjack your way there in no time. And you can give my regards, and my regrets, to this king of yours."

"I can't return without you," Jix said simply. "And I know that you can't be forced. Therefore you will have to go of your own free will."

"I will do no such thing," Mary said, with some indignance.

Jix had nothing further to say about it.

With their conversation done, Jix gathered the Afterlights from their golf games. "Mary will speak to you now," he told them. It was all he gave as an introduction. Then, just to make sure there was no question as to who was calling the shots, he said, "Our plans are still the same."

Mary ignored him and began her speech, making sure she addressed these Afterlights by looking into as many eyes as she could, and smiling, always smiling, so that they knew she only wanted the best for them . . . although sometimes it took convincing, for so few Afterlights really knew what was in their own best interests.

"Some of you have been lost for quite a while," she began, "and some of you for only an instant. Well, I am here to tell you that no matter how long you have been lost, you have all been found—and I promise you that I will make your deaths joyful and fulfilling from now until the end of time. That's why I'm here. And if divine providence saw fit to awaken so many of us before our time, then there is a reason for it. Together, we will find that reason."

Then, as if by that same divine providence, something extraordinary happened. More Afterlights began to arrive! They looked a little haggard, as if they had been running. They would have been breathless, had they been alive.

"Mary?" one of them said. "It's Mary! Look! Look! It's Mary!"

They ran to her, pushing past all the others, and hurled themselves into her arms, nearly knocking her over. She recognized many of their faces—these were her children—or at least what was left of them. There were a few dozen at most. Some spoke of a tentacled monster that had chased them away from a playground, but she didn't give their tale much credence. If there was one thing she learned about Everlost, it was that tales often grew very, very tall.

If the other Afterlights had not yet been won over, this did the trick. How could they not see her as their salvation? The devotion of her children was a better testimony than anything she could say.

"All is well," she told them. "All is well." And it was only going to get better.

"We should just leave," Jill said to Jix as they hid behind the miniature golf Taj Mahal, making sure Mary couldn't hear them. "We don't have to go to the City of Souls, we can go anywhere we want."

"No," Jix told her, and it just made her furious.

"Who cares about your stupid mission? You failed. It's over. Deal with it!"

Jix took a long look at her. He reached out to touch

her face, and although he thought she would pull away with anger, she closed her eyes and purred.

"Please," she said, using the *P* word she once claimed was not a part of her vocabulary. "Please, let's get away. Just you and me. I'll even start furjacking if you want me to."

Jix had to admit that it was tempting, but he couldn't leave now. He had to see how this would all play out. "Maybe soon," Jix said, "but not yet."

Now Jill pulled away, returning to her fury—which was a much more comfortable place for her. "Why not?"

"Because Mary is right, I think. Maybe there *is* a reason why there was this *'Gran Despetar,'* this 'Great Awakening,' but it may not be the reason she thinks."

"So what? Why does it matter?"

"It matters if it convinces her to come with us to the City of Souls. I still have faith she will choose to come."

Jill laughed bitterly. "You don't know Mary."

"No," said Jix. "But I know the only thing more seductive than power . . . is greater power."

A few miles away, Milos paced the bank floor, kicking everything in sight—the account desks, the teller windows. Nothing broke, but he kicked it anyway. He wished it *would* break. Destroying something—anything—would give him great satisfaction at this moment.

On the floor, just in front of the closed vault door, sat Moose, who had not stopped crying since he heard about Squirrel's tragic end. "He didn't desherve it," Moose wailed. "He didn't do anything wrong. He jusht did what *you* told him to do."

"Do not be such a tearbaby! It happened, it's over, and there is nothing to be done."

"Itch 'crybaby'!" yelled Moose. "You get everything wrong!"

Milos kicked over a chair, sending it flying past Moose, but Moose didn't flinch and the chair didn't break. "Save your anger for Mikey," Milos told him. "He's the one who told the scar wraith to extinguish Squirrel."

At the mention of Mikey's name Moose clenched his fists and his Afterglow turned a furious red. "I hate Mikey," Moose growled. "I want him dead."

"He *is* dead," Milos reminded him.

"Then I want him worse than dead. I want him extinguished too!" Then he began to cry again. "I can't believe Squirrel's gone. What am I going to do without him?"

Milos gently patted Moose on the shoulder. "We will have our revenge," Milos told him. "I promise."

Moose's sobs soon subsided into muffled cries, and now Milos could hear the faint voices and pounding coming from behind the thick vault door, which now held almost two-hundred Greensouls that should have been sleeping Interlights. Milos had no explanation for the awakening. It terrified him—and all of them were now banging around in there, demanding explanations. Milos was not ready to let them out. He was simply not in the frame of mind to fight the miserable battle to win them over, convincing them to trust him. Let them stay in the vault for all he cared.

He longed to go back to his old ways, skinjacking for profit, selling his services to whatever Afterlights he came across—and there were plenty of them east of the

Mississippi. He could leave all this behind and forget it had ever happened. That's what he was thinking when he heard someone rattling the bank doors.

He spun to see who it was, fearing that Nick had led the scar wraith to them. If it was the scar wraith, they would never get in; the glass doors, which had crossed into Everlost along with the rest of the bank, were double-locked from the inside. But instead of an enemy at his threshold, the visitor was the most welcome sight he had ever seen.

It was Mary standing there behind the glass, framed by the door, the way she had once been framed by the glass coffin. He should have realized she would have awoken when all the other Interlights had. Milos had come to believe she had been spirited somewhere far away by the Neons, but he had held on to the hope that he would be able to find her once she awoke. He never dreamed she would be the one seeking him out.

Milos stood there, still afraid to make a move toward the door, not knowing how angry at him she would be . . . but no one kept Mary waiting. He went to the door, fumbled with the locks, and opened it.

"Hello, Milos," she said. Her voice was neither warm nor chilly. He had no idea how to read her. Behind her was a large vapor of Afterlights, but Milos wasn't concerned with them. "Well, aren't you going to invite me in?"

He let her in, locking the door behind her. For a moment he was at a loss for words. All he could think to say was, "Sorry about your dress."

She brought her hand to the tear in her satin gown, directly above her heart. "It couldn't be helped," she said.

"But it's an important memory to keep. It reminds me of the good you've done." She paused for a moment, then said, "I heard about the train. Jill told me everything."

Milos had played this moment over and over in his mind dozens of times, all the excuses, all the explanations he would give her . . . but when the moment finally came, there was nothing he could say except this: "I'm afraid I've made a mess of things."

"Yes, you have," Mary said. Then she turned to Moose, who hid his weepy eyes in shame. "Why is he like this?" Mary asked.

"Something happened to Squirrel," Milos explained. "He was extinguished by a scar wraith."

Mary snorted in a most unladylike way. "There is no such thing. You should read my books again and refresh your memory."

"I'm sorry, Mary, but there is. I saw the scar wraith with my own eyes, and I saw Squirrel extinguished. I think that is what made all the Interlights wake up."

Mary allowed all this to sink in. "So . . . scar wraiths are real . . . and one is loose in this city. Is it seeking out Afterlights to extinguish them?"

Milos shook his head. "It just wants me," Milos told her. "And now I think it will want you, too." Then he added, "It is controlled by a boy who used to travel with us named Mikey."

At that, Mary's eyes shot to him, looking as wild as Mikey's had, almost as if there was some sort of resemblance. It was so unnerving Milos had to look away.

"You say his name was 'Mikey'?"

"Yes."

"And did he have a last name?"

Milos only shrugged, but Moose, through his sobs, said, "McGill. Mikey McGill. Like the monster. He said he *was* the monster. He also said he was related to you. He lied about a lot of things."

"Of course he did," said Mary, seeming a little less confident than she did a moment ago. "Anyone unstable enough to use a scar wraith to do his dirty work would lie about anything."

Once again, there came more pounding from behind the vault door.

"And who is in there?" Mary asked.

Milos offered her the slightest of smiles. "I've been reaping for you," he told her. "You wanted more Afterlights . . . so I have been creating accidents, forced crossings."

Mary put her hand against the vault door, perhaps to feel the vibrations of those pounding on the far side. "How many?"

"A hundred and eighty-three," Moose told her. "I've been keeping count."

"You did want me to gather new souls, yes?" Milos asked.

She took a long moment to consider it, looking at the closed vault door almost as if she could see through it and into the hearts of every Afterlight within. Then she turned to Milos and at last she smiled. Then she gently took him into her arms, and whispered into his ear.

"You've done a wonderful thing," she said. "I can forgive you for all the rest now, because I know your heart is in the right place."

Milos felt a wave of relief wash over him. He never realized just how much he needed her forgiveness.

"A hundred and eighty-three . . . ," said Mary, still pondering the vault door. "Well, it's a beginning, but I think we'll need to start thinking on a grander scale."

"Grander scale?" asked Milos.

She gave him a gentle kiss on the cheek but said no more about it. "Open the door, then close it behind me, Milos. I'll need some time to quell their fears. Do you have any of my books handy that I might give them?" But Milos sadly shook his head. "Just as well," she said. "Things have most certainly changed in Everlost. Perhaps it's time for me to write something new." Then she went into the vault, determined to make these new children her own.

Jix waited with Jill just outside the bank with the Neons and their Greensouls. They had no idea what was going on inside, and Mary took an uncomfortably long time.

"What if Mary doesn't come out?" the Bopper asked. "What then?"

Neither Jix nor Jill had an answer for him.

When Mary finally did come out, she was not alone, but came with Milos, Moose, and a huge vapor of Afterlights — more Greensouls, who looked uncertain, but clearly had already put their trust in Miss Mary Hightower.

Jill would not even look at Milos, and he had nothing to say to her either.

"Let us hold no animosity toward Milos," Mary told Jix and Jill. "He has worked hard to create crossing opportunities, and to save as many souls as he could from the living world. Whatever bitterness is between you, it must now end."

Jix agreed, and Jill nodded a bit more reluctantly.

"Good," said Mary. "Now, Milos has given me some grave news. He has informed me that a scar wraith has come to San Antonio."

The Afterlights close enough to hear gasped, and word of the scar wraith spread, blending with the rumors of the tentacled beast.

"A scar wraith," said Jix. "Interesting. Such a creature would be a living vortex between worlds. It could explain many things."

"And," Mary continued, "it poses mortal danger to every Afterlight." The next part seemed a bit harder for her to say. "Therefore . . . this might not be the best place for us to be."

Jix sensed an unspoken request in her voice. There was something she needed from him. Jix knew what it was, and only now was he willing to give it. He bowed his head respectfully, and said, "I am at your service, Miss Hightower. Whatever you want to do now, I will make sure that it is done." Then he added, "All these Afterlights are yours to command."

"Thank you," she said, "but I do not command, I protect."

Jix bowed his head again. "My mistake."

Mary looked out at the Afterlights all waiting for guidance, then she turned back to Jix, offering him a smile that seemed to him both warm and cunning. Very catlike.

"I want you to tell me about this king of yours," she said, "and the City of Souls."

CHAPTER 30
Something About a Chicken

*T*hey're going to find your son soon," a voice said loudly inside the woman's head. *"I want to prepare you for the worst. . . ."*

The woman was taken by surprise. When her son was not among the kids who had been rescued from the playground, she feared the worst, but hoped that perhaps he wasn't on the playground at all. Perhaps he was in the nurse's office or the bathroom. But no one had seen him in those places—and now there was this strange voice in her head.

"I can't imagine your pain, but you're not alone. I'm here to comfort you."

"Who is this?" the woman said to the voice in her mind.

"I'm a spirit sent to tell you that your son has reached his destination."

"What do you mean 'his destination'? Who is this? How are you inside my thoughts?"

"I'm here to comfort you in your time of sorrow. You can mourn your loss, and cry that you'll never see him again in this life, but don't mourn for his spirit—because I saw him go into the light with

my own eyes, and there was a smile on his face brighter than I've ever seen! He got where he was going . . . and he's happy."

A few moments later, a police officer approached the woman with a pale look of such sorrow, she knew the news was very, very bad. He took off his hat and she looked away from him even before he began speaking. Yet in that horrible, horrible moment the strange visitation had given her something that freed her spirit to soar beyond the here and now. Even as her body was racked with sobs from the news of her son's death, her spirit soared with an absolute knowledge that he was now home in the truest sense of the word, and that there was something more than this.

When Allie pulled out of the poor woman, Mikey could only stare at her in amazement. "That was the most beautiful thing I've ever seen."

Allie looked at him strangely. "You could hear?"

Mikey shook his head. "I didn't need to. The look on her face told me everything. Look at her now." They turned back to see the woman still standing just outside the police line. She still cried, but beneath it there was a smile on her face, a tiny ounce of peace and contentment behind her tremendous loss.

Mikey and Allie were alone in Everlost now. Clarence had fled the scene. The moment he realized what he had done to Squirrel, he ran. Although all the living were clamoring about a scar-covered hero who rescued everyone, Clarence clearly did not feel like a hero.

"Go after him, Nick," Mikey had said. "Don't let him out of your sight."

Nick was more than happy to do it. Mikey would have done it himself—he *should* have done it himself, but at that moment, he was being selfish. He had not yet had his true reunion with Allie, and the last thing he wanted to do was to leave her before even saying hello. It was only after Nick was gone that Mikey realized his mistake. Nick was the only one who knew Milos's hiding place. Now they couldn't go after him until Nick returned.

The strange scene before them was now a blend of triumph and misery. The many who were saved, the one child who was not. As much as he and Allie wanted to leave, they couldn't because this was where Nick would rendezvous with them, hopefully with Clarence. So they climbed to the top of the freshly crossed jungle gym, for its highest platform gave them the best view of anyone approaching in either world. Since the whole playground was now a deadspot, they could rest from their troubling adventure and not have to worry about sinking.

Living-world commotion surrounded the disaster site around them. But as Mary herself once said, Afterlights can tune out the living world if they truly want to—and at that moment, Mikey and Allie saw and heard nothing but each other.

They held each other tightly, saying comforting things.

"Everything's going to be okay, now that you're here."

"We'll make everything all right, together."

And when Allie leaned her head gently against Mikey's chest, he focused as intensely as he could on the memory of his heart to make it beat gently in her ear. Now their afterglows had combined into a uniform lavender glow, proving they were connected, proving they were one. It was almost like being alive.

Allie knew that time was elastic in Everlost. It moved as quickly or as slowly as the thoughts in one's mind. But in this moment, she wished it could stop completely and leave them both there in an eternal embrace. It was perhaps the closest Allie had ever come to Mary's way of thinking, for being here with Mikey, whispering gentle things and listening to his heartbeat, would be her perfect eternity.

Nick was terrified of forgetting again, for this time if he forgot, he would lose Mikey and Allie and never find them again. Yet this time, he knew things were different. He didn't have someone like Milos telling him lies, confounding the few things he thought he knew.

He followed Clarence to a dimly lit bar that smelled of stale cigarettes and old varnish. It was the kind of saloon that was open before noon on a Friday. A place for career alcoholics, people who thrived in dimly lit places, hiding from illumination of any sort.

There were only a few customers sitting at the bar, each in their own personal clouds of woe. An old flickering TV reported on an earthquake in Africa.

Nick tried to sit on the barstool next to Clarence, but kept sinking through it, so he stood there, constantly shifting his feet to keep from sinking. The floorboards here were thin and staying aboveground was a challenge. Clarence didn't look at him, but he knew Nick was there.

"Go on. Sink down to hell for all I care." Ice clinked in his amber drink as he took a long gulp.

"Hell's not down there," Nick told him. "Just the center of the earth."

"Well, then," Clarence said. "Pleasant journey. If you meet Jules Verne, give him my regards." From the end of the bar, the bartender gave Clarence a sideways glance, so Clarence pulled out a broken Bluetooth headset, and fixed it to his ear. "I learned this trick while traveling with Mikey," Clarence told Nick. "Makes my brand of crazy seem the same as everyone else's."

The fact that Clarence put on his ear prop was a good sign. It meant he was willing to talk, so there was hope of bringing him back from whatever dark place he was now in.

"Your friend Mikey knew what my touch could do, but he didn't tell me. He turned me into a murderer. Worse than a murderer."

"I think," said Nick, "they call that manslaughter or wrongful death, don't they? I mean, when it's an accident or out of ignorance, or something."

Clarence turned to Nick, studying him with his Everlost eye. "You're a lot smarter than you were back in the cage," Clarence said. "You look better too. Back then you were a thing, now you're almost a person."

"Thanks . . . but 'almost' is still 'almost.'"

"Yeah, well, we're all almost something."

Nick pulled his feet out of the ground, nearly losing his balance.

"Stop that. You're making me nervous. And when I get nervous . . ." Clarence didn't finish the thought. He just grabbed his drink and took a swig, then stood from the bar. "Looks like someone once croaked in a booth back there. Unlucky for him, lucky for you."

Sure enough, there was a corner booth that had a bright little deadspot on the seat just big enough for an Afterlight to sit on. They went to the booth and sat across from each other.

"You tell Mikey I'm done with this nasty business," said Clarence. "I want nothing to do with any of you anymore."

"I understand," Nick said. "But—"

"No buts!" Clarence slammed his drink down so hard an ice cube leaped out and slithered across the table like a snail. There were tears in Clarence's eyes now, both the living and the dead one.

"When I touched that boy, I felt something. Something awful. Something I can't describe."

"We all felt it," Nick said.

"You may have felt it, but I caused it." Then both his eyes seemed to go far away. "Something changed out there. I don't know what it was, but something in the world changed because that kid didn't deserve what I did to him—and the powers that be know that I did it." Nick watched as a tear fell from his Everlost eye and disappeared through the living world table.

"What if," said Nick, not even sure what he was going to say yet, "what if you were that kid and you were told you could change the world, but you would have to sacrifice yourself to do it?"

Clarence chuckled at the thought. "I believe that question was already asked a long time ago, and that creepy kid did not look anything like Jesus to me."

"But you do think that something changed. . . ."

"I don't know whether it's good or bad."

"What if it's neither?" suggested Nick. "What if we get to make it one or the other?"

Clarence finished the rest of his drink and crunched on the remaining ice. "You're a pain in my derriere, you know that?" Clarence said. "Derriere, that's French for 'butt.'"

"I figured."

Clarence took a long look at his empty glass, his unkempt clothes, and his Everlost hand, which, to his left eye, was nothing more than a shriveled lump.

"You know, I wasn't always like this," he said softly.

"Neither was I," Nick replied. "But maybe . . . maybe we'll both find who we once were."

Clarence looked at him, perhaps seeing more than just the chocolate. Nick thought he caught the slightest hint of a nod, but then the bartender called over.

"Hey! Hey, you in the corner!"

On TV, the news had switched away from the quake, and now was reporting live from the playground disaster. A teacher being interviewed spoke of a disheveled, scar-faced man who had saved them.

"Hey!" yelled the bartender. "Are you the guy?"

Clarence sighed. "Yeah, I'm the guy."

"That's great, man. Hey, your drink is on the house!"

"That's good, because I can't pay for it anyway."

Then Clarence left with the invisible chocolate boy before the bartender could call the media.

Nick met Mikey and Allie back at the playground. Clarence kept his distance, hiding his face because reporters still swarmed the accident scene in search of the mysterious scarred hero. Nick then led them halfway across town to the crossed bank, only to find it deserted. The vault was empty and not a single Afterlight was in sight.

"Milos could have left the city by now," Mikey said, furious at himself for not going after him right away. "He could be anywhere!"

"I don't understand," said Nick, peering into the empty vault. "It was full of sleeping spirits. The 'Angels of Life' couldn't have carried them away—there were too many."

Then they heard a small voice somewhere behind them. "That's because they all woke up."

Allie recognized the voice right away. "Lacey?" Allie searched the bank, and found her hiding under the teller counter. She sat knees-to-chest, looking numb. Looking lost. Allie told the others to stay back. The last thing that Lacey needed was an audience. Then Allie knelt down to her and gently asked, "What happened, Lacey?"

"All the kids we reaped woke up. Mary woke up too, and she came to take them away."

"Mary's awake?" It was too much for Allie to process. How on earth could Mary be awake? It hadn't been nine months. Allie had never heard of an Interlight waking up prematurely.

"I was glad Mary woke up at first, because I thought for sure the bad stuff would stop," Lacey said. Then her voice got soft as if she was afraid Mary might hear. "But then I heard them all talking. Mary *likes* what Milos did. How could she like it? How could she?" Lacey looked up to Allie, her eyes pleading for an answer.

"I don't know" was all Allie could say. Then she looked up to see Mikey and Nick peering over the counter. They had both heard. She couldn't imagine the mixed feelings they must have had—Nick so in love with Mary for so long, in spite of all the awful things she'd done; Mikey struggling to reconcile the memory of his sister with the self-righteous power-hungry spirit she had become. And they didn't even know the worst of it. Only Allie did, for only she had seen into Mary's mind.

Allie returned her attention to Lacey. "Do you know where they were going?"

Lacey shrugged. "Kind of. But it didn't make sense. I heard them talking about chickens. 'It's a chicken,' they said. 'We're going somewhere far away, and it's a chicken.'"

Allie went off with Nick and Mikey to puzzle all this out. Clarence stayed to entertain Lacey, who, amazingly, was not frightened by his creepy appearance. She had dozens of questions about both sides of his face—like whether or not he needed glasses, and how do you find glasses that have half-crossed?

Allie took Nick and Mikey into the vault, and they sat there, a summit meeting of three questionable superpowers: a skinjacker, an ex-ogre, and a part-time monster.

"This is going to be hard to hear," Allie told them, "but you need to hear it. And then we have to decide what to do."

Mikey took her hand and smiled at her, but Nick just looked down sullenly. "I'm remembering more and more about Mary," he said. "I kind of wish I didn't."

Allie wasn't sure how much Nick remembered, and how much Mikey even knew about that fateful day the bridge blew up, so she told them how she helped drag Mary, hair-first, out of Everlost, and into the living world. "When Mary was crammed back into the living world, she had a body. She was flesh and bone . . . at least she was before Milos re-killed her. And while she was alive . . . I skinjacked her. I saw Mary's deepest thoughts. Everything she hoped for, everything she believed, everything she planned to do." Allie hesitated, not wanting to say it, but knowing she had to. "Mary believes she was put on earth to bring an end to the living world."

Both Nick and Mikey just stared at her.

"What do you mean . . . end?" asked Mikey.

"End means end. Complete and total destruction. She wants to kill everyone and everything. She wants to bring down every building, burn every forest, empty every ocean of life. She wants to turn the earth into a dead planet. . . ."

Nick looked to her with eyes almost as pleading as Lacey's. "But . . . why would she want to do that?"

"Because to her, Everlost is the only world that matters."

Mikey nodded, finally understanding his sister's twisted logic. "And once the living world is gone . . . anything worth keeping will cross. . . ."

"Exactly," said Allie. "Imagine a world that's nothing but the memories of a dead one. That's the future Mary wants. She wants no future at all."

No one said anything for a while. Allie silently fanta-sized that they could close themselves in that vault, and just make the rest of the world go away. But that would be no better than what Mary wanted, would it? So this was their great reunion. Things were much different now than the last time the three of them were together. Allie had thought she was dead, Mikey had been a full-time monster determined to be king of the world, and Nick was just an Afterlight boy with a small smudge of chocolate on his face. For a place that was supposed to stay the same forever, quite a lot had changed for them in Everlost.

Mikey was the first to speak. "She can't do anything without skinjackers."

"No," said Allie, "she can't." As a skinjacker, Allie knew that more than anyone. She knew how easy it was to change things in the living world by skinjacking just the right people at just the right time—and there were many ways to end the world if you could slip into anyone anywhere and take them over. But without skinjackers, Mary was completely power-less over the living.

"So it's not her we have to stop, then," said Mikey. "We have to end her skinjackers before they end the world. We have to extinguish all of them."

"No!" The three of them turned to see Clarence standing on the vault threshold. "No! I won't do it! You can't make me do that!"

Mikey stood up. "What if it's the only way to save the world?"

"Then the world's gonna end!" Clarence pointed an accusing finger at Mikey. "You didn't blot someone out of the universe! You didn't feel his soul die. I would rather see everyone go down the tunnel to judgment than ever see another person snuffed into nothing!"

Mikey glared at Clarence's cold Everlost eye, but then backed down, looking beaten, perhaps even ashamed. After all, Mikey brought Clarence as a weapon. It was Mikey's fault his weapon misfired.

"The little girl wants you," Clarence told Allie. "She's already bored with me."

"Tell her I'll be out in a minute."

Silence fell once more when Clarence left, until Nick, who had been mostly silent, said, "Maybe they all went to Rhode Island." Allie and Mikey looked at him strangely, and he shrugged a chocolate shoulder. "'Rhode Island Red.' It's a chicken."

Allie sighed at the thought. "Lacey must have gotten it wrong."

"Maybe it's some kind of secret code," suggested Mikey.

"Well, if we're going to stop them, we're going to have to figure out where they went."

Even though Allie had no need to breathe, she forced her lungs to fill, and let out a long slow breath. "What if we *don't* have to find them?" she said. "What if there were a way to stop Mary's skinjackers without having to know where they've gone . . . just where they've been?"

Mikey shook his head. "I don't follow."

Allie closed her eyes and shook her head, there was an idea taking form in her thoughts that she did not dare consider, so she shook the thought away before she could even put it into words. "Never mind," she said. "I don't know what I was thinking." Then she went to Lacey, and asked her to point out the direction Mary and her new vapor of Afterlights had gone. While Lacey couldn't help with a destination, she had no trouble pointing out a direction. They were heading southeast out of San Antonio.

"Body of Christ!" said Clarence, and they all looked at him strangely. He just stared back at them in disbelief. "Don't you know your Latin? Corpus Christi, Texas. 'Body of Christ'—although that's one body I'm sure never set foot on the Gulf Coast. Not even on vacation. If this crazy Mary of yours went southeast, then she's headed toward Corpus Christi."

"Right," said Allie with a sick little grimace. Where else would Mary would go after rising from the dead?

CHAPTER 31
The Road to Corpus Christi

Since the moment Mary left the safety of her towers more than three years ago, she had felt something pulling her westward. At first, she thought it was the strength of curiosity, a calling to know what lay in the mysterious western Everwilds. But Mary had never suffered from a curious soul. No, there was more to this western gravity—and gravity is exactly what it was. She was compelled by some unknown force to take her and all her children someplace west. It was a place she would know only when she arrived.

Remembering that had helped her stay the course, but Mary was at a crossroads now, a tipping point, and all because of this scar wraith. The touch of a scar wraith was to be feared. Such a vile spirit had no place, no purpose in the world other than to defeat the effort of good souls like herself, and although her heart said west, fear of the wraith—and maybe even of a resurrected Nick as well—was driving her off her true path.

Still, in their southeastern march to Corpus Christi, Mary took the lead, for she always took the lead. There was an old road that had been torn out to build a four-lane high-way. This was the road they used, and since they did not have to worry about the maddening softness of the living world, they traveled with relative ease.

"It's wise of you to come with me to the City of Souls," Jix told her as they traveled toward the gulf shore. "It will place you at the right hand of the king." When he spoke, he often stood a bit too close to her, practically whispering in her ear, the sly voice of temptation.

"His Excellency believes in the magic of oracles and of mystics. Right now he has a nasty little spirit who serves as the royal vizier, an advisor, interpreting the stars and giving prophecies—but you could take his place. He's the one who told the king about you. He's the one who wanted you captured because of the threat you posed."

Mary crossed her arms smugly. "I pose no threat to spirits who have good intentions."

"All the more reason to come to the City of Souls," Jix said. "If your intentions are pure, things will only go well for you."

Temptation. It was a tricky thing to grapple with, for it was hard to sort out one's own personal motives. This kingdom was clearly greater than any Mary encountered in all her years in Everlost. To have access to such a powerful leader and thousands of Afterlights already collected and subdued could be a major step toward her goal. In time she could replace the king and establish her own benevolent rule of kindness and orderly law. But if she went, it would also be fear of the scar wraith driving her, and Mary Hightower had never allowed herself to be motivated by fear.

"You make a persuasive argument," she told Jix, but never gave him a definitive answer. She knew it was in her best interest to keep her options open and to keep questionable spirits like Jix dangling at the end of her finger.

Jix, however, was no fool. He knew he was being strung along, but he also knew the longer she kept him on the line, the more she risked entangling herself.

He had not lied to her. If her intentions were pure, she most certainly would do well in the City of Souls, for the king, as arrogant as he was, had a soft spot for simple, honest intentions.

What Jix didn't mention was the cost of unpure motives.

If Mary's intentions were as dangerous as Jix suspected they were, the king would know, and deal with her swiftly and effectively. So, bringing her to the City of Souls would solve the problem of the Eastern Witch one way or another. And no matter what happened, Jix would be rewarded for bringing her there.

This girl was a powerful personality to be sure, but Jix couldn't help but believe that the feline predator always had the advantage.

Many things became clear to Mary on the trek to Corpus Christi. Her new illumination began when she finally admitted to herself that her own success was entirely dependent on the cooperation of her skinjackers and their commitment to her cause. Which also meant that everything now depended on Milos. In spite of his previous failures, he was now her greatest asset. While Jill was capricious, Jix enigmatic, and Moose, damaged by the loss of Squirrel, Milos was the one she could trust. His devotion was almost embarrassing. He would wait on her hand and foot if she allowed it, but she knew it was best for all involved if he maintained some dignity.

"There are difficult decisions to be made," Mary told Milos, as they reluctantly rested on the second night of their march. It was an overcast night. Rain pelted the living world tickling their insides, and the Greensouls claimed to be exhausted, refusing to believe they didn't really need sleep. Their combined afterglow made them a target if the scar wraith was in pursuit, so Mary posted lookouts in all directions, and wandered through the resting horde, giving comfort and courage to those in need. Through all of it, Milos kept her company.

"What are your thoughts on the City of Souls, and this so-called king?" she asked Milos, as they did their rounds.

"I think the ruler of an ancient kingdom will treat you as a piece of furniture," he answered, clearly having given it plenty of thought himself. "Bringing you there will serve only one person's interests, yes?"

"Yes," agreed Mary, knowing exactly to whom Milos was referring. "And Jix is hardly a 'person,' is he?"

She looked around to make sure Jix was not in earshot. He often turned up when one least expected him to, dimming his afterglow to make himself even more stealthy. "Jix already has the loyalty of those belligerent 'Neon Nightmares.' He may betray us if he's given the chance."

"He may," Milos quietly responded. "But I have every faith in your ability to turn even betrayal to your advantage."

Milos's undying faith in her through these dark moments

of doubt was just what Mary needed—and so she had no qualms about giving Milos what he needed as well, which was her affection. When he put his arms around her, she allowed it, and when he kissed her, she kissed him back with just the right amount of intensity she imagined a boy such as he would want.

"If only you could skinjack," he would tell her. "In living flesh we could feel deeper, truer passion than this."

But Mary was quick to respond. "There is no truer passion than passion of the soul." Each time they were together, his afterglow would turn the lavender blush of love, but Mary's would not.

"Someday Milos," she told him. "Things are so complicated for me now, but someday . . ."

He accepted the promise of love, fully believing it would come—perhaps because Mary believed it might come too. Surely if he were to do all the things she hoped he would do for her, then she would love him with all her soul. And if not, he would, at the very least, have earned an eternity of heartfelt pretense.

Much later, when Milos had gone off to check in with the lookouts, Jix snuck up on Mary as she looked off into the night, stalking her as he always did.

"A fine night," Jix said to her.

"Perhaps," said Mary. "But the rain is a nuisance."

"Rain gives life. The Mayans worship rain."

"If you're a skinjacker," Mary pointed out, "then you are not Mayan. Wherever your body sleeps, it does so in a very modern world."

"My ancestors were Mayan," he told her. "The king has taught me to appreciate the old ways."

"Yes, of course," scoffed Mary. "Human sacrifice and bloodsport."

Jix was not put off by her remarks. "There is none of that in the City of Souls. There can be no sacrifice, because no one dies, and while there are sports, there is no blood."

Mary tried to imagine this "great city," then realized she really didn't want to. "Why aren't you with Jill?"

"Every soul needs moments of solitude," he answered. It got Mary wondering if perhaps their devotion to each other was just a matter of convenience. Perhaps they could be separated. They would both be much more effective skinjackers if their attentions were not focused on each other. Mary was still pondering this when Jix blindsided her with something she was not prepared to discuss.

"Una pregunta," he said. "One question: Allie the Outcast told me you wish to end the living world. I want to know if it's true."

Mary looked into his invasive eyes, paralyzed for a long moment. She had not shared the full depth of her vision with anyone. But Allie, that horrid shrew, had skinjacked her and violated her mind, stealing her deepest thoughts. Mary knew she had to choose her words very carefully.

"I'm impressed that she would spread such a rumor," said Mary, "that she would think me capable of such a remarkable feat."

"I believe you could end the world," Jix said, "with the right friends." But there was no way of telling from his tone of voice how he felt about it.

"You have quite an imagination," said Mary.

"Not really. But I see what I see."

"And what do you see?"

"I see that you have absolute faith in the things you do. Sometimes the gods are pleased by an undying faith in one's vision . . . and other times they are angered."

"Well, we wouldn't want to anger the gods," Mary told him, trying her best not to be too condescending. "My aim is to protect my children," she said. "Whatever Allie told you, I do not care about the living world in the least."

Jix nodded, accepting her words at face value. "If the children are your only concern, I'm sure you will find all the safety you require in the City of Souls." Then he left her to continue her soulful moment of solitude.

She was glad that she could put him off without having to lie—for what she said was absolute truth: She didn't care about the living world, which is why she had no problem bringing about its end.

The following day, Mary was still reeling from her conversation with Jix. All through the day's march, she was tense and preoccupied. At first she had seen Jix as a spirit filled with silent and small self-interest, but now she realized he could either be the key to the bright new future of Everlost, or the key to her undoing. It all depended on whether or not he had the capacity to truly see and understand her vision. If she went with him to the City of Souls, he could make or break her, depending on whether he believed his gods were pleased, or angered by her intentions. No Afterlight should have that kind of power over her.

That night, with the lights of Corpus Christi, and the Gulf Coast just a few hours away, Mary took Milos aside before dawn. Before she left, she made sure that Jix was occupied. He was with Jill and one of the younger Greensouls—a Hispanic girl that Jix had a soft spot for. Jill, Jix, and the girl were like a little family now, which was fine as far as Mary was concerned. His attentions to his little pride made Jix less aware of Mary's actions, which meant he was less likely to catch her by surprise.

"There is something I must tell you," she said to Milos, when they were far enough away to be sure no one else could hear. "Something marvelous that I can share only with you."

He kissed her and brushed her hair from her face. "I'm listening."

"I had a vision, Milos. I had a vision at the moment of my second death. As I died in your arms, as I transitioned, it came to me. I wanted to tell you the moment I came into Everlost but sleep came too quickly—but I held on to it, I remembered it, and I can't keep it to myself any longer. But if I tell you, you must promise to keep it our secret."

Milos nodded, hanging on her every word.

"My vision was of a war. Not in Everlost but in the living world. And happily, it will be the last war ever fought. In fact, it will end war in the living world forever. Isn't that wonderful? No more pain, no more bloodshed. The living world will finally know true peace from now until the end of time."

"It is a spectacular vision," said Milos. "I can think of none better."

"And here's the best part," Mary told him. "You and I

have been chosen to make it as short and as painless as possible. You and I and your team of skinjackers will bring a glorious end to this war, and usher in a bright new day. Not just in the living world, but also in Everlost."

Milos kissed her again. "What do I have to do?"

But she didn't answer him quite yet.

"Do you love me, Milos? Do you love Everlost?" she asked him, as if she and Everlost were one and the same.

"You know I do."

"Then when the time comes, you must do whatever I ask you to do without question or hesitation."

His answer was to glance at the knife-tear in her dress. "I already have, remember? I would hand you the universe if I could."

Which was nothing less than she was asking.

In her book *My Struggle: The Quest for a Perfect World*, Mary Hightower writes:

"Every Afterlight fears the ocean, and well they should, for Afterlights have zero buoyancy, and plunging into a living-world sea means a trip to the center of the earth. In Everlost no one walks on water—and yet it never ceases to amaze me that Everlost boats still float simply because it had been their purpose in life.

This proves beyond a shadow of a doubt that everyone and everything blessed to be in Everlost has a divine purpose. I have found mine, dear reader; it is to reach out to you! Together we can make Everlost the shining world of glory it is meant to be. All it takes is a willingness to leave behind that which is old.

My hand is outstretched to you across treacherous waters, but I know you have the courage. Come to me!"

CHAPTER 32
The Hand of Judgment

Mary and her vapor of obedient but anxious Afterlights found eight tall-masted racing yachts in the Corpus Christi marina that had crossed into Everlost, thanks to a hurricane that had devastated the Gulf Coast. Jix had calculated that a five-day journey across the gulf of Mexico would land them in the Yucatan Peninsula, and Chichén Itzá, the great City of Souls.

Naturally the Afterlights were wary, but Jix assured everyone there was nothing to fear. As jaguars are one of the few cats that love water, Jix had often sailed on scouting expeditions for the king. He acted as if he was a master of the mast, and it helped put the others at ease. He was the first to climb aboard one of the yachts, then he turned back to speak to Mary and her entire vapor.

"We are here at the start of a new journey," Jix announced. "All that remains is for you to accept my invitation, on behalf of all your Afterlights . . . and travel with me to the City of Souls.

"Well," said Mary, offering him a smile, "since it appears the Good Lord has granted us eight vessels for the voyage, how could I say no?" And although it was expected that Mary would be in the lead yacht, Mary politely deferred to Jix.

"You should lead us, Jix," Mary told him. "It is your vision, your leadership that will bring us to the City of Souls. I insist that you take the lead vessel." Then Mary announced, "All those who wish to travel with Jix should join him now in the lead yacht."

Many of the Neons joined Jix on his vessel, and so did Inez, the girl that he had unintentionally brought into Everlost. He was pleased that she chose to join him, for although it wasn't forgiveness, it was at least a moment of healing trust. Jill made a move to join him, but Mary held her back.

"Milos, you go with Jix," Mary said. "I'd like Jill to come with me. We've barely spoken since I've been awake, and we have so much to discuss."

And although Jix longed to have Jill with him, he knew he needed to allow Mary to call the shots to strengthen the illusion that she was in control.

Jix positioned his crew around the yacht, and to everyone's amazement, the yacht sailed out of its slip the moment the various posts were manned. There was no wind to fill the sails and yet the yacht moved through the water, for the sails themselves held within their canvas fibers a memory of every race in which they had competed. Although the living-world water left no wake behind it, the ghost-yacht rode joyfully on the powerful memory of its purpose.

"You see," Jix called back to the others still waiting on the dock. "There's nothing to worry about!"

Jix took his yacht out of the marina, doing simple maneuvers in the bay just to demonstrate to those on shore how easy this was going to be . . . but the moment they were in open water, something went wrong.

The boom swung wide, capturing the memory of a transverse wind, pulling the entire yacht into a sudden starboard lurch. When Jix looked back at Milos, he saw the rope coiled tightly around Milos's wrist to keep him tethered to the mast. Although it couldn't be seen from the dock, he was the one pulling the boom out of line.

"I am truly sorry for this," Milos said. But clearly he was sorry about nothing, for he pulled the rope even harder, forcing the yacht past the tipping point. The Neons on board screamed and grabbed for one another, but it was no use. They were hurled off the yacht into the sea, disappearing beneath the living-world waves without the slightest splash. Foul-Mouthed Fabian didn't even get the chance to utter a single four-letter word. All of them plummeted with the full force of gravity toward the bottom of the bay and into the depths of the earth. Jix tried to hold on to little Inez, but she was tossed out as well. The last he saw of her were her pleading eyes before she disappeared beneath the water.

Jix tried to stay on the yacht, but the force and the speed of the sudden capsize was too great for him. He lost his grip and plunged into the unforgiving water, and all he could feel now as he dropped deeper and deeper in the water of the bay was the depth of the betrayal, and how badly he had underestimated the ruthless, diabolical Eastern Witch.

No one watching from the dock saw the cause of the "accident." All they saw was a swiftly capsizing boat, and more than fifty Afterlights lost. There were gasps and wails from all those assembled—but no one's cries were as loud or as pained as Jill's.

Mary gathered as many children as she could into her arms. "Turn away," she told them. "Don't look. You mustn't look."

In a few terrible moments, all the Afterlights that had set out with Jix were gone. The yacht was still floating, but now it floated upside down. Then, in a moment, a hand appeared from beneath the water, climbing to the upturned hull. It was Milos.

"Look at his arm," someone shouted. "It got tangled in a rope!"

"Thank goodness!" said Mary. "Let's see if there are others."

But there were none . . . and in a moment, Milos skin-jacked the driver of a passing motorboat and was powering his way back to them.

Through all of this Jill's screams continued, and she had to be held back from hurling herself off the dock and into the deep. Mary grabbed her and with a physical force she rarely displayed, she pushed Jill back against a boathouse, slapping her across the face.

"Let him go!" Mary yelled at her. "Jix's journey is not yours. He is nothing but a mewling beast bound for the center of the earth now. Is that what you truly want? To go down with him? Have you forgotten that you are a skin-jacker on the verge of changing the world? Yes, mourn your loss, but don't throw yourself away!"

And for the first time in both life and in afterlife, Jackin' Jill crumbled to the ground in tears.

Mary now turned to the others who were all frightened and confused. She spoke commandingly, but lovingly. "Today, we have witnessed something horrible . . . but I believe we have also witnessed the hand of judgment . . . because I have reason to believe Jix was selling us into slavery to a foreign king."

"That's not true," wailed Jill, but her voice was weak, and her objection ignored.

"Sadly now, we'll never know for sure," Mary told her children, "but from this moment on, I pledge to you to protect you from such evil designs. Our path is, and has always been, to the west. We will not lose our way again."

Mary had them all hold a minute of silence for the souls lost to gravity, and when the minute was over, she called Moose forward. Moose had been given a special task to take his mind off of Squirrel. He now presented to Mary six Afterlights he had gathered from the crowd. Four boys, two girls. They were all Greensouls, products of the Great Awakening. They varied in ages. The youngest was nine and the oldest was fifteen. Mary smiled at them once they were gathered.

"You may not have realized this," she told the six of them, "but you are very, very special. All Afterlights are special, of course, but you have a purpose and a destiny that makes you more important than you could possibly imagine."

The youngest boy raised his hand as if he were in a classroom. "Does it have to do with the way we get stuck inside living people?" he asked.

Mary smiled and the warmth of her smile seemed to light the overcast day as brightly as the sun. "You are skinjackers, and part of an elite team now. Milos, Moose, and Jill will show you how to use your powers." But when Mary turned to Jill, Jill was gone. Mary searched the dock and the living world beyond it, but she was nowhere—and Mary wondered if perhaps she was too harsh on the poor girl. Surely she would realize that Mary had her best interests at heart, and return. Regardless, Mary could not allow this to distract her. There was still one more thing to be done.

"Little Richard," she called, looking for him in the crowd. "Will you come here, please?"

Little Richard pushed his way through the crowd, his bank now jangling with coins Mary had asked him to gather from all the Greensouls.

"You lost many friends today, didn't you?"

The boy nodded.

"I want you to close your eyes, make a wish for them . . . and once you've made your wish, kiss the bank, and hand it to me."

Little Richard did as he was told. He made a silent wish, kissed the bank, and put it in Mary's hands.

Then she cast the piggybank full of all the Greensouls' coins into the sea.

CHAPTER 33
Creature Discomforts

Jix had plunged to the bottom of the bay. He had seen the others helplessly disappear into the ocean floor beneath him. There was nothing he could do to save them, but he knew he might be able to save himself. It would take split-second timing, the sum of his skills as a skinjacker and the largest amount of luck he had known. He knew it was his only chance. As he fell, nearing the ocean floor, he spread out his arms wide and kept his eyes open for something alive, but there was nothing.

Then, just at the moment of impact on the ocean floor, he felt it: a sea slug not much larger than his finger, squirming in the mud. He leaped toward it, bringing his arms together and squeezing his spirit in upon itself like a collapsing sun, until he found the primitive nervous system of the slug and invaded it, flooding its tiny consciousness with his soul.

Darkness. Numbness, an emptiness of all thought and feeling, and absolutely no sense of time. It was the hardest thing he ever had to bear, to hold his full consciousness in the primitive flesh of a tiny spineless creature. But he did it. He did it long enough to sense a passing crab and he quickly leaped into that. Jix's consciousness was so great that he killed the sea slug the moment he left it.

Now he was held in the exoskeleton of the crab and it felt no better than the slug. But he had some sensory awareness now. There was a fish swimming by him. He could feel it on his antennae. And so he leaped to that. Again, the crab died from the weight and loss of his consciousness.

Now inside the fish, he swam away from the school and, seeing a large shape moving in front of him, he leaped directly inside its mouth and found himself inhabiting a harbor seal. The seal was able to hold his spirit without dying, and at last, he had enough familiar senses to navigate his way to the surface.

When he broke surface, he looked around with the eyes of the seal. Mary and all her children were long gone, as he suspected. This desperate journey through small creatures had taken him much longer than it seemed, for those creatures were unable to comprehend something as complex as time. He had no clue if this was even the same day.

There was a challenge before him now, and although he lived for challenge, he needed to truly prepare himself this time. So he swam close to shore, leaped from the seal to a human, then skinjacked his way all the way to the Corpus Christi Zoo.

There, he furjacked himself the most majestic jaguar he could find, releasing it out into a stormy twilight.

The smells, the sights, and sounds of life through the senses of the cat rejuvenated him, and brought him back to his true self. Independent. Alert. Knowing his needs and knowing how to meet them.

He killed a deer in the nearby woods and ate its sweet meat, relishing every bite. Then, when he was full and satisfied, he rested and took stock of his entire situation. His existence had always been comfortable, he had always held a clear picture of himself, his duties, and his place in a world. He saw that world as a place so full of turning gears he had no hope of comprehending how things fit together, so why even try?

Now things were different, however. Now he wasn't just looking out from inside of the clockwork. Instead, he was actually seeing the final motion of the escapement—the ticking hands of the clock itself.

And it was a doomsday clock.

Both his feline and human instincts told him to let it be. It was not his problem, or his place to interfere. If the living world was destined to fall, let it happen, let it pass into history once and for all. Who was he to try to save it?

But on the other hand, if the living world were lost, then there would never again be great cats to furjack . . . and couldn't it be that hearing the actual ticking of the clock gave one the responsibility to stop it?

Chasing Mary, however, would lead to another confrontation, which he knew he would lose. He was not so proud to think that he could best her alone. She was master of what she did. Smarter. Slyer. If he were going to face her, he was going to have to have more cards stacked on his side. He'd have to set a new plan in motion.

He raised his nose to the air, and sniffed in the night— more out of habit than anything else. . . , He never expected he'd pick up the wet-lightning scent of skinjacker in the air.

It couldn't be Moose or Milos—they were long gone, and this scent was coming from the city itself. He followed the scent into Corpus Christi, and tracked it back to where he least expected. The city zoo.

Jill knew this was the closest she would ever come to being with Jix again: hiding within the flesh and fur of a jaguar. She was ashamed of it, but at the same time it gave her comfort. She knew the longer she stayed in the cat's body, the more she risked being bound to it, but she didn't care. Let it happen. She had no desire to leave or to be anyone or anything else anymore, and, as Jix had guessed, her spirit was in perfect tune with the cat. Wearing fur made her feel more complete than wearing skin.

She dozed for just a few minutes at a time, licking her emotional wounds. Then when she opened her eyes, she saw another jaguar—a male one—eyeing her curiously.

"Get lost!" she tried to say, but it came out as a half-hearted roar.

Still, the other jaguar just stared at her with eyes that seemed to peer even more deeply than feline eyes should. She thought she recognized something there, and her heart held for a long beat, then pounded powerfully just as the male jaguar pounced, not just knocking her over but knocking her out of her furjacked skin. Now she was back in Everlost, rolling, almost sinking in the living world as she tumbled—and there he was, beneath her, above her, all around her as she rolled.

It was Jix! Jix, hugging and laughing, nuzzling and cuffing her. Jill had to convince herself she wasn't dreaming inside the cat. This was real, and Jix was truly there!

"How . . . ?" asked Jill. It was the only word she could get out.

"I really do have nine lives, *verdad?*" he told her, with a wicked grin. Then they pulled themselves out of the dirt of the jaguar pit before the living world left them too deeply grounded. They walked the paths of the zoo alone at dawn, and Jix told her everything. How Milos had caused the yacht to capsize. The way he watched so many of the Neons and poor Inez vanish into the depths. He told her of the slug and the crab, the fish and seal—the boy of so few words now spouted forth more than he'd ever said at one time. Then when he was done, he paused, regaining his stoic composure, and said, as plain and simply as he could, "You must go back to Mary."

"I won't!" Jill told him, the suggestion feeling like its own betrayal.

"Listen to me," Jix said. "Right now we have no eyes or ears among her Afterlights. And her vapor will be growing. You must go back to her, prove to her you are still loyal— even kill more of the living to prove your loyalty if you have to—but you must get back into her inner circle."

"She has six more skinjackers now," Jill told him. "She won't need me."

"She will. You have experience, the new ones don't. And your experience makes you very valuable to her. So play her game, do her dirty work . . . and find the real names of all of her skinjackers."

"I can give you two names right now," she said with a smirk. "Vitaly Milos Vayevsky, and Mitchell Terrence

Moessner: Milos's and Moose's real names."

Jix regarded her with wonder. "You've always known their real names?"

"Not always," said Jill. "But when you're a skinjacker, it's a good idea to find out the true identity of your friends, just in case they become your enemies."

Then Jix said something he had never said before, either in life or in Everlost. "I love you," he told Jill.

"Then you're an idiot," she replied, and kissed him hard enough to hurt the living.

CHAPTER 34
Separate Ways

They furjacked the jaguars once more, and headed northwest by night beside the highway, constantly sniffing the air for the scent of skinjacking and perhaps something even more exotic. They found it at dawn, just twenty miles out of Corpus Christi: a powerful scent indefinable and terrifying, like the deep fumes of tornado-torn earth blended with the bitter noxious tang of imminent death, an unearthly scent that could turn a herd into a panicking stampede. "I believe it's the smell of a scar wraith," Jix told Jill.

He convinced Jill to wait out of sight, because he suspected anyone traveling with the scar wraith would know Jill and instantly see her as an enemy. Then he quickly put the cat into a deep sleep, peeled into Everlost, and climbed back up to the highway.

There they were: Allie, the wraith, the Chocolate Ogre, and two others that Jix didn't recognize. One was a small girl with loose laces, and the other a boy who hung close to Allie, in a protective sort of way. Jix might have been wary if he hadn't already chosen to be on their side.

They stood in a face-off, the little girl hiding behind Allie. "He's one of them," she said.

"Stay back," said the boy close to Allie, and Jix could swear he began to grow horns, or perhaps antennae. No, definitely horns.

But Allie, who knew, or at least suspected, that Jix's intentions held no danger for them, asked, "Are you here to help us, Jix, or cause us more problems?"

"We share the same problem," Jix told her. "Her name is Mary."

Allie hesitated for a moment, then asked, "So where is she?"

Jix chose not to answer that question because it didn't matter. "Elsewhere," he said. "I'm sure she and her vapor circled around to the north just to avoid you. And even if you do find her, you won't defeat her. She's too cunning, too smart, too good at what she does. You will not stand a chance against her."

Allie crossed her arms. "We'll see about that."

But Jix took a few steps closer. "How many times have you faced her?" he asked. "How many times have you failed?"

"This time will be different," the chocolate boy said.

"How will it be different?" Jix asked, but none of them had an answer. *Good*, thought Jix. Because when facing a spirit like Mary Hightower, knowing you knew nothing was the best place to start.

"And we have another skinjacker on our side," Jix told them. "I believe you know her."

* * *

Jill put her cat to sleep next to Jix's, joining them, and they all spoke through the morning, sitting in the shade of a crossed oil well that had burned into a charred knot many years before. The decisions they reached were not easy, but Jix was persuasive in his simple, obvious logic.

Fact: The seven of them could not hope to battle Mary and her maniacal vision alone.

Fact: Mary's skinjackers were her weakness, for she needed them to do her bidding in the living world.

Fact: His Excellency the Supreme King of the Middle Realm would be a powerful ally against her. True, Mary's power was a viral kind of charisma that could practically melt flesh from bone, but the king had acquired certain powers in Everlost as well. It might be enough to swing things in their favor.

When the conversation was done, Allie, Mikey, and Nick went off to consider their options, Jill went off alone, if only to escape from the company, and Jix sat with Clarence — not close enough to be accidentally touched, but close enough to make it clear that Jix didn't fear him. They both watched Lacey as she played tic-tac-toe alone in the deadspot dirt. It gave Jix a pang of sadness, because she reminded him of Inez — the girl he killed. The girl he could not save. He imagined every little girl would be a reminder, from now till the end of his memories.

Jix regarded Clarence, considering his battle wounds, considering the sparking line that held together the living from the lost side of his face. It was terrifying to behold, but it was also remarkable. To Jix, Clarence was very much like an Everlost coin: undeniable proof that the universe had tricks it was not ready to reveal to anyone.

"Go on, stare at the monster," Clarence said bitterly, misinterpreting Jix's unblinking gaze. "Gawk at the nasty child-eating bogeyman scar wraith."

"No," said Jix, "I don't see you as a monster. We are both oddities. I have respect for that." Clarence waved off the prospect of Jix's respect, but Jix was insistent. "Listen to me," Jix said. "I've come to think it's no accident you are the way you are. There is a purpose for you in all of this. I sense it—and if there's one thing I'm good at, it's sensing. You already saved many people, and yet you still feel unfulfilled. It means you still have more to do in that purpose, I think."

Both the living and the lost halves of Clarence's face smiled, but it was a smile of apology. "I used to believe things like that," he said, "but in my experience it all goes belly-up in the end. I hate to burst your bubble, but I don't have a purpose . . . and when I finally go down that tunnel to the pearly gates or wherever, I'm going to slap God silly for not giving me one."

Jix nodded, accepting Clarence's point of view without judgment. "Do that if you must," Jix said. "But I suspect it will all be much clearer when you are there."

A few yards away, Jix's sleeping jaguar stirred and Clarence turned his living eye toward it. "Better skinjack that thing before it wakes up and eats me."

"Chichén Itzá!" said Allie. "The City of Souls is at Chichén Itzá! I should have figured out it had nothing to do with a chicken."

"I won't go!" yelled Mikey. He could not be calmed. He raged and stormed, and as he did, his anger gave him all nature of deformities. Extra hands and arms, boils bubbling the size of golf balls on his face. Mikey didn't just wear his heart on his sleeve, he wore it all over his body in frightening manifestations of fury.

"Calm down and think about it!" Allie told him. "What Jix proposed makes sense. You can't go where I'm going—and anyway, I won't be alone, I'll have Clarence—"

"who will wipe you out of existence if he touches you," reminded Mikey.

"So I'll be careful. And you shouldn't be worrying about me—you'll have your own mission to worry about."

"Some mission!" griped Mikey. "I will not go down to the City of Souls to grovel at the feet of some stupid king!"

"Hey," said Nick. "I'm going there too—and I'm not complaining."

"You're too stupid to complain," growled Mikey.

"That," said Allie, "is not fair!"

"No, he's right," said Nick. "I'm not the boy I used to be. Maybe I never will be—but at least I'm not so selfish as to—"

"Selfish? You think I'm *selfish*?" Boils bubbled on Mikey's face and popped like pizza cheeze. "I'll show you selfish."

"Stop it!" yelled Allie. "Now you sound like the McGill."

Then Mikey's face became a pale lava flow over mournful pleading eyes. "Do you know how hard I tried to find you? And now that I did, you're going to leave? I might never see you again!"

"That's true," said Allie. "But there are more important things than us being together."

"No," yelled Mikey, "there aren't!" and he stormed away. Allie started to go after him, but Nick stopped her.

"He'll be okay," Nick told her. "He needs to explode a little bit." They watched him as he burst into different unpleasant shapes beneath the hazy morning sun.

Allie sighed. "I hate it when he explodes."

"Actually, I think you love it."

Allie had to smile because he was right. She thought back to the days on the *Sulphur Queen*. Back then Mikey was so proud to be the One True Monster of Everlost, reveling in every display of hideousness. She could not remember the moment her general disgust was replaced by understanding, and eventually love. No doubt such things sneak up on a person. She knew, in spite of everything, her feelings for Mikey were greater than the most miserable incarnations of his stormy emotions. Love, Allie concluded, wasn't blind, it simply saw alternate dimensions.

Allie turned to Nick. "So . . . do you still love her?" she asked. "Do you still love Mary?"

Nick didn't speak right away. She could tell he was struggling to find an answer. "I love . . . how she wraps the world around her finger so gracefully you can't imagine it anywhere else. I love the determination she has to do 'the right thing'. . . . But I will never understand how she can see ending the world as 'right.'"

Then Allie asked the big question. "If it comes down to it, and you have to destroy her . . . would you do it?"

Nick looked down. "It's no worse than what you're

being asked to do." He thought a moment more, and added, "I know I can't save her from herself. When the time comes, I'll do what must be done. I promise."

Allie leaned in and gently gave Nick a kiss on his cheek . . . and although her lips came away puckered with chocolate, there was now a single spot on Nick's cheek through which his true self shone through.

The sleeping jaguars had been spotted by the living, and had already been wrangled by animal control, leaving Jill fleshless. Now she leaned against the oil well, arms crossed, looking impatient. Allie found it awkward and unpleasant to be in cahoots with Jackin' Jill, and clearly the feeling was mutual. They spoke to each other, keeping a distance, as if either one might smack the other if she got too close.

"How come you're not with Jix?"

"I won't go near that thing he's with," Jill said. "The sooner you and the scar wraith get on with your mission, the better."

"How about *your* mission?" Allie asked. "Going back to Mary . . ."

Jill folded her arms a little tighter. "Mary won't be so hard to find. That hoard of hers shines too brightly to hide when they're out in the open—especially at night."

Allie dared to take a step closer. "So I guess we're working together now."

"It's like they say," Jill told her, " 'my enemy's enemy is my friend.'"

"We don't have to be friends to work together."

"Good," said Jill, "I'm relieved. So when I find out the

names of Mary's new skinjackers, how do I get you the information?"

"I've discovered a method of instantaneous communication, that can reach all of us without even having to know where we are," Allie said. "It's called e-mail."

Jill laughed. "That's so easy, it's almost disappointing. Shouldn't we have to communicate by magical smoke signals or something like that?"

Allie smiled in spite of herself. Jill had a point, whether she realized it or not: In Everlost, Afterlights always had to do things the hard way, from communication to transportation. It was easy to forget the advantage they had as skinjackers, having all the resources of the living world at their disposal.

"I'm setting up an e-mail address that we can all check regularly," Allie told her. "It's stopmarynow@gmail.com."

"Cute."

"All you have to do is send the names of the skinjackers to that address. You do know how to use e-mail, right?"

"Who do you think I am, Mary?" said Jill. "They had e-mail when I went into a coma."

"Sorry." Allie looked over to Jix, who was still talking to Clarence. Jill and Jix's complete devotion to each other reminded Allie of her own relationship with Mikey . . . in a dark-side-of-the-Force sort of way. "I'm glad you found something you like better than killing people," she told Jill.

"Don't knock it till you've tried it, Pollyanna." Then Jill gave her a nasty, knowing wink, and sauntered away.

Allie tried not to think about what Jill had said. She had other business right now. Lacey was still off by herself playing tic-tac-toe in the dirt, toward the edge of the deadspot. That sad-eyed expression never left the girl's face. Allie went over to her.

"Having fun?" Allie asked.

"Maybe. I guess," Lacey answered. "When I was with Mary, I played tic-tac-toe every day with some boy. The exact same game over and over again. It felt good to know what would happen next, but at the same time it didn't feel good at all. Isn't that weird?"

"No," said Allie. "I understand." Then Allie reached into her pocket, and pulled out something that had been sitting there, waiting for years. An Everlost coin. When Allie held it in her hand, the coin stayed cold and inert. As long as she could skinjack, the coin wouldn't work for her. But it would work for Lacey. Allie held it out to the girl. "Would you like to have this?"

Lacey looked at the coin warily. "Mary said we should make a wish with it and throw it away—she said it wasn't good for anything else—but you know what? I think she was lying."

"It will get you out of Everlost," Allie told her.

"Will it take me home like the ruby slippers?"

Allie thought about the question. "Yes," she told Lacey. "Not the home where you've been, but the one you're going to."

Lacey shrugged. "I don't remember the home I came from, anyway. All I remember is Everlost, Mary, and tic-tac-toe." Lacey looked at the coin, still afraid to take it. "They say skinjackers can see the tunnel when people go in, and they know what's there. Can you tell me?"

Allie shook her head. "We can see the tunnel, but the light at the end is too bright to see what's there. . . . But I'll bet you still remember how it felt in the tunnel, before you came to Everlost, don't you?"

Lacey looked off into the sun to remind her. "I remember feeling . . . kind of good about it. But then I tripped over my laces and fell."

"Maybe you'll feel good this time too."

Then Lacey grabbed her arm, tightly as if something might grab her at that very moment and take her away. "But what if it's a trick? What if it's a lie? What if the light's bad—or what if it's fake and there's nothing there at all? What then?"

Allie grabbed Lacey and held her close, trying to comfort her, but how do you comfort someone from something you're not sure of yourself? "I don't know what's in the light," Allie said. "Only the people who get there know for sure. . . . But I do know this: Everyone who has ever lived has gone down the tunnel, and everyone who ever *will* live will go there too. So you're in good company."

"Not everyone gets where they're going," Lacey pointed out. "What about the souls who sink?"

"They'll get there eventually, even if eventually means a long time."

And then Lacey said, "Squirrel didn't go into the light. He didn't go anywhere at all. What about him?"

Allie closed her eyes. She never liked Squirrel, but he didn't deserve to be extinguished. "Well," Allie said, "that's the exception that proves the rule."

She held Lacey for a moment more, and when she let

go, Lacey seemed comforted. More than comforted, she was calmed. She was ready.

"Will you hold my hand until I'm gone?" Lacey asked.

"Of course I will."

They stood with Allie holding her hand, then Lacey held out her other hand, and Allie placed the coin in the middle of her palm.

"It's warm," Lacey said.

Allie smiled. "Make a wish."

Lacey closed her palm, holding the coin tight, and in an instant they were both bathed in bright light coming from the end of an impossibly long tunnel. Lacey looked into the light, letting go of Allie's hand, and she gasped. "It came true!" And then she was gone, shooting down the tunnel into a blinding eternity.

Jill, who had seen the whole thing, gave Allie slow applause. "Very touching," Jill said. "I may have to skinjack someone just so I can hurl."

CHAPTER 35

Dark Cumulus

A ny journey worth making is more meaningful made on foot. And crossing the desert is a time-honored tradition of any holy pilgrimage."

This was Mary's decree as they marched up from south Texas, keeping away from roads and other hints of civilization. It was, she decided, the best way to steer clear of the scar wraith. The path they cut took them north of San Antonio, and they began to pick up stray Afterlights that had scattered after the Neons had attacked the train. The collective afterglow of her army was a beacon attracting Afterlights for miles in all directions, and when her scattered flock realized that it was Mary, they came running. Not all of them found their way back, but their numbers increased every day.

Mary soon announced that her vapor of Afterlights had grown so large, they could now consider themselves a full-fledged cumulus. It was more than appropriate, because her cumulus was a storm of living light that continued to gather strength as it pushed ever forward—and this time Mary refused to rest for Afterlights who thought they needed to sleep.

They numbered more than five hundred by the time their relentless march reached Odessa, Texas.

Only now did Mary allow her children a rest from their travels. There was an old sports arena in Odessa that had been torn down when the new coliseum was built. The old arena was now the most substantial deadspot that the small city had to offer. With so many Afterlights under Mary's wing now, it was a perfect-size space for a temporary respite, and an effective center of operations for her new skinjackers' first mission. The trick was figuring out what that mission should be.

As it turned out, Moose was very helpful in this regard. While Moose had never been accused of being a genius, he was actually a whole lot smarter without Squirrel around, and more highly motivated by his loss than by his presence. He was very clever when it came to skinjacking reconnaissance. In other words, Moose gathered information and intelligence about Odessa and what sorts of marvelous things might be accomplished there by a motivated team of skinjackers.

Mary turned the arena's press box into her center of operations. From here she could look out over the whole arena, and keep an eye on all her children. There was a fine basketball court below, and a few basketballs had even crossed with the arena when it was imploded. Now a spontaneous basketball game had erupted. Many Afterlights played, more were content to be spectators, and others began to spread out into the stands, finding their own particular patterns of behavior. Mary watched the repetitive games and conversations; comfort of familiarity taking root in this unfamiliar environment. It was all about habit, Mary knew. It was all about consistency. For this reason Mary was not at all surprised when Jackin' Jill showed up in Odessa. She knew Jill was a creature of habit too.

"Of course you're still one of us, Jill," Mary said, giving Jill a warm welcoming hug. "I understand your pain, and I forgive you."

Jill nodded but said nothing because she knew if she did, it would be a bitter accusation. Mary might forgive her, but she could never forgive Mary for having tried to send Jix down. She wished she could announce to Mary that the trick had failed, and that Jix hadn't sunk, just to see the look on Mary's face. It would almost be worth the fallout.

Mary took Jill's silence for embarrassment at her emotional outburst back on the Corpus Christi dock. "Let's forget the past," Mary told her. "After all, I do owe you a debt of gratitude. I won't easily forget that *you* were the one who first began reaping souls!"

Jill couldn't meet her eye. It was not something she was proud of. Jill had done it for her own selfish reasons, of course, to secure her own position—first, within Pugsy Capone's corrupt inner circle of Chicago hoodlums, and then, once Mary took over, she reaped to keep herself within Mary's inner circle. Milos had accused Jill of enjoying reaping. Well, he was right. The stalking, the hunting, the adrenaline rush of a successful kill was as thrilling to her now as it had ever been. But Jix, with the slightest caress of her spirit, had redirected those energies. Jill was still a mistress of the hunt, with a strong taste for violent mayhem . . . but not for murder. She no longer craved the spilling of human blood, for it was all too easy. She was beyond that now; it was unworthy of her skills. But taking down Miss Mary High-and-Mighty—now *there* was challenging prey!

"So, is that what we'll be doing?" Jill asked. "More reaping?"

"Yes and no," Mary told her. "More like *world building*. You see, Jill, there are many places in this world that really ought to cross into Everlost so that eternity can preserve them."

"World building . . ." repeated Jill.

"Yes. We'll select places a bit more substantial than that sorry little playground Milos brought into Everlost. Of course, it goes without saying that any place that crosses will bring with it any number of souls—many of them youthful enough for us to reap into our protection."

"So then . . . the new skinjackers are all with the program?" Jill asked.

"They will be," Mary told her, "once they've had time to gain the kind of broad perspective that you and I have. But for now, there's no real need to trouble them with details that might confuse them. That's best left to those of us who truly know what we're doing, don't you agree?"

The skinjackers had been given the spacious privacy of the home-team locker room, perhaps to bolster their spirit of camaraderie. When Milos saw Jill, he folded his arms and put forth the most gloatingly superior smile Jill had ever seen.

"Well, well," said Milos. "Look what the cat dragged in."

Jill could have stomped his grinning head straight to the center of the earth, but somehow she managed to keep her cool. "You finally got an English expression right." She would never, ever forgive Milos for capsizing the yacht, but the fact that she already despised him made it easier to mask how much more deeply she loathed him now. She was constantly fantasizing about all the ways she could end his existence or at least make him suffer. But she also knew she had to keep such dark thoughts to herself. Her job was to infiltrate and observe. She consoled herself with knowing that revenge would be more satisfying the longer she waited.

Milos introduced her to all the new skinjackers—including their star pupil, a fifteen-year-old in an ROTC uniform.

"This is Rotsie, from the Benson High fire," Milos told her. "He is a natural at soul surfing and . . . what do you call it?"

"'Information retrieval,'" said Rotsie.

"Yes. He can go into a fleshie's mind and instantly pull out any information he wants."

"Pleased to officially meet you," he said, respectfully shaking Jill's hand. "I'm sorry about your friend—the one who drowned."

"He didn't drown," Jill snapped. "He sunk. And anyway, it's old news. What's done is done."

"We've been training for our first mission," said one of the other skinjackers, a girl that seemed to be bleeding sparkles out of her nails and eye makeup, and who was given the uninspired nickname "Sparkle."

"Mary had a vision," another skinjacker said.

At the mention of Mary's so-called vision, Moose, alone in the corner, grunted, but offered no follow-up.

"Right, Mary's vision," said Milos. "She has foreseen that this city's gas main will explode, and take out several square blocks downtown."

"Really?" said Jill.

"Yeah," said one of the other boys. "So Mary wants to send us out before it happens, and stop it."

Milos then gave Jill a secret wink out of view of the others. "Yes. We must 'stop' it."

If Jill had blood, it would have boiled.

At dawn, on the first Monday of the new year, Mary and all her children waited in the streets of Odessa, all eyes on the natural gas plant, where the accident would occur.

"It's a good thing we're here," Mary told them. "Gas explosions are terrible things. They kill thousands every year."

"I'm glad you're in charge again, Miss Mary," said one of her tried and true Afterlights. "Milos actually had us make bad things happen instead of stopping them."

"Don't judge him too harshly," Mary told the child. "Who could blame him for trying to save the living from their sorrow-filled world?" Then she turned to the others and spoke loudly enough for all of them to hear. "We may not succeed today in stopping the accident, for visions of the future are very hard to change. But if the cause is lost, at least we will be able to run in and save as many children as we can from the light."

Then she sent forth Milos and the skinjackers to do everything within their power to make things "right."

Milos led the way, making sure each of them knew their

own small part of the plan. Moose and Jill, of course, were aware of the larger picture, but not how it all fit together. Only Milos and Mary knew the full extent of the operation, and how devastating this "accident" would be—how many hundreds would die, so that every youthful soul could be reaped. Knowing that she trusted him to pull this off meant everything to Milos, and as he marched into the plant, skin-jacking the senior engineer, he smiled at everyone he passed, for he knew today would be glorious!

PART FIVE

Stealing Life

Philosophical Interlude with Arnie,
the Grand Inquisitor

How easy is murder when one calls it by a different name? How much easier is it for the conscience to condone "reaping" than "killing"—and when one knows that death isn't the end, does it stop the killing hand for fear of retribution, or does it simply make it easier to kill, because, if life continues, how can murder be murder at all?

*"Kill them all, for the Lord knoweth them that are His."** That was the creed of the medieval crusaders, cutting down everyone in their path, the good and the bad, content in the knowledge that God would sort them out in the hereafter. They believed themselves holy warriors, bringing glory and reward with every bloody slash of their swords.

Mary Hightower, a girl from a more civilized age, needed no sword to do her holy work. Her weapons were much subtler. Her weapons were skinjackers, and the body of anyone on earth she wanted them to possess. And since her skinjackers could possess anyone, that made Mary Hightower the most powerful, and most dangerous person on earth, living or dead.

---

* Arnaud Amalric, Archbishop of Narbonne and Grand Inquisitor under Pope Innocent III, 1204 AD.

EVERFOUND

Was that a tap on your shoulder? Do you sense some unseen spirit whispering in your ear, announcing the end of everything you know? If you do, then Mary is close by, waiting for you with a loving smile, and her hordes are there as you fall, ready to catch you, and hold you, and keep you. Forever.

But not yet . . .

CHAPTER 36

Holding Patterns

On New Year's Eve—the same night Mary first arrived in Odessa—Allie was arriving in Baltimore. Travel in Everlost took forever, but all it took for Allie to get from south Texas to Baltimore was a fleshie, a plane ticket, and a connecting flight. All it took to get Clarence into a first-class seat was a skinjacker who could provide him with cash, and an expensive suit to make him look the part.

Allie was never proud of using skinjacking as a method of stealing. But if there was anyone who needed a spiritual Robin Hood, it was Clarence.

"You make me feel like a person again," he told Allie before they boarded that first plane. "I'm not sure that's a good thing."

Allie had skinjacked a well-dressed middle-aged woman who very well could have been Clarence's wife. As Clarence no longer had any ID, she had to skinjack a couple of security guards to get him through. Easy as pie.

As they circled the airport waiting to land in miserable weather, the turbulence became so severe it nearly knocked Allie out of her host.

"Sorry to ruin New Year's Eve for all you good folks," the captain announced, "but I guess the old year is hurling hailstones at Baltimore. I promise to have you down before the ball drops."

Allie could feel the tension filling the living—even the seasoned travelers. Allie felt tense as well, but it had nothing to do with the rattling of the jet. Her turbulence would start after they landed.

Time was of the essence, but the task was daunting. So Allie did something she rarely did. She took care of herself. After they landed, Allie skinjacked a wealthy woman with nowhere to go. Then she lavished upon herself and Clarence the finest New Years' dinner Baltimore had to offer. Afterward they retired to their respective rooms in a penthouse suite.

But while Clarence slept, Allie did not. She opened the laptop of her host, and spent the night scouring the Web for information—and when old news reports proved insufficient, both she and Clarence hit the streets in the morning, hoping to dig up all the facts they could on the tragic tale of a Russian immigrant boy who was not entirely dead.

Vitaly Milos Vayevsky.

Born in St. Petersburg, Russia. Emigrated with his family to the United States at the age of eleven. Fell from the roof of a five-story apartment building at sixteen. A tree broke his fall. But not entirely.

He suffered massive internal injuries and a subdural hematoma that left him one step short of brain-dead. He spent more than a year in a long-term care facility, and then, when insurance and money ran out, the decision was made to take him off the machines that monitored his faint life signs.

Prognosis: grim.

The doctors gave him just a few weeks to live in such a nonresponsive vegetative state. His parents brought him home, for his mother was determined to make her son's final days peaceful. However, those days turned to weeks, turned to months, turned to years. And now, in a bedroom, in a fourth-floor apartment, in a working-class neighborhood of Baltimore, the body of Vitaly Milos Vayevsky slept . . . while his soul journeyed in a world between life and death.

Each day, the drip, drip, drip of the intravenous feeding tube marked time for the family. His younger sister went off to college, graduated, married, and had a son that she named for him. Milos was an uncle, but he would never know.

From time to time, when the sight of him brought too much pain, his father would suggest they turn off the feeding tube so that he could quietly fade away. No one would ask questions, and maybe it would be best that way. Each time it was suggested, however, Milos's mother would flatly refuse. This, she knew, was her penance; her punishment for allowing Milos to play with those boys on the roof that day. And so she would change the bedpan, and sponge him down, and clip his nails, and treat the bedsores, always holding on to the faint, faint hope that one day her boy might wake up.

Eight a.m. A Baltimore boulevard lined by low-rise apartment buildings, and covered with a fine dusting of snow that threatened to stick. Trash trucks already rolled down the street, pounding a week's worth of waste in their hoppers, and collecting dry Christmas trees from the curb. It was the first Monday of the New Year, and at the very same moment that Mary and her horde waited in the streets of Odessa for a gas explosion, Allie and Clarence stood on a Baltimore street corner, on the brink of a very different mission.

Clarence wore a long cashmere coat, looking like a million bucks. His stylish leather gloves hid the burns on his left hand, and protected Allie from his touch. While his retro fedora didn't exactly hide his facial scars from the living world, it cast them behind a bold new fashion statement. Beside him Allie inhabited a FedEx delivery girl, whose flimsy coat did not protect her from the cold. She held a small package.

"I know I'm here for moral support," Clarence told Allie. "But I wish there was something more I could do."

Allie offered him a slim, shivering smile. "It's all right," Allie told him. He had been invaluable in tracking this place down, but she knew from the beginning that she'd have to go in alone.

"Do you want to tell me what's in the package?" Clarence asked.

Allie looked at the small package in her hands. She had gone to a lot of trouble to secure its contents, and she didn't really want to talk about it. "Tools of the trade," she told him. "Does it really matter?"

"I guess not," Clarence said. "I'll be waiting for you when you get back."

Allie found the first step forward was the hardest, but the next was easier. One step at a time, she made her way down the street in the borrowed body of the delivery girl and went to the front door of an apartment building she wished she never knew existed.

Mrs. Vayevsky always jumped at the sharp, loud buzz of the apartment intercom. Who would be buzzing up at this time of the morning? She reached to the intercom and pressed the button, leaning close as she spoke.

"*Da?* Who is it?" Perhaps her husband had forgotten his key. It certainly wouldn't be the first time . . . but an unfamiliar voice came back at her through the squawk box.

"I have a delivery for the Vayevsky family."

Delivery? The woman thought, *Since when do they deliver at eight in the morning?* "Fine. I buzz you. Apartment 403." She concluded it must be a late Christmas gift from overseas. Relatives back home never seemed to remember that getting packages halfway around the world took many weeks.

She waited by the door until she heard footsteps reach the fourth-floor landing, then opened before the knock.

"For the Vayevsky family?"

The delivery girl stepped in, which surprised the woman. FedEx always lingered at the threshold. The intrusion unsettled her, but then perhaps this girl was just new. She handed the package to Mrs. Vayevsky.

"Do I have to sign?"

"That won't be necessary," said the girl.

Then suddenly Mrs. Vayevsky felt her mind spinning into an unfamiliar place. Her hands now held the small package, yet it felt as if she didn't have control of her own hands or any other part of her body anymore. *Something is wrong here,* she said in Russian, but only in her mind, for her lips couldn't form the words.

Then another voice in her head said something in very clear English,

"Sleep."

Mrs. Vayevsky felt herself obeying the command, spiraling away from consciousness into sudden slumber.

Allie took full control of Mrs. Vayevsky, and as she did, the delivery girl collapsed to the ground. Allie had knocked the girl so deeply unconscious, nothing could jar her awake. Allie gathered the sleeping delivery girl, and tried to put her into a chair—but now, in the body of Mrs. Vayevsky, Allie found picking the girl up very hard to do. The woman had knee troubles, she had back troubles, she was weak and worn and carrying a little too much weight. In the end, the best Allie could do was to drag the girl across the floor, and prop her up against a wall.

Allie estimated Mrs. Vayevsky to be in her mid-fifties. She had salt-and-pepper hair, and lined, careworn eyes. Allie had thought she might be a bit younger, but perhaps she had gotten old before her time because of the things she had been forced to endure.

Allie straightened up her stiff back and had a look around. The furniture was modest; worn but still livable. A TV with color issues played a morning talk show. Allie turned it off. A hallway led off toward three bedrooms.

First the master bedroom came into view, with a queen-size bed that had not yet been made. The second bedroom had been converted into a sewing room. And the third bedroom sat behind a closed door at the end of the hallway.

Allie took a deep, shuddering breath, reached for the knob, turned it, and then slowly pushed the door open.

The curtains were half-closed and a wide swath of morning light cut across the room. There were pictures on the wall, each one featuring a smiling boy whom Allie recognized, although the pictures all showed him younger. There was a desk clean of all dust which held several books between marble bookends: *Catcher in the Rye, Ender's Game*, and all three *Lord of the Rings* volumes. It proved that this room once belonged to a very real, very normal boy, before that boy became what he became.

Allie continued to let her eyes move around the room. Concert posters on the wall. Trophies on shelves. She forced her eyes to look everywhere but at the center of the room. Then, when she had nowhere else to look, she zeroed in on an intravenous stand which held a bag of milky fluid. She lowered her eyes from the bag and followed the tube which snaked down into an arm. The hand at the end of that arm was bent back at the wrist, with fingers that curled in on themselves, fully atrophied from years of disuse. Then she took a deep breath and raised her eyes to see his face.

Allie gasped at what she saw.

In the bed lay a sallow-faced, sunken-cheeked man. Not a boy, but a man. Beard stubble covered him, four or five days of growth, for regular shaving was not a priority under the circumstances. His lips were stretched, his mouth slightly open, and above his pale forehead, his hairline had begun to recede.

Allie's first instinct was to think that there had been some mistake, that this couldn't be Milos—yet she knew it had to be. While Milos had remained sixteen in Everlost, his comatose body had not. He had been in this coma for almost eleven years. Milos was a man pushing twenty-seven.

She had to look away, and when she did, she caught her own reflection in a mirror. But it wasn't *her* reflection, it was that of the woman whose body she had stolen. The woman whose son now lay in the bed before her.

Allie looked down to the package in her trembling hands. Before she could change her mind, she ripped the package open and pulled out the syringe.

If someone had told Allie that she would commit a premeditated act of murder, she would not have believed it. She would have spouted off all the reasons how she could never be capable of such a thing—that no matter how dire the circumstances, she would find a better way. She was so naive, so arrogant to think that the laws of necessity and unthinkable circumstance could not apply to her. She could tell herself that this was an act of mercy, but that would be a lie. This was an act of war. An act of terrorism. It was nothing less than an assassination.

If I do this, Allie told herself, *I am no better than Mary. I will have sunk to the worst possible place a person can go. After this moment, I will be a cold-blooded killer and it can never be taken back.*

So the question was, did Allie Johnson have the strength to sacrifice all that was left of her innocence if it meant she might save the world?

The answer came to her like a burst of courage from a wellspring deeper than she knew she had inside herself.

I would sacrifice everything I am, everything I believe, to save the living world.

And so, with tears filling her eyes, she took the cap off the syringe, found a vein in Milos's arm, and injected a massive dose of poison into his withered body.

Mrs. Vayevsky opened her eyes to see the delivery girl looking down at her.

"Are you all right, ma'am?" the delivery girl said.

Mrs. Vayevsky was now lying on the couch with no memory of how she got there. She sat up feeling weak and lightheaded. "What happened?" she asked. "Have I fainted?"

"You're fine," the delivery girl said. "I'm sure there's nothing to worry about." She offered Mrs. Vayevsky the faintest of smiles and a glass of water, which she drank with a shaky hand. "You should rest," the delivery girl said and she clasped Mrs. Vayevsky's shoulder a little too hard, for a little too long. "I'd better be going now."

"The package . . . ," said Mrs. Vayevsky.

The delivery girl pointed. "It's on the table there. Like I said, there's no need to sign for it." Then the delivery girl left, quietly closing the door behind her.

When Mrs. Vayevsky felt strong enough to stand, she went to the table to find the package had already been torn open. Had she done that before she fainted?

Inside, of all things, was a Russian nesting doll. Its familiar shape—like a squat bowling pin—and brightly painted surface, made her smile. It was the kind of simple wooden toy she had played with in her youth, a reminder of a much simpler time. On the outermost shell was the painted figure of an old man, but each shell opened to reveal a smaller, younger man inside, until finally in the very center was a wooden baby no larger than her pinky. The gift came with no card, no return address, no clue as to who sent it, or why. All the same, she knew exactly where it needed to go.

She headed to her son's room and set all six shells of the nesting doll side by side, smallest to largest, on Milos's desk, admiring the colors and the workmanship it had taken to create the lacquered figurines. Then, when she turned to glance at the bed, her expression changed.

Without even touching him, she knew. Without holding a mirror to his lips to check for breathing, she knew.

She sat in the chair beside the bed, wrapped her arms around her chest, and began rocking back and forth, sobbing his name over and over. She wailed with the deepest grief she had ever known . . . and yet somewhere within that grief was secret gratitude that after so many years, she had finally been given permission to cry.

CHAPTER 37

Skinless

It happened in an instant. One moment Milos was skinjacking a worker, preparing to blow the entire gas main, and the next moment, he wasn't skinjacking at all. He was just standing on the plant floor, slowly sinking into the living world.

Something had changed.

He could sense it—a sudden lightness, a sudden disconnection. The living world, which always seemed a bit blurry and faded, seemed even more so now—one step further removed. There was a panic in Milos, and with it came a sense of irretrievable loss that he could not put into words. He tried to deny it, refused to even think about what it might mean, and he attempted to skinjack the worker again. He stepped right through the man, and out the other side. Milos did not feel flesh, nor did he hear a single thought.

"No!"

He leaped again and again, but it was like leaping at shadows. Finally Jill and Moose peeled out of their hosts, and stared at him.

"What's wrong with you?" Jill asked.

"Nothing," Milos insisted. "Get on with the mission."

But neither of them moved. Now the other skinjackers were peeling out of their hosts as well, wondering what was going on, and Milos was at the center of their attention. He screamed in fury, and leaped at every living blur that moved around him, but it was hopeless.

"I'm stopping the mission," said Jill.

"No, you can't stop the mission. I'm the lead skinjacker. I give the orders."

"Sorry," said Jill, "but you can't be the lead skinjacker if you can't skinjack."

Mary's children were overjoyed that the disaster was prevented. Mary, however, was not—but she was wise enough not to show her disappointment. If Milos had been able to rupture the gas main, the resulting explosion would have taken out several residential blocks. The story would have been much different. The fact that he could no longer skinjack posed a whole set of problems she would have to quickly address.

Yet even though this mission had been botched, Mary was a girl with a positive outlook. In spite of her frustration, she couldn't help but see the glass as half full. She looked out at her huge cumulus of Afterlights, and quickly came to realize that far from being a failure, the morning had, in an unexpected way, been a grand success. Her children all believed that the disaster had been averted because of the skinjacker's efforts—which meant they now believed fully and completely that Mary had the power to see and to change the future. After today, they would trust her decisions even more than before, and follow her guidance without question. In this case "failure" made her stronger. Thinking about it lifted her spirits, and left her ready to prepare the next mission—which she knew would be a resounding success. She would make sure of it.

For eleven years, Milos had taken his ability to pop in and out of the living world for granted. To do something as simple as grab himself a burger if he wanted to, or, if the whim struck him, to ski down a white, powdered slope in the body of a fleshie who actually knew how to ski.

Deep down he knew it couldn't last forever, but Everlost has a way of making one dismiss tomorrow as just another version of today. He never considered what existence without skinjacking would be like, so he wasn't prepared for the shock of his body dying.

For Milos, it was nothing short of horrific. The constant hunger, with so little food to satisfy it. The slow drift of memories being lost. The relentless chiseling away of one's identity. How could ordinary Afterlights stand it? What made it worse was the speed at which a skinjacker reverts— as if making up for lost time. Memories didn't just fade, they were sucked out into a vacuum. Milos suddenly realized his mind, which had been so sharp, was now an open box, and if he took out a memory to treasure, or even to just ponder, it was lost by the mere act of thinking about it. In just one day, he had forgotten his last name—which he had remembered all these years—and he quickly came to realize with increasing dread that he had no yardstick with which to measure the depth of the things he had already forgotten.

"Get over it," Jill had told him, clearly thrilled at the prospect of his misery. "Learn to be ordinary, I'm sure you'll excel at it."

But it was more than just being ordinary. When one knew the exhilarating power of dual citizenship in two vastly different worlds, losing connection to one of those worlds was like losing one's limbs. It had never occurred to Milos before, but to the "ordinary" Afterlight, the living world might as well have been the moon, for it was just as unreachable. How could anyone exist with such disconnection?

Milos went to Mary, knowing that she would have some wisdom and some comforting words for him, as she always did . . . but when he went into the press box to talk to her, he found that she already had company:

Rotsie.

The two of them sat facing one another. Rotsie was all smiles and Mary laughed at a joke that Milos hadn't heard. A vending machine that had crossed with the arena was still partially stocked, and so the two of them were sharing a can of Coke, passing it back and forth between them. Watching Mary's lips touch the same can that Rotsie had just drank from made Milos's afterglow falter. It felt like his body was dying all over again. Rotsie noticed him first.

"Hello, Milos," he said, seeming both arrogant and self-conscious at the same time. It made Milos feel uncomfortably off-balance. He had to remind himself that Rotsie was the intruder here, not him.

Mary took a moment to gather her thoughts, then stood, smoothing out her shimmering gown. She sauntered to Milos, and took one of his hands in both of hers, clasping it tightly.

"Milos, I am so, so sorry." She didn't move to embrace him, she just held his hand. "I know you're strong, I know you'll get past this."

"Yes," said Milos. "We'll get past this together."

Mary's smile became a little slim, then she squeezed his hand, and let go.

Rotsie, who still hadn't stood up, said, "I just want you to know, I have every respect for you."

Milos had no response to this.

"What Rotsie means," Mary explained, "is that it won't be the same without you on his skinjacking team, but we'll all have to manage."

"*His* team?"

"Well," said Mary, turning her eyes to Rotsie and offering him a smile that should have been aimed at Milos. "I had considered putting Jill in charge, but she doesn't exactly work and play well with others. Then I considered Moose, but he's much more of a follower than a leader, wouldn't you agree? Rotsie, on the other hand, already has the respect of the new skinjackers."

"But . . . but I can still lead the team," Milos insisted.

"Denial doesn't help anyone," Mary told him. "Circumstances have changed. Your body has died, and we all need to face that." Then Mary sat back down, took the can from Rotsie, and took a long sip of soda, savoring the flavor. That's when Milos realized that this was more than just a shared can of soda. It was like a champagne toast between the two of them, to celebrate a decision that had already been made in Milos's absence.

"Why don't you go down to the arena floor with the other Afterlights?" Mary suggested, indicating the endless basketball game below. "You could watch the game—maybe join in if you like. You've been so busy for so long, it's been forever since you've played anything at all. Why, I bet if you thought about it, Milos, you could find something you'd like to do more than anything else. One special thing that would keep you content."

"Think of it as retirement," Rotsie said. "I'm sure you'll find something useful to do."

"That's right," echoed Mary. "Useful and fulfilling."

"No," insisted Milos feeling his last ounce of hope fading away. "Please, Mary . . . you still need me. . . ."

Mary sighed and rose again as if it was an effort. Finally she gave him an embrace and a kiss, but none of it held the passion it did before. The embrace was perfunctory, a mere requirement of common courtesy. And the kiss was a peck on the cheek. He felt the way a beloved pet must feel the moment before being "put down."

"Please, Milos," she said. "There's no need to make this so . . . awkward."

Finally Rotsie stood. "Why don't I escort him out?"

But Milos would not allow the humiliation of being kicked out by Rotsie. Milos backed away, holding Mary's gaze, hoping she would look away in shame, but she didn't, because Miss Mary Hightower wasn't ashamed of anything she did. Ever.

"I will go," Milos said. "I will go and make myself . . . useful." And he left, turning all his attention to the supreme task of remembering his name.

CHAPTER 38

Blame It on Mavis

One by one, Jackin' Jill had teased out the real names of Mary's new skinjackers—even though Mary had insisted they all take on nicknames to keep their identities secret. Mary was shrewd, but Jill was far more cunning, and she was already feeling the thrill of the hunt—a different kind of hunt, but, in its own way, rewarding. She knew who they all were within a few days, and then she memorized their names, knowing that even if she found a way to write them down, she could not take the list with her when she skinjacked.

AmberAguilar

Now all that remained was getting the information to Allie. Jill hated the fact that she was on Allie's side now, and she had to remind herself that she was on nobody's side but her own. This next part turned out to be harder than finding out their names. There simply was no way for Jill to sneak off and send the information to Allie. She was under the constant scrutiny of Rotsie and the other skinjackers. She couldn't get away from Mary's structured little world without raising suspicion. Finally she came up with a plan.

"These skinjackers are pathetic," she told Mary. "They need more training, or they'll be useless—and they need more skills to make up for the loss of Milos."

Mary, who was preparing to march west from Odessa with her horde, was aggravated by anything that might delay them. "You'll train them as we go," she told Jill.

"How? There's nothing west of Odessa for miles. We need fleshies to train them, and the only fleshies around are in this town."

Finally Mary relented, allowing them a training day, and the next morning they went to downtown Odessa.

JonathaN goldstein

Although Moose and Jill were the most skilled skinjackers among them, Rotsie insisted on taking charge. "We'll practice soul surfing," Rotsie said, "and increase the distance we can jump."

"You can do that, but I want to teach partialing."

"What's that?" Rotsie asked.

Jill gave an exaggerated roll of her eyes. "Don't you know anything? It's when you take over just a part of a fleshie. A mouth, or a leg, or an arm."

"What good is that?"

"Sometimes it's all you need, and it's faster when you're in a hurry, moron!"

Then he grabbed her wrist angrily. It would have hurt if they were skinjacking. "I am your superior," Rotsie said. "You will treat me with respect."

Jill saw all the other skinjackers, including Moose, looking at her to see what she would do. A battle of wills would not help the situation, so she gave him a salute, just exaggerated enough to be defiant, but just real enough for him to have to accept it. Then she made a mental note to list his name in all caps for Allie, so she'd go after him first.

DAMON McDANIEL

Rotsie and Moose went off with the four kids who had the most trouble soul-surfing, and left Jill with the boy who always raised his hand, earning him the nickname "The Teacher's Pet," or just "The Pet," and a Korean kid they called "Seoul-Soul," but that quickly became "SoSo."

Luke Nguyen

The problem with having these two was that they were too focused. As Jill explained partialing, they watched, and listened, and Jill suspected they would constantly be peeling out of their practice hosts, seeking her approval. What she needed were a few solid moments with nobody watching her.

"We need to get out of the street," Jill told them, "and find a place where people aren't moving so much." She looked down a row of shops, and said, "There—that gift shop. It's the perfect place."

But The Pet raised his hand. "Uh, excuse me, but won't it be easier if people are sitting down? Like maybe in the Starbucks next door?"

"Why would I want to make it easier?"

They walked right through the glass front of the gift shop, a store full of china figurines, and leftover Christmas decorations at half price. The floor was thin, and they had to struggle to keep themselves from sinking. Jill pointed to two fleshies in line. "Half-jack those two," she told them. "Hide behind their minds without taking them over, then focus on one hand, and make that hand take something and slip it into their pocket without them knowing."

"That's shoplifting," said The Pet.

Sebastian Var]ner

"Are you a skinjacker or aren't you?" snapped Jill.

"I hate to tell you this," said SoSo, "but I stink at half-jacking. Most of the time they know I'm there, and they freak out."

"Practice makes perfect," said Jill. "Now do it before you sink!"

SoSo looked at the fleshie, clenched his fists, and leaped inside. The Pet did the same to his fleshie, and both disappeared.

The moment they were gone, Jill made her move, jumping right through the wall into the Starbucks—which wasn't just full of people sitting down, it was full of people with computers. Without a second to lose she jumped into the closest one—a fat guy with way too much facial hair, and the instant she was inside—

—Down twenty points, stupid stock market, sell sell sell—

Jill knocked him unconscious and took over his body. It had been a long time since Jill had used a computer, and they had changed considerably. The keys were smaller, the screen bigger, and the maddening touchpad was nothing like a mouse.

She managed to close the stock market window, and found a mail icon. She clicked it, played around with the menu until she opened a new blank e-mail. Then she got to work typing out the names—but when she looked at her hands, she saw only her two index fingers extended, and she couldn't make her other fingers touch the keys. This idiot didn't know how to type! He could only hunt-and-peck, and although Jill knew how to type—she had learned as a child from an old Mavis Beacon typing program—her own ability could not override the fat guy's lack of muscle memory.

C'mon! Faster! Faster! But no matter how quickly she tried to type, she kept having to correct errors, and find the right keys. Jill calmed herself down and concentrated, knowing that frustration would only make it worse.

Maril;ou DiLuzio

Six names. Twelve words. And yet it took almost two minutes to type them. Finally she was done, and she went to the top of the screen, filling in the e-mail address.

stopmarynnow@gmail.com

Then she hit send, made sure that the e-mail uploaded, then peeled out of the fat guy, jumping back through the wall and into the gift shop.

In the living world SoSo was having trouble with his fleshie. The poor woman was screaming and flailing her arms, knocking things off shelves and breaking them like the proverbial bull in a China shop. Finally SoSo pulled out. "See," he told Jill. "I told you I suck at half-jacking."

The Pet peeled out a moment later. "Maybe we should try this in a place where things won't break."

"Forget it," Jill said. "You're a couple of screw-ups. We'll try partialing some other time." Then they left, with Jill confident that her mission was accomplished—and it would have been, had there not been a typo in the e-mail address.

CHAPTER 39

Ghost Town

Bad luck, bad karma, and plain old human error.

There was no other way to explain what happened in Eunice, New Mexico, just west of the Texas border. Until today, the town was little more than a spot on the map: a quiet and unremarkable place, with a population of about twenty-five hundred. In terms of industry there was a single factory that employed more than half the population: a plastics facility that manufactured lightweight components for fighter jets and smart bombs.

Protests were occasionally staged by activist groups who claimed that the people of Eunice were complicit in the creation of machines of death, and that the town would eventually get what was coming to it. Karma, the protesters said, would come a-calling.

Of course, no one took the protests seriously. It wasn't like the people of Eunice were warmongers—and besides, the plastic fittings the plant produced were not destructive in and of themselves: They were just small parts of larger puzzles assembled a thousand miles away.

Under the circumstances, it was very difficult to piece

together the unlucky string of events that befell the town of Eunice, but it all began with a tanker truck. Such trucks rolling in from Odessa were a regular site at the plant, since the plant needed regular shipments of trimellitates, polybutane, and other raw materials needed to make their particular type of plastic.

One tanker truck, however, never made it to the plant. To the best of anyone's knowledge, the driver lost control of the wheel while approaching the town. A heart attack was suspected. The tanker truck plowed into an electrical station and ruptured, and as the electrical station blew, a dense cloud of fumes billowed into the air. While burning polybutane would have been a health hazard and general nuisance, it would not have been deadly. However, due to some clerical error back at the chemical company in Odessa, the tanker was full of methyl isocyanate instead, a chemical used in pesticides that's only marginally safe to begin with, and when tossed into a fire, the resulting gas cloud would be lethal to anything downwind . . .

. . . Which was the entire town of Eunice.

The gas cloud caught everyone unawares, and in half an hour had taken out the whole population.

Bad luck, bad karma, and plain old human error.

What no one could explain, however, was how every building in town—even the ones that were nowhere near the accident—had been burned to the ground.

"We were unable to stop this tragedy," Mary told her children, "but somehow we must find joy within the sorrow."

Mary chose not to tell her children that the "accident"

was caused by her own skinjackers. Jill and Moose were sent to make sure that precisely the wrong chemical came to Eunice at precisely the wrong time, while her other skinjackers were sent to set roadblocks in and out of town — believing their efforts would stop the disaster. Instead, they succeeded in keeping the population from escaping.

Her children didn't need to be troubled with the details. As the living who dined on fine steaks shunned all thoughts of the slaughterhouse, Mary's children needed only to consider the plate before them . . . and theirs was a plate of compassion and of salvation.

The moment the cloud began to spill forth in the living world, and it was clear that there was nothing that could be done to stop it, Mary sent forth her children to catch the dying as they crossed. Those who were older, and could not be unbound from their path, were simply left to get where they were going. However, every child and teenager was grabbed at the precise moment of crossing and brought into Everlost.

With so many children at work, the final tally would clearly be impressive. Countless souls were now in transition, sleeping on the small deadspots where their living bodies had expired. They needn't sleep for nine months, though, for Mary had come up with a plan to use the very force of evil that threatened her. She would lure the scar wraith into another extinguishing moment at the time of her own choosing, and create yet another Great Awakening. As to who would be extinguished, it didn't really matter. She knew that most of her children would be willing to make the ultimate sacrifice if she asked.

"This place must be purified," Mary told her skinjackers, once the toxic cloud had done its damage and had dissipated. "Purified by fire." And she sent them out to burn the dead town of Eunice to the ground.

Now the fire raged all around Mary's children. Some walked right into the flames just to know how living-world fire would feel. They could sense the intensity of the heat like a faint fever, but nothing more. Soon the living world had been burned away like so much chaff, revealing the treasures of the town of Eunice.

"Eternity will preserve what it will," Mary told her children. "That which is worthy, that which is loved, will be blessed into Everlost."

The little round gazebo in town hall park crossed. So did a statue erected to honor World War II veterans. A church with beautiful stained glass windows and a corner café were now a part of Everlost too. Not many homes crossed, but particular objects from them did. A stuffed animal here, a bicycle there. A clarinet, a rocking chair. Everlost was now littered with odds and ends resting on tiny deadspots and the occasional larger structure. And of course, there were the souls in transition.

When all the sleeping Interlights were gathered, they were laid on the benches of the church and counted. A hundred and seventy-eight in all.

Satisfied, Mary turned to Little Richard, whom she had taken on as her personal assistant. "Let every Afterlight go forth and find an object of desire," she told him.

"Huh?"

She sighed. "Just tell everyone to pick one thing that's

crossed over—but only one. I will not condone greed."

"Yes, Miss Mary." Then he went out to spread the word.

Emergency vehicles had begun arriving from every direction in the living world, and the skinjackers abandoned their hosts, returning to Everlost. Each of them carried with them the smell of smoke and the exhaustion of the living bodies they had inhabited.

Moose was the only one who had not yet returned, but Mary was not too concerned. He was easily distracted. More than likely he was either scavenging for crossed objects, or watching the town burn.

Mary, always an insomnoid, looked out from the beautiful, freshly crossed gazebo at the wonderful ruins of Eunice that night. All her children had found deadspots around the center of town, and either slept, or were engaged in various activities. Only the church was off-limits, for it was full of Interlights.

Mary had assigned two Afterlights who seemed content to tell knock-knock jokes to each other, to be the sentinels of the church.

"When the rest of us leave, you will stay here to guard the ones who sleep," Mary told them. "And when they awake, you will be in charge. But always remember that it is I who am in charge of you." Then she had given them a volume of her newest book, penned by hand and painstakingly copied for them by a girl with perfect penmanship who Mary had chosen as her personal scribe.

"Read this," Mary had told the two jokesters. "Read it daily and when these new souls awake, please have them read it too."

This was a key part of Mary's plan. In each place she went, in every location she tore free from the living world, she would leave a team of Afterlights to tend to the sleeping Interlights left behind. Then when they awoke they would have a town to call their own, and would be welcomed into Mary's extended community.

Yet 178 new Afterlights was just a tiny drop in the bucket. There were more than six billion people in the living world, and one-fifth of those were young enough to be saved by Mary. Even if she did this every single day it would take thousands of years to complete the job. That simply wouldn't do. The war she had spoken to Milos about simply had to happen: The living had to be turned against one another, but she was still not exactly sure how to bring that about.

As she stood, looking out from the gazebo, a wind blew in the living world, dragging the smoke from the smoldering town westward. Mary could feel her own westward pull as well, stronger now than ever before. The answer to everything lay in that direction, just ahead of her, just past the horizon. Somewhere out there was the center of this strange gravity, and when she found it, when she stood right in the middle of it, she would know exactly what to do.

As she pondered the days ahead, looking out at the smoke, and her Afterlights shining through it, she saw one Afterlight coming toward her. One who wore a helmet. Moose had finally returned, and hopefully with a good excuse as to what had taken him so long . . . but as he got closer, Mary could sense that something was very, very wrong.

* * *

It had been a pretty bad football accident that landed Mitchell "Moose" Moessner's body comatose in a Pittsburgh convalescent hospital, paralyzed from the neck down. Wilted flowers attested to the fact that he was visited regularly, but no one was visiting him at the moment that Allie "the Outcast" Johnson put his physical self to rest. Unlike Milos, he had not suffered brain damage. In fact, Moose's brain should have been functioning normally, and yet he had never come out of his coma. It made perfect sense to Allie; consciousness could not exist here while his consciousness was elsewhere.

Moose could have skinjacked his own body if he had chosen to . . . if he had, he would have woken as a quadriplegic with no hope of motion below the neck, and no hope of even breathing for himself. Still, he could have done it, reclaiming some version of his old life. Now, however, that was out of the question.

There were many things that Moose feared: hell, the scar wraith, but God help anyone who witnessed the fury of Mary Hightower. As far as Moose was concerned, her anger was the most frightening thing in the universe—and for the first time ever, he was glad he was wearing a helmet, because he truly believed her rage could make his head explode.

"How could I have been so stupid?" Mary seethed. "How could I have been so blind to not know the truth from the moment Milos lost his ability?"

"Maybe itch a coincidench?" Moose's eyes were full of tears, but fortunately his face mask hid them, and Mary was not looking too closely.

"If you think that, then you're a more of a fool than I thought you were."

He had lost his ability to skinjack only minutes after crashing the tanker truck into the electrical station. And since then he had been hiding, afraid to come back.

Mary paced back and forth in the gazebo. "This is Allie's doing—I'm sure of it—and it's all Milos's fault! He should have sent her down the moment she was captured instead of making her the blasted figurehead of the train. He brought this on all of us!"

"Not really," said Moose, trying to defend him, because Milos was beyond any ability to defend himself. All of his attention was now on a deck of cards he had taken from one of the other kids. Milos spent all of his time shuffling it, and looking for one-eyed jacks.

"What I want to know is how she found your bodies," Mary said. "She must have known your true names!"

"Not neshisharily . . . ," said Moose.

"Stop contradicting me!" Mary paced with such a storm of emotion, Moose half expected lightning to crash all around them. Finally Mary turned to look at Moose and saw the tears in his eyes. She softened just a bit. "I know this isn't your fault. It's unfair that you have to be the one to suffer."

Moose nodded and the tears started to flow more freely, no matter how hard he tried to hold them back.

"You may go now," she told him. "I'm sorry for your loss."

He left sobbing in tears that were as great as the day that Squirrel was extinguished. But his tears were not tears of sorrow. They were tears of joy. Although he was always a team player, the weight of being a skinjacker in the service of Mary Hightower was more than he could bear. He didn't care if he lost his memories and his mind the way Milos had—in fact, he would prefer it. As he left Mary, he could already feel it all slipping away, so he went forth into the ruins of Eunice, searching among the crossed odds and ends, until he finally found himself a football . . . because the prospect of throwing and catching a football from now until the end of time was Mitchell "Moose" Moessner's idea of heaven.

Mary gathered the remaining skinjackers. They numbered seven now, including Jill. "We are under attack," Mary told them, "and we must strike back with full force as quickly and severely as possible. We must find the body of Allie the Outcast, and we must send that body to the grave."

No one answered immediately. These new skinjackers had no frame of reference, no idea who she was talking about. It just infuriated Mary even more.

"Her coma would have begun after a car accident, north of New York City, not quite four years ago. That is where we will begin our search. I will need a volunteer."

Rotsie immediately raised his hand, and Jill gave him a look of utter disgust. "Don't be stupid," Jill said. "You don't even know what she looks like." Then she turned to Mary. "If you need someone to do some pest control, it might as well be me."

This gave Mary pause for thought. It was out of character for Jill to volunteer for anything . . . but then perhaps

Jill's hatred of Allie rivaled her own. Or perhaps it was because Jill knew that she would be next on Allie's list.

"Sorry," said Rotsie, "but I think I'm better equipped to handle something like this."

"Yeah, right," said Jill dismissively, then turned back to Mary. "Even if you wanted to send him, you couldn't — you need Damon to lead the group, don't you?"

And suddenly Mary saw Jill in an entirely new light. "Indeed, I do need Damon," she said, keeping her eyes tightly trained on Jill. "I didn't know you knew Rotsie's real name. How ever did you come across it?"

Jill opened her mouth to speak, but nothing came out. Then The Pet politely raised his hand and said, "We told her our names. She said it was important in case we ever forgot it, that someone should know."

Mary offered a smile that was anything but pleasant. "I wonder why you would say that, Jill, when you know that skinjackers don't forget their names like other Afterlights."

"You're . . . you're blowing this all out of proportion," Jill said, looking more and more worried.

"Do you know that I never knew Milos's and Moose's real names? I never felt a need. But I'll bet *you* knew their names, didn't you, Jill?" This time Jill said nothing. As far as Mary was concerned, her silence convicted her.

"I will ask you this once," Mary said. "And your answer will determine how you will be dealt with." She paused, letting the severity of the situation sink in, then she asked, "Did you give Allie the names of my skinjackers?"

"You had Milos flip that boat and sent more than fifty kids down!" Jill accused.

Mary did not lose her cool. "Did you give Allie their names?"

She looked to support from the other skinjackers. "The tanker truck today was no accident either! Ask her!"

Mary couldn't tell if Jill's accusations rattled the others, because she wouldn't take her eyes off of Jill. "Answer the question," Mary asked calmly, then she waited, knowing that every criminal, if given enough time, will confess. Jill was no exception.

"Yes," Jill said, in arrogant defiance. "And now that she knows who they are, she'll pick them off one by one until you have no skinjackers left."

So there it was: proof positive that Jill was a traitor. Well, if Jill's accusations had won any points with the skinjackers, she had lost them now.

"Treason," said Mary, "is the highest crime in any civilized society. I will try to treat you with compassion . . . but it will be difficult, even for me, to show you mercy."

TO: FurbyXXL@Odessa-access.com

FROM: MAILER-DAEMON@Odessa-access.com

SUBJECT: Returned mail—see transcript for details.

*** ATTENTION ***

Your e-mail is being returned to you because there was a problem with its delivery.

----- The following addresses had permanent fatal errors -----

<stopmarynnow@gmail.com>

----- Transcript of session follows -----

>>> DATA

<<< 5401 5.8.1 <stopmarynnow@gmail.com> . . . Relaying denied

5401 5.8.1 <stopmarynnow@gmail.com> . . . User unknown

<<< 504 5.0.0 Need RCPT (recipient)

Final-Recipient:RFC8232; stopmarynnow@gmail.com

Action: failed

Status: 5.1.1

Remote-MTA: DNS; gmail.com

Diagnostic-Code: SMTP; 5401 5.8.1 <stopmarynnow@gmail.com> . . . Relaying denied

Return-Path: <FurbyXXL@Odessa-access.com>

Received: from imo-ma04.tx.Odessa-access.com with ESMTP id MAILSMTPRLYDA051-3bba5bda1598379;

From: FurbyXXL@Odessa-access.com

To: stopmarynnow@gmail.com

Subject: Names of the six skinjackers

Status: FAIL

CHAPTER 40
Pittsburgh Stealer

Nothing from Jill.

So far Allie had found only spam at the "stop-marynow" e-mail address, and she was beginning to worry. Had Jill even found Mary? Had she switched sides again? There was no way of knowing. So here they were, sitting in the lobby bar at a Pittsburgh airport hotel, Clarence dressed in his new fancy fashions, and Allie in the body of a flight attendant with big hair. They had no destination, and no way to find out what was going on with Mary and Jill, or with Nick, Mikey, and Jix. Right now, Allie would have settled for those smoke signals Jill had joked about. Even that would be better than nothing at all.

Through all of this Clarence had been a rock to lean on—even if she couldn't physically lean on him without being extinguished. He was such a troubled, imbalanced person when it came to taking care of himself. Yet when the well-being of others was at risk, he rose to be whatever the occasion needed him to be.

"Seeing Everlost was always a curse," Clarence had confided in Allie. "Ruined my life. Worse than the scars. A person can live with scars, but to live with things that no one else can see . . . ?"

Outside flurries had begun to whip across the glass front of the hotel, blown by a bitterly cold wind. Since being in Everlost, Allie had learned to appreciate the things she felt while skinjacking. Cold, heat, comfort, discomfort, hunger, thirst, and even indigestion. After experiencing the painless numbness of Everlost, all the things a living body could feel were a blessing.

"Well," suggested Clarence, a little sheepishly, "We could go back to San Antonio and find victims of Milos's accidents that were left in comas. We know the new skinjackers had to come from those accidents."

"No," said Allie. "I will not end lives on a hunch. I need to know for sure." To be honest, a part of Allie was glad that Jill hadn't responded. She didn't know if she could steal the life of a stranger. She knew Milos, she knew Moose, and knew the threat they had posed . . . but somehow stealing away the physical life of a total stranger would be much more difficult.

Clarence sighed. "Well, being as we have nowhere else to go . . ." Then he reached into his pocket and pulled out a piece of paper. "Your friend Jix thinks I have a purpose. I think maybe this might be it." He handed the paper to Allie. "See, while you were out taking care of business, I was doing my own research—'cause you know what they say about idle hands . . ." The paper had an address scrawled on it. A hospital in Memphis, Tennessee.

Allie took a deep shuddering breath. "Who's at this hospital, Clarence?"

The living half of Clarence's face puckered into something resembling a smile. "You are," he said.

Allie had tried to put it out of her mind. The thought of returning to herself, the dream of skinjacking her own body had been there, burning a hole in her mind the way that Everlost coin had sat heavy in her pocket until she gave it away. Since the moment Allie knew that her body was still clinging to life, she knew this day would come, but rather than dreaming of a joyful reunion of spirit and flesh, she feared the moment. She had good reason. Her family had made a life without her, and returning now would be difficult for all of them. The sight of Milos and Moose was disturbing to her as well. Milo's body had been in a severe state of atrophy, and Moose was completely paralyzed. Even if they could have returned to skinjack themselves, why would they have? An existence as a free spirit was better than being bound to a body with no hope of recovery, wasn't it?

But what if her body were undamaged?

What if she could just slip back into it and resume her life?

"Once you skinjack yourself," Jix had told her, "that's it. You're bound to your flesh until the day you die." If she ever did it, she knew there would be no going back . . . so for Allie it was best never to know the state of her body. That way, she would never have to decide.

Yet in spite of all the reasons not to go, she and Clarence boarded a flight to Memphis, and Wolf River Convalescent Hospital.

CHAPTER 41
Punishment and Crime

It was decided that sending Jill down to the center of the earth was much too kind a fate for her. Punishment for treason, Mary decided, should include far more suffering than that. As a skinjacker, Jill could experience pain while in a living body, but physical torture was far too barbaric for Mary's taste. Then it occurred to her that true punishment could only come if Jill was forced to linger within an undesirable host long enough to permanently bond with it.

Standing in the crossed gazebo, with her entire cumulus of Afterlights filling the park around her, a jury of twelve announced their verdict, without the messy inconvenience of an actual trial. Then Mary pronounced the sentence.

"Jackin' Jill, you have been found guilty of treason and high crimes against the universe," she proclaimed. "Your punishment is to be bound to the body of a pig for the rest of your natural days."

Through all of it, Jill had said nothing either in defense or in objection. Primarily because she had been gagged.

A suitable pig was found on a nearby farm. An animal

that would neither be slaughtered nor die anytime soon. It was the farm's prize breeding sow. Three times a year the sow was bred with a healthy male pig, producing sizable litters—and were Mary not bringing the world to a much-needed end, it would live and breed for at least another eight years. The sow had become so fat, it couldn't support its own weight, so it barely moved anymore.

With Mary present to witness, the skinjackers hurled Jill into the pig, and surrounded it. Each time she tried to escape, they hurled her back in until she was too exhausted to peel out anymore. After a day, when it was clear that Jill was bound to the sow for the rest of the animal's days, they left her there alone, except for the male pigs in the next pen, longing for the day they got to keep her company.

After Jill's sentence was carried out, Mary brought her remaining skinjackers together for a solemn meeting in the café that had crossed. Rotsie was not with them, because Mary had already sent him off in search of Allie's body. Sparkles was appointed the temporary leader of the skinjackers, because she had been the head of her cheer squad, and some leadership experience was better than none at all.

In the café they sipped the last of the crossed coffee, and shared a piece of cherry pie that had also crossed. There was a sense of despair among them—the accusations Jill had made had clearly chipped away at their confidence. Mary knew a decision had to be made. She had done her best to shield them from the difficult work ahead. Perhaps that had been wrong. Perhaps her skinjackers needed to know the full extent of what they had been called on to do. She couldn't deny that she feared this moment . . . because although she had unshakable faith in herself, she did not have such faith in those around her. Jill had turned on her — she couldn't assume that everyone would share her vision.

Before Mary could speak, The Pet raised his hand like a good schoolboy, and asked, "Is it true the things that Jill said? That you did those things on purpose?"

Mary sighed. She would not lie to them. "A traitor like Jill will say anything to cast blame away from herself," she said, "including the twisting of a noble act into something despicable." They waited for more, clearly not satisfied with the answer. Well, it was time they got a glimpse of the larger picture. "Prepare yourselves for what I'm about to tell you. It is neither pleasant nor pretty, but it will lead to things more wonderful than you can imagine."

"Tell us," said Sparkles. "We can take it."

Mary steeled herself and told them as plainly as she could. "The living world will soon be coming to an end."

There. She had said it out loud for the first time, and she found there was magic in saying it, for now that it was out in the open, it made it more real.

Then, to Mary's amazement, The Pet said, "I knew it!"

It caught Mary by surprise . . . but then she realized that she shouldn't be surprised at all — for hadn't the living world trained them for its own eventual demise? Didn't the living world speak of Armageddon and grand cataclysms in everything from sermons to the silver screen? Now her skinjackers focused on her with such intensity that Mary actually felt her own afterglow begin to burn brighter.

"You have been chosen to be the shining heralds of a new world."

They didn't bat an eye at this, either, for didn't every soul long to believe that he or she was singled out for a special divine purpose?

"You will be asked to do things that frighten you—things that will test your resolve—but I know you have the courage to do all the things you are called to do."

They began to puff up with pride, for didn't every soul long to believe that they had courage to face the most difficult of tests?

Mary's afterglow now pulsated with searing purpose, and she realized something remarkable! Mary always believed that her ability to gather and galvanize others was the result of refined charm and grace, but it was more than that: It was a power, every bit as potent as her brother's! While Mikey had the mystical power to repel anyone, Mary had a mystical ability to attract!

Now that she truly understood it, she was able to focus the scorching radiance of her soul and reach out with it. Tendrils of silver light now touched the afterglows of her skinjackers, bonding with them, gripping them, making their energy just an extension of her own, thereby turning their doubts into conviction. She didn't persuade them, she didn't force them. She didn't need to. Why would they need persuasion when they suddenly found their own beliefs were secretly replaced by Mary's?

"We'll do what we have to do, right, everyone?" said Sparkles, and everyone agreed.

Mary smiled at them, and they soaked in her joy as if

her beaming smile were the life-giving rays of the sun. Mary knew there would be no stopping her now. The western pull to her mysterious destination was stronger than ever, and she knew they would reach it soon. It seemed to Mary that every blow levied against her served only to further her cause. Jill's betrayal hadn't crippled Mary—instead it forced her hand, making her reveal her full plan to her skinjackers—leaving them bound to her spirit, and to her cause. And with Allie out there as an ever-present danger, rather than demoralizing Mary, it simply made her speed up her timetable. Thanks to Allie things would be moving much more quickly now.

Everything was aligning to lay a golden path before Mary now—a path she was ready to take, without looking back. The living world's end would be swift. Although she wasn't quite sure how, she knew there were many, many ways to bring about sudden, sweeping destruction. It was winter now; the living would have to enjoy their frostbitten fields and bone-chilling winds . . . because their world would never see the spring.

"Gather the others," she told them. "We leave now, and we don't rest until we reach our destination."

"What's our destination?" SoSo asked.

"Anywhere I say it is," Mary told him, and all of them agreed to follow, none of them knowing that any choice they had in the matter was snuffed the moment they were touched by Mary's beautiful tentacles of light.

CHAPTER 42

Sense and Sensibility and Skinjackers

Wolf River Convalescent Hospital in Memphis, Tennessee, overlooked Wolf River Lagoon, Mud Island, and the Missisippi River beyond, but the patients in the long-term maintenance ward had no interest in the view. They had no interest in anything at all.

The nursing staff knew better than to remove the offerings of loved ones unless they became a fire hazard. Mylar balloons, potted plants, and all sorts of bright decorations filled the many rooms of the ward, as if it were a perpetual party ... but nothing could mask the oppressive silence of the place.

Allie Johnson hadn't begun her convalescence here—but when the family moved to Memphis, they had Allie brought here, so they could still be close to her. The thought of abandoning her in the New Jersey facility was unthinkable. They had last come to visit on Christmas—the busiest day of the year, when relatives came out of the woodwork to sit in the lonely rooms, making them a little less lonely for a while.

On Christmas Day, just as on other special occasions, Allie's family lavished love upon her comatose body in every way they could. Her older sister trimmed and painted her nails, both fingers and toes, while playing Allie's favorite music. Her mother brushed the tangles out of her hair and gave her a haircut. Her father did the hard work of massaging her knotty muscles, softening them for the day they might be used once more. According to the doctors there was no brain damage—no reason why she shouldn't wake up. Except that she hadn't for four years.

Then her mother sat down and read yet another chapter from Jane Austin's *Sense and Sensibility*. She believed it was Allie's favorite book, but that was entirely untrue. Allie just thought the guy who starred in the movie had been cute. Then, after the reading was over, the melancholy began to set in as it always did, until it became too potent, and they decided it was time to leave. Her mother gave Allie a gentle kiss on her forehead, affixed a Christmas card to a bare spot on a wall already full of greeting cards, then promised to return on Valentine's Day.

As evening fell, families poured out the front door, no more comforted than when they came but at least feeling they had done the right thing. The ghost of Christmas present soon became the ghost of Christmas past, and silence descended in each room once more, punctuated only by the beeps and whirs of the machines that monitored and pumped and infused and labored to keep dozens of people existing in this strange state of living death.

"I'm not afraid of dying," Allie told Clarence, as they stood in front of the hospital, in the middle of the day, more than two weeks after her parents' Christmas visit. "For more than three years I thought I already was dead. I just want to know how bad off I am."

"Sounds like you're a little afraid of living."

"The only thing that scares me," said Allie, a little bit brusquely, "is a world ruled by Mary." Then she skinjacked a passerby.

"I'll be back soon," Allie said.

"If you're not, I'll understand."

"I said I'll be back!"

Then she turned and strode into the hospital.

Five minutes later she was in the body of one of the long-term care nurses, moving through the ward to room 509, which, according to hospital records, was where Allie's body lay in repose. "Repose"—that's what they called it here. A nice word for a terrible state. She waited until the other nurse on duty was occupied, then she took a deep breath . . . then another . . . then a third, as if she were about to go underwater. Then, still skinjacking the nurse, she stepped into the room.

Furniture was minimal. The greeting cards on the wall added a nice touch, but some of them had fallen, and now lay haphazardly on the ground, making it clear that decorations were not a high priority for the staff. Well, why should they be? There was no need for comfortable amenities here. The two soft chairs and the hotel-grade painting on the wall weren't there for the patient, they were there for visitors, to make *them* feel comfortable. None of it mattered to the living dead.

Allie forced herself to look at the figure in the bed before she lost her nerve. The sight took her breath away, as she knew it would.

It was bad, but not that bad.

It was shocking, but not all that shocking.

The girl in the bed was remarkably close to her memory of herself. Still, it was chilling. It was like seeing a ghost before you actually believed in them.

"Hello, Allie," she whispered.

Allie-in-the-bed did not respond. A feeding tube ran into her nose, but she had expected that. Her skin was pale, almost translucent. She had expected that, too. What she didn't expect were the painted nails and the state of her hair—not a gnarled mess, but brushed back from her face. A series of machines beeped and clicked and whirred. One machine had fat tubes stretching to each of her extremities, and pumped up rubber bladders of air, then let them go flat again with a slow hiss. Allie realized it was to help her circulation, but it gave the illusion that her arms and legs were moving ever so slightly.

The car accident had left its mark on her. There was a long, jagged scar across the right side of her forehead that went down her right cheek, and seemed to go under her hairline—but it was long healed. Other than that, her body and face were intact.

As she stepped closer, she began to feel the pull, like a secret undertow, tugging her forward. The closer she got, the stronger it became.

"Come home," her body silently said to her. *"My flesh is yours. I ache for you. I long for you to come home, dear sweet Allie, and make us both whole again."*

And now, in the presence of herself, she finally realized what she feared above all else. She feared the call of her own flesh.

"Come back to me, Allie. Be me, Allie."

The call of her body was now a riptide so strong she felt she would abandon the struggle against Mary just to leap inside it and be whole again. Would she leave Mikey, to grow up and grow old without him? And if she did, would she be able to live a normal, fulfilling life, knowing of all the things that existed in the places she couldn't see? Or would she spend her life trying to find the rabbit hole that would get her back to her own peculiar wonderland?

"You want this. It's right. It's natural. Leave this unnatural state while you still can. . . ."

But the voice wasn't coming from the bed at all, it was coming from her mind. And yes, everything it said was true, but some things were more important than fixing her own divided self. So she stood there within the nurse, keeping her spirit away from her body. It was painful. It was heart-rending. But still she resisted the riptide until she knew she could resist it as long as she had to.

Now she finally understood why she had to come. Until she faced herself, she was only running away . . . but to look at her own unseeing, half-open eyes and choose not to see through them again—that made her stronger and more determined than she'd ever been before. If there was a time to return to her body, it could not be now. If there was a time to go home, that time would have to wait. Allie still had work to do.

"Something wrong?"

Allie was startled by the voice behind her. She turned to see the other ward nurse standing in the doorway. Short cropped hair and a tired smile. "I saw that you weren't at your station," the other nurse said. "Is there a problem with this patient, Daisy? Do you need some help?"

"No, no," said Allie, and she knelt down. "I was just picking up some of the cards that had fallen. It's a shame — she's so young."

The other nurse sighed. "There's no rhyme or reason to these things. All we can do is make her comfortable."

"Right. And who knows, maybe she'll wake up someday."

The other nurse gave her that tired smile again. "Stranger things have happened." Then, seeing the tears in Allie's eyes, she said, "Go back to your station, Daisy. I'll pick up the rest of those cards."

Allie left, but she didn't go back to the nurse's station. She walked straight to the elevator, and took it down to the lobby. She would be happy to be out of this place, and in a different body — one that didn't remind her of hospitals. She looked down at her nurse's uniform, where the name "Daisy" was brightly embroidered on her breast pocket, and she resolved to skinjack the first nonmedical person she saw once she stepped out of that elevator . . . but the only person there when the elevator door opened was another nurse getting in. That's when Allie noticed something. . . .

The name "Daisy" was on the other nurse's uniform too.

As the elevator closed behind her, Allie realized that Daisy wasn't her name at all; it was the name of the company that manufactured the uniforms. Any other nurse would have known that.

Unless that nurse was being skinjacked.

* * *

Rotsie didn't like being in a woman's body, but it was the only one available, and a good soldier uses every resource at his disposal. He had never met Allie the Outcast, but his image of her had been larger than life. Yet here, lying on the bed before him was an ordinary girl. She was not larger than life at all. She was fragile, and easily put out of her misery.

It had all been easy enough until now. He had learned of her location by simple trial and error. He located the original accident report, and by skinjacking various people in various accounting offices, he followed the paper trail from an emergency room, to a hospital in New Jersey, to this hospital in Memphis.

At first he thought he might use a weapon—something suitable for an execution—but, although he would never admit it, he wasn't too keen on the sight of blood. In the end he decided a simple suffocation would do the trick. No mess, no noise. He leaned over Allie's body, took a pillow from behind her head, fluffed it a bit, then pressed it down over her face, already imagining how he'd announce to Mary that his mission had been accomplished.

The elevators were too slow, so Allie raced up five flights of stairs. The nurse she was skinjacking was not in the best of shape, and she was out of breath and dizzy by the time she reached the fifth floor. Allie could feel something happening to her, and she couldn't tell whether it was the nurse's body reacting to Allie's own panic or the feeling of her real body dying.

She burst out of the stairwell and raced down the hall-way to room 509. In the room, the nurse who had sent her out was suffocating Allie with a pillow. The body in the bed was bucking and quivering, but at least that meant she was still alive!

Allie didn't waste a moment. She let loose an angry wail and hurled herself at the nurse, knocking her over and taking her down to the ground. The pillow went flying. They struggled on the ground, but Allie had an advantage, having caught her by surprise. She hit the woman over and over until the murderous nurse's eyes went from steely anger to confusion and panic. Allie instantly knew the skinjacker had left her.

Then, before Allie could reassess, she was lifted off the ground by a very big, very bald male orderly who had the same look of determination the nurse had a moment ago.

"Mary wants you dead," the skinjacked orderly said, and pushed her up against the wall. "And I *always* complete my mission."

Allie didn't answer him. Instead she leaned forward and bit his nose so hard that he screamed. The pain was enough to knock him out of the orderly. Allie peeled out as well, to get a good look at the true face of Mary's assassin.

He was a tall kid in some sort of military uniform. Right now he was ankle-deep in the thin floor, trying to keep from sinking through. They made eye contact, but only for a moment.

Then they both heard the footsteps of hospital staff running toward the room, drawn by the commotion. In the room around them, the two nurses and the orderly still wailed and whimpered in their own personal shock and awe.

The assassin skinjacker staggered, slogging through

the ground, struggling to keep from sinking, and reached toward an approaching guard, hoping to skinjack his way back into the living world.

Well, if this tool of Mary's thought he could out-skinjack Allie, he had something else coming! Allie focused on the fleshie he was reaching for and leaped, zooming right past him, and skinjacked the fleshie before he could. She felt him try to get in, but couldn't because Allie was already there. He just bounced off like a pinball. Now Allie leaped to the next closest fleshie, and again she got there before the murderous skinjacker. And then she did it again, out-racing, out-jacking, outsmarting him every single time.

Finally, as she neared the elevator, she peeled back into Everlost to see where he was. Each one of Allie's preemptive skinjackings had left the assassin mired deeper in the floor. Now he was in the green linoleum tiles to his knees, and was near panic as he tried to keep himself from falling right through.

Just then, an elevator door opened before them—and there was a single fleshie inside. Allie hesitated, pretending she didn't see the man in the elevator, and the assassin threw himself forward toward the unsuspecting man. This was exactly what Allie was hoping the assassin would do! The moment he crossed the elevator threshold, Allie launched over him and skinjacked the man in the elevator first!

Now, ensconced in flesh, and seeing only the living world, Allie couldn't see the assassin skinjacker anymore—but she could feel him trying to get inside, desperately fighting to grab hold, but he couldn't get in. Allie had him exactly where she wanted him.

"Mission accomplished," she said. Then she hit the button for the top floor and the elevator began to rise.

Rotsie was furious. This girl had played him for a fool and now he knew he was in serious trouble. The fleshie in the elevator had already been skinjacked and the moment the elevator began to move, Rotsie realized the extent of his folly . . .

. . . because when the elevator went up, he didn't.

With nothing to grab on to, the living world elevator rose away from him, and he found himself plunging down a dark elevator shaft. He hit bottom, but didn't stop, because the living world could not provide enough resistance to catch his plummeting spirit. He found himself falling through the bottom of the elevator shaft, then through the basement, then through the first parking level, then the second.

Finally the thick cement floor of the second parking level caught him, but he was embedded all the way to his neck. He could feel the concrete of the building's foundation in his chest—not painful, but thick and oppressive, like heavy congestion. He could feel poles of iron rebar passing through his gut like skewers, and he could already feel his feet in the densely packed earth beneath the foundation. As much as he tried to pull himself out, each movement just pulled him farther down until his chin was in the concrete as well, then his mouth, then his nose, then his eyes, then his scalp, until the surface world was history and everything around him was darkness and he knew the only place he was going from now until the end of time, was down.

* * *

Allie, rather than feeling traumatized by her run-in with Mary's assassin, was filled with even more determination to stop her. She skinjacked a girl waiting at a bus stop, and met up with Clarence in a coffee shop. He was scouring newspapers, getting every last detail of Mary's latest disaster.

Clarence was beside himself when he heard what happened at the hospital. "I knew I shoulda come with you," he said. "I'll stay here in Memphis and protect your body, 'cause if I don't . . ."

"No," said Allie. "Mary doesn't know her assassin failed, so she won't send out another one for a while. That buys us some time."

"But when she does . . ."

"Then I'll deal with it," Allie told him. "If it happens, it happens—but while I can skinjack, I need to stand against Mary any way I can."

"In that case, have a look at this." Then Clarence showed her the latest headlines.

Allie thought it would be more on the toxic gas cloud, and fire in the town of Eunice—clearly Mary's hand at work—but instead it was something new. The town of Artesia, New Mexico, about seventy miles west of Eunice, had suffered a deadly tainting of the water supply. Being that Artesia was so close to Roswell, nut jobs were already coming out of the woodwork, insisting that it was aliens.

"It's ghosts, not aliens," Allie said. "People need to get their conspiracy theories straight."

"Read the next part," Clarence said, pointing to the bottom of the page.

Allie read on. Apparently the death count was relatively

low . . . which, if this was Mary's doing, didn't make much sense . . . until Allie saw how many people had been hospitalized . . . and were still in comas. . . .

Allie dropped the newspaper on the table as if it were also tainted.

"My God! She's making more skinjackers!"

Clarence took back the newspaper with his good hand and pondered the article, but it was clear he was pondering something else entirely. "I said I would never want to extinguish another soul," he said, "but if there's one spirit I'd be willing to wipe out of existence . . ."

He didn't need to finish his thought for Allie to know who he meant. "Whatever the consequences?" asked Allie.

Clarence nodded. "Whatever the consequences."

Allie took a deep breath. "Let's hope it doesn't come to that."

An hour later they were on a flight headed toward New Mexico and Mary Hightower.

PART SIX

Ruin Nation

Historical Interlude with Angry Gods and Insufficient Sunscreen

The living see only ruins. They see crumbling temples and a stepped pyramid rising out of a dense forest that, year by year, struggles to consume it. To the living, the place is ancient history, full of colorful custom, furious gods, and countless vendors selling trinkets—all very interesting, but irrelevant to a modern world. Still, the many touristts who come to the great Mayan city of Chichén Itzá can't help but feel a sense of mystical presence within the ruins that transcends time and space. No one who has ever visited Chichén Itzá will ever forget they've been there, and those who wander the ball court, and the great field that surrounds the pyramid, aside from getting a nasty sunburn, can't help but sense a spiritual connection to something unseen. They leave knowing they've had some inexplicable experience, never realizing that they have just crossed through a crowded, bustling city of seventeen thousand invisible souls.

CHAPTER 43

The City of Souls

From: memphisbelle95@yahoo.com

To: stopmarynow@gmail.com

Subject: 2 down

Hi, it's Allie skinjacking. Milos and Moose are dead. Jill, are you there? We need those other names! Jix, I hope you made it to the City of Souls, and that you're all okay. Tell Mikey and Nick hello. And be careful, all of you!

Allie

Back on New Year's Eve—the same day that Allie and Clarence first boarded the plane to Baltimore—Nick, Mikey, and Jix sailed for Chichén Itzá. They took the smallest of the Everlost racing yachts from Corpus Christi Marina, solemnly passing the hull of the doomed boat, which still floated upside down. They sailed southwest across the Gulf of Mexico, toward the Yucatan Peninsula. That first day, and all through the night, Mikey stood at the yacht's bow. The sun rose to his left at dawn, and he felt it shine through him, adding golden accents to his natural afterglow. Their boat did not pitch and roll with the motion of the sea; rather it glided as if skating on ice, regardless of what the living sea did around it, leaving no wake to mark their passage. Their journey offered no bursts of sea spray, no bow lurching to meet the waves. It was an indignation of Everlost that ocean voyages were stripped of their drama.

This was the first time Mikey had been at sea since his days as the McGill, and he couldn't help but feel a little nostalgic. Back then, his greatest pleasure was to be miserable in every possible way. Things were so much better now, but he did occasionally have an urge to wallow. This sleek sailing yacht was nothing like the dank rusty bulk of the old steamship, the *Sulphur Queen*. He couldn't say which he liked better: the rude character and brute force of the old vessel, or the sleek majesty of the yacht. Perhaps he'd be most at home with a combination of both. If the yacht's sails were windtattered, if its polished brass and varnished wood were scarred from a hundred successful voyages, it would have suited him, because character should always come before beauty.

Jix, who knew full well what was in store for them, chose not to brief Mikey and Nick until the fourth day, when the Yucatan shoreline was already visible on the distant horizon, and changing their minds ceased to be an option. Then he sat them down in the galley, and told them all they needed to know about the City of Souls and His Excellency, the Supreme King of the Middle Realm.

"It is a very old city," Jix told them. "And he is a very old soul. From a time when things were very different. When we arrive, you will be formally announced and I will present you." Then Jix paused, knowing the next part would be difficult to swallow. "I will be presenting you to the king as gifts."

"Excuse me?" said Mikey "Did you say 'gifts'?"

"It's the only way to get you into his court. Otherwise you will be confined to the ripening caves for years, until you forget your past and remember nothing but the City of Souls. "

"I'm nobody's property," grumbled Mikey, growing himself a pair of inadvertent fangs that he drew back once Nick glared at him.

Jix showed no emotion in his response. "If you wish to stop your sister, then you will do as I say. The king will become your ally only if you approach him with absolute humility, then win him over."

Nick sighed. "Then we're in trouble. Mikey doesn't do humility."

"If all goes well, you may not be palace slaves for long." Jix thought for a moment, pondering what he should say and what he shouldn't. "His Excellency has another name," Jix told them. "They call him 'the Unremembering King.' It has to do with his memory. The things he remembers and the things he doesn't."

"So he forgets things?" scoffed Mikey. "Big deal. Who isn't forgetful in Everlost?"

"No," said Jix patiently "He's not forgetful, he's *unremembering*. There's a big difference, and you will know that difference. It is the very core of his power."

"What does that mean for us?" asked Nick

"It means that he will have a very short attention span

for you," Jix explained, "and when he tires of treating you as playthings, he may unremember you into a position of power. But take care, because there are others who seek power in the City of Souls. . . ."

"Like you?" asked Mikey, almost an accusation.

"I," said Jix, "will be the least of your troubles."

Upon seeing the approaching yacht, winged messengers went soaring over the forest toward the city, and by the time the yacht neared shore, an army numbering a thousand was there to capture the intruders, whoever they were.

"His Excellency believes in excess," Jix told Nick and Mikey, as they sailed closer to the waiting army.

Mikey and Nick were less than thrilled by the huge battalion of tribal warriors, each armed with nasty-looking sharp objects. Although they knew the weapons technically couldn't hurt them, there was nothing pleasant about being riddled with arrows, or impaled by a spear, or hacked by a machete—and if this king was as resourceful as Jix said, perhaps he had found a way to inflict pain, or at least unrelenting discomfort.

"They'll recognize you, right?" asked Nick. "Because you work for the king."

Jix mewled a little, then said, "Not necessarily." Then he turned to Mikey. "Quickly—explain to me your power. What kind of things can you turn yourself into?"

"I can't make myself something real, if that's what you're asking. I can't be a giraffe or a jaguar or an elephant—it has to be something I make up, and I'm never sure how it's going to look."

Jix pondered that, fiddling with his whiskers. "I think we can work with that."

Five minutes later, the yacht had run aground, and the entire army had lowered their weapons, gawking in awe at a creature that was part vulture, part fish, and part iguana, with scales like golden kernels of maize. Taken together, they were four of the holiest of Mayan symbols. The only thing holier was the boy riding the beast: a jaguar spirit, and what appeared to be his dark, oozing shadow riding behind him. When the strange beast leaped off the boat onto shore, none of the warriors dared to disturb it, because clearly it was sent from the gods. Then when the creature turned itself into a boy, the guards picked up their weapons once more, but only to protect the three boys, and escort them inland to the City of Souls.

Jix spoke to their escorts in a language that baffled Nick and Mikey. "It's Mayan," he explained. "The language of the kingdom. But don't worry; the king speaks English."

"How could he learn a language that didn't exist before he died?" asked Mikey, who knew that an Afterlight's set of skills could never surpass his or her fleshly education.

"He didn't have to learn it," was all Jix offered as an explanation.

They marched on well-worn dirt paths that had crossed into Everlost. The forest around them was filled with trees that lived, and trees that had crossed. It seemed Everlost had much more of a footprint here than in the North.

They marched through the night, and just after dawn they came to a high stone wall that stretched out in either direction for as far as the eye could see, and in the center of the wall was a triangular wooden gate, barring their entrance.

Mikey and Nick suspected that an ancient city might have such a wall, but what they saw atop that wall made it clear that this wasn't just an ancient city, it was an Everlost city. All along the ramparts were strange-looking spirits, their mouths open wider than normal mouths, like living gargoyles, and their feet—if they even *had* feet— were embedded in the stone. They all wore brightly colored headdresses full of feathers and gold, and there were hundreds of them, probably enough to stretch all the way around the city.

"The wailers," said Jix, with an exasperated sigh.

At the sight of the approaching crowd, they began to shriek, their eyes fixing on the three new arrivals. Then, in a minute or two, those screeches resolved into song, sometimes dissonant and sometimes harmonic. Their song was in Mayan, and was strangely hypnotic.

"They are announcing us to the king," Jix explained. "Telling their impressions of each of us—but I suspect the king won't be listening. He never listens to the wailers anymore. He's lost interest in them."

"What are they saying?" asked Mikey.

"They're talking about me," Jix said. "They're saying that I look familiar, yet very suspicious. . . . Now they're talking about Nick. They say that you are made of rotten tree-resin, and you're highly suspicious. . . . Now they're talking about you, Mikey. They seem to like you."

"Really?"

"Yes," said Jix, "but they're very suspicious of spirits they like."

The song continued, and the army, which was apparently used to this, waited with practiced patience.

"Now they're debating whether or not you should be thrown into the Cenote," Jix explained. "That's a bottomless pool that goes to Xibalba, the Mayan underworld . . . although I suspect it really just goes to the center of the Earth."

"Thanks for sharing," said Mikey.

That made Nick laugh, which was something, because Mikey was never known to make anyone laugh.

The strange song of the wailers soon changed, becoming more melodic, building toward a crescendo. "They're singing the song of opening," Jix told them. "When they're done, the guards will open the gates."

"How long will this take?" asked Mikey.

"As long as they feel like," said Jix. "The wailers are a pain."

And sure enough they went on singing for another half hour, until finally they reached the last note which, since Afterlights need no air to sing, lasted four whole minutes. Then the song came to a dramatic end and the gates began to swing open. Immediately Nick and Mikey were struck by light and color so bright they had to look away.

"Welcome," said Jix, a little bit proud, and a little embarrassed, "to the City of Souls."

No one who has seen the City of Souls is ever the same. There are sights and sounds to boggle the most worldly mind and fill it with both elation and terror. Spirits with the colorful wings of parrots soared overhead in formation, dancing in the sky, while on the ground below, Afterlights adorned with gold, jade, onyx, and impossibly bright feathers engaged in all sorts of joyous activities. Troops of dancers stomped and gyrated in circles everywhere. Crowds moved in swarms, seeming to have no purpose other than moving and swarming. Magicians performed amazing feats and jugglers hurled balls of flame high into the sky. The entire city was a single massive party that had raged for eons and showed no signs of slowing.

"As I told you," Jix said, "the king likes excess."

"Right. More is more," said Mikey.

"No," said Jix, "as far as His Excellency is concerned, 'more' is not nearly enough."

Nick was so bewildered, he couldn't speak. While he still remembered nothing of his life, he had a momentary flash to a trip he had taken with his family to Las Vegas. He recalled the dazzling assault of light, color, and sound—sensory overload, everything competing violently for his attention. Well, the City of Souls was so much more intense, it made Las Vegas feel like a lazy Sunday suburb. The sight of it would probably kill the living—or at the very least drive them insane.

It was only as Mikey and Nick looked closer that a darker side of this eternal celebration revealed itself. The dancers, so full of rhythm and grace, needed no voices to perform. So they no longer had mouths. The many street singers, so full of joyous vocal tones, didn't need to see their audience. So they no longer had eyes. The artisans, who worked only in color and texture, had no need for ears. And the wandering minstrels, who had no need to ever put down their instruments, now had their instruments growing right out of them.

"Eww!" said Mikey, a bit embarrassed that he, master of all imaginable monstrosities, actually said "Eww."

"Well . . . uh . . . they seem to be . . . happy," Nick offered, uneasily. "It's kind of like an extreme version of Mary's 'perfect day.'"

"We all find our place in the City of Souls," said Jix, looking around at the strange living mosaic. "But none of this is for their pleasure. It's all for the king's amusement. This entire place is *his* perfect day."

They came around a huge temple and before them stood the pyramid of Kukulcan, the feathered serpent god, which was engraved in gold on every side. While the living world saw the pyramid as a crumbling ruin, in Everlost its limestone was smoothly chiseled and shining white.

However, it wasn't the sight of the pyramid that stopped them in their tracks. It was the object behind it.

"No!" gasped Mikey. "It can't be!" Mikey felt himself beginning to turn inside out, but swallowed, keeping his innards from switching places with his outards.

"This could be really, really good," said Nick, "or really, really bad."

There, moored to the top of the great pyramid of Kukulcan, was the largest gas-filled object ever built by man. The *Hindenburg* sat in the heart of Chichén Itzá, its sliver skin reflecting the tropical sun, looking like it belonged there.

"Hmm," said Jix. "I've never seen that before. I guess the king found a new way to get around."

CHAPTER 44

Zero Recall

The Unremembering King had the power to create a barrier of wind in a world that had no wind, in order to keep certain intruders from crossing the Mississippi.

The Unremembering King could speak any language instantly upon hearing it.

The Unremembering King could bring lightning from the sky to make his own afterglow shine brighter than anyone else's.

Such tall tales were common in Everlost, but when it came to Yax K'uk Mo', The Supreme King of the Middle Realm, every tale was true. He had been in Everlost for many thousands of years, and his true name and true life were long forgotten . . . until one day, he unremembered the fact that he wasn't a Mayan king. So suddenly he was. And as a king he felt he should set up court in the halls and temples of Chichén Itzá, and declare dominion over all lands that had once been Mayan. He unremembered that he had no actual claim to those lands—yet by the awesome power of his unmemory, every Afterlight existing in those places instantly believed that he was their king without knowing or meeting him.

And shouldn't a Mayan king have power over the heavens and glow brighter than all the other Afterlights? So suddenly he did, because he couldn't remember that he shouldn't. Naturally it was easy for him to speak all languages when he couldn't remember a single language he didn't know. It was the same way with the flying red-winged spirits. Being from Mesoamerica, he had never seen people with red hair, and so when he did, he thought them beautiful, like the red-crowned parrot of the Yucatan jungles. He unremembered that these spirits didn't have parrot wings, and so all spirits he saw with red hair instantly grew wings the color of their hair, and could fly—which thrilled the spirits, unless they had a fear of heights.

The power of unremembering made King Yax the mighty ruler that he was—and when it came to unremembering, the only limit to the things he couldn't not do, was his imagination.

Unfortunately, King Yax did not have much of an imagination, so mostly he just spent his time being amused by Mayan sports, loud parties, and admiring his own glow.

Lately, however, his attentions had been elsewhere.

For many years an ironsmith had been laboring to create a statue in his image by melting down the coins of all fresh souls who came to his kingdom. Until recently it hadn't been much of a statue—a thin, headless, and armless thing on a huge black obsidian base. There simply had never been enough metal to finish it—and in Everlost, nothing else made of metal melted. Things were annoyingly permanent.

But the coins, which behaved like nothing else in Everlost, *did* melt. Where, then, was a king to find more coins? It was useless trying to unremember his lack of coins, because, try as he might, he couldn't forget he had none left.

And then the giant silver balloon arrived with two foreigners bearing the greatest gift he had ever received. A bucket full of coins! And not just any bucket—this bucket was bottomless! As soon as it was empty, all one need do was look away, and when one looked again, the bucket held however many coins as there were souls present. His latest ironsmith quickly got to work, and whenever the coin supply was depleted, the king threw a party in the Temple of the Jaguar, until the bucket filled itself once again, and then he threw everyone out.

The king's ironsmith was a large boy who had the misfortune to die while wearing a blue luchador mask—a wrestling disguise that covered his whole head, leaving him looking somewhat like an executioner. No one knew what he looked like under the *lucha libre* mask, and no one ever would. The blue luchador worked tirelessly melting down the coins, with gloves on his hands to protect him from the coins' magic. Then, as the metal cooled, he pounded them flat into thin skins that were then applied to the surface of the statue and shaped by hammer into a perfect likeness of the king.

"Add more muscle," he would tell the luchador, for he had long since unremembered how scrawny he had once been. "The gods will be pleased," he would often say, for a Mayan king was a reflection of the gods, so the more glory that he heaped upon himself the greater the joy of the gods—or so he reasoned. Overseeing this project was so important, he gave his vizier control over the kingdom—everything but allowing him to sit on the throne—primarily because the throne had been moved in front of the forge to face the statue. The vizier—a sort of mystical spiritual advisor—was more than happy to run the kingdom.

As the statue neared completion, the more obsessed with it the king became. He had unremembered that the statue was a worthless tribute to his own arrogance . . . and by the power of his own unremembrance, he turned something worthless into the single most important object in the world.

Upon arriving, Jix, Mikey, and Nick were brought directly to the forge. Had the vizier been able to intercept them, things might have gone differently, because he had a tendency to make visitors disappear before ever reaching the king—but the vizier was with the king at the time, so couldn't prevent His Excellency from seeing them.

The vizier, however, behaved very oddly today. The moment the new arrivals were brought into the forge, the vizier hurried behind the statue to hide. The king might have wondered why, if he weren't so absorbed in watching the metal-molding luchador build his glorious likeness.

Jix walked into his field of vision, and the king seemed annoyed. "Your Excellency," said Jix. "I have returned with gifts from the North." He spoke in English so the king would respond in the same tongue.

"Oh," said the king. "It's you. Didn't we just send you on a mission?"

"That was more than a month ago, Your Excellency."

Nick hung back with Mikey and watched the interchange, trying to take in everything around him. Nick studied the king, his shiny black onyx throne, the statue, and the diligent luchador—even the vizier, who peered out every few moments from behind the statue, so hidden in shadows he could barely be seen. Nick's gut told him that something was very wrong here, but he couldn't put his finger on what it was. As for the king, Nick found him to be overadorned and so full of himself that he might just explode in a flurry of glitter. He had straight hair, as dark and shiny as raven feathers. He wore a golden headdress, golden wrist cuffs and golden anklets, and a golden skirt that went almost to his knees, and the way his hair was cut in bangs straight across his forehead, it made him look like a very short, very tan, very shiny Mr. Spock. Other than the gold adornments, though, the king had no other clothes. It was clear that these objects were all add-ons, and didn't cling to him as Everlost clothes would. Nick suspected that he either crossed naked, or in a loincloth beneath his golden skirt—but Nick was definitely not curious enough to check.

"Your assignment was to bring us the Eastern Witch," the king said to Jix, "but neither of these two look like her, unless she is very clever with disguises."

"DON'T TRUST THEM!" screeched the vizier from behind the statue. "CAST THEM DOWN TO XIBALBA. THE STARS TELL ME THEY WILL BRING YOUR DOOM."

While Jix looked concerned, and Mikey just annoyed, something about the vizier's voice tripped in Nick's mind. His thought processes had gotten better, but he was still not fully himself. There were memories and thoughts bouncing around his head that had not found a suitable place to cling . . . and one of those loose memories was the sound of the vizier's voice. Was it his imagination or did the vizier sound familiar?

The king just reclined on his dark stone throne, dismissing the fearful prophecy with a wave of his hand, as if swatting away a gnat. "We see no stars; it is daytime." Then he turned to the luchador. "It is daytime, isn't it?" But apparently he had been in there for so long, he had no idea.

"Why does he keep saying 'we'?" Mikey whispered to Jix. "Are there more than one of him in there?"

"No," Jix whispered back. "Royalty always does that, even if there's just one."

"We do not approve of secret conversations," said the king. "We demand to know what you are talking about!"

"We're talking about the Eastern Witch, Your Excellency," said Jix. "She is a powerful enemy: She broke through your barrier of wind, and at this moment she threatens to destroy the living world."

"What do we care about the living world?" said the king.

Suddenly Mikey stepped forward and spoke brashly. "If she does it, then thousands, maybe millions, will be under her control, and she will declare herself Queen of Everlost."

The king raised an eyebrow. "It speaks!"

"I'm not an 'it,'" growled Mikey.

Jix grimaced, but the king merely gave his gnat-chasing wave. "Of course you're an 'it.' You are an 'it' until we say that you are not."

Mikey opened his mouth to say something, but the king

cut him off. "Being an 'it' makes you an object, and we don't ever remember seeing an object move of its own free will. No, we don't remember that at all."

Then all at once, Mikey was frozen in place, unable to move, standing as stiff as the statue, thanks to the king's unremembrance.

"Now, then," said the king, "what is this other gift you bring me?"

"A boy of chocolate," said Jix.

The king smiled. "This is something new." He rose from his throne and approached Nick, looking him over, dabbing his finger to the tip of Nick's nose and then tasting the chocolate on his fingertip. Then the king laughed. "We should forget that there aren't more spirits like you!" the king said. "And perhaps we'll forget them in different flavors. Coconut, strawberry, tamarind . . ."

"Please, Your Excellency," said Nick, thinking quickly, "I am one-of-a-kind, and if there were more, I wouldn't be the special gift that I am. One flavorful spirit for the one true king."

The king considered it. "Very well. But we may choose to unremember your flavor if the royal taste buds tire of chocolate."

"That," said Nick, "would be fine with me."

"DESTROY THEM," hissed the vizier, still hiding behind the statue. "THROW THEM INTO THE CENOTE RIGHT NOW."

The king sighed. "Our vizier doesn't like you, but we have yet to pass judgment." Then he turned to Mikey, who was still unable to move. "Your chocolate friend's wisdom has saved you. We shall unremember that you are an object that cannot move." And in an instant, Mikey was no longer frozen in place.

"So," said the king. "We assume that the jaguar-boy would not bring us a gift that did nothing." The king folded his arms, looking intently at Mikey. "We order you to impress us!"

Jix nodded to Mikey, and Mikey transformed into various spontaneous creations. The king actually applauded.

"We are truly amused! The gods themselves would be amused!"

Mikey transformed back into himself, and folded his arms in the same superior way that the king had done.

"You shall be my personal mascot!" said the king. "I shall parade you on a diamond-studded leash and you will become whatever creation I desire."

Mikey stared at him, eyes bulging furiously, growing more and more veins.

The king matched his anger, staring into those bulging eyes. "Do I sense that my mascot has become unruly? Perhaps I should listen to my vizier's advice."

"YES, YES!" yelled the vizier. "LISTEN TO ME AND SEND THEM TO XIBALBA!"

Mikey's eyes bulged just a little bit more . . . and then, to everyone's amazement, Mikey got down on his knees, then on all fours, and spread himself out on the floor before the king.

"I will be a rug before your feet, your Excellency, from now until the end of time, if you agree to battle the Eastern Witch." Then he transformed himself into something flat and furry. He would have resembled a bear-skin rug if he didn't have a dozen eyes.

The king looked at him a bit disgusted. "We have enough rugs," he said. "But we like the way you think." The king tapped his lip, as he considered the rug-boy before him. "We've changed our mind. If you will entertain, with brand new forms that we have never seen before, We shall agree not to put you on a leash if we can help it."

Mikey transformed back into himself, and bowed. "Your Excellency has a most gentle and merciful spirit."

"Of course we do," the king said.

"But about the Eastern Witch . . . ," Mikey said.

"The Eastern Witch will wait until we feel like dealing with her."

"CAST THEM DOWN NOW," the vizier cried out. "DO IT, BEFORE IT'S TOO LATE!"

The king shook his head. "Our vizier is having a bad day."

It was Jix who spoke up. "Your Excellency, pardon me for being so forward . . . but I think that any spirit who has a mind to condemn me and my gifts, should do it to my face."

"Very well," the king said. He snapped his fingers to the blue luchador. "Fetch the vizier for us."

The luchador put down his metal-working tools, went behind the statue, grabbed the vizier, and although he tried to escape, he was much smaller and weaker. The luchador was able to lift him up by his armpits and bring him to the king, in spite of the way he squirmed and kicked.

"We present to you the Royal Vizier," the king said, and Nick just stared at him in disbelief. Finally, that stray bouncing memory stuck in his mind like a spit wad, and he said, "Vari?"

The small, curly-blond boy looked at Nick with that permanently pinched face he always had when he had served as Mary's rotten little toady.

"CAST THEM OUT! SEND THEM DOWN! XIBALBA! XIBALBA!" Vari screeched.

The king was hugely amused. "You know each other?"

"Vari used to serve the Eastern Witch," Nick said.

"Well, now," said the king. "At last our day has become interesting."

The path that brought Vari to Chitchén Itzá was a strange one. He had shed his name of "Stradivarius," pretending to be the McGill when he sailed in the *Sulphur Queen* across the Atlantic Ocean, but that didn't last very long. He might have been an excellent violin player, but he was a lousy monster. Still, he had seen the wonders of Atlantis . . . and then had been thrown out. He had seen the glory of Pompeii . . . and had been exiled from it. He had strode the halls of the great library of Alexandria . . . and had been tossed down its thousand steps and told never to return by the Afterlights who inhabited it.

While Pinhead—his second-in-command—had found a cushy job giving guided tours of the Tower of Babel, Vari had no such luck. Wherever he went, he eventually wore out his welcome because he was so painfully irritating. Sure, everyone enjoyed the melody of a well-played violin, but it was hardly worth putting up with the boy who played it.

He thought he might fit in with a horde of young Vikings because he looked somewhat Scandinavian. But after only a month, he was set adrift aboard a perpetually burning Viking funeral ship.

Eventually, he got picked up by the *Titanic* which had been taken over by a gang of angry dead Icelandic youth, who seemed content to do nothing but hunt narwhal . . . but since narwhal had never been known to cross into Everlost, nothing was ever caught. He got a gig as the second violin in the *Titanic*'s string quartet, but there was only so long he could stand playing "Nearer My God To Thee" over and over, with no actual hope of hitting an iceberg and sinking. Eventually he hatched a mutiny plan, which failed miserably, and, once more, he was set adrift—this time in a lifeboat.

After several months at sea, he landed on the Yucatan Peninsula, where he was caught by the king's army and brought to the king. Vari quickly learned that his knowledge of the world made him a valuable spirit to the king. At last he was appreciated.

Since time immemorial, the king's vizier had been a pudgy Toltec girl who told fortunes by reading entrails of goats—which were extremely hard to come by in Everlost—and while fortune cookies always yielded undeniable truths, goat entrails were a little bit iffy. Once Vari told the king about the Eastern Witch, the king (at Vari's suggestion) hurled the Toltec girl into the Cenote and put Vari in charge of all prognostication. Now, as the king became more and more entranced by his statue, the kingdom fell more and more into Vari's hands, which is exactly what he wanted. Things had been looking up for Vari. Until today.

To: stopmarynow@gmail.com
From: Bobwurldtravlur@aol.com

Subject: We're in the City of Souls

It's Jix. Good work Allie with milos & moose. Worried about Jill. King hard 2 convince 2 join us. Mikey says stay safe, allie. Guess what? Hindenburg is here.

Sent from bob's iphone

After several days home, Jix was getting increasingly anxious. Home simply did not feel like home anymore. All the noise and excitement seemed to pale now that there was something truly worthy of his attention. And someone. Jix would skinjack tourists on a regular basis, using their iPhones, or whatever they had, to check the e-mail address that Allie set up, hoping for a message from Jill, but usually the "stopmarynow" mailbox was either empty or had an update from Allie. The fact that no e-mails had come from Jill was a very bad omen, and made him want to get back to a place where he could help her, or at least find her. He knew that Mikey felt the same about Allie. The distance, and the lack of interest from the king in their cause, made them feel helpless.

From past experience, Jix knew that the king could be conjoled into doing many things if he thought it was his own idea. Such cajoling, however, could take months. Usually time was not an issue, but they didn't have months. The one good thing was the airship. It could provide them with a fast means of getting them where they needed to go, if only the king would see how serious the threat was. If not, Jix resolved that he, Mikey, and Nick would take it themselves . . . although without the king, his power of unremembrance, and his army, their chances against Mary Hightower were slim.

Johnnie-O and Choo-choo Charlie had no idea where or what Chichén Itzá was when the *Hindenburg* arrived. All they knew was that being there was heaven on earth. The angels—who turned out not to be actual angels at all, but redheaded kids with wings—brought the drifting airship down from the heavens. The arrival of the giant airship was enough to bring the king out to personally greet them, thinking it might be the long-awaited arrival of the gods. When they turned out not to be gods, the king's vizier adamantly insisted they be sent to Xibalba, but he was overruled when Johnnie-O presented the king with the bucket of coins. As far as the king was concerned, that bottomless bucket was more valuable than all the gold in Everlost. It was, in short, the greatest tribute that the king had ever received.

"Let it be known," announced the king, "that We are generous to those who are generous with us." Thus, Johnnie-O and Charlie were rewarded with a team of personal servants, and a never-ending feast in the Hall of a Thousand Columns. All manner of crossed food and drink were set before them on a continual basis, and since Afterlights never got full, and never gained weight, it was a perfect, if somewhat overindulgent way to spend eternity. Charlie even stopped singing long enough to stuff his face.

They had been happily dining for more than a week when Nick showed up in the City of Souls, and when Johnnie-O saw him, he embraced Nick like it was a family reunion. However, their tender moment ended abruptly once Nick opened his mouth.

"We need to convince the king to go after Mary," he told Johnnie.

"What are you, nuts?" Johnnie said, his mouth stuffed with something that tasted like chicken. "Forget it. Mary's not our problem anymore."

"She's *my* problem and that makes her your problem."

"We don't work for you anymore," Johnnie-O said. "We quit."

Nick grabbed him, getting chocolate all over his shirt sleeve. "If we stay here, Mary will eventually come to the City of Souls with enough Afterlights to overthrow the king. Can you imagine this place under Mary?"

Johnnie-O scowled at him. With Mary in charge, the city would no longer be the endless party that it was, and there wouldn't be an eternal smorgasbord for him and Charlie. "Why do you keep ruining my death?"

Nick turned to Charlie, trying to reason with him as well, but Charlie just smiled back as he ate, saying nothing.

From the outside world's perspective, it might have appeared that Choo-choo Charlie had completely lost his mind, but in truth, he had never been more at peace with his place in the universe. Now the songs that had been coming out of his mouth were merrily rolling along in his head instead, swirling into one another. Although all the words of all the songs were different, the meaning to him was the same.

You're ready, Charlie, the songs said. *It's time to move on.*

He knew it since he first began to sing, and he could have taken a coin from the bucket, held it in his hand, and completed his journey at any time. He didn't want to do that to Johnnie-O, though. He couldn't leave Johnnie alone. But as long as he had the songs in his head, he didn't mind waiting—even if he had to wait until the end of time. Now he understood how the souls at the center of the earth felt. He was one of them now, full of patience, perfectly centered in himself, even without being centered in the earth.

It was only now that Nick was here, that Charlie felt he could leave Johnnie. So, on the evening that Nick arrived, Charlie left the Hall of a Thousand Columns and went to the forge. The king was out, making Mikey perform transformations for the king's closest personal flatterers, which included the luchador, so no one was guarding the statue. Charlie thought he was alone. He had no idea that he had been followed.

He walked closer to the statue, skillfully crafted from the thousands of coins collected from the souls of Chichén Itzá, and the coins taken from the bucket. The statue looked like King Yax K'uk Mo' but that was just a clever lie. No amount of disguise could hide the truth from Charlie. You could melt the coins down, pound them out, and make them look like some king's face, but it didn't change what they were. They were the way out.

"Charlie . . . ?"

He turned, surprised to see Nick standing there.

"What are you doing here?" Nick asked.

Charlie found that he had no words to explain all he was thinking and feeling, so instead he began to sing.

"Should auld acquaintance be forgot, and never brought to mind . . ."

Then before he could change his mind or be pulled away, he reached out his hand . . .

"*Should auld acquaintance be forgot, and days of auld lang syne . . .*"

. . . and he touched the statue.

"Charlie, no!"

But the deed was done. A coin-size piece of the statue vanished, and a tunnel appeared before him with a light at its end, both bright and warm. Suddenly all the memories that had been lost to Charlie came back to him.

Something was talking in his head now too—not a voice, but a feeling. It was something he knew he was meant to share, but his mind was so full of memories of the life he had lived, it was hard to make room for the words that were fuzzily forming in his head. Still, he tried to get them out as best as he could, because he knew he didn't have much time.

"Fat Alamo . . . the Trinity . . . Ground Zero . . ."

"Charlie?"

"Hey, that's right! Charlie really is my name! How about that?"

Then he shot down the tunnel into the light and got where he was going.

CHAPTER 45
Mikey, the God

There was only so much Mikey could take, so many petty transformation requests from the king and his flatterers that he could stomach. He had once told Clarence that he was not a circus monkey, yet this was his role in the court of King Yax, and although the king promised no leash, he might as well have been on one. Jix had told him to have patience, but that had never been, nor would it ever be, one of Mikey McGill's virtues.

When he tired of showing Mikey off around the city, the king boarded his sedan chair, carried by four strong subjects, each with one shoulder substantially lower than the other. He made Mikey walk.

"Come, changeling," the king said, "we shall return to the forge to witness the completion of the statue, and you shall entertain us with your transformations there."

They made their way through the dancing, singing, partying crowds, and as they crossed the huge grass square, where the shadow of the pyramid fell, Mikey came across Jix.

"This isn't working," he told Jix, lagging far enough

behind the king so he couldn't hear. "I can change myself into too many things—he'll never get bored."

"Yes, it's a problem," Jix admitted.

"And I have a solution," said Mikey. "But I need you to distract the king so I can get away."

"Not now, I'm busy" said Jix. "The king's vizier has vanished, and I have to find him."

"Why?" said Mikey. "Vari's a weasel. If you can't find him, it's good riddance. I'd be happy to never see him again."

"Yes, but weasels are sneaky," said Jix, "and he's likely to pop out of the mulberry bush at the worst possible time."

"Look for him later. Distract the king now," Mikey said. "I promise you'll be glad you did."

And so reluctantly, Jix made his way to the front of the sedan chair.

"Your Excellency," Jix said. "I need to discuss with you the . . . uh . . . the Inca threat to our southern border."

"What Inca threat?" asked the king. "Why weren't we informed of this?"

While behind them, Mikey slipped away.

Ten minutes later, the City of Souls was besieged by a creature standing atop the pyramid, and was rocked by a voice so loud, that it shook the ground.

"YAX K'UK MO'!"

All eyes turned to the pyramid, where a fearsome plumed serpent with searing jade eyes peered down from the pyramid peak.

"YAX K'UK MO'!"

The creature looked very much like the carvings and

mosaics of Kukulcan, the single most powerful Mayan god. Of course, it did look a little bit different from the artwork, with few extra eyes in the wrong places—but who could expect human artists to capture the likeness of a god?

The king, who was still being briefed by Jix on the nonexistent Inca threat, rose from his sedan chair, shaking in such terror that all his gold rattled. "We are being summoned by the God of the Elements!"

"YAX K'UK MO'," the god commanded, "YOU HAVE ANGERED THE GODS, AND HAVE MISTREATED MY MESSENGERS. I SUMMON YOU NOW TO MY PYRAMID. DO NOT KEEP ME WAITING!" And the god breathed out fire for emphasis.

Still trembling, the king left his sedan chair and struggled to climb the steps of the pyramid while his entire kingdom watched.

"We are here, Lord Kukulcan," said the king as he arrived. "We will do whatever you desire."

"FIRST OF ALL," the glorious feathered serpent said, "YOU WILL NO LONGER REFER TO YOURSELF AS 'WE.' IT'S ANNOYING. YOU ARE AN 'I,' JUST LIKE EVERYONE ELSE."

"Yes, Lord Kukulcan."

"AND YOU WILL TREAT MY MESSENGERS FROM THE NORTH WITH RESPECT, AND HEED THE THINGS THEY SAY, OR I SHALL PUT THE MIDDLE-REALM IN WORTHIER HANDS."

"Yes, Lord Kukulcan."

Then the god addressed the entire kingdom. "KING YAX K'UK MO' WILL LEAD YOU INTO BATTLE

AGAINST THE EASTERN WITCH, BECAUSE IT WILL PLEASE ME TO SAVE THE LIVING WORLD FROM DESTRUCTION."

"Yes, Lord Kukulcan," said King Yax. "Whatever you say, O God of the elements, O God of healing, O God of rebirth, O God of—"

"—ENOUGH OF THAT!" said the serpent. "NOW GO AND DO AS I SAID!" Then the serpent roared and hissed and spun and vanished in a fiery burst of flame.

When the god was gone, everyone turned to the king for direction, but it took all his strength just to get down from the pyramid without falling.

As all eyes were on the king, nobody noticed the boy running down the stone steps at the back of the pyramid, trying to make the last of his feathers go away.

Once properly motivated, the king wasted no time in preparing the journey to battle the Eastern Witch. Fearing that someone would install themselves as king in his absence, he decided to take the entire population with him. He even unstuck the wailers from the city wall. "Where I go, the kingdom goes," King Yax declared, struggling to use the word "I."

Since Afterlights can squeeze themselves into any confined space, with virtually no added weight, the king ordered the entire population into the vast infrastructure of the *Hindenburg*—even those with wings, just in case they decided to fly the coop on the way. He installed the completed statue of himself in the stairwell landing, because it was too big, and too tall, to get any farther into the ship. "All my subjects will see its glory as they come up the gangway stairs," he proclaimed.

While the City of Souls piled itself into the great airship, King Yax gave "the messengers of Kukulcan," an entire temple, and a phalanx of guards to protect them.

To Nick, however, it felt more like house arrest. Mikey paced, Jix tried to hide his anxiety by grooming himself, and Johnnie-O, who was depressed that Charlie was gone, did nothing but complain.

. . . Fat Alamo, the Trinity, Ground Zero . . .

Charlie's words stuck in Nick's mind. He could have dismissed them as the randomness of a spirit in transition, but he knew that one never thought more clearly than at the moment before disappearing into the light. Watching Charlie leave Everlost struck Nick harder than anyone else's exit. He knew he should have been happy—after all, it had been Nick's entire purpose to free the souls stuck here—but watching a friend go was always difficult to bear.

Every day Nick was more and more himself. His fingers were emerging from the chocolate. Spots of white appeared on his shirt. Bit by bit, Nick was coming back from the brown. With it, however, came a sense of responsibility, and the kind of heartache he felt upon seeing Charlie go. It was almost easier being the simpleminded ogre, who understood little and had no depth to his emotions.

Since Nick had been given the cryptic message—if it was even a message at all—it left him as the new unofficial leader of the group. It had been a long time since Nick had been in a position of leadership.

"The king thinks the gods will direct him to Mary

Hightower," Jix said. "Which I might believe if the gods had actually spoken to him, but they didn't." He glanced over to Mikey, who got defensive.

"What are you looking at me for? I got him to go to war with my sister, didn't I? Isn't that what we were trying to do?"

"We need to figure out what Charlie was trying to say," Nick reminded them.

"Why?" said Johnnie. "Why bother? I say we stay here after the freakin' blimp leaves, and eat all the food king 'Yakin' Kook Moon' leaves behind!"

"No, Nick is right," said Jix. "We can't just ignore it. If it came from the light, then it's a message from the gods."

"You mean God!" said Johnnie. "I might not remember my life, but I do know I went to Sunday school, so I know there ain't a whole bunch of 'gods,' there's only one, unless you mean the holy Trinity, which is kinda like one divided into three—and hey—I'll bet that's what Charlie meant. He saw the Holy Trinity when he looked into the light!"

Nick shook his head. "He couldn't have seen anything yet—the tunnel's like an air lock. By the time you see what's there, it's too late to tell anyone."

"So the gods must mean something else," said Jix.

"God, not gods!" insisted Johnnie.

Nick threw up his hands. "God, gods, or whatever," said Nick. "Right now, it doesn't matter whether it's Jesus, or Kukulcan, or a dancing bear at the end of the tunnel. What matters is that we have a clue, and we have to figure it out."

"Why?" Johnnie asked again. "Why does God—excuse me, I mean 'the Light of Universal Whatever'—why does it just give us a freakin' impossible clue? Why can't it just tell us what we're supposed to do?"

"Because," said Mikey, "the Dancing Bear wants us to suffer."

But Jix had a different opinion on the matter. "I think the Universe wants only to point us in a direction, not tell us what to do. If it tells us, then we're not really choosing. It only means something if we choose it."

"Yeah, but if we're supposed to save the stinkin' world, why make it so hard?" said Johnnie. "In fact, why make us do it at all? If 'the light' is all-powerful, then 'the light' oughta save the world itself, and leave us alone."

"Maybe it doesn't want to save the world," said Nick.

Mikey laughed bitterly. "If that's what you think, then why are you even here? You should join my sister; you're in love with her anyway."

"Just hear me out," said Nick. "Mary wants to destroy the living world. We want to save it. The 'Universal Whatever' is willing to accept either outcome, so it makes the odds fifty-fifty."

"'Fifty-fifty'?" said Mikey. "If you ask me, Mary's got the advantage right now."

"So if you were the light at the end of the tunnel, how would *you* even out the odds?" Nick asked.

"I'd tell the losing side to get a clue!"

"Or," said Nick, "you'd *give* them a clue . . ."

Nick's thought left everyone speechless. Suddenly the temple around them began to actually feel like a temple, and although none of them worshipped at the same altar, there was a sudden singularity of purpose that bound them.

. . . Fat Alamo, the Trinity, Ground Zero . . .

"It's places we've been," said Mikey. "It has to be. Ground Zero is what the living call the place where Mary used to live. You know—the towers that gave her her name. And Jix was at the Alamo, right?"

"So maybe we're supposed to go back to those places," offered Nick.

Johnnie pointed an oversize finger at Mikey. "I ain't going back nowhere unless it's where I started. And anyway, it don't explain the Trinity."

Jix scratched his whiskers and gave it more thought. "*Álamo* is Spanish for a kind of tree. . . ."

"So we're looking for a fat tree?" asked Mikey.

"Perhaps." Jix went over to one of the guards "*¿Dónde hay un álamo gordo?*"

The guard shrugged. "*Los álamos son todos delgados.*"

Suddenly something caught in Nick's mind with such force, he thought his brain might be ecto-ripped right out of his head. "What did you just say?"

"I just asked him if he knows where—"

But Nick cut Jix off. "Los Alamos . . . Alamogordo! My God, I know what it means. I know *exactly* what it means!" They all looked at him, waiting, and Nick tried to keep his voice steady. "There's this town in New Mexico called Alamogordo. It's kind of famous if you're a geek, and I think I was one, when I was alive. The thing is, Alamogordo has its own 'ground zero.' I imagine it would be like a giant deadspot—perfectly round."

"Charlie and I saw that!" said Johnnie-O. "We passed right over it. It was weird—full of static and stuff."

"That's only two out of three," Jix pointed out. "It doesn't explain 'the Trinity.'"

"Not THE Trinity—just 'Trinity,'" Nick explained. "That's the name of the site!"

"You figured it out!" said Mikey, slapping him on the back. "That's good news, isn't it?"

Nick swallowed nervously. "Trinity was a military test site." And as he thought about it, all his remaining chocolate began to harden and crack like fused desert sand. "Mary's going to the place where they tested the first atomic bomb."

In her book *My Struggle: The Quest for a Perfect World*, Mary Hightower writes, "Destiny is the sum of the choices that God knows we'll make."

For once, Allie the Outcast doesn't disagree, but she adds, "Not even Einstein can do that kind of math."

PART SEVEN

Journada de Muerto

E=MC²

PART SEVEN

There are about three hundred billion stars to a galaxy, and more than eighty billion galaxies in the known universe. That means that if only one in a million planets can support life, and one in a million of those actually *has* life, and one in a million of *those* planets has *intelligent* life . . . then there are at least one and a half million civilizations out there.

Of course, chances are they'll never find one another, being so spread out in time and space. Yet all of these civilized worlds have distinct similarities when it comes to the works and wisdom of the living, namely, the "befores" and "afters" that define every intelligent world:

before and after the harnessing of fire

before and after written language

before and after the smelting of iron

But above and beyond all of these is the single most important milestone of all: before and after a world discovers the ability to lower the number of life-sustaining planets by one.

On July 16, 1945, the human race reached the single most important man-made moment in its history. In the *Jornada de*

EVERFOUND

Muerto—"Journey of Death"—desert, near Alamogordo, New Mexico, mankind discovered the power to end all life on earth. Until that moment, it had only been an idea, a mathematical calculation in the minds of geniuses who could theorize a step beyond the average individual. But on that fateful day, the smartest minds in the world, funded by the wealthiest nation in the world, toward the end of the most devastating war the world had ever known, turned theory into reality.

The first atom bomb, modestly called "The Gadget," was detonated, in the single greatest moment of earthly invention and destruction, for the power to create always goes hand in hand with the power to destroy. The twenty-kiloton blast firmly put the blade of self-annihilation into the hands of mankind, and from that moment on, nothing on earth would ever be the same.

The bomb was not beloved, but even so, the universe could not ignore such a world-altering event, and so at the very instant The Gadget was dropped from its tower and detonated, the entire blast zone crossed into Everlost, becoming the world's largest deadspot, perfectly round, and perfectly preserved. And at ground zero, the very center of the deadspot, sat the bomb itself. While its atoms had been shredded in the living world, in Everlost, The Gadget sat a millimeter above the Journey of Death desert, poised at the last microsecond before detonation, waiting at that final moment of infinite possibility.

Waiting, perhaps, for Mary Hightower.

CHAPTER 46
The Sum of All Tears

Mary Hightower and her huge cumulus of Afterlights crossed the Nevada desert, pulled by Mary's conviction that something spectacular lay ahead of them. They carried with them more than twenty Interlights whose bodies lay comatose back in the town of Artesia. If all went according to plan, every single one of them would awake as a skinjacker.

On a bright chilly January morning, Mary stepped from the living-world desert, and onto the Trinity deadspot. Mary was not a girl easily impressed. She had seen many things in her deathtime, but nothing could prepare her for this moment. All around them, on a deadspot that stretched for more than a mile, was a treasure trove of crossed objects. The ground was a giant repository of random items. Chairs and cars and toys and clothes and books and boxes and basically every type of manmade object imaginable stretched for as far as the eye could see. Flashes of static, like tiny forked lightning, sparked around them every few seconds; phantom branches of light, shooting between metal objects.

Clearly this wasn't just a deadspot; it was some kind of

vortex. In all her years in Everlost, bargaining and trading with finders for crossed items to keep her children in perpetual comfort, she had never had seen so many things. Not even her brother, during his monstrous days filling the cargo holds of the *Sulphur Queen*, had ever accumulated this much! Mary had no idea where it had all come from, but that didn't matter. All that mattered was that it was here now, for her, and for her children.

"Is it real?" one of her younger children asked.

"Of course it is," Mary answered. This was not exactly what she had imagined when she pictured the place she was being drawn to, but in its own way it was better. It was very clearly the center of gravity, the focal point of the world.

Mary and her children wandered through the maze of crossed belongings, spellbound by all the things around them.

"What is this place?" her children asked.

"The heart of Everlost," she told them. "We're finally home."

Mary, as it turns out, was not the first to stumble upon the Trinity vortex. Another resourceful, if somewhat waterlogged, spirit had gotten there first.

After the attack on the train, hundreds of refugees had scattered. Only some of them had rejoined Milos. The rest formed their own vapors and went their separate ways. Many had been reabsorbed into Mary's growing cumulus as they stormed across Texas into New Mexico, but one group, numbering close to a hundred, had been shepherded by none other than Speedo.

Speedo never fancied himself much of a leader, but because he had been close to Mary, because he was the train's conductor, and because he had been the only non-skinjacker with special privileges, he was the one his group of refugees turned to for guidance.

"Well, Mary wanted us to go west, so we'll go west," he had told them. He didn't know what he would find there, but it sure beat hanging around to be attacked by the Neons again.

What a marvelous surprise it was to stumble across the giant deadspot, just a few weeks later. It was a Finder's delight — and Speedo, who was still a Finder at heart — knew a great business venture when he saw one. Why, with all this stuff, he would be the wealthiest Finder in all of Everlost! So, like an old-fashioned prospector, he staked his claim and had his Afterlights begin the monumental task of cataloging all his new finds.

He had no idea what this place was, but to Speedo, it didn't matter. He had big, big plans for his business empire . . . but it all came crashing down when Mary Hightower showed up. All his Afterlights instantly abandoned him in favor of Mary, and there he stood, his hopes dashed, and his claim jumped. Speedo suddenly found himself, both literally and figuratively, all wet.

Mary was, of course, surprised to find Speedo there, but pleased as well, because it added quite a few more Afterlights to her growing cumulus. She would soon have to come up with a new word for them. Thunderhead, perhaps. "A thunderhead of Afterlights." She rather liked it!

"Thank you so much," she told Speedo, "for taking care of these children and finding this wonderful place for me."

"Right," said Speedo, "for you." There wasn't a trace of his typical over-wide smile on his face.

Around them, Speedo and his squad had begun to separate things into piles. One pile caught Mary's attention. At first glance it appeared to be a pile of bodies.

"What on earth?"

"Oh, don't worry," said Speedo. "I know what it looks like—but they're just plastic."

"Plastic?"

"Yeah, I know. Weird, right? Lots of weird things here." Then he got a little bit quiet. "But that's nothing. I'll show you the weirdest thing of all."

The plastic personages scattered about the deadspot might have seemed odd if one didn't know where they came from. The fact is, it was common for many nations to use test dummies to discover the effects of a nuclear blast on the human body. Entire communities were evacuated and test dummies were installed in the homes, and then bombed. The communities were usually old military housing, but sometimes not. There were entire islands in the South Pacific blown to radioactive smithereens, along with the abandoned homes of those who once lived there.

And, of course there were the wartime attacks on Hiroshima and Nagasaki that not only took things, but people as well. In those two deadly blasts, more than 100,000 souls were instantly sent into the light, bringing a tragic end to a painful war.

. . . But the things consumed by nuclear fission in those cities, as well the things incinerated in every nuclear test ever performed, did not leave the universe entirely. They came here: ground zero of the first cataclysmic blast—the one that made all the others possible, and therefore will forever bear the burden of all things lost.

The Trinity vortex was the repository of nuclear memory.

To Mary, whose lifetime had not included such things as nuclear fission, it was all new. She knew the living world had found extraordinary methods of large-scale destruction, yet she had no idea the extent of it. . . .

. . . But as Speedo led her deeper into the deadspot, Mary began to tingle. The gravity that had pulled her here felt stronger than ever before, and she knew, without ever having to ask, that Speedo was leading her to the center of the Vortex.

"Have a look at this," Speedo said. They came around one of Speedo's sorting piles, to reveal a clearing about fifty feet across. In the center was an object hovering just above the sand. To Mary it resembled some sort of metallic jar turned upside down or maybe a child's top. It was dull green, with wires all over it and it stood more than ten feet high.

"It looks sort of like a space capsule," said one of her skinjackers.

"We think," said Speedo, "it's a bomb. . . ."

"Really? How very interesting." Mary approached it, with her skinjackers close behind her. The thing looked heavy, it looked complicated.

Then The Pet raised his hand, but this time didn't wait

to be called on. "Uh, Miss Mary . . . I think it might be some kind of nuke."

"And what is that?" she asked.

"You don't want to know," said The Pet.

Mary took a step closer to the object. "Maybe I do." Then she reached out and touched the surface of the bomb.

Inanimate objects have their own peculiar form of memory. It's nothing so linear as living memory; it's more like the sum of the intentions of those who created it. However, when it came to the memory of "The Gadget," it held in its soulless shell a whole lot more.

The instant Mary touched it, she was flooded with a searing vision of every atomic blast ever created on earth, from here to the Marshall Islands, to Japan, to Siberia, to all the poisoned underground caverns all around the world. The memory of every blast filled her mind, and in that single instant Mary knew! She understood the power, the scope, and the potential. She knew what these silent objects could do and how quickly and how completely they could do it.

She pulled her hand back, her eyes still blinded by the memory of the blasts. It was almost as bright as the light at the end of the tunnel but, oh, so much better! Then, when her vision cleared, she turned to her Afterlights, who were all looking at her, waiting for her. She knew this was the moment she had been waiting for. Her entire existence was leading to this.

She sent out her loving tendrils of light to her skinjackers.

"I need you to find out how many of these devices there are in the living world. Find out where they are and how we can gain access to them. Skinjack anyone you have to."

"And then what, Miss Mary?" asked The Pet.

She gently touched his face and smiled. "And then we save the world."

CHAPTER 47

Thunderbird Persuasion

```
To: stopmarynow@gmail.com
From: bighairbertha@aol.com
Subject: must stop mary
```
It's Allie again. Mary is out of control. We're Tracking her down in New Mexico. Tell Mikey I'm okay. Come soon. Need all the help we can get.

```
      Allie
```

There had been no word from Jill, so Allie and Clarence had no choice but to intercept Mary. They flew into West Texas, and Allie skinjacked the driver of a fast car, switching drivers and vehicles every few hours, with Clarence riding shotgun.

They followed Mary's clear path of destruction; the remains of Eunice, then Artesia. Then they followed the highway west.

"If we can isolate her, and get her away from her skinjackers, I can take her down," Allie told Clarence.

"And," asked Clarence, "if it doesn't work?"

"If it doesn't work, we always have plan B."

Plan B was not something to be discussed, but they both knew what Allie was referring to. The touch of a scar wraith. If ever there was a soul in need of extinguishing, it was Mary Hightower . . . and yet Allie instinctively knew that the premeditated ending of someone's entire existence, even Mary's, was a last resort. Ending the physical lives of skinjackers, that was bad enough . . . but intentionally extinguishing a soul? Squirrel had been an accident, but if they willfully extinguished Mary, it would be a crime against the universe, and perhaps the one act that was truly unforgivable. For that reason, it was a last resort.

Allie, who was skinjacking, couldn't see into Everlost, but Clarence had the benefit of double-world vision—so it was Clarence who saw the deadspot, just past the town of Alamogordo.

"I don't know what that is, but it doesn't look good," he said.

Allie pulled over to the side of the road, and, making sure her fleshie was still asleep, she peeled out. Once in Everlost, she saw the massive deadspot in the far distance.

"Whatever it is," Allie said, "Mary would have seen it if she came this way, and would have gone to check it out."

Up ahead there was a restricted military access road, leading to something called Trinity Site. The name sounded familiar to Allie, but she couldn't recall where she'd heard it before.

"Well," Allie said, "it looks like I'm gonna have to skinjack someone with military access."

They returned that afternoon. Allie had skinjacked an

Army officer, and let Clarence take the wheel, because only he could see the deadspot with his Everlost eye while Allie was skinjacking. They approached from the north. From Allie's perspective, all there was to see was a stretch of dark fused sand, more than a mile or two across, but Clarence's perspective was quite a bit different.

"They're here!" Clarence told her, in a panic. "They didn't just come through here, they're still here! We've gotta . . ." Clarence pulled sharply to the right, and stopped the car abruptly, then he breathed a sigh of relief. "We're okay—I don't think they saw us."

"Won't they see us now?"

"I got it covered."

Then, when Allie tried to peel out, she found it difficult.

"Lift your butt about six inches off the seat," Clarence told her. "*Then* try to peel out."

It worked, and once she was back in Everlost, it all became clear. Clarence had parked the Jeep in the exact same airspace as a vintage pickup truck that had crossed into Everlost. The living-world jeep was hidden from view within the footprint of the larger pickup truck. Allie now found herself sitting in the passenger seat of the Everlost pickup, while the body of the Army officer remained asleep in the Jeep—and as long as he stayed asleep, and didn't get out, no one would see him.

Allie couldn't believe the collection of junk around her—a lot of it sorted into piles and stacks, some of which towered over her head—and between the stacks were vehicles parked every which way. Most of them seemed to be from the 1940s or 50s.

A few of Mary's children were wandering about, but the deadspot was so cluttered, and the branchlike flashes of St. Elmo's fire were so distracting, that Allie and Clarence were able to slip out of the pickup truck without being seen.

There was more activity deeper in the deadspot, but the farther in they moved, the harder it was to hide. Clarence had it easier, since he could hide at least the living-world parts of his body within larger Everlost objects.

"If your plan was to get captured, you're doing a great job," Clarence told her from within a pile of air conditioners.

The current plan was to isolate Mary, and push her down into the living world, because unless they planned to extinguish her, that was their only choice. It meant that, for Allie, this would be a one-way mission. Allie would be going down with Mary.

"We're going to have to lure her to the edge of the deadspot," Allie told Clarence.

"And how do you propose we do that? If you show your face, they'll grab you and bring you to her, right there in the middle, not at the edge. And if I show my face . . ."

"Right; they'll all run, and Mary will surround herself with Afterlights to protect herself."

They pondered their dilemma, until an answer came from a very unexpected source.

"It's not fair!" said Speedo as he moved farther and farther away from the center of activity, wanting to get as far from Mary as he could. "This was *my* claim, I found it. It's mine."

"Yeah, but we're back with Mary now," said Sandman,

who used to be in charge of the sleeping car. Now he was in charge of collecting beds for the Artesia Interlights, many of whom were suspected to be skinjackers.

"So what?" said Speedo. "It's still not fair." He kicked a pile of air conditioners, making the top few tumble. For a moment, he thought he saw something moving in the pile, but he knew it was just his imagination.

"Maybe I should tell Mary how you feel," said Sandman.

"No," said Speedo fearfully. The last thing he wanted was for Mary to know that he was not with the program. "No, I'll be okay. I just got to get used to the idea."

"Better get used to it fast, because now that she's here, everything's going back to how it used to be." Then Sandman strode off in search of more beds, leaving Speedo alone with his thoughts.

Disgusted and dejected, Speedo leaned against a '57 Thunderbird convertible and reached down, trying to scrape the muddy sand from the soles of his wet feet.

"It's not fair . . . ," Speedo mumbled again, and, to his surprise, someone answered.

"Of course it's not fair."

He spun to see, of all spirits, Allie the Outcast sitting in the passenger seat of the bright red T-bird.

"Mary treats everyone unfairly," she said, "and somehow she makes you feel like that's exactly what you want. I'm glad you aren't falling for it anymore."

Speedo's first instinct was to run and tell Mary . . . but then, why should he? What did he owe Mary? All this time he had chauffeured her around by car, by zeppelin, by train—and how did she repay him? By jumping his claim.

"Don't . . . Don't hurt me" was all Speedo could think to say.

"I couldn't if I wanted to," Allie said. "The worst I could do would be to send you down, but I won't do that, Speedo, because I think you finally get it." Then she patted the driver seat beside her. "Come on, hop in."

Speedo looked around to make sure they weren't being watched, then got in. He didn't use the door, he just hopped over it the way he imagined James Bond would, and slid down to the plush leather seat of the convertible with a wet *sploosh*.

"Put your hands on the wheel," Allie said. "Go on."

"Why? I'm not going anywhere," he said.

"You could be," Allie told him. "This car and everything on this deadspot could be yours again."

Speedo sighed. He knew where this was going. "But only if I turn against Mary, and join up with you, right?"

"Not even that much," Allie said. "All you have to do is get Mary to come to the edge of the deadspot."

"And then?"

"And then nothing. I'll take it from there."

Speedo shook his head. "If I do that, and you do something to her, everyone will know I helped you."

"I think you're clever enough to get Mary here without anyone knowing you helped me."

Then, as Speedo looked at the various piles around them he got a flash of inspiration. "We're in the north part of the deadspot right now, but I think I can bring her to the southern edge. Can you be there in an hour?"

Allie nodded, and with their plan set, Speedo left with

the firm knowledge that Allie was right: He was clever. Extremely clever.

At the heart of the deadspot, they had already begun deconstructing the piles and moving furniture to create open-air living spaces for the hundreds of children under Mary's protection. A special dormitory area was set for the Artesia Interlights, and they were set on comfortable beds made with military precision, making it clear to everyone how important these new skinjackers would be once they woke up.

Mary had set up her own personal parlor right in the middle of everything, with the bomb as a centerpiece like a piece of modern art. Meanwhile, her five remaining skinjackers formed a think tank, planning trips to Washington, the Middle East, Russia, and everywhere else they were likely to find the keys to Armageddon. The real work, though, would come once they left Ground Zero, and truly educated themselves on the many twisting paths of this journey of death. Certainly, even with arms treaties, there were more than enough nukes to kill the living world.

"I like what you've done with the space," Speedo said, as he walked into Mary's parlor, "and I've found just the thing to make it complete."

"What did you find?" Mary asked.

"It's a surprise," Speedo said. "You're gonna absolutely love it!"

He led her to the southern edge of the deadspot, right at the boundary of the living world. "This was the first place we sorted," Speedo told her. "When I saw this, I immediately thought of you."

At first Mary thought he was referring to a sorted pile of shiny metal objects, containing everything from corkscrews to silver cups to trophies.

"Thank you, but I don't need a trophy to satisfy my ego," Mary told him.

"No, not that stuff, I'm talking about this!" He led her around the shiny pile to a cluster of desks, then he pushed a few desks aside to reveal an old fashioned roll-top. He rapped it with his fist. "See that? Solid oak!" And his over-size smile stretched from ear to ear, revealing more teeth than any person should have.

Mary clapped her hands together, thrilled at the sight of it. "How thoughtful of you, Speedo."

"Well," Speedo said, "I figured you'd be writing some more. I mean, there are so many more Afterlights to educate, right?"

Mary approached the desk, but as she did, a figure leaped out of nowhere, knocking her down. And Speedo reacted with the same surprise as everyone else.

Allie knew she would have only one shot at this. She took Mary to the ground, and they landed right at the edge of the deadspot. Although Mary fought back, Allie rolled them both off the deadspot, and into the living world.

Her children tried to rush to Mary's aid, but then Clarence stepped out of the pile of desks, threatening to touch anyone who interfered. Their fear of the scar wraith was stronger than their need to help Mary.

Mary struggled against Allie, but Allie was stronger.

"First you kill my skinjackers and now you dare to

attack me?" Mary said as she struggled. Allie pushed down on Mary's shoulders, and she began to sink.

"Your time on earth is over," Allie told her. "You can try to sell the kids down there on your cause, but I don't think they'll listen." Now Mary's shoulders were in the ground, and when she tried to roll, Allie held on, leaving them both wedged in the earth. Yes, it would be a one-way trip for Allie, but it was worth it. "Oh, and by the way," said Allie, "I met your assassin in Memphis. He's sleeping with the magma now."

"That's nothing compared to what we did to your friend Jill." And then Mary oinked like a pig, which, in its own way was satisfying . . . although it didn't bode well for Jill.

Then all at once Mary stopped struggling. Perhaps, thought Allie, she was resigned to her fate. But then Mary smiled.

"If you must know," Mary said, "we've been expecting you." Then a blur came up behind Clarence—a living blur in an Army uniform. It was the officer that Allie had left sleeping in his jeep. He swung a tire iron at Clarence's head and knocked him out cold. Instantly, Mary's children flooded off the deadspot, grabbed Allie, and pulled Mary out of the ground before she could sink any farther.

Then, to Allie's horror, the army officer took out his pistol. "Sorry, dude, but Mary says I gotta do this."

Allie turned away. There came the awful sound of a gunshot, and Allie knew it was over. Her one chance of ending the reign of Mary Hightower had failed.

CHAPTER 48
Suicide King

Bad luck, bad karma, and simple human error.

These are the things to which Allie attributed her catastrophic failure to defeat Mary Hightower and save the living world. Had she been lucky and been able to squeeze out a few more seconds . . . had she not committed the crimes of killing Milos and Moose . . . and had she not been so irresponsible as to leave that Army officer where he could wake up, and be seen by a skinjacker, it would have all gone differently. She was now held by four Afterlights and put into handcuffs that had come to the vortex from one blast zone or another.

Before her on the ground lay Clarence, his blood seeping from his head into the ground. She had looked away, because she had not wanted to see it. All she saw was the flash of light as he got where he was going. . . .

But if he was dead, then why was his chest still rising and falling? How could he still be breathing?

That's when Allie saw the body of the Army officer on the ground, the gun still in his hand. He hadn't shot Clarence, he had turned the gun on himself! And beside him in Everlost, the Asian boy who had skinjacked the man, and forced him to take his own life, was now crouched beside his body, shivering.

"Don't make me do that again, Miss Mary. Please don't make me do that again."

"It's all right, SoSo. It's going to be all right now."

Mary went over to him, and Allie saw the strangest thing—Mary's afterglow seemed to stretch out, enveloping him, making his own flickering glow grow steady and bright. In seconds he appeared comforted and relieved of his burden.

"If you had any thought of escape by skinjacking," Mary told Allie, gesturing down to the dead man, "it won't be possible now. There's not a living soul around for miles, except of course for your friend here."

Allie realized that there wasn't all that much blood coming from Clarence's head at all, but he was still out cold.

Now that Mary was no longer being threatened, she was calm and genteel. "You really are to be pitied, Allie. Such potential, such skill, but you've squandered it all—and for what? Just to settle your petty rivalry with me."

Allie had a lot to say to her on the matter, but Mary had made sure Allie was gagged just in case she might say something that Mary didn't want her precious children to hear.

"I do believe in rehabilitation, Allie. I believe you can be brought back from that angry place you've been, and see the light. So I shall give you one more chance. . . ." Then Mary moved closer to Allie, and as she did, Allie felt something strange happening to her. She felt something coil around her just as it had done to SoSo. It was a surge of Mary's afterglow, wrapping around her like an anaconda, squeezing her, trying to merge with her own, until Allie could no longer resist it. . . .

. . . And suddenly, Allie understood!

She saw the *rightness* of Mary's vision! How Mary had struggled for so long to create a perfect world—for wasn't that the goal of every society, every culture, every spirit from the beginning of time? To build the perfect world? And not just any world, but one filled with the spirits of children untainted by a life of disappointment and compromise; souls rescued at the purest and brightest moment of human potential! Such a world wouldn't be complete without things and places to fill it as well. After all, shouldn't the universe be given the golden opportunity to choose which works of man deserve to remain perfectly preserved forever?

Why, the living world was merely a womb! Yes, the pains of birth are great, but oh, the reward! In the end, the womb must become barren, so that Everlost can shine as the glowing product of love's labor. It was the perfect formula for eternity: Everlost equals the product of Mary and her children—soon to multiply exponentially!

Allie's eyes were wide with understanding now . . . except for one thing.

Mary was wrong.

Even though Allie's soul had been injected with Mary's overpowering vision, as beguiling as moonlight, Allie knew that Mary's light was false—a trick, just like the glow of the moon, which is nothing more than a dead rock reflecting the light of something far greater than itself.

The living world is not a womb, Allie would have told

Mary if she could. It's the nursery, the school, the home, and the hearth. It is the source of all possible futures. And Everlost? Everlost is no more and no less than the portraits that hang on life's walls. This would be a bland and bare universe without Everlost, but like a portrait, its place is on the side, not in the center.

Mary's coiling of Allie's soul did not win Allie over. Instead, it transformed Allie's hatred of Mary into pity . . . for Allie realized that Mary could never escape from the dark place in which she existed. There would never be a doorway of illumination for her. How could there be doorways when you're blind to everything but the walls?

Their spirits were now so intertwined that Mary could sense exactly what Allie was feeling—and what Allie now felt coming from Mary was a virulent, deadly kind of hatred. The kind of hatred that ends worlds.

Mary pulled back, separating her light from Allie's. Then she looked Allie dead in the eye and said, "I've given you one last chance to do the right and proper thing, but now I know there is nothing right or proper left inside you." She turned to the Afterlights beside her.

"Would you be so kind as to bring the sarcophagus?"

They brought over an old-fashioned refrigerator. It was the kind with rounded edges, and a solid latching handle, like a car door, but unlike a car door, there was no way to open it from the inside. It was powder blue, a friendly color for an object that now had a very sinister purpose.

A team of Afterlights stood it upright at the very edge of the deadspot and opened it, revealing that the shelves inside had been removed.

"Consider it a protective shell," Mary told her. "A more civilized way to send you to the center of the earth." Then she glanced over at Clarence, who still had not stirred. "It would be cruel of me, though, to send you down without making sure you understood that it was not my intention to kill, or even hurt, your friend the scar wraith. We did need him unconscious, however. You see, he'll be doing something very important today. Something terrible, but also something wonderful. It is my belief that the good far outweighs the bad."

And then she called for Milos.

Shuffle. Deal three. Toss, toss, toss. Choose.

The Three of Clubs.

Shuffle. Deal three. Toss, toss, toss. Choose.

The Nine of Diamonds.

Shuffle. Deal three. Toss, toss, toss. Choose.

The deck is missing the Jack of Spades.

He knew not because he counted the deck, but because it was the only card that never came up when he played Three Card Monte. It disturbed him that something could cross into Everlost incomplete. What disturbed him more, however, was that the missing Jack of Spades was a one-eyed jack. There were only two of them in a deck; the Jack of Spades and the Jack of Hearts. Although it terrified him for reasons he had entirely forgotten, the whole purpose of his game was to find them. Fear overtook him every time he chose one of the three cards to flip. Terror overwhelmed him when that card turned out to be the Jack of Hearts, with that evil eye peeking out sideways at him. And then such intense relief when he shuffled it back into the deck, only to start looking for it once again.

The other Afterlights had come to know him now as Monty, for the Three Card Monte game that he constantly played by himself, never letting anyone else choose the cards. Although many Afterlights knew his real name, they preferred Monty to Milos because Monty didn't bother anyone.

That's why, when Mary called for Milos, he didn't respond right away. It took someone tapping him on his shoulder to make him look up from his cards and accompany his escort to where Mary waited.

"Milos, there you are!" Mary said when he came to her. He smiled, remembering that, yes, that had been his name.

"I am at your service, Miss Mary," he said, then offered her something he never offered anyone. "I shall deal you the three cards and you can try to find the one-eyed jack, yes?"

"Not now, Milos," she said gently. "But I do have something else I'd like you to do." And then she leaned forward, and kissed him with such warmth and affection, it reminded him how much he loved her, how much he had done for her, and how much he still would do. It brought a trace of his failing memories back from the cloud that had enveloped his mind. Then she put her cheek against his, and whispered in his ear, "I need you to touch the scar wraith, Milos."

Milos followed Mary's gaze to the living man lying on the ground just a few feet away. Instantly Milos realized that this was the one-eyed jack he so feared, yet felt so drawn to.

"I need you to touch him, Milos . . . to wake up the new skinjackers who sleep."

Tears began to well in his eyes and he looked to Mary and pleaded. "Will you do that thing that you do to the others? I've seen it. The way you touch their souls. Wrapping. Melding. Making them want whatever you want. Will you do that for me?"

But Mary shook her head. "I can't do that to you, Milos," she said. "The choice to sacrifice yourself for the greater good must be your choice alone."

"But it's what I want," said Milos, his tears flowing more heavily now. "To be one with you, if only for a moment."

Mary did not meet his gaze. "I will ask you, but I will not coerce you."

Milos bit his lower lip and wiped his tears with the back of his hand, embarrassed for his display before all the others.

"Well, then," he said, "why don't we let the cards decide." He went to the roll-top desk that Speedo had so proudly offered to Mary.

Shuffle, deal three, toss toss toss.

When he was done tossing the cards over one another, he steeled himself and chose the card to the right. He held it before him for a moment, seeing only the back, then he flipped it, and when he saw what it was, he laughed. It wasn't the Jack of Hearts, or the missing Jack of Spades . . . it was the King of Hearts. The one with the sword through his head. The suicide king.

He turned to Mary. "Do you love me?" he asked.

Mary hesitated, and said, "I will remember you more fondly than almost anyone I've ever known."

Milos sighed, realizing that fondness was as good as he was ever going to get.

With everyone watching, and Allie shaking her head, trying to speak behind her gag, Milos dropped his cards and they scattered. He would not need them anymore. He then knelt beside the one-eyed jack that had extinguished Squirrel. Milos knew he had done things in this world that were unforgivable. He knew that if he ever went into the light, he would face the most severe of consequences. He wasn't sure what those consequences would be, but he feared them all the same. Yet all of those deeds had only been to make himself worthy in Mary's eyes. Now he had to accept that nothing would ever make him worthy—not even this—but this would bring him closer than he had ever been before. He wondered if he could live with that. And then realized that he wouldn't have to.

"I sacrifice my existence for you, Mary. I do this of my own free will." Then he reached down, firmly clasped the hand of the unconscious scar wraith . . . and in a single, silent moment, Vitaly Milos Vayevsky ceased to exist.

Once again pangs of mourning rippled through the world, just as they had when Squirrel was extinguished. In every ocean, massive rogue waves rose from the sea, curling and crashing in places where no ship sailed, so no human eye could see. In the polar ice caps, every glacier calved tons of ice, losing face. And in the Jornado de Muerto desert, a hurricane formed, turning, against all logic, clockwise instead of counterclockwise, and remained fixed over the Trinity site, its clear, cloudless eye the exact size of the deadspot. The storm didn't just rage in the living world, but in Everlost as well, where there were never such storms.

Again, a sudden, sharp pain wracked the gut of every Afterlight, and it was so severe this time that everyone doubled over, collapsing to the ground.

No one felt the pain more than Mary. It was worse than that knife wound that had re-killed her, worse than anything she had ever felt or ever imagined.

"What have I done?" she wailed. "What have I done? What have I done to myself?"

When the pain had passed, her vision cleared to see the storm raging just beyond the edge of the deadspot and her children surrounding her, terrified. Then, as she rose, regaining her bearings and her poise, she realized that both Allie and the scar wraith were gone.

Clarence had been jarred back to consciousness the moment of the extinguishing. The blow to his head had addled his brain, however. He wasn't quite sure where, or when, or even who he was, and his head hurt something awful, like the worst of hangovers. When he turned, the first thing he saw lying on the ground beside him were objects that had fallen from the pile of shiny things just a few feet away. A trophy and a silver martini shaker. Having not known where they came from, he concluded this indeed must be a hangover, and the martini shaker was probably the cause of it. Between the trophy and the shaker was a single playing card: the Jack of Spades.

Beyond that were dozens of ghosties, all doubled over, moaning in pain. The doctors had said the ghosties weren't real, and in his confused state, he thought that maybe they were right. He knew how to make them go away, though.

All he had to do was cover his dead eye with his dead hand and he couldn't see them anymore.

He stood up, feeling dizzy, as if he were in a fun house and the world was shifting beneath his feet. With his dead eye covered, all he saw was a massive plain of fused sand with clear skies above it, but the angry swirling maelstrom of a hurricane raging beyond the perimeter. A few yards to his right was a dead soldier with a gun in his hand, and far away, straight across the patch of fused sand, was a jeep.

Clarence didn't know very much at that moment, but he did know this was not a place he wanted to be. So, with his dead eye covered and his good eye to lead the way, he staggered across the dark expanse of fused sand toward the jeep.

At that same moment, Allie was incapacitated by the pain, but she knew it gave her an advantage. While the others were doubled over, Allie stumbled over to the Afterlight who had handcuffed her, and thrust her hand into his pocket, retrieving the key. Ignoring the pain in her gut, she jammed the key into the small keyhole, turned it, and freed herself from the handcuffs, dropping them on the ground.

"What have I done?" she heard Mary wailing as storm clouds began to billow beyond the deadspot. Allie tried to advance on Mary, but the pain ended as abruptly as it had begun and everyone began to recover. Allie would not make the same mistake twice: Hurling herself at Mary now would result in the exact same situation she had been in a moment ago. She saw that Clarence was gone, and if she escaped, there would come another time, and another place, to battle Mary. Maybe next time luck would be on her side. And so

Allie retreated, running along the edge of the deadspot, until she heard a sound peaking above the surge of the storm. It was the drone of engines. Something was approaching, still unseen behind the storm, and she knew it was headed her way.

High up in the catwalks and deep infrastructure of the *Hindenburg*, the crowded souls of Chitchén Itzá went about their perpetual party, for they had known nothing else for so very long. The mourning pang hit with such unexpected ferocity that they were broken out of the rhythm of revelry, and it took several minutes for them to get things going again. The warriors, crammed like sardines into the passenger promenades, used the pang to help fuel them for battle. "It is a strike against us by the Eastern Witch," they told one another, "but we shall strike back with twice the force!"

Johnnie-O was at the helm—not because he could fly the thing, for he had never even been in the control room before, but having been trapped aboard for so long while the airship was adrift, it gave him "squatters rights" to pilot it now. Besides, his large hands appeared very confident on the wheel. King Yax had been with him for most of the trip, because the views from the control room were spectacular, but the king must have lost interest, because Johnnie-O hadn't seen him for over a day. Instead, Nick, Mikey, and Jix were in the control room with Johnnie, getting their first glimpse of the Trinity vortex ahead, when the mourning pang struck.

"That was worse than before," said Jix, understating the obvious, as he recovered.

"Do you suppose it was Mary who was extinguished?" Nick said, trying to mask his concern.

"No," said Mikey with authority. "Remember, she's my sister and we crossed into Everlost together. If she was extinguished, I'd feel it."

None of them wanted to guess who might have been the victim of this extinguishing, for any speculation led them to answers they didn't want to consider. Then, as if to give weight to their worries, a sudden rainstorm in the living world hid the view before them and penetrated the ship, pouring through their spirits with such severity it made them shiver. And yet, they could also hear the rain on the Ship's skin.

"*No es possible!*" said Jix. "The storm is in both worlds!"

And the *Hindenburg* began to violently lurch in the raging wind.

In the clear eye of that swirling storm, at the southern edge of the deadspot, Mary and her children had all recovered from the mourning pang, but a sense of dread still filled every soul. Although she was far from the cluster of beds where her latest batch of Interlights had been laid, she knew that they had awoken in this second Great Awakening, and she would soon know how many of them were skinjackers.

The living-world sands just beyond the edge of the deadspot had become inundated so quickly by the rain that it looked like an ocean out there, rather then a desert. Even if they wanted to leave now, they couldn't, for the living-world sand had become so soft and wet that they would all sink after only a few steps.

"The storm covers the whole world," someone said.

"Nonsense," said Mary. "It will pass like all storms."

The immediate order of business was to locate Allie, but before Mary could organize her Afterlights into a search posse, something within the storm stole their attention. Some children pointed, some even fled, but most took their cues from Mary, and stood their ground as an impossibly huge object emerged out of the blinding sheets of rain, like a planet plunging from the heavens toward them.

Mary instantly knew it was her airship—and it was coming in too fast and too low. The *Hindenburg*'s nose pushed forth into the airspace of the deadspot, then the low-hanging control gondola, and the ship's entire underbelly, hit the ground hard, scraping along, knocking over everything in its path until finally it came to rest like a massive beached whale.

When Mary looked into the windows of the passenger compartment, she saw faces—hundreds of faces. All of them angry. All of them foreign. Then, when she lowered her eyes to the windows of the control room, she saw, standing beside the pilot, three spirits she never thought she'd see again.

Mikey, Jix, and Nick.

Mary turned to her children, who all looked to her for strength and solace, and she said to them, "Run!"

CHAPTER 49
The War of Souls

"Now, *that's* what I call an entrance," said Johnnie-O. Then, with his flight mission accomplished, he immediately climbed the ladder up from the control room, and into the hull of the ship, to fight his way through the crowds to the gangway. Mikey, Jix, and Nick, however, who were less linear in their thinking, simply jumped out of the control room window, and were the first ones off the ship.

Everyone expected King Yax to lead the advance against the Eastern Witch, but the king was still nowhere to be found. With so many souls packed within the higher reaches of the airship's aluminum skeleton, it was very possible that the king was wedged in with all the humanity, and had yet to make his way out. No one knew for sure.

Without the king to order his subjects about, command of the siege was left to Jix. This was fine with him. While Mikey could play the occasional deity, and Nick could be their conscience, Jix was, and always would be, the hunter. True, he was not a pack hunter, but he did not mind having more than a thousand warriors under his command. Jix had seen fear in Mary Hightower's eyes when they landed, and for the first time in a long time, he felt the excitement a jaguar feels the moment it smells blood.

With Mary and her children in full retreat, Jix ordered his warriors to pursue them, subdue them, and force Mary's surrender. There were several problems, however:

1) The gangway stairs were designed for the leisurely departure of first-class guests, not for an entire Mayan civilization;

2) The warriors had to avoid touching the statue of the king on the way out, lest they accidentally make a more permanent exit, and;

3) The belly-flop nature of their landing left only one of the two gangways in a position to open, forcing the furious fighters to exit single-file.

Thus, Jix had to wait until he had enough warriors to lead, so it wasn't exactly like storming the shores of Normandy.

With Jix in charge of the battle, Mikey's mission had narrowed to a single objective.

"Allie!" he called.

Let the others face his sister. He had motivated the king to bring them here, and he didn't need a monstrous transformation to frighten Mary's children, since they were already running away, so Mikey's job was done.

"Allie!" He could sense that she was here somewhere, and the feeling was so strong, he knew she must be close! "ALLIE!" But all he heard in response were the war cries of the exiting warriors and the rain and winds of the two-world storm.

* * *

Allie, it seemed, was destined to be restrained in one way or another. First on the face of a train, then bound to the body of a coyote, then cuffed and gagged by a girl bent on destroying the world. Once she had freed herself from the handcuffs and recognized the sound of the approaching engine, she thought she could guide the *Hindenburg* in, but the ship came in so fast, no one in the control booth saw her directly in its path.

Now she was pinned to the ground beneath the airship, and with the clatter of warriors coming down the gangway stairs, and the roar of the storm, and Mikey bellowing her name, her own cries fell on ears deafer than the king's artists.

When Nick had seen Mary through the control room window, he felt more himself than he ever had before—but the old feelings surfaced in him in full force. He knew Mary was his weakness, but seeing Mary's face told him something crucial: He was Mary's weakness as well.

Now, as he strode through the piles and random objects filling the Trinity deadspot, he could feel more and more of the chocolate that plagued him flaking away. It was now just bits of a hard shell on the outside, rather than the thick mud that used to fill him. His tie was still caked with the stuff, but his shirt was mostly white now, and his pants mostly gray. His face only had brown patches here and there. He knew that as long as he held on to himself and stayed in the company of those who knew him, he would be fine.

He once dreamed of reforming Mary—perhaps not in the same way that Mikey had re-formed him from the blob of molten chocolate he had become—but he *had* hoped to change Mary from the inside out, opening her eyes to a better way of existing. He had wanted to show her a new concept of "right." Now, however, Nick's hope was much more humble. He just wanted to stop her, and render her powerless. If he could even just make her doubt herself, it would give them an advantage.

He wondered what she'd say to him when she finally faced him. . . . But he was more curious as to what *he* would say to *her*. Regardless, he sensed this confrontation would be the last time he would ever face Mary Hightower, whatever the outcome.

Finally Jix and the first wave of warriors—perhaps a hundred or so—went racing past Nick, their weapons raised, and Nick turned to look back at the great airship behind him. Was it his imagination, or had the *Hindenburg* begun to move?

Speedo, hiding behind a pile of furniture, was the first to see the *Hindenburg* unexpectedly start to rise, because he had his eyes trained on it from the moment it landed.

"Oh, no, you don't!" he shouted, and ran toward it. The *Hindenburg* was his. He had traded for it fair and square long ago—but like everything else, somehow it became Mary's and he had become a mere chauffeur, piloting her around. Well, he let his airship go once, he wasn't going to let it get away again.

He raced for the gangway stairs as the engines grew louder. Oddly dressed warriors were falling from the gangway, having not expected the ship to suddenly lift off. As the ship rose higher, Speedo climbed on the roof of a Cadillac, and leaped to the gangway stairs, clinging with the tips of his fingers. Speedo was not a particularly strong boy, but in Everlost physical strength is less about physique, and more about determination. He pulled himself up to the bottom step of the gaping gangway, and climbed into the ship. Pushing his way past agitated warriors, he made his way straight to the control room.

"Get out of my cockpit," he yelled at a figure adorned in gold, at the ship's helm.

Then, when the figure turned to him, Speedo recognized him from his earliest days with Mary, and he stared in disbelief.

"Vari?"

"Don't call me that!" said Vari. "I am His Excellency, the Supreme King of the Middle Realm. Hear my name and revel."

Sadly, King Yax K'uk Mo' was no longer a passenger on the *Hindenburg*. He had only himself to blame for putting his trust in his power-hungry vizier. Vari knew the jig was up the moment Nick and Mikey arrived. The king was likely to throw him into the Cenote for lying about his connection to "the Eastern Witch." Vari couldn't stay under the rule of the king, and didn't want to go back into the service of Mary, who treated him like the small child that he was, so Vari went into hiding. Then, when the king ordered all his subjects onto the airship, Vari hid in the ship's air vents, waiting and watching.

The king spent most of his time in the control room with

Johnnie-O, enjoying the view below. When there was no one he had to impress, the king often removed the heavy, restrictive gold adornments he wore, all the way down to the ragged little loincloth he had died in a thousand years ago. Although the huge windows of the control room offered spectacular views, this was not one of them. Johnnie-O's interest in seeing the king in his underwear was as close to Xibalba, the Mayan underworld, that Johnnie-O ever cared to get, and so he left the airship on autopilot, going off to brief Nick, Mikey, and Jix on their progress, until such time as the king made himself decent again.

Once Johnnie-O was gone, Vari, who, had been watching from an air vent, made his move.

As King Yax looked out of the open window, Vari dropped into the control room, catching his former boss off guard.

"Vizier?" said the king, for King Yax knew no one's actual name. "What are you doing here?"

"Saying good-bye," said Vari. Then he reached down, grabbed the king's bare feet, and flipped him out of the window, enacting a quick political *coup de drop*. Once the king had been dispatched, Vari retreated into the air vent again with all the king's gold, planning to bide his time until he could get Mikey, Nick, and Jix off the airship as well.

The king was understandably outraged as he fell from the sky, and swore all manner of retribution against his vizier, once he solved the predicament of falling a thousand feet with no deadspot to land on. Although there were many, many things he could unremember to get himself out of this situation, the king was not the brightest bauble in the headdress. He concluded that if there were no such direction as "down," then he couldn't possibly fall, could he?

"I don't remember there being a 'down,'" King Yax said. "I don't remember it whatsoever."

The problem with that particular unmemory is that it instantly transported him to the only place on earth where "down" does not exist. Namely, the very center of the earth, where the only direction is "up."

Thus, King Yax K'uk Mo' avoided many long years of sinking, and promptly became the central-most soul in a very different party than he was used to.

"Mikey! Over here!"

Mikey heard Allie call out to him the moment the *Hindenburg* began to rise. The great airship lifted off the ground, and he saw her rising to her feet from beneath it. He ran to her, wrapping his arms around her, and he found himself growing another set of arms, and another and another just to hold her. He could not embrace her enough.

"I thought you had been extinguished," Mikey said. "I couldn't bear the thought of it."

"It was Milos," Allie told him. "Your sister made him do it."

Mikey shook his head and said something he'd been feeling for quite a while. "She's not my sister anymore," Mikey told her. "Megan McGill's been gone for a long, long time."

Mikey held her in his multiple embrace, and although he wanted to make this moment the only moment that mattered, he knew he couldn't. So he pulled in his extra sets of limbs, and said, "Nick thinks the first atomic bomb is at the center of the vortex."

Allie looked at him, horrified, finally realizing what this place was. "Well, it can't go off, right?" she said. "I mean, this is Everlost—it can't be destroyed."

"Unless," he reminded her, "its purpose was to be destroyed . . ."

In the *Hindenburg* control room, Speedo still stared at Vari in a gold skirt, trying to wrap his mind around it. "The Supreme who? The king of what?"

Then the ship hit the double-world storm, and the *Hindenburg*'s nose began to drop. Vari looked at the controls around him, baffled, so he turned to Speedo. "I command you to take me to the City of Souls!"

"You command squat," said Speedo, finally sticking up for himself against those who would order him around. "This is my airship, and you are just a passenger. Got it?"

The nose dipped farther, and Vari nodded nervously.

Speedo, who had been a true master of the airship's helm, quickly took the controls, adjusting the elevator wheel until the inclinometers were level and the ship had stabilized. He paused then, but only briefly. He now had his ship back— and although it meant abandoning his claim on the deadspot, he resolved not to return to Mary. Not now, not ever.

"We need to get more altitude, and we can't do that in this storm," Speedo told Vari. "We'll go back over the deadspot—it's quiet in the eye. Then, by the time we reach the far side, we'll be high enough to make it through the storm."

Speedo turned the ship around, and it began to rise as it crossed back over the deadspot.

Jix knew something had gone terribly wrong when he saw the *Hindenburg* soaring overhead with its gangway still open and the occasional warrior tumbling out. He looked back to take stock of the limited number of warriors with him now. There were thousands upon thousands of souls to fight Mary Hightower, but that meant nothing if they all were aboard an airship that was flying away.

Now, Mary's children were coming out of hiding all around Jix, and there were lots of them—many more than the warriors who actually made it out of the airship. It looked like Mary's children realized that too, because they didn't seem frightened anymore. In fact, they were closing in.

Johnnie-O never got to the gangway before the ship took off. He got close, but something along the way stopped him. It was the statue of the king. Johnnie remembered how, when he and Charlie had first flown over the deadspot nearly a month ago, the airship had filled with sparks and silent lightning. Now, however, all the electrical charges seemed to be focused around the statue, creating pleasing patterns of light. Pleasing, at least, to him. Johnnie-O found himself mesmerized, unable to look away, and while the warriors had been frightened by it, sticking close to the stairwell wall on their way to the gangway, Johnnie could not stop looking at it.

Old thoughts began to play in his head. *"It's gotta mean something, don't it, Charlie? The fact that I'm not a complete blithering idiot like you?*" Although Johnnie-O didn't know what the meaning was, he couldn't help but think that his destiny, like Charlie's, was somehow tied up with this statue.

He was so enthralled by it that he never even felt the ship leave the ground. It wasn't until he heard a commanding yet whiny voice behind him that he broke out of his trance.

"Why are you staring at that statue?"

He turned to see what at first he thought was the king, but quickly he realized it was Vari wearing the king's clothes.

"None of your business," said Johnnie-O. "Get lost."

Vari took a step forward, trying to look taller than he was. "I am your king now. All who disrespect me shall be cast down to Xibalba." Then Vari looked at the statue. "When we return to the City of Souls, we will find your bucket of coins in the forge, and make a new face for the statue. *My* face." He paused for a moment, then added, "And as punishment for your disrespect, you will be made to do it, by dipping those big fat hands of yours into the molten metal."

That was all Johnnie-O had to hear. Suddenly the sparking statue didn't look beautiful to him, it looked hideous. "You know what? I got a better idea." Then he grabbed the statue's obsidian base with those same big fat hands, and knocked it over.

"No! What are you doing?"

Then Johnnie kicked it down the gangway stairs.

"Stop! I order you to stop!"

"Sorry. I don't take orders from obnoxious, snot-nosed twits."

Now the statue lay half in and half out of the airship, wedged against the gangway stairs' support strut. With the airship halfway over the deadspot, and still gaining altitude, that last step off the gangway was a very long one.

"Don't you dare!" said Vari.

"What are you gonna do about it?" He kicked at the base until the statue became unstuck and began to totter.

"No!" Vari hurried to save it, but Johnnie-O stuck his foot out, Vari tripped over it, and he went flying into the statue.

"Nooooo!" The second Vari touched the statue, he vanished in a rainbow twinkling of light, getting to where he was going, whether he liked it or not—and the force of his momentum tipped the statue off its precarious balance. It fell from the gangway, plunging to the deadspot far below.

"Ha!" said Johnnie-O. "That'll show him. Xibalba, my butt!"

Then Johnnie, happily humming "Anchors Aweigh," climbed back into the ship, and sat down, leaning against the stairwell wall. He knew that in those brief moments something had changed . . . because there was now nothing in the world he wanted to do more than to sit there and have his own private sing-along.

Clarence covered his dead eye, but he couldn't cover his dead ear enough to drown out the sounds all around him—and the various burned parts of him kept bumping into things that weren't there, making his trek to the jeep slow and difficult. His dead ear heard children calling to one another, and orders shouted in other languages. There were sounds of battle, and the roar of engines high above. And then there came a heavy, decisive *thud* very close to him.

Still dizzy, still foggy in his thoughts, Clarence began to remember things. He remembered that the ghosties weren't in his mind, they were real. There was an invisible war going on—and he was a part of that war. He remembered a boy with a face like a cat. Jix. Jix had told Clarence that he had a purpose—but the sounds around him were so chaotic, at that moment it was hard to imagine anything had a purpose at all.

Far far ahead, sat the Jeep—but with all these sounds crashing around him, he couldn't stop himself from taking a peek with his dead eye. Immediately the barren desert wasn't barren anymore. What he saw didn't make any sense, though, because it was the exact same thing he saw before he covered his dead eye.

A trophy and a martini shaker.

Only this time, they were both huge. He made his way closer to the strange objects. The trophy was not a trophy at all, but a statue, and it was sparking wildly with multi-colored electricity. The other object wasn't exactly a mar-tini shaker. It was shaped like one, but a bit stouter—and it wasn't silver; it was dull green, with lots of wires. It was also upside down, and standing on its head, but closer observa-tion revealed that it was hovering just above the ground.

There was something missing from this picture, wasn't there? Yes! There had been a playing card between the tro-phy and the shaker!

Then, all at once everything that was missing in his mind came back to him. He knew where he was. He knew what that green thing was. He had seen pictures of it as a child. And now, as he approached the very center of the deadspot—the heart of the vortex—he realized that Jix had been right all along. Clarence did have a purpose! There was a reason why he was the way he was—why he had to suffer through the ridicule of living this half-life of suffering—because what needed to be done today could be accomplished only by him: someone with an unnatural presence in both worlds. Ever since the day his flesh was seared and he was given his vision of Everlost, every thought he had, every phrase he uttered was somehow incomplete. *He* was incomplete, but today in this place, at this moment, completion was finally at the tips of his fingers. The playing card was missing, but it was only a placeholder—a reminder that he was the one-eyed jack between the here and the hereafter.

With his Everlost hand, he reached to his left, gripping the statue firmly. Then, with his living hand, he reached to his right, toward the bomb. He didn't touch it, for his living hand could not touch an Everlost bomb. Instead his living hand reached right through it, as if it wasn't there. He stretched his fingers out as far as he could, and when his fingertips reached the core of the device, an electrical charge ran from the statue of fused coins, through Clarence, and into the memory of the bomb. And in that moment of infinite possibility, the statue, Clarence, and The Gadget all did exactly what it was their purpose to do.

CHAPTER 50

Straight Up, with a Twist

In the living world, the detonation of a thermonuclear device has very predictable, very devastating, consequences. But Everlost is not the living world. Add to that detonation tens of thousands of Everlost coins, and you never know what will come pouring out of your martini shaker. All you can know for sure is that whatever the cocktail, it will be exactly what the universe requires.

At the moment of detonation, a tunnel opened, a thousand feet high and a thousand feet wide, leading to a blinding light and the Unknowable Place beyond it. Mary's children and the warriors they battled instantly knew the tunnel was there. Those whose forms had changed, now changed back; those who had forgotten their names, now remembered. Every single one of them heard the light calling them by name, and suddenly all the things they had been asked to do in Everlost seemed unimportant when compared to this new directive. So together, and yet each on their own terms, the warriors and Mary's children leaped into the tunnel, completing their journey, and getting where they were going without fear or regret.

At the moment of detonation, Johnnie-O's hands shrunk back down to normal size and he ran down the gangway stairs. When he saw the tunnel, he leaped joyfully into it like a skydiver, and shouted, "Bring on the dancing bear!" while Speedo, now dry for the first time since arriving in Everlost, found himself right at the edge of the event horizon, and the most important decision of his existence. Like all the others, he felt the call of the light, but the ship was far enough away for him to resist it. He knew he could sail the *Hindenburg* away if he wanted to, and return to being a finder for as long as there were things left to find. Then he realized that such a decision would deny everyone aboard their chance to leave Everlost . . . so he turned the rudder and steered the *Hindenburg* back toward the deadspot, and into the tunnel, piloting himself, and thousands of endlessly rejoicing souls directly into the light.

At the moment of detonation, Mary Hightower, who had lost track of all her children in the midst of running away from the invading force, found that she was alone, and back where she started: the exact spot where she had asked Milos to sacrifice himself. When the tunnel formed, calling to her like a furious parent, she chose to be the petulant child. Grabbing the handcuffs that Allie had left on the ground, she locked one end around her wrist and the other end around a car's door handle, so that no matter how hard that light tugged on her, Mary wasn't going anywhere.

At the moment of detonation, Allie became the selfish one, holding on to Mikey with the full force of her will as the light called to him. Mikey knew, however, that this was an irresistible force.

"Please don't go," Allie whispered in his ear.

"I don't want to," Mikey whispered back, "but it's time."

They both wished that they could stand there, holding each other forever—and as if to answer them, the light gave them a precious gift. It took that elastic Everlost moment, and stretched it, making it feel like an entire lifetime. Intense. Fulfilling. Complete. And when the timeless moment was over, Mikey kissed her one last time, then let go, and disappeared into eternity, leaving Allie with five words she knew she would never forget:

"I'll be waiting for you."

And at the moment of detonation, the last of Nick's chocolate vanished, and Nick opened his arms wide, waiting, waiting, and waiting some more . . . until he realized that the light was not ready to take him, and that he was not ready to go.

When all the souls who needed to complete their journey had done so, the tunnel imploded in upon itself and the light disappeared. Clarence stood at the center of Ground Zero, with one hand reaching for a statue that was no longer there, and the other hand held firmly in a spot where the memory of a bomb used to be.

The raging storm was gone now, dissolving as quickly as it had formed, and Clarence sensed there was a balance in both worlds that hadn't been there before, and he knew that whatever he had done had been successful. He knew not just because he felt it in his heart, but because his left hand was now unfeeling, his left ear unhearing, and his left eye unseeing. He was no longer a scar wraith, just a man with scars that were reminders of the many lives he had saved. All he could see, feel, or hear was the living world, and he smiled because he knew that this was as it should be. His only regret was that he wouldn't get to say good-bye.

Clarence left Trinity site with a new determination to repair the mess he had made of his life. If he could save one world from destruction, and another from domination, then fixing up his life oughta be a cakewalk.

CHAPTER 51
Westinghouse Blue

Mary knew what had happened. Somehow the dark conspiracy had taken all her children from her. She had defiantly looked into the beckoning light, and when the light retreated, she knew she was alone. But not entirely.

"Hello, Mary."

She turned to see Nick. There was not an ounce of chocolate on him now—not even the small smudge he started with. Mary found that she wanted to hate him—to hate all of them, but she found that she didn't have the strength.

"Just leave me alone," she said, letting her copper hair fall before her face to hide him from view.

"So why do you think the light won't take us?" asked Nick.

"It will take me," Mary confessed. Then she held up her hand, showing that it was cuffed to the door handle of the car she sat beside. "But I won't go."

Nick looked around on the ground until he spotted the key, then he knelt beside Mary, undoing the cuffs and setting her free.

"I've loved you for a very long time," Nick said to her, "in spite of all the bad stuff that's happened between us. Why do you think that is?"

"I'm not answering your questions, Nick. I have no answers."

"I'll tell you why, then. Because you let me see who you *could* be. Not who you were, not who you became, but who you might become. Which means the Mary I love, in a way, hasn't even been born yet. But she could be now."

Mary finally looked up at him, feeling that painful twinge of love that had plagued her for so long. She couldn't handle that unforgiving feeling alone.

"I want to talk to my brother," she said. "I want to talk to Mikey."

"He's gone," said a voice behind Nick.

Mary looked past Nick to see that Allie had arrived. Jix was there too, and so were her own skinjackers. They had all heard what Nick said, and were looking at her with a putrid mix of fear and pity. She tried to reach her tendrils of light out to snare them, but realized that the persuasive power she always had, which had grown into a mystical force, was now gone. It had been stolen by the light. All that was left of her afterglow now was a faint luminescence, no more remarkable than anyone else's.

The Pet spoke without as much as raising his hand. "I'm sorry, Miss Mary," he said, "but I quit."

She could see in the rest of their faces that The Pet was speaking for all of them. She turned to Nick, who still waited patiently for an answer to his proposition. "You don't need to be Mary Hightower anymore," he said. "You could be Megan Mary McGill . . . all you have to do is accept that you were wrong."

Mary told him nothing, because there was nothing more to say. Her choices were simple and clear.

"Thank you, Nick," she said, and she kissed him, allowing herself to savor the moment, and lock it into her memory. Then she turned and walked toward the edge of the deadspot, where the old blue refrigerator stood. She pushed it over, watching it fall backward onto the sands of the living world. In this position it did, indeed, look like a sarcophagus. For the first time she noticed the brand name on the door: *Westinghouse*. Mary could have laughed, for it occurred to her that this would be the only "West" that she'd be going. She grabbed the heavy latching handle and lifted open the door.

"Mary, no!" said Nick.

But Allie grabbed his arm. "This is her choice."

Mary knew there wasn't much time, for the refrigerator had already begun to sink. She took one last look at Everlost, the world that had almost been hers . . . then she stepped inside the cramped, claustrophobic space, and laid down on her side, pulling up her knees so that she could fit.

All you have to do is accept that you were wrong.

For Mary Hightower, there could be no such admission. If she could not be in a world where she was the very definition of right, then she would not be in that world at all. She would rather be in a world of one. And so, as her last act as a citizen of Everlost, Mary Hightower pulled the door down, hearing the latch firmly lock into place, and sealed herself into solitary darkness from now until the end of time.

* * *

Nick could have gone after her and pulled her out before it was too late, but Allie was absolutely right. This was Mary's choice. The others were already turning their backs, and Nick found himself furious at them. "No!" he yelled, holding back tears. "We will watch this! We will give her the dignity of watching this."

And so they all stood in a circle around the sarcophagus in silence as it sank slowly into the ground, until the last bit of it disappeared beneath the desert sands on its long, lonely journey into the earth's unyielding embrace.

PART EIGHT

EverEnding

Paradoxical Interlude with Physicists and Lobstermen

Quantum science says that all that we believe is solid is 99.99 percent empty space. It only seems solid because that's what our senses are designed to tell us.

Astrophysics says that 27 percent of the universe is dark matter. In other words, stuff that is measurably there, but for some reason no one can see it and no one knows where it is.

Cosmic String Theory says that there aren't just three dimensions, but that there are actually eleven—but most of them are unable to be perceived from where we sit, no matter how comfortable our chair is.

And in the jagged coastline of Maine, people often have been known to say, "You can't get there from here," even when you can see the place right across the inlet.

In short, there are mysteries of science and of soul that will never be understood no matter how hard we measure, no matter how strongly we believe, no matter how deep our think tanks and how high our aspirations. But as anyone will tell you—for we all know this within our hearts—the impossible happens and grand cosmic mysteries are solved on a regular basis, although most of the time the solutions lead to even greater mysteries.

There is a place, however, where all the mysteries have been solved, and all the answers have been given, and there is nothing anywhere left to know. You can find it if you try, if you are true of heart, and strong of will, and know beyond all else that it is a world you wish to live in.

And when you get there, give my regards to Mary Hightower. On second thought, don't.

CHAPTER 52
World After Mary

So what should we do with all this stuff?" Allie asked Nick as they looked out at the Trinity deadspot, sitting fifteen feet high on a sofa piled on top of a dozen other sofas.

"Leave it all here," said Nick. "If anyone left in Everlost needs furniture, we'll know where to send them."

Allie could see in Nick a kind of peaceful resolve, but also a certain sorrow deep in his eyes. Or maybe it was just a reflection of her own sadness at having to give Mikey over to the light. Both she and Nick lost someone they loved today, but in very different ways.

"I'm sorry," Allie said.

"Don't be," Nick told her. "You know what they say — what doesn't kill me makes me stronger, right?"

"Well, sure," said Allie. "But being that you're already dead, I don't know if that applies."

Nick laughed. "You don't have to worry about me. The light didn't take me, but it did give me some pretty cool door prizes."

"It took away the chocolate, for one," Allie said.

"Yeah, but that's only part of it. I remember now, Allie. I remember everything! Who I was, who I am, and even who I will be."

"Oh, so now you can see the future?"

"Not exactly," said Nick. "But I know my place in it."

"And that would be . . . ?"

Nick smiled at her. It was a genuine smile. "I'm the new Mary."

Allie leaned away from him and the sofa shifted treacherously on the pile. "That's not funny," she said.

"No, I'm serious," Nick told her. "That's why I felt so connected to her. It was in her heart to help and protect everyone who came to Everlost, but she couldn't separate herself from her calling. Once it became all about her, it got sick and twisted until it destroyed her and almost destroyed the world."

"So how do you know that won't happen to you, too?"

Nick shrugged. "Because I turned to chocolate. Because I was melted and got put back together again. Because I saw what happens when you believe you're the most important person in the universe. It all sort of humbled me, you know?"

Allie thought about that, remembering how helpless she felt inside the coyote. She had always been an ambitious girl, but that awful experience had taught her that there were more forces at work in a balanced world than her own willpower; there was nature, there was wisdom, there was knowledge and understanding. Without life's humbling experiences, Allie could have been just like Mary Hightower.

Allie looked off to where Jix talked to the skinjackers.

Not just SoSo, Sparkles, and the lot, but the new ones that Mary had so successfully created too. Twenty-three of them, to be exact.

"Do you believe that everything happens for a reason?" Allie asked Nick, as she watched them.

Nick sighed. "I looked right into the light and I still have no idea."

"Well," said Allie, starting to climb her way down from the mound of sofas. "Just in case, I'm going to treat everything like it does." Then she went to join Jix.

"We'll go back to your towns, and find your sleeping bodies," Jix told all the skinjackers, as Allie approached. "Some of you will choose to skinjack yourselves and go back to your lives. But some of you I think will be brain-dead, or too badly broken, and you'll choose not to."

The new skinjackers stared at him in total shell shock, and understandably so. When it came to comforting words and bedside manner, Jix did not get high marks.

"Listen," said Allie, bridging a little bit of the distance between them and Jix. "It's gonna be okay either way. And if you decide to stay in Everlost as skinjackers, well, maybe it was meant to be that way." Then the questions started flying. All the things they wouldn't ask Jix, they now threw at Allie.

"Can I skinjack someone skinny?"

"Will I turn into a cat?"

"What if I skinjack a movie star?"

"Can we skinjack one anothers' bodies?"

"Will I turn into a cat?"

"Am I still lactose intolerant if I skinjack?"

"Will I forget who I am?"

"What if I turn into a cat?"

"Hijole!" said Jix, throwing up his hands. "Look what you've started."

"All questions will be answered," Allie told them. Then she added, "And for those of you who end up staying in Everlost, there are some pretty amazing things you can learn to do. You can be like guardian angels, and really do some good in the world."

"Or," mumbled SoSo, shamefully looking down, "you can destroy it."

"Somehow," said Allie, "I don't think that will be a problem anymore."

They all walked together to the town of Alamogordo, and there, on a corner as ordinary as any in the world, they said their good-byes.

"We're staying here in town for a day or two," said Jix. "I want to teach the new skinjackers the basics, in case they decide to stay. Mary's skinjackers could use some training too."

Allie gave him a hug, feeling the velvet softness of his fledgling fur, now a little bit thicker than when they first met. "Thank you for freeing me from the train."

"Sorry about the coyote," he said. "It was all I could find at the time. Now that I know you, I would say that you are an eagle spirit, and eagle spirits do not do well in canine bodies."

"I really should come with you," Allie said. "You shouldn't have to train them alone."

Then Jix gave her a sly, feline smile. "Who says I'll be alone?" he said. "Sparkles told me where I can find a highly skilled skinjacker . . . although I hear she's quite a pig." Then he went off with the other skinjackers to the rodeo, an excellent place to practice soul-surfing.

Nick had found himself a backpack at the Trinity vortex, which he filled with odds and ends he might need in his travels. He also picked up a vintage leather jacket that he now wore over his dressy shirt and tie. "If the Supreme King of the Middle Realm can wear gold over his loin cloth, then I can wear this."

Allie took a long look at him. "So what now?" she asked.

"Well, there's a whole bunch of Afterlights in Atlanta, and I hear Mary left a church full of them in Eunice. In fact there's got to be Afterlights all over the world, not to mention the ones arriving every day. And if any of them lost their coins, I know an empty Mayan city, where there's a bottomless bucket of them."

Allie shook her head, impressed by this brave vision of his own future.

"I remember the first time I saw you," Allie said.

"I thought you smelled me first."

"Right," said Allie. "The chocolate. But then I saw you as I sat up in the dead forest, thinking I knew you. At the time, I thought I must have seen you through the windshield when our cars crashed. . . . But that wasn't it. I think, way back then, I was seeing you as you are now. Isn't that funny?"

"Not as funny as the way I always complained, and the way you always bossed me around!"

spare change, and out of the change, Nick retrieves a funny-looking coin with a faded face.

"You'll want to keep this," Nick says, and puts it in Kyle's shirt pocket as well. "Be careful not to lose it."

Now as Kyle looks at the people around him — how they don't see him, how they actually walk past him, and some walk right through him, he realizes the truth.

"I'm . . . dead?"

"I'm sorry, Kyle. I'm also sorry that you didn't make it into the light, but you will. In the meantime, I know a place you can stay for free right here in New York. You can even have your own apartment there. The only rules are that you have to do something different every day, and you can only 'rent' for one month at a time."

"Why? What happens at the end of the month?"

"At the end of each month, you check with the coin," Nick says. "It will tell you if you're ready to move 'uptown.'"

And although it doesn't make much sense to Kyle yet, he follows Nick. Something inside Kyle tells him he can trust this kid — that Nick truly has his best interests at heart.

"So this place I'm staying . . . ," asks Kyle. "Am I gonna like it?"

"I think you'll love it," says Nick, with a smile that's just a little bit mischievous. "And you won't believe the view!"

on a street corner in the middle of the day. He looks around, and the world seems strange. Sounds are hollow, people pass by as blurs, and the colors all seem muted except for him, his skateboard, and the spot that he's on. He turns to see a boy sitting on the curb across the street, also in perfect focus, watching him. As he goes over to the boy, he notices that there's something wrong with the ground. It feels as if it's melting beneath his feet.

The boy who's been watching him smiles him and stands up. He wears pressed pants and a leather jacket over a white shirt and a dark tie.

"What's going on here? Am I dreaming? Am I drugged?" the skateboarder asks.

"Neither," says the smiling boy. "You'll want to tell me your name now. I'll write it down in case you forget it."

"Very funny," says the skateboarder, and yet as he tries to say his name, it takes him a moment to pull it up. "Kyle."

"Nice to meet you, Kyle. I'm Nick." He shakes Kyle's hand, writes his name on a piece of paper, then sticks it in Kyle's shirt pocket. "Do you remember what happened?"

"Yeah," says Kyle, scratching his head. "I came out of that alley, and almost got hit by a garbage truck."

Nick shakes his head. "Hate to tell you this, Kyle. But it wasn't, 'almost.'"

"No way, man. That's not even funny."

The smile never leaves Nick's face. "Check your pockets," he says.

"What for?"

"You'll see."

Kyle reaches into his pocket and pulls out a bunch of

Still, the couple do their best to make the most of it. The mother paints the girl's nails, for her sister is in college and can't be there to do it. The father goes through his ritual of massaging her muscles to keep them soft and supple, for there's still a faint and far-off chance that she'll need them again someday. The mother reads yet another chapter from *Sense and Sensibility*, and then when melancholy sets in, the father goes to pull up the car, for he doesn't want to make his wife walk in the storm.

The woman gets up to look out of the window, her heart sinking at the sight of quivering branches on winter-bare trees. She wishes that Valentine's Day—that every holiday—could be different for them, but she knows that it probably never will be. Resigned to that fact, she turns to look at her silent daughter in the bed, only to see her daughter looking right back at her.

"Hi, Mom," the girl says, her voice weak and raspy.

"Allie?" The woman hurries to her daughter, sitting in the chair beside her, taking her curled hand, and holding it—and for the first time in a very, very long time, that hand squeezes back.

"Sorry I've been gone for so long," Allie rasps.

"It's okay, honey," the mother says. "Oh my God, it's okay." Tears burst from the woman's eyes, falling more powerfully than the rain outside. They are tears of joy, because finally, after all these years, she's been given permission to cry.

Picture this:

A skateboarder in New York City awakes to find himself

498

The leopard's white, spotted fur seems to glow in the waning gibbous moon. The cat is hungry, but it does not attack. Instead, it reaches with its paw, grabs the gate of the pen and pulls it closed until it latches, making sure it couldn't get out if it tried. Only then does the leopard bare its fangs at the sow.

The sow doesn't move. It couldn't if it wanted to, so instead, it stares into the leopard's eyes as the leopard slowly moves forward, opens its mouth wide, and digs its powerful fangs deep into the sow's neck. . . .

A few minutes later, at the sound of a strange roar, the farmer grabs his shotgun and heads out toward the pigpens, where his worst fear is realized. A wild animal has gotten into the pen. The strangest animal he's ever seen in these parts. His prize sow is dead, and somehow locked in the pen with its body is a huge white cat, furiously bouncing around the pen, unable to escape.

"Now I've seen everything," he says.

. . . But in truth, he hasn't seen everything. Because he doesn't see the two invisible spirits embracing right beside him, then racing off into the Everlost night.

⁂

Picture this:

A hospital on Valentine's Day in Memphis, Tennessee.

A sparse gathering of families have remembered their silent loved ones today, including the parents of the girl in room 509, who arrive shortly after work and tape a Valentine's Day card up on the wall. It storms outside; icy rain hitting the window, making it rattle. Not the most inviting of Valentine's Days; not the most inviting of settings.

CHAPTER 53

Portraits

Picture this:

A farm in west Texas. It's night. Animals in the barnyard are on edge. Something has them spooked and the farmer doesn't know why. He double-checks the pens, but loses concentration for a moment, then goes inside, never realizing that in that moment of disorientation, his hands, under someone else's control, had unlocked the pen of his prize breeding sow.

In the pen, the sow awakes. Not the sow, but the girl within the sow, who is beginning to forget that she is a girl. She does not want to consider the misery that she has been put through these many, many weeks. The slop she has been served to eat, the stench of the pen, and the massive immobile weight of her own bloated, porcine body.

Then she hears the gate of her pen slowly creak open. She is hit by a new sharp smell, and adrenaline fills her, for the instinctive mind of the pig knows the smell means grave danger. She turns her head enough to see bright eyes looking at her, reflecting the distant porch light like yellow marbles.

A snow leopard.

They embraced and held each other for a long time.

"Don't forget me," Nick said. "No matter where your life goes, no matter how old you ever get. And if you ever get the feeling that someone is looking over your shoulder, but there's nobody there, maybe it'll be me."

"I'll write to you," said Allie, and Nick laughed. "No really. I'll write the letter then burn it, and if I care just enough, it will cross into Everlost."

"And," added Nick, "it will show up as a dead letter at that post office Milos made cross in San Antonio!"

Allie could have stood there saying good-bye forever, because it was more than Nick she was saying good-bye to. She was leaving behind four years of half-life in a world that was both stunningly beautiful, and hauntingly dark. And she was saying good-bye to Mikey. *I'll be waiting for you,* he had said. . . . Well, if he was, maybe she wasn't really saying good-bye at all.

Nick hefted the backpack on his shoulder, "Shouldn't you be heading off to Memphis?" he said. "You'd better hit the road . . . Jack." Then he chuckled at his own joke, and walked off.

And although he was just an ordinary Afterlight, Allie couldn't help but notice as he strode down the street, that he wasn't sinking into the living world at all.